W9-CYB-534

Waitin' For The Train To Come In

Copyright © 2013 David Garnes
All rights reserved.

ISBN: 1434863689
ISBN-13: 9781434863683

Waitin' For The Train To Come In

A Novel Of World War II

David Garnes

Indian Pipe Publishing

2013

Dedication

For Ruth and Jim

In Memory

Prologue: October 2003

Bill eased his red Corolla into the darkened driveway, the car's headlights momentarily catching the glimmer of the large silver globe in the side garden. The purple asters that surrounded its base appeared to have survived the October New England nights, at least so far. That would change with the first killing frost.

Stretching his legs as he slowly stepped out onto the asphalt, Bill arched his body and raised his arms, clasping his stiff fingers together over his head. The trip had been longer than usual because of restoration work on the Merritt Parkway, though he still preferred this prettier turnpike to the Interstate. He didn't like the 18-wheelers that sped by on the New England Thruway.

The Merritt reminded him of much earlier trips, back when he'd first moved to New York in the Fifties, when you'd continue north into Massachusetts on old Route 5, past tobacco fields and roadside stands selling corn and flowers and yellow summer squash. Today he'd driven at a steady speed of 60 on the historic parkway, under elaborately carved low stone bridges covered in vines, through an endless red and gold canopy of overhanging ash and beech and sugar maples.

He walked slowly to the front porch, rubbing his lower back, and checked the mailbox for any stray items that might have eluded the stop-delivery request. Unlocking the door, he walked into the familiar dim foyer. Though he'd been up several times in the past few weeks, it was a shock once again to find it darkened and still— no radio playing one of those music-of-your-life stations, no light visible in the kitchen down the hall, no familiar song coming from the piano in the den. He'd gotten used to Jinx not being there; his brother Gary had been happy to add his mother's dog to the menagerie of strays up at his place in the Berkshires.

Walking up the stairs to the second floor, Bill paused at the landing and looked at the photographs on the marble-top table. Some of the pictures he remembered from his grandmother's old house across town. He always stopped on the landing, perhaps as a way of acknowledging the faces smiling out at him. He wasn't a cemetery visitor.

He picked up a large picture in a fancy silver frame, a group shot taken at his brother's wedding some years earlier. Nan, in a fancy flowered hat, in the center, flanked by her two male grandchildren. In the back, his aunt Belle and Abe. His mother and father stood smiling on the right, Alan towering over Laura and everyone else. Now only Bill and Gary—the 'boys,' as Nan would say—were left.

He glanced at another photo at the back of the table, a small snapshot of Alan and him taken during the war. Both were dressed in Navy whites, Billy's little suit bought as a surprise for his father when he was home on leave from boot camp. Bill studied the picture, then turned away and continued upstairs to his mother's room.

The maple bedroom set, an Art Deco design from the Thirties, gleamed in the semi-darkness and he recognized the aroma of Chanel #5, along with some disinfectant he couldn't identify. He wondered again just where they'd found her. By the time he made it up to Springfield she was at Baystate Medical in a coma, and he'd never talked with her again—to her, but not with her.

He rummaged through the deep top drawer of the bureau for a couple of pieces of jewelry his cousin Sandra had asked about. "That amber set I gave her years ago, the summer of the circus fire" she'd said. "You remember, she used to wear the earrings a lot."

He did remember, and he found the jewelry eventually, jammed in the back along with many other stray pieces, as well as mirrors, numerous lipsticks, handkerchiefs, his and Gary's old class rings, bobby pins, faded coins, combs, shirt collar tabs, little velvet boxes containing her good jewelry. 'Laura's top drawer' had become a joke in the family. If you'd lost something, look for it there.

He shut the drawer, placed the amber set on the glass top, and reminded himself to take it easy on the stairs. He'd stumbled and fractured his ankle at his apartment last year and had been in a cast for weeks. Downstairs in the den he lifted the lid of the piano stool and leafed through a handful of sheet music, mostly standards from the swing era, the songs his mother had sung around the house throughout his childhood.

Sitting on the bench, Bill picked up a photo from the top of the piano, a sepia-colored shot of Laura standing in front of a microphone, white flower pinned in her long hair, a small band of tuxedoed musicians seated behind her. They weren't performing, just posing rather solemnly for the camera, frozen in time like softly focused cutouts from another age. Look at us, they seemed to say, here we are and now we're gone. Most were young, maybe one or two pushing forty, but they all had that sophisticated, lacquered look that even dressed-up teenagers seemed to affect back then.

He glanced at the song sheet propped up on the piano, "Sentimental Journey," with a faded image of bandleader Les Brown and a very young Doris Day on the cover. Inside, there were notations in what looked like his mother's more recent, spidery handwriting. He wondered if she'd been practicing for some local benefit or old-timers reunion. Or maybe a veterans' celebration. She'd kept busy during her long widowhood.

Folding the sheet music, he carefully placed it back on the piano holder, turned out the light, and walked down the hallway. He wandered from room to room, checking on the rest of the house, his mind filled with tunes and images and other ghosts of the past.

PART I

SPRING 1943

*On March 1, the British Royal Air Force drops 900 tons of bombs in one-half hour on the city of Berlin

*_Oklahoma!_, Rodgers and Hammerstein's landmark musical, opens on Broadway

*Norman Rockwell's painting of "Rosie the Riveter" appears on the cover of the _Saturday Evening Post_

*American airmen captured in the "Doolittle Raid" on Tokyo are beheaded by the Japanese

*The #1 tune on the _Billboard_ chart is "I've Heard That Song Before" (Harry James Band, vocal by Helen Forrest)

*German spies land from a U-boat on Long Island, N.Y., are captured, and summarily executed

Chapter 1: Laura

It had been a bad day, right from the beginning. Hay fever season had blown in, and Laura awakened in an irritable mood. Her eyes itched, her nose felt like it was packed with cotton, and the sharp sinus pain above her eyes made her cringe when she turned over.

Alan, already dressed, was sitting on the edge of the bed, smoke from his cigarette curling in thick circles inches from her face. She pulled the covers over her head.

"I know I haven't shaved, but do I look that bad?" Alan scratched at the sheet stretched over her face.

"No, I just have a headache."

"Want me to pull the shades back down?"

"It's all right," she replied, lowering the sheet. Alan leaned over and, stretching his big frame, crushed his cigarette in the glass ashtray on his side of the bed. She caught a whiff of Wildroot in his hair, and that made her feel better.

"You're up early for a Sunday," she said.

"I couldn't sleep."

"Why not?" But she didn't really have to ask.

"Nothing. Just couldn't." He paused. "It's that...you know, what we were talking about last night."

They'd had the same conversation the day before and the day before that. She did understand how he felt about enlisting, but it was only a matter of time before the draft would start for married men with children, and that would settle everything.

"Alan, I know how you feel, I mean it, but what's a few months? Can't you just wait? Or is it that you want...?" She stopped herself before finishing that question, and he pretended not to have heard.

"Come on, lazybones," he said, rising from the bed. "Shake a leg. Still want to take a ride down to Connecticut?" She wasn't in the mood today, but she'd been asking for weeks if he'd like to visit her folks, just the two of them.

"Sure, I guess we should. The kids already up?"

"Billy's reading in his room, and Gary's downstairs. I think he's with my mother, or maybe he's playing fetch with Lucille out back. Come on," he added from the doorway "I've made coffee. That'll help your head."

She massaged her temples and swung her feet to the side, feeling for her pink mules.

And so the day had begun.

❧

Later that afternoon, after they'd returned from Hartford, she was standing in the bathroom, washing her hands. She examined herself in the mirror, smoothing her neck and checking the mass of black hair cascading to her shoulders for a stray strand of white. The harsh light accentuated faint smudges under her eyes, but that was to be expected. She was, after all, nearly thirty.

Suddenly, the circles seemed to darken and pouch. Furrows appeared on her forehead, and the skin along her jaw line sagged. In a second or two, the image disappeared, but she remained transfixed, staring at herself wide-eyed until the hot water from the running faucet steamed the glass into an opaque reflection that could have been anyone's.

She splashed water onto the mirror, scrubbed it furiously with the hand towel, and ran into the hallway. Her first impulse was to wake Alan, but she didn't want to disturb his Sunday nap. The kids were playing a game in the back room, and she hesitated to go downstairs and bother their grandmother and aunt.

She had to get out of the house for a while. Tiptoeing through the kitchen, she carefully opened the door to the landing and walked down the winding back stairs of the two-story house, careful to avoid a creaky step next to the door that led to her in-laws' kitchen.

The cool air felt good as Laura stepped onto the porch. She hoped Lucille didn't come trotting along, but the old terrier was probably deep in sleep under the lilacs at the far end of the backyard.

Heading out to the street, Laura walked on the wet grass to avoid making noise on the tar driveway. The day had been unusually mild, with afternoon showers that left the tulips heavy with moisture and the ground damp and worm-ripe for the occasional darting robin. Now, as early evening approached, fog enshrouded the valley, blanketing the wide Connecticut River and extending into the residential neighborhoods up the hill from downtown Springfield. Laura was glad she'd grabbed Alan's old poplin jacket from the hook on the landing.

Reaching State Street, the main thoroughfare, she walked to the bus stop on the next corner. She'd left her purse at home, but a skirt pocket yielded a quarter and a dime, enough for three tokens and change.

Laura turned around, wondering if anyone had followed her. *Followed her?* She began to laugh, feeling suddenly like a jailbird on the run, or a spy in a Hitchcock movie. Or maybe just a little kid running away from home who hadn't even thought of where to go. Well, that part was true—she didn't know what to do next.

Deciding to take a walk instead of waiting for the bus, Laura crossed the street and approached the big wrought-iron entrance gate to the college. On the opposite side of the quadrangle, several empty benches under the tall sycamores beckoned. She just needed to be alone for a while. She was never alone.

Skirting the green of the tiny campus of American International, Laura watched a bunch of neighborhood kids playing kickball, a new version of baseball that even Billy liked. Besides swimming, it was one of the few sports her older son seemed to enjoy.

Regular classes had already ended for the term, so the quad was empty of college kids. She wondered if there would be a summer session this year. Probably not, with so many boys in the service.

She picked a bench next to a massive forsythia, a few remaining yellow blossoms still visible against the deep green of the ivy-covered building behind it. The bench was still warm from the fading afternoon sun. Laura closed her eyes and leaned back, sorting out the events of the day.

☙❧

She and Alan had left on the train for Hartford around noon, the kids all set for a visit to the zoo at Forest Park with their aunt. Belle was great that way, and Laura never felt guilty leaving them with her, or with Nan. Both boys were crazy about them.

It was a nuisance having to take the bus downtown and then board a train, but Alan didn't want to risk driving the car from

Springfield to Hartford. Pleasure trips had been discouraged and then banned by the government five months earlier—a year into the war—and they might get stopped over the border with their Massachusetts plates, especially on a holiday weekend.

Pulling out of busy Union Station, the train meandered south along the Connecticut River. Soon they were passing acres of makeshift tents, their white cheesecloth billowing in the late spring breeze. Inside, millions of young tobacco plants were already flourishing in the rich riverbed soil of the valley.

"Wish we could open the windows," Laura said. "It looks so nice out there." The compartment was stuffy with smoke and particles of dust, the glass on the stuck windows filthy.

They'd been lucky to get seats. The trains were never empty anymore. Even today there was a mob of recruits, still in their civilian clothes, headed south, probably to Fort Dix or Fort Monmouth in New Jersey. They acted like a bunch of kids on an outing. Laura wondered if they'd managed to attend their high school graduations.

Arriving in Hartford, she and Alan took a bus from the station over to the West End, where Laura's parents still lived in the big brick colonial of her childhood. The wide street was quiet and shady, with a center strip still lined with majestic elms. Dutch elm disease had begun to take its toll, and she wondered how long it would be before the magnificent trees were gone.

Elizabeth Park was just a block away. It was a bit early for the roses, though this spring had been unusually warm. As a kid, Laura had loved playing under the arbors that dotted the manicured landscape, watching wedding parties gather on Saturday mornings in June to have pictures taken among the thousands of blooming bushes.

She was surprised today at her father's appearance, though her sister Ceil had warned her. "Dad's failing but he won't see a doctor, and mother's pretending everything's just fine." He'd retired from Aetna a few years ago, and as far as she knew didn't do much of anything now. She had a momentary feeling of guilt at how she'd lost track of her parents' weekly routine.

She wondered what they talked about these days. They'd never had much to say to each other when he was working and she and her sister were still at home. "Oh, I have my ladies' clubs, and your father putters around in the garage," her mother replied when

Laura asked a few months back. He didn't do any yard work, though the beds and gardens had already been worked on. She wondered how much they paid to keep the place up. Plenty, she thought ruefully, thinking of the small victory garden she and the boys were planning for the backyard at home.

"So, Alan, how's the job at Westinghouse?" her father asked. She could have predicted the course of the conversation. It always began with this question, and eventually got around to her, and then to the kids. Sometimes, when small talk lagged, they even asked about the dog. That's when she knew it was time to leave.

They were seated in the backyard. Her mother had served lemonade, though something didn't taste quite right, like maybe she hadn't added enough sugar or the lemons weren't ripe. She wasn't looking so good, either, Laura noticed. But they were both in their early sixties, and you had to expect some changes at that age.

She had a sudden image of both her parents years ago at their summer cottage on the shore, her father in that tight black bathing suit with the scooped out strapped top that exposed his chest and accentuated his privates. She'd been embarrassed by that as a kid, as well as a particular beige jersey sleeveless tank suit her mother wore that clung like a second skin to every curve and crevice of her shapely figure.

How funny to imagine them so young, she thought, glancing at the top of her father's head, shiny and mottled, and at her mother's veined hands. Still has nice legs, though, she noticed. Laura had inherited those, as well as her mother's dark, luxuriant hair.

"And you, Laura, are you keeping up?"

She never knew quite what her father meant by that phrase, and she never asked. Instead, she answered, as she always did, "Oh, I'm just fine."

When he'd first started asking that question, she'd imagined that he was making a comment about her new life with Alan. Both her parents had warned her about the adjustments she should expect if she married him. They'd never quite accepted the fact that she hadn't settled down with a boy from a well-heeled West Hartford family, any number of whom she could have had.

"Look, your father doesn't mean anything by it," Alan always said. "He's just not good at small talk." Still, she'd never been quite comfortable visiting, and she was also aware that neither of her parents showed real interest in Billy and Gary. What a difference from Nan and Belle.

The conversation had moved on, as she knew it would, to the perfunctory inquires about the boys. Laura let Alan answer. At some level, even after a dozen years, she still hoped that they'd warm up to him if they'd only get to know each other better. She shifted her gaze down the long expanse of lawn to the playhouse.

She and her sister Ceil had spent many hours in that little house, pretending to be on vacation, hosting tea parties for their friends, reading balmy afternoons away. On hot summer nights, they often slept on little cots that they moved outside the playhouse when the lights went out in her parents' bedroom. The girls' dog and cat, both long gone, would usually join them, though Jinx the spaniel was the more steadfast of the two. Pam invariably prowled off during the night.

They used to put on shows down there for the neighborhood kids. She remembered one where she dressed in the playhouse and emerged dramatically in one of her mother's discarded dresses, a short red satin number. She'd sung "Ain't She Sweet," ending with that complicated hands-on-knees Charleston step it had taken her hours to master. She loved performing, even back then.

It looked like the glass in one of the windows of the playhouse was missing. She was tempted to walk down to see and then decided not to. She didn't want to look inside at the tools and garden equipment her father stored there now.

Suddenly finding herself close to tears, she rummaged for her handkerchief in her black leather bag, which reminded her that it was Memorial Day weekend and she needed to get out her white purse and summer clothes.

"Do you have a cold, Laura?" her mother asked.

"No, you know, just my usual allergy. It makes me tired, too. In fact, we probably should be going."

Alan looked over at her but said nothing. Her parents didn't seem taken aback, but with them you couldn't tell.

On the bus ride back to the train station, Alan asked her what had happened.

"I don't know," she replied. "I suddenly just wanted to get away. I never know how I'm going to feel coming down here—you know that—but it's always a letdown. Always. Not because we fight"—though there had been a few episodes of unpleasantness over the years—"but there's always some kind of, well, letdown, that's the only way to describe it. There's a point where we just have nothing to say, you know?"

She didn't add that today, for some reason, she'd also felt an overwhelming sadness. For what? Her childhood? The noticeable aging of her parents? Everything was so changed, and she was afraid of more coming. She was glad the conversation hadn't turned to the war and Alan's precarious draft status. But her parents never brought up anything of consequence, so no fear of that.

Later, on the train, she asked, "What did you mean when you said, 'Nothing lasts forever' when you and Dad were talking about Westinghouse?" She wished she'd been paying more attention to the conversation, but she had noticed that particular remark.

"Oh, I don't know. Just that, I guess."

"Fibber."

He laughed. "OK, I guess I meant that I don't intend to stay working there, certainly not forever."

She let it go at that and looked out the grimy window. The train was passing a convoy of army vehicles on nearby Route 5, truck after truck covered in green-khaki canvass. The flaps were tied back in the rear of a few, and through the openings she could see young men—soldiers in fatigues—peering out as the train passed. This somber group, unlike the chatting recruits on the trip down, looked like so many cattle on their way to the stockyard. She shuddered and shifted her gaze to Alan.

He'd dozed off and had that funny look on his face when he was asleep, mouth open and eyebrows raised. She watched him for several seconds, feeling irritated and tender and scared, all at the same time.

ॐ∽

"Lady, watch out!!"

Starting, Laura roused herself on the college bench, the image of Alan earlier in the day replaced by that of a real soccer ball heading toward her from across the quad. She jumped up and deftly caught the ball before it sailed over her head.

"Nice one, Mrs. Stewart!" She recognized one of Billy's friends and waved. Then she raised her foot and gave the ball a good kick, sending it high in the air toward the group of boys. She laughed and took a bow as they all applauded. Adjusting her skirt and tossing back her hair, she turned and walked around the edge of the green.

Back on the street, she met the Pringles, an elderly couple who lived in a pretty stucco bungalow up the street. They were each holding big ice cream cones.

"Bet I know where you've been," Laura said.

"Yup, and it's good, too," said Mr. Pringle, one of Laura's admirers, a member of what her sister-in-law Belle called "your old coots fan club." Mr. Pringle was always making remarks about her appearance, little comments that, coming from a younger man, would have made her uncomfortable. But she'd decided old Mr. Pringle was harmless.

"Well, vanilla will do, but I prefer chocolate," his wife said, delicately dabbing at her mouth with a handkerchief. "No chocolate available this week." She sighed and peered at Laura. "What are you doing out by your lonesome, my dear?"

Mrs. Pringle was somewhat of a gossip. Laura wondered if she'd seen her kick the ball. Her skirt had flared up a bit more than she'd expected.

"Just taking a stroll. Have to watch my figure, you know."

"Oh, you've nothing to worry about in that department," Mr. Pringle said. He glanced at his wife, giggled, and added, "Wouldn't you say, dear?" He licked his cone.

Mrs. Pringle ignored him. "And how are Billy and Gary?" she asked.

"Both boys are just fine. We're getting ready for Billy's birthday tomorrow. He'll be ten."

"My, my, time surely does fly. None of us are as young as we used to be." Mrs. Pringle was giving her the once-over. She'd noticed her billowing skirt for sure and, probably, Alan's oversized jacket.

"Well, we don't want to keep you from getting supper ready for everyone," Mrs. Pringle said. She took her husband's arm.

"Supper? Oh, I don't know, Mrs. Pringle, I may just let them go hungry tonight," Laura replied lightly, turning and not waiting to see her neighbor's reaction.

Wrapping Alan's jacket tightly around her in the growing chill, she continued on home. Shielded street lamps cast a muted glow in the fast-diminishing twilight. The green and yellow city buses were finishing up their weekend runs, while a few cars, headlights half-blackened, made their way slowly along State Street. Laura wondered if anyone in the house had missed her. Maybe Lucille, if she wanted to be let in.

From one of the houses, she could hear the faint radio sound of Harry James' trumpet on "How Deep Is the Ocean?," an Irving Berlin tune she used to sing back in her band days. Unconsciously, she began to hum along.

Overhead, the drone of a fleet of B-17s from nearby Westover, heading eastward, was a nightly reminder of the war raging across the Atlantic. Occasionally a dog barked, one yelp setting off a cacophonous chorus from other zealous guardians perched on front porches or sniffing the trunks of trees bordering the sidewalks and streets. The steady buzz of katydids, newly emerged from the soil and ready to mate, thrummed in the carefully tended yards and gardens of the houses on the hill.

Laura walked faster, realizing that she did need to start supper as soon as she got home. No food, and they'd all realize she wasn't there, for sure. She'd even asked Belle and Nan to join them.

She tried to make up a funny story to tell her younger son about what she'd been up to. Gary wouldn't get it if she said she'd just wanted to be alone. Billy, on the other hand, would, and not only because he was older. He just understood things.

By the time Laura reached home, it was nearly dark. The heavy scent of lilacs filled the air as she walked up the drive. She was tempted to stroll down to the backyard, but she heard the jingle of Lucille's collar as she lumbered down from the porch.

"All right, old girl. Come on, let's go in." Laura reached down and put her cheek against the top of the terrier's fuzzy head. "Guess they didn't miss either one of us."

She was right about that. The kitchen was dark, as though no one had been about since she left. She exchanged the jacket for her apron hanging on the pantry door. There was the sound of a radio and the boys' voices coming from Billy's room, but no sign of Alan's having stirred.

She went into the bathroom, quietly closing the door and pulling the chain on the lamp above the mirror. Blinking in the sudden glare, she examined her reflection. Not great, but at least this time there was no old crone gaping back at her. She turned off the light.

Heating baked beans to go with the ham they'd had the night before, Laura rummaged through the pantry cupboard and found a can of B&M brown bread in the back of the top shelf. The kids would like that, and she could even put out a big slab of butter from what was left of last week's rationing. She wiped the dust off the can—it must have been up there since before the war— and carefully cut out the top with the opener, gently plopping the bread onto a plate. It looked and smelled all right.

Examining the dark, moist cylinder, she wondered how it got into the can in the first place. Was it poured and then baked inside the tin?

The bread reminded her of the clipper ship in the bottle on her father's desk back home. She'd never figured out the mechanics of that mystery either. "Magic," he always said, until he finally explained it to her one afternoon when he'd found her holding the bottle and peering with one eye into the narrow opening. She couldn't remember if it still sat on his desk, next to the green banker's lamp.

Laura continued to stare at the bread. *In a little while*, she thought, *this perfectly shaped object is going to be cut to pieces, pulled apart by the fingers of two hungry boys, and chewed into nothingness. And it's been sitting so quietly by itself all this time.* She felt like crying again.

Laura closed her eyes and massaged her temples. She had hoped the walk would help, but it hadn't.

Chapter 2: Billy

Billy crept out of bed and walked softly across the room. From down the hallway came the flourish of organ music and the slow, torturous opening of a creaky door. *"Inner Sanctum Mysteries,"* intoned a familiar voice, *"brought to you by Palmolive Shaving Cream. Welcome to another session of mystery, murder and madness."*

Billy carefully took the striped pullover vest that Nan had knitted from his bottom dresser drawer and pulled it on over his pajama top. The wool itched, but he soon forgot his discomfort as the plot of tonight's episode unfolded. Stretched out on the scatter rug next to the half-opened bedroom door, he settled in, straining to hear every word.

A man and lady who spoke with English accents were driving along a lonely road when their car suddenly died. Somewhere in the distance a dog howled. *"I'll go back to that cottage we passed and get help,"* said the man. *"Oh, Nigel, do be careful,"* the lady replied, the slamming of the car door echoing in the stillness. She clicked on the radio just in time to hear an urgent bulletin. *"A patient has escaped from the local asylum for the criminally insane. He is a convicted ax murderer and is considered dangerous. Stay inside and bolt your doors. We repeat, stay inside."* The dog howled again, followed by a thumping outside the car. *"Nigel, Nigel? Who's there? Who's there?"* the English lady cried.

Suddenly, Billy's mother's voice interrupted. "Alan, mind if I switch the station? It's almost time for Walter Winchell."

"Go ahead," replied his father. "I'll tend to the furnace. I'll be up in a jiff."

Billy shivered and ran back to his bed. He buried his head under the pillow and tried to forget about the ax murderer on the lonely road. But then he imagined his father making his way down the winding backstairs to the musty cellar with its dark corners and cobwebs and scurrying mice. He wished Lucille would pad in from the living room and jump up on the foot of the bed.

The living room was quiet now except for the music of some band. Nan and Belle had come up for dinner but had gone back downstairs when Jack Benny's show was over.

"Come on, Mother, I've got to work the matinee shift tomorrow," Belle said. "No rest for the wicked, even on Memorial Day. And the thought of those kids running up and down the aisles. Yikes. I've got a headache already. Thanks for dinner, Laura."

"The ham and beans hit the spot," Nan added. "And we haven't had brown bread in a good while. With real butter at that!"

Gary had already been sent off to bed, but Billy was in no hurry to say goodnight. Since there was no school tomorrow, he was hoping to stay up past his usual eight o'clock bedtime. But his father had been firm.

"Off you go, Billy," Alan said after another hour or so. "You know the rules. And you've got a big day coming up, birthday boy." Billy glanced over at his mother.

"Gary's already been asleep for an hour," Laura said, as though that explained everything. At night she always deferred to his father's word. He knew it was no use arguing. Besides, he could tell his mother was out of sorts. He wondered where she'd gone off to a few hours earlier without telling anyone.

As he walked off to bed, Billy could hear Gary across the hall, not asleep at all, singing one of his favorite commercials. *"Halo everybody, Halo!"* he piped in his little voice. *"Halo is the shampoo that glorifies your hair, Halo everybody, Halo!"* He could drive you crazy with these jingles.

Billy stuck his head in the doorway and shushed, "Go to sleep!"

"Shut up, Billy!" Gary hissed back. *"Rinso white, Rinso bright, happy little washday song!"*

Now, after a few minutes hidden under the covers, Billy stopped thinking about the murderer from the asylum. Too warm now, he sat up and wriggled out of his vest. Carefully folding the wool blanket so that it rested at the foot of the bed, he considered taking off his flannel pajamas, at least the top. But then he'd probably wake up later with an asthma attack, wheezing for breath, unable to lie down, hoping for morning or a few hours of sleep. He didn't want to begin the day like that. Not when tomorrow was his birthday.

"I was born in 1933, and you were born in 1938," he'd said to Gary that afternoon. "I'll be ten and you're still five. So, tomorrow I'll be two times as old as you." Gary hadn't really understood what that meant, but Nan smiled when Billy told her what he'd figured out.

"Yes, I guess that's true," she said. "My goodness, I wonder how many times older that makes me than the two of you. Can't do my figures that high, I'm afraid."

Maybe he could sneak out for a drink of water, though he knew he'd have to be quiet and not let anyone hear him, at least not until he was already in the bathroom. And if Lucille was still awake she'd perk up her ears. But she was probably dozing at the foot of his father's chair, her Scottie tail occasionally twitching in reaction to a sound effect from the radio or an exciting dog dream.

After counting to 100 three times in a row, once backwards, Billy gave up. He turned over and opened his eyes. The white sharpness of the full moon, softened by a few wispy clouds, cast a pale light across the room. The wallpaper opposite his bed, a panorama of clipper ships, sails billowing against the blue sky, reflected the spidery pattern of the gauze window curtain.

Billy smoothed out the top sheet and began thinking about the presents he'd be getting tomorrow. He'd made out a list and memorized it so that when anyone asked he was able to say exactly what he wanted. He knew he'd receive games and a few other toys from his Aunt Belle. Mrs. Brown always gave him books, and she'd asked him what he'd been reading the other day when he was out back by her house. He hadn't put any clothes on his list, but that's what Nan would buy him anyway. What he wanted more than anything was a Viewmaster like the one he'd seen downtown in the toy department at Johnson's.

Just as he was imagining presents carefully piled on his chair at tomorrow's birthday dinner, there was a flash of light against the side of the house next door. The familiar putt-putt of Sal's red Ford got louder as the sedan made its way along the Mazzarellas' gravel driveway. Even from the second floor, Billy could hear the knocks and pings that continued after the car's motor died.

He quickly jumped out of bed and squatted by the bedroom window, propped open a few inches at the bottom. The orange glow of Sal's cigarette was visible inside the car. Sal had told him earlier in the day that he was going bowling and then maybe to a movie. He wondered which one he'd seen. And if he had gone alone or with a friend.

"They've got *This Gun for Hire* with Alan Ladd at the Paramount, Sal," Billy said. He always knew the schedules of all the theaters downtown. "Maybe Belle can get you in for free."

"Nah, I don't want no crime show. Any war movies on?"

"*Action in the North Atlantic* is at the Capitol. Humphrey Bogart's in it. It's about U-boats."

"Hey, that sounds good. He was swell in *Casablanca*." Sal smiled and poked Billy's shoulder. "Thanks, chief. See you later."

Billy's legs were starting to fall asleep from his crouching position at the sill. He shifted his feet and inched the window up a bit further. Now he could hear the faint sound of band music coming from inside the darkened car. Sal always played his radio real loud, so he must have lowered the volume when he turned into the drive.

The car door opened and Sal stepped out into the driveway. His high school team jacket was open, and his t-shirt glowed white in the faint moonlight as he yawned and stretched his arms over his head. Billy thought he saw Sal glance up his way, but he wasn't sure. Sal flicked his cigarette into the grass and walked onto his back porch. He opened the squeaky screen door and disappeared into the darkened kitchen.

Billy waited for the light to go on upstairs in the bedroom directly across from his own. Sometimes Sal left the shade raised, but tonight he reached up and pulled it down, scratching at his stomach with his other hand. Faint shadows appeared as he moved around the room. Billy continued to watch the window, massaging his toes to keep them warm. Pretty soon he could tell that Sal had begun his exercises by the rhythmic motions of his silhouette on the shade. And then after a few minutes the lights went out.

Billy shifted his glance to the left, to Angie's window. Her shade was pulled, too, but there was a faint pink glow from the light of her lamp, which meant she was still reading in bed. Angie's parents let her stay up a lot later than Billy, even though she was just a year older. When they were younger, Angie and Billy used to stand in their windows after bedtime and talk in a kind of sign language. That didn't happen anymore, but they spent a lot of time together after school and on the weekends. Angie was still his best friend.

Suddenly sleepy, he got back into bed and curled into his favorite position, on his side, legs tucked up, one arm under the pillow. As he began to drift off, he faintly heard a familiar voice bark from the living room, *"Good evening Mr. and Mrs. North and South America and all the ships at sea!"* That meant it was already 9 p.m. *"FLASH!"* shouted Walter Winchell, tapping on some kind of mechanical key that made everything he said sound urgent. *"Yamamoto is dead, reported on Tokyo radio as having been shot down somewhere over the Pacific!"*

This *was* big news, since everyone knew Admiral Yamamoto had planned the attack on Pearl Harbor two years ago. Billy wondered if it meant the war was ending, or at least the part of the fighting in what they called the "Pacific Theater." He couldn't understand why it was called a "theater." Trying to figure that one out again, he drifted off.

☙❧

During the night Billy had a dream. He was sitting on a bench in a dark room along with men in khaki outfits. All of them were clutching straps above their heads. It was very cold. Suddenly a door in front of them opened, and Billy realized they were high above the ground. They were flying in an airplane, and now he understood that he was a paratrooper getting ready to jump. He turned to check his chute, only to discover he wasn't wearing one.

Strangely, there was no noise in the hold, and everything seemed to be happening in slow motion. Outside the open door another plane appeared and began to pass them. The window of its cockpit seemed to be only a few feet away. Sitting in the co-pilot's seat was an old Japanese soldier wearing a lot of medals, his white silk scarf waving in the air. As his gaze met Billy's he held up a birthday cake and grinned like the evil Japanese soldiers in "Terry and the Pirates." Then he began to cut the cake with a big ax.

Suddenly, bullet holes shattered the front of the plane. Blood splattered over everything. With a surprised look on his face, the old pilot and his plane fell silently from sight, white smoke trailing against the clear blue sky, scarf floating in the air toward Billy's face.

He awoke with a start. It was just beginning to get light, and he was freezing, and Lucille's stubby tail was brushing against his cheek.

"Lucille," he whispered. "Move. Get up, Lucille."

But Lucille was deep in her own dream, so Billy eased himself sideways from under the sheet and crawled to the foot of the bed. He retrieved the folded blanket and quickly covered them both.

Looking at the grayish pink dawn outside his window, he suddenly remembered he had turned ten years old during the night. Billy stopped thinking about his General Yamamoto dream and concentrated instead on the day ahead and the party that he'd be having at dinnertime. He reached down and placed his hand on Lucille's fuzzy back, glad to be safe in his own bed.

Chapter 3: Belle

Belle was half dozing when her alarm went off, its relentless buzz finally jolting her fully awake. *Let it ring*, she thought, *Nan'll never hear it*. Then she remembered with a start that it was Memorial Day. Maybe Alan was trying to sleep in upstairs. She reached over and knocked both the clock and her ashtray to the floor.

"Shit...So much for that," she said aloud. She swung herself to the side of the bed and leaned down to retrieve the still-ringing clock and the pink shell ashtray she'd brought back last year from Atlantic City. She collected the cigarette butts from the floor and wiped up the ashes with a Kleenex.

It was 7:30, earlier than she'd usually get up on a late workday. She didn't have to be at the theater until noon, but she'd promised her mother they'd go to the cemetery before she caught the downtown bus. She lay back on the bed, covering her legs and feet with the rumpled winter spread she still hadn't put away. It was a bit chilly, but the cool breeze from the slightly open window felt good.

Belle could hear Nan already bustling about in the kitchen. She wasn't light on her feet, but she moved like someone half her age. Funny how she and Alan usually referred to her as Nan, same as almost everyone else. She was the grandma everyone wished they had. When Billy came along and all the attention shifted to him, well, that did it. The adults followed his lead and started to call her "Nan," maybe because they still wanted to be one of her favorites, too.

"Belle, dearie, are you up?" Nan was peering around the open door, wiping her hands on her apron. Belle had finally gotten her to stop singing snatches of songs at this particular time of day—"You Are My Sunshine" was one of Nan's wake-up favorites—but that had taken time. Belle wasn't at her best in the morning.

"Getting up!" she answered. She swung herself off the bed and walked over to her mother. "Good morning, sweetie," she said, giving her a hug. Belle knew Memorial Day was always difficult for her. even with Billy's birthday and all.

Belle had her usual breakfast of toast, coffee, and a Chesterfield. Then she went back to her bedroom to get ready for the day. She decided she'd have time to do her hair after the cemetery. She picked out a pale rayon turban that covered her pin curls, a white cotton blouse and, with some second thoughts, a new pair of pleated beige gabardine slacks. She slipped on her wooden-heeled wedgies, applied some lipstick and returned to the kitchen.

She was having her second cup of coffee and another cigarette when Nan appeared, pocketbook in hand. She'd changed to her dark blue crepe and a tam with a green feather.

"Don't you look nice," Belle said. She waited for Nan's response.

"Thank you, dear. So...you're all set?"

"Yep, all set."

"Belle, your blouse is very pretty, but those pants..."

"Slacks, Nan, they're nice gabardine slacks. Two ninety-eight at Forbes."

"I know, but it seems so unladylike...pants."

"Mother, I know I'm a lady and you know I'm a lady. I'm not going to get all dressed up when I've got to change again later. I'm wearing these nice gabardine slacks. Come on, let's go."

Nan gave a sigh of resignation, but she patted Belle's arm as they walked down the front porch steps. Despite the mild weather, Nan was wearing her light woolen coat, a silk scarf and brown cotton gloves. Belle had her sweater flung over her shoulder. She needed both hands to hold the geranium and vinca arrangement that Nan had carefully potted earlier in the week.

They walked under newly leafed elms and oaks shading both sides of the wide street. The houses, a mix of bungalows and larger multistoried structures with porches on each floor, reflected the quietness of the holiday morning. A few birds chirped and the odd squirrel scurried away at their approach, but that was all.

Red and white squares flags with a blue star in the center were displayed in many of the windows they passed, reminders to Belle of all the kids she'd grown up with who were serving overseas. As they approached the Hathaway house, she dreaded seeing the gold star—signifying the loss of a loved one—that had probably already replaced the blue. Donnie Hathaway had been reported killed in action several weeks ago, somewhere over North Africa.

Belle thought of Alan. Still at home, but for how long? She shivered and hugged the flowerpot closer to her chest.

"What is it, Belle?" asked Nan.

"Just a little chilly, that's all," she answered, smiling and nudging her elbow against her mother's arm. "You were right, after all, to wear your coat."

Sure enough, she spotted the altered flag in the big picture window as they reached the Hathaways' stucco cottage. The gold star was indistinct but unmistakable behind the evaporating dew on the glass pane. Belle and Nan exchanged glances. "Dear, oh dear," was all Nan said.

They cut over to Oak Grove Avenue. A short distance ahead of them, the cemetery's black iron entrance gates were already open in anticipation of the busy day ahead.

As they walked under the massive brownstone arch, Belle thought of the countless times she and Nan and, in earlier days, Alan, had brought their birthday and holiday offerings. Alan hardly came any more.

Belle remembered her father as a solid lap and the smell of a smoking pipe, but to Alan he was just a name and a yellowed photo in an oval silver frame on Nan's bedroom bureau. He'd died just after the last war, in a construction site accident. Twenty-five years ago, to be exact, when she was eight and Alan only five. When they were kids Alan used to ask Belle questions about him, but no more.

The grave lay under a big sycamore at the crest of a grassy rise, past the huge crypts and ornate monuments to the dead of an earlier era. Nan picked up some twigs and a few of last year's leaves and wiped the stone with her handkerchief. *William Fraser Stewart*, it read, *August 2, 1882-July 5, 1922*. It always chilled Belle to see that name—Billy's name now—carved in stone.

She stepped back and stumbled on her wedgies. "Goddamn dangerous shoes," she muttered under her breath.

"It's so pretty here, isn't it?" Nan said.

"Yes, dear, that it is," Belle replied. *But so what if you're dead and gone and don't know the difference*, she thought. It was a lovely spot, though, in its own quiet way. Strangely calming. Maybe that was the point. Soon they'd be back to do some planting for the summer.

Belle gently placed the pot next to the stone. She handed Nan a clean handkerchief and took her arm. They stood for a moment over the grave, the silence broken only by the scolding of birds unused to early morning intruders.

On the way out, they passed a few other holiday visitors, busy fixing plants and getting water from the low faucets on the corners of the graveled pathways. A little boy, younger than Billy, struggled to stick a large American flag in the ground at the head of a grave already decorated with a smaller one, placed there by the local chapter of the Veterans of Foreign Wars.

ॐ◌ॐ

Back home, Belle hurried to get ready for work. She removed the pins from her hair, quickly combed it out, and fixed her face at the bathroom mirror. She envied Laura her naturally wavy hair. One less thing to have to do every night. She grabbed her dried stockings from the shower rod. She hated the heavy feel of the rayon on her legs, but she wasn't going to risk her last pair of nylons traipsing up and down the dark aisles of the theater. She reminded herself to buy a new bottle of leg make-up for the warmer weather ahead.

"OK, Nan, I'm off. I'll be back in time for Billy's cake. How's this?" Belle did a couple of quick turns. "Better?" She knew Nan liked the look of her uniform, its neat pleated skirt, white blouse, low pumps, and dark blazer. Some days she wore her street clothes and changed into the spare outfit she kept at the theater, but today she was coming straight home after work for Billy's party.

"Lovely, dear. Now, be careful." Belle was never sure what she was supposed to be careful about—the weather, a runaway bus, a tall, dark stranger?—but Nan said this to everyone. She kissed her goodbye.

"Oops, wipe your cheek, hon," Belle said. Everyone liked to kiss Nan, so she often bore traces of lipstick on her face—except, of course, on her own unpainted lips. "OK, so who visited you today?" Belle would often ask, pointing to a telltale crimson smudge.

She dashed out the front door and down the steps and then realized she'd forgotten about Billy. She turned back onto the porch, opened the door to the separate second floor entrance, and walked up the stairs. Laura came from the kitchen, wiping her hands on her apron. Every hair in place, as usual, but she looked as though she'd been crying.

"You all right?" Belle asked.

"Yes, fine, just didn't sleep well."

"I came to wish Billy a happy birthday. Not here, huh?"

"No, he and Gary are out playing somewhere. Maybe next door at Angie's."

"That's fine, I'll catch him tonight. Save some cake for me. Got to run, sweetie."

"See you, Belle," Laura replied. She added, "I'll talk to you later."

Walking to the corner to catch the downtown bus, Belle wondered what that was all about. She knew that Alan had been staying out late some nights. And he was drinking too much, but that wasn't anything new. She'd get the scoop later from Laura.

The buses weren't running as frequently because of the holiday, and there were few cars on State Street. An old dark blue Dodge approached and slowed down. A cute-looking sailor, still in winter blues, leaned out the passenger's side and yelled, "Hey, headin' downtown?" The driver and another guy in the back seat were also in uniform.

"Thanks, fellas, some other time. Got to go straight to work."

They laughed, waved, and drove off. Home on leave from boot camp, Belle figured. She wondered where they'd be by the end of the summer. On the Atlantic? Pacific? Alive somewhere, she hoped. She rummaged in her purse and lit a Chesterfield. Nan would kill her if she knew. But at least she was wearing a skirt. Talking to sailors and smoking on the street was bad enough. In pants it would be enough to send her straight to hell, for sure.

The bus finally arrived. Belle gave the driver a quarter and said, "Three please." He handed her two tokens and dropped a third in the glass receptacle, where it clinked as it hit others at the bottom. Holding on to the metal rims of the seats to balance herself, she walked deftly down the aisle.

The bus made good time as it clattered downtown, past the college and the shops at Winchester Square. Lights were on in the big brick Indian Motorcycle plant, a huge building extending an entire block.

Heading down the hill that led to the center of the city and the Connecticut River, they passed the Armory and its acres of sprawling buildings, some of them dating from colonial times. Activity there, too, she noted.

Everything was so different now. She wondered how much her friend Betty was being paid to work the holiday. "Belle, give up that lousy job at the Paramount," Betty told her all the time. "So what that you're the assistant manager? The pay is crappy and your boss, the guy with the hands, is a jerk."

But Belle had decided to stay on until she made up her mind about school. If she wanted to take a college class or two, it would be easier to work a schedule at the theater that would allow her to attend during the day. Meantime, this job paid the bills, and so far she'd been able to keep Mr. Simpson in line.

She got off the bus just before it turned the corner into Lyman Street, near its last stop at the train station. She walked to the side of the theater, retrieved a hefty set of keys from her purse, and let herself in through what used to be the stage door back in vaudeville days. Belle enjoyed opening up. It gave her a feeling of really being in charge, and she liked that.

She turned on all the lights, checked the ventilating and heating systems, and reviewed the staff worksheet. She wondered if Maisie, the ladies' room attendant, would show up, and in what condition. Besides Maisie, there were nine others on the afternoon shift. That wasn't counting Mr. Pomerang, the organist, who wouldn't come in until just before the first evening show. She reminded herself to ask him if his floor switch had been repaired. Last week he got stranded halfway between the basement and the stage when the console lift got stuck.

Belle was sorting the cash for the box office and candy counter when the loud buzzer at the old stage door entrance startled her. That would be Stan. He'd been the projectionist since talkies came in. She locked the office door behind her and made her way backstage down the hall with its exposed brick wall and naked light bulbs.

"Hiya, Stan," she said as she opened the door. "You going to have Bobby go out and get some coffee when he gets here? Tell him to get me one and a BLT, would you?" Bobby was a high-school kid who helped Stan and did other odd jobs on the weekends and late afternoons. She hoped the lunch shop wasn't closed today.

By the time she unlocked the box office door for Lorraine, everyone had arrived. Maisie looked like hell, bags under her eyes the size of pillows, but she was sober. There was already a line forming outside. *This Gun for Hire* was a surprise hit, already held over for a second week. Belle hadn't seen the movie yet from start to finish, but maybe she'd work on Laura and see if she could take Billy to an early show during the week.

She knocked on the door of the little cubicle at the front of the sidewalk lobby. "Ready, Lorraine?"

"All set, Belle."

She moved around to the sidewalk. "Good afternoon, folks, the box office is now open. Please have your money ready, change if you've got it, and enjoy the show."

Today would be easy. No Simpson, only a few hours of work, and then Billy's party. Belle walked briskly back into the theater, checking her stocking seams in one of the mirrors that lined both sides of the wide, tiled entrance lobby.

Chapter 4: Laura

After spilling half a pint of milk inside the refrigerator, Laura burned her finger on the stove and then dropped an egg on the floor. She bent down with a spoon and cup to try to salvage the mess, but it was no use. Lucille, hoping for an unexpected treat, shuffled over to investigate. Ignoring Laura's cries of "Shoo!" she gave a cursory sniff or two and then turned and walked away, leaving sticky paw prints on the shiny linoleum.

"Boys, come on. Up!" Laura yelled. Alan was still sleeping, but as far as she was concerned he could get up, too. She wasn't feeling particularly charitable this morning.

She could have seen it coming. "Alan, why now?" she'd asked again the week before when he'd brought the subject up. "You've gone this long without enlisting. Why now?"

"You know my letter's coming," he replied. The government had recently announced that the ban on drafting married men with children would be lifted later in the summer.

"Besides," he added, "I might as well go in now. Christ, I'm getting nowhere at the plant and I hate it. That last promotion was probably it. I'll be thirty soon and then what? Another 35 years at Westinghouse and a gold watch when I retire?"

"Thirty's not old."

"Come on, Laura, we don't even have our own place. Do you I like that we rent a floor in my mother's house? And the same shitty job for another ten years? I'm stuck. Maybe I can learn something in the service. They say a lot of new stuff—machines and inventions—are being developed in the military."

"All right, I guess I understand. Don't swear. It's a shock, that's all."

She couldn't argue with his logic. He was miserable, and she was concerned about the time he was spending away from the house at night. It wasn't good for the kids. They usually weren't even up to see him when he got home. On second thought, maybe that was just as well. His drinking was beginning to concern her. Belle had even asked her about it the other day.

"If I enlist, I can pick the Navy. Maybe I can get into some kind of electronics—radio or radar on a ship. Something like that. And then I could even go to school afterwards."

She noticed that he didn't add that maybe being on the water was safer than getting shot at in the desert or in a jungle on some godforsaken island. That's what everyone said about the difference between the Army and the Navy. And it would only get worse for the soldiers in Europe when the rumored invasion of Italy or wherever finally came. As for the Marines, she wasn't sure what their rules were regarding age and marital status, but it seemed to be the most dangerous branch. She realized she didn't know much about the military at all.

The Navy meant that he'd probably be farther away, most likely in the Pacific. And the war with Japan was going to go on longer, that's what Gabriel Heatter predicted on the news last week. Still, Laura felt she'd rather see him "somewhere at sea," as the commentators always said. "Somewhere" seemed safer.

Laura heard a door close downstairs. She looked out the kitchen window and smiled when she saw the feather on Nan's hat fluttering as she walked down the drive with Belle. She was about to open the window and ask Belle to check the back porch to see if there had been a milk delivery, but she wasn't in the mood for even a wave.

She wondered when Alan would tell Nan he was enlisting. Belle already suspected. Maybe his mother did, too. Laura thought Nan always knew way more than she let on. She just pretended everything was fine. Who knows, maybe she really did think things were swell, at least mostly swell. Nan had lived a long time. If it worked for her...

Laura walked down the hallway. Gary was still in bed. "Up, young man, right now!" She turned and looked in Billy's room. He was just finishing getting dressed.

"Happy Birthday, honey," Laura said.

"Thanks, Ma. Breakfast almost ready?"

"Yup, go on in," Laura said, knowing he was wondering if she'd remembered his special birthday breakfast.

She opened the door to the bedroom at the end of the hall. The room was stuffy with the smell of stale smoke and sleep. In the semi-darkness she could see Alan's feet sticking out of the covers at the bottom of the double bed.

"Awake?" she asked softly.

He grabbed her and pulled her down on top of him.

"Whoa!" Laura whispered. "Hey, I'm cooking breakfast." But she allowed herself a moment of feeling his stubble against her cheek and the warmth of his body under hers. He thrust her hand against his pajama bottoms.

"The kids are waiting," she said, knowing that he knew that, too. She moved her hand away. *You're ready when it's not the right time,* she couldn't help thinking. *Why not last night?* She got up from the bed and straightened her dress and apron. She left the door open as she returned to the kitchen.

"OK, French toast for Billy The Birthday Boy!" she said. "Go get your little brother. His breakfast'll be cold."

❧❦

Later in the morning Laura had the house to herself. Alan had promised Nan he'd straighten up the basement. Billy would have been expected to help, but since it was his birthday Alan excused him. Just as well, Laura thought, it would only end up in a scene of one kind or another. He and Gary had gone out to play, Lucille clumping down the stairs after them. Billy was probably at Angie's next door and Gary with his new little friend, Jimmy.

Laura heated up the oven and began to mix the batter for Billy's favorite cake. It was called "victory cake" in the new cookbook issued by the government, but Laura had also seen it described more enticingly in a magazine as "yum yum cake." Everyone liked it, and it required no butter, no eggs and no milk. She had gotten some sugar from Nan—folks in the neighborhood were always giving Nan a bit extra for her tea—and she still had two squares of chocolate left over from last month.

She decided to fix the spaghetti sauce while she was at it. Laura prided herself on her sauce. Even Mary Mazzarella next door once said, "This gravy very good! You sure you're not Italian 'way back?"

No one could make meatballs like Mary, and Laura was determined to get the recipe. She'd once asked for it, but instead Mary had made a big batch and presented it to her.

One day she brought up the subject with Angie. "Do you ever watch your mother make her meatballs?"

"Nah, Mrs. Stewart," Angie replied innocently, "I never pay attention when she cooks. Besides, she moves real fast and doesn't even have anything written down." She smiled sweetly at Laura.

Stirring the sauce, Laura turned on the radio in time to catch Bing Crosby's 15-minute morning show. She loved the mellow sound of his voice, and he could sing anything—ballads, western songs, Hawaiian. Did he ever get as nervous as she used to before a performance? Everything he sang seemed so effortless.

Laura wondered what the coming weeks had in store for Alan. For all of them. She went over and over the conversation they'd last night in bed.

"What do you mean, already? It's definite? You've *already* enlisted? You mean the next thing is that you'll be called?" she asked incredulously. Alan had finally confessed that he'd actually gone to the recruiting station two days before. That explained why he had come home early on Friday, claiming he didn't feel well. She hadn't really believed him; he was never sick enough to miss work.

"Yep, it's definite," he answered. "They said I'll get my orders in a week or two."

"How could you do that without telling me?"

"What was the point of telling you before? Anyway, I had told you, kind of. Come on, Laura, you knew that I was planning this. Now it's done. The Navy took me."

They had stopped talking when they heard a tap on the half-open bedroom door. Gary was standing there, scratching his eyes and holding the back of his pajamas. Sometimes he wandered down to their room if he had a bad dream, but they had taught him always to knock.

"What is it, Gary?" Laura asked, wondering how much he had overhead. She quickly got up and led him to the bathroom.

She wasn't, in fact, completely surprised by Alan's news. He'd been hinting for weeks. But she was scared.

She'd be OK with money, especially if she went to work at the Mutual. The insurance company had lifted its restriction on hiring married women the previous month. Because of her earlier experience at the Travelers in Hartford, Laura knew she could get a job there anytime she wanted, and she'd been planning to do that. But not so soon, and not because she really had to. Now she had to. She'd make an appointment to go for an interview next week. She had no idea what a sailor's pay was, but not a heck of a lot, that much she knew.

She was adding Mary's meatballs to the simmering sauce when Bing Crosby began to sing "Stardust." She paused and closed her eyes. That was the song playing the night Alan asked her to dance at the Atlantic Beach Casino at Misquamicut, down on the Rhode Island shore. She and her sister had driven over from the family cottage at Black Point, on the Sound. She'd noticed him right away, several inches taller than anyone else in the big ballroom.

Had it really been only a dozen years ago? Along with the cottage, the dance hall had been blown out to the sea in the '38 hurricane. She had sung there for a couple of summers after she turned sixteen. Sixteen. It all seemed like a million years ago.

As the song ended, she heard a "Yoo hoo, it's me!" in the front hallway. Her hands were wet and smelled of garlic from the meatballs, so she wiped her eyes and face with her apron.

"Coming!" she cried as she rushed through the living room in time to meet Belle at the top of the stairs. Laura didn't want to have to explain everything just now, so she was relieved that her sister-in-law had only come to wish Billy a happy birthday. She'd get Belle alone tonight at the party and tell her.

Laura walked briskly back to the kitchen. She turned down the gas heat under the sauce, washed all the dishes and tidied up the counter. She took a wet mop to the linoleum and wiped away the stickiness and Lucille's paw prints. The cake was cooling on the top of the fridge, out of the dog's reach, and the frosting—"fluffy frosting," made of honey, vanilla extract and egg white—already made and waiting to be spread. Laura took off her apron and hung it behind the pantry door.

Alan would be up from the cellar soon, and he and the boys would be wanting lunch. She'd make sandwiches—that would finish off the ham—and perhaps a Waldorf or some other kind of salad. She had plenty of apples. It seemed surprising that fruit and vegetables hadn't been rationed, at least not yet. Maybe homegrown produce wouldn't be a problem. It was all very confusing.

Laura walked to the bathroom and, soaking a Kleenex in witch hazel, blotted her eyes to take away the puffiness. She'd learned that trick from one of the movie magazines Angie was always bringing over for Billy. Stretching her mouth wide in an exaggerated smile, she inspected her teeth. She was proud of their whiteness and perfect shape. Then she washed her face, brushed her hair, applied fresh lipstick, and gave herself a final inspection in the mirror. Not bad.

Laura wanted to look especially nice for Billy's party tonight. She knew he liked having a pretty mother, and she decided she'd wear her green silk. It was too dressy for the occasion, but he liked it. She hung the dress on the closet door, humming as she carefully stretched some wrinkled pleats on the skirt. It would do without an ironing.

She started to sing "Stardust" as she headed back to the kitchen. Laura kept her voice in shape by singing every day, even if she didn't get a chance to sit down at the piano. She missed performing, especially now that Gary wasn't a baby anymore.

Instead of starting lunch, she went into the living room and pulled out the bench to the small upright she'd brought from home when she and Alan married. She flipped up the keyboard cover and began to try a new song, "I Had the Craziest Dream." After hearing Harry James' recording last week on the radio, she'd bought the sheet music at Woolworth's. The melody she could pretty much play by ear—she could manage anything if she knew the tune—but she needed the sheet music for the words. Soon she was lost in the music.

"Say, I like that. Can I have this dance?" Alan had come up behind her and was nuzzling her neck. She reached around and stroked the back of his head.

"Sure can, mister, but we'll have to hurry. I have a husband and kids to feed."

She got up and they did a few turns around the room. The back of Alan's shirt was damp, and she could smell the familiar scent of his body. Laura closed her eyes.

Outside, Gary yelled something in his shrill little voice, and Lucille's hoarse bark answered back.

"Hey, you're all sooty from the cellar," Laura said to Alan, moving back. "Go wash up, I'll call the kids and we'll eat." She took his head in her hands and gave him a kiss. "Sailor," she said. He patted her behind as she walked off to the kitchen.

Chapter 5: Alan

Alan heard Laura singing as he made his way up the back stairs from the cellar. He knew it wouldn't take her long to recover from the night before.. On the other hand, maybe she wasn't that upset at his leaving. Not exactly happy, perhaps, but ambivalent? Ready for something else? He didn't want to think that and, besides, he wasn't sure about anything these days.

Walking down the hall, Alan paused at the door to the living room. Laura's back was to him, long black hair swaying with the motion of her head, right foot caressing the piano pedal, fingers moving across the keyboard in a blur of gleaming red polish. She was singing a song about a dream. He tiptoed close to her and kissed her behind the ear. She smelled of the scent she always wore—My Sin—and he was glad when she turned and smiled up at him.

He headed for the bathroom and a quick shower before lunch. It was good to get sweaty and grimy once in a while. In a way, he missed that at the plant. And he hated feeling caught in the middle of management disputes with his friends. He could feel the tension sometimes when he was with the guys from his old department, even though none of them reported directly to him.

"Hey, we're still friends, right?" he'd asked Joe, his work buddy, after his promotion was announced last year.

"Yah, sure, but it's going to be funny to see you in a shirt and tie and all," Joe replied. "That'll go over big with the boys at the bar." Alan hadn't really thought that moving up to management, even a lower rung, would change anything except his paycheck and what he did at his desk.

But it had. He didn't eat lunch with his old crowd anymore, and he rarely saw them during the day. He left at the blast of the three o'clock whistle only on the days when he was the car pool driver.

When he did occasionally stop in later at the High Life across the street from the plant, most of the guys he knew were long gone, including his ride, and he'd end up drinking with whoever was left standing at the bar. Too often that meant taking a bus home, where he was greeted by Laura's icy welcome, a grudgingly heated-up dinner, which he ate alone, and awkward glances from Billy. Lucille still slobbered all over him and Gary was always eager to tell him about his day. Often, however, both boys were already in bed.

Alan finished drying himself and stood in front of the bathroom mirror, smoothing his hair back with a silver-plated brush, one of a set Nan had handed on to him. The monogram "WFS', etched in a fancy, old-fashioned script, was one of the few tangible reminders of his father.

"Daddy, Mommy says lunch is ready," Gary announced at the bathroom doorway. "She says I have to wash my hands." Billy stood behind him.

"OK, Buster, get busy," Alan replied, tousling Gary's hair. "You waiting, too, Billy?" he asked.

"I guess so," Billy replied. "But I'm really not dirty."

"Better do what your mother says. And Gary, don't let me see any dirt on the towel. It's supposed to go down the drain with the soap and water."

Standing behind his younger son, Alan finished brushing his hair, still thick, darker now from the long winter. He checked his hairline and examined the bristles for loose strands. By the end of the summer his hair would have turned nearly blond. Then he realized that this year it would all depend on where he was. Standing watch on a destroyer in the frigid North Atlantic wouldn't do it, but maybe he'd end up on a sunny deck somewhere south of Pago Pago.

"Oops, sorry," he said as he backed up and bumped against Billy. He kept forgetting how big Billy was getting. Nan said he was taller than Alan had been at his age. "But no smarter than his father," she always added, though everyone knew that in Nan's eyes Billy could do no wrong. And in fact he probably *was* smarter than just about anyone in the family. Sometimes he looked at Alan with the eyes of an old man, all-knowing and judgmental.

As they were finishing their left-over lunch, Gary said, "Daddy, will you play with us?"

Laura looked over her shoulder from the sink. "What a good idea!" she said. "What do you say, dad?"

"Sure, what'll it be?"

"Catch, catch!" Billy can play, too!" Gary shouted.

Alan looked over at Billy. Billy, avoiding his glance, focused on Laura.

"There you go," said Laura. "Sounds like fun to me!" She didn't acknowledge Billy's expression of dismay. "Now, go on, the three of you, and I'll finish the dishes. I'll be out soon. Go on now."

"I don't know where my glove is," said Billy. "I'll try and find it later."

"I do, I do! It's in your closet, 'way at the back. I saw it. I know where it is!" Gary raced away to Billy's room, Lucille barking and trotting after him. "I'll get everyone's!" he shouted from the bedroom.

They walked down the back stairs and into the yard, Gary racing ahead with Lucille, Billy straggling behind Alan. The day had turned warm, more like a morning in late June, and the grass seemed greener than it had just a few days earlier.

The backyard of Nan's house was deep, with a few tall evergreens, a budding apple tree, and lilac and forsythia bushes. toward the rear, a large rectangular patch lay fallow, awaiting the planting of this year's victory garden. Beyond, a high picket fence, always heavy with roses in June, separated the yard from the rear of Ada Brown's property, which faced the adjoining street. To the right was the Mazzarella house, with its artfully arranged flower beds, a plot where Mr. Mazzarella planted his vegetables, and a large rectangular grape arbor, a cool and shady refuge during the hot summer months.

"Remember what happened last year, guys," Alan said. "We need to be careful."

Late in the summer a wild throw from Billy had sent Alan racing backwards into a corner pole, splitting it and sending part of the arbor roof crashing to the flagstone paving. Luckily, most of the grapes had been picked, but several vines were broken.

Mr. Mazzarella had reacted with good humor. "Is OK, is OK," he had said, waving his hand in dismissal, probably not the way he'd have behaved if Billy or Gary had done the damage. He'd have been shaking his scary finger at them—a stump resulting from a long-ago accident—and cursing in Italian.

"OK, Billy, you stand there. Gary, you come closer," Alan said.

They began to toss the ball. Alan liked the feel of his glove, worn and pliant from all the years he'd played in high school and later on the team at the plant. No more of that, at least for this summer, and probably the next. But then again he wouldn't have felt comfortable playing anyway. He couldn't think of anyone from management ever being on the team, so it was just as well that he'd be gone. Another awkward decision he wouldn't have to make.

After Billy dropped the ball several times, Alan walked over to him. "Here, let's see the glove. Needs some work." The glove had been a birthday present last year but hadn't seen much action. Alan kneaded and punched it. "OK, try it now."

"Daddy, do that to mine, too," Gary said.

"Sure, give it to me." He worked on Gary's small glove a bit, pretending to shape it. "There you go."

They resumed playing. Billy wasn't a bad catcher, but he needed to practice his throwing. Alan wanted to stop and give him some tips, but decided not to. Next time. Though Gary was having trouble making his catches, Alan noticed with satisfaction that he had a natural way with the ball.

Lucille had decided she'd be Gary's helper. "Lucille, no!" Gary yelled as she raced after the missed ball. She'd retrieve it like a good terrier and then run back to Alan, growling and wagging her tail when he tried to take the wet ball from her mouth. That was a dog game they played long ago, when Lucille was in her prime.

A loud creaking of the fence at the back of the yard drew their attention, and this time Alan missed his catch. Ada Brown was re-fastening the latch on the little gate Alan had made for her years ago. "No sense in you both walking around the block to visit each other," he'd told Nan. "Now you're just a gate away."

Mrs. Brown turned and began walking toward them. She was wearing very high heels, but she managed to navigate the still-damp lawn with surprising ease. The skirt of her light blue dress swayed, drawing attention to her still-pretty legs and the gold bracelet that circled her ankle. *Boy, she must have been a knockout when she was young*, Alan thought, not for the first time. No one knew Mrs. Brown's exact age, but Nan said she had at least a good ten years on her. That made her somewhere well on the other side of 70.

"Hi Mrs. Brown," said Alan. "Please, Alan, do call me Ada," she'd once asked him, but he never did. No one he knew ever called Mrs. Brown Ada, not even Nan. He supposed her husband must have, but he was part of Mrs. Brown's past. He'd died out West and Mrs. Brown had returned to Springfield, where she'd spent her childhood. She'd bought her little house and apparently put her earlier life behind her. If Nan knew more, she wasn't telling.

"Good morning, Alan. And good morning, boys," she replied. "What a lovely day." Billy smiled and greeted her. Gary waved and waited patiently, ball in hand.

"Warming up for the game today?" she asked. "Where are the Red Sox this week? In St. Louis?"

"Yeah, they're playing the Browns," Alan said. He knew Mrs. Brown was an avid Sox fan.

"Well, I'm off to catch the bus to Amherst to visit my friend Grace," Mrs. Brown said. "But I couldn't go without seeing Billy on this very special day." She reached under the coat she was carrying and handed him a big wrapped package. "Happy birthday, my dear. You may open this at your party. I'm sorry I won't be there."

"Gee, thanks, Mrs. Brown," Billy said. He dropped the glove and took his present. He examined it briefly and then put it safely under one of the small firs. No doubt a book, or maybe a couple of books, Alan figured. Mrs. Brown was very kind to Billy, sometimes maybe too generous, but money didn't seem to be a problem. She was a good influence on him, after all, and he loved spending time at her house.

"Stop by if you get back in time," Alan said.

"I may be late, but, if not, I surely will. Now all of you have a wonderful time on this glorious day." Lucille had run up and was waiting patiently to get her friend's attention. Mrs. Brown knelt down and gave her a hearty rub under her chin. "Hello, darling," she said. "Now you stay here and watch these men play, hear?" Then she stepped onto the paved drive and walked briskly toward the street, heels tapping on the asphalt, tightly waved red hair glinting in the sunlight. Touched up every single week at the beauty parlor, according to Nan.

"C'mon, can we play now?" Gary asked.

They resumed their game, Alan encouraging Billy when he made a good catch and trying to ignore his awkward throwing stance. Lucille had grown tired of chasing the ball and was resting under a forsythia, her coat jet black against the mass of yellow blossoms.

The porch door across the driveway opened, and Mary Mazzarella appeared, balancing a brush, comb and bowl against her ample chest. Angie followed behind her. The screen door banged shut.

"Angie, don't let that door slam! Happy birthday, Billy!" Mary yelled. She was wearing a black dress that didn't hide her pudgy figure. On her feet were pink bedroom scuffs with big puffy pom-poms. Mary couldn't be much older than Belle or Laura, but she seemed to be from another generation, more like the elderly Italian ladies from the south end of Main Street, with their headscarves and dark clothes and grocery satchels. Though she never wore make-up, Alan thought Mary was pretty in her own way, with her thick black hair and little gold earrings.

"Happy birthday, Billy, from me, too," said Angie. She was absorbed in one of her movie magazines.

"Thanks, Mrs. Mazzarella. Thanks, Angie. Are you and Sal coming to my party?" he asked.

"Yep, the cake and presents part. What're you doing now?"

"Nothing. Playing catch."

"Want to do something when my hair is finished?" Angie asked.

"Uh, OK," Billy replied, looking at Alan.

Alan said, "Let's play until Angie's ready." He threw the ball to Gary.

Angie sat on a chair as her mother began to braid. First she brushed and parted Angie's long black hair, dipping the comb in the bowl of water and shaking off the excess. Then she arranged three thick strands on one side before rapidly intertwining them into a tight overlapping pattern. She then turned Angie's head a bit and repeated the process, her little hands moving rapidly and methodically.

"Billy, heads up!" Alan yelled. But the ball sailed past him, landed deep in the backyard and rolled under a dense thicket of junipers. Lucille decided she'd rested long enough and took chase.

"OK, Billy, OK, go ahead," Alan said. "That's enough."

"Wait, Daddy, wait! I want to play more, " Gary cried.

"We'll play, you and I. I was just telling Billy he can go."

Billy took off his glove, picked up his present from Mrs. Brown and ran up the stairs to join Angie and her mother.

"OK, buddy come on, let's see you throw. Bend your elbow like this." Alan raised his arm and walked over to show Gary how.

Chapter 6: Billy

Billy held his baseball glove in one hand and his wrapped present in the other as he waited for Mrs. Mazzarella to finish Angie's hair. When Angie moved, her mother smacked her on the head, gesturing heavenwards with one hand and mumbling something in Italian under her breath.

"Hold still, you!" Mrs. Mazzarella yelled again. Her fat wrist was red and the skin pinched from the barely visible elastic bands that soon would be used to fasten each braid. She gave one of Angie's earlobes a decisive twist.

"Ow, Ma, that hurts!" Angie cried. She rolled her eyes at Billy.

"Maybe I'll put my stuff away," Billy said. "Angie, come on over later. 'Bye, Mrs. Mazzarella."

"Bye bye, dear. You have a nice birthday, you hear me? You havin' my meatballs tonight? Tell your ma heat long time."

Billy put the unopened present on the dining room table. He went into his bedroom and threw the glove back into the closet. Then he retrieved it, got on his hands and knees and nudged it under his bureau until it was far in the back and out of sight. When he returned to the kitchen, Angie was at the door.

"Hi, Angie, come on in," said Laura. Billy figured his mother been about to frost the cake, hidden now in the pantry. He'd seen her run in there when he'd opened the back door.

The sauce was still simmering on the stove. "Smells good," Angie said. "Just like my ma's."

"Why, thank you, Angie," replied Laura. "Now, you're coming over for cake tonight, aren't you? You and Sal? Around 6:30."

"Yep, I'll be there, and I'll remind my brother. Hey, Billy, let's go out in the yard."

When they got downstairs, Angie picked up a small bag she had left in a corner of the porch. "I have a surprise. Let's go somewhere." She headed down the stairs, then turned. "Hey, I know, let's go up to your attic."

They went back inside and climbed the creaky back stairs. Billy retrieved the key from its hiding place under the umbrella stand on the second floor, and they made their way up the narrower stairs to the attic. He unlocked the door and pulled on the frayed tassel of the old floor lamp that stood by the entrance. An amber glow filled the immediate area, but the corners of the big open space remained dim. At the far end, the small dormer windows at the front of the house provided some additional light.

It was always exciting to go up to the attic, a place that even now Billy preferred to visit with somebody following close behind him, at least at night. When he was smaller he never went alone. There was always a moment before he turned the lamp on when he wondered who or what might be lying in wait behind the big old standing mirror or the dusty horsehair sofa.

He and Angie walked to a corner near one of the windows, where an old Persian carpet covered the rough plank floor. This secluded nook was their favorite place, except in the hot days of July and August when they preferred to be in the yard. But on a stormy and windy afternoon in the early summer or fall, with the rain splashing the window and tapping the roof, it was the ideal spot to read or enjoy games. When they were younger, they played dress-up in clothes from Nan's old trunks or cut out costumes for Angie's movie star paper dolls.

"Close your eyes. Don't open them until I say it's OK," Angie said.

Billy sat on the rug cross-legged, careful not to stretch his blue jeans too tight at the knees. Laura had told him they'd have to last through the summer. He felt a loose strip of rubber on the sole of his sneaker and started to pick at it. Then he remembered that they'd have to do, too. "They're not even selling those in the store," his mother said. "No rubber." He could hear Angie fussing with the paper bag she'd brought along.

"OK, ready. Open your eyes!"

At first he couldn't make out anything. But then he followed Angie's eyes and saw the tiny pieces of metal glinting on the edge of the rug, a small rubber ball sitting next to them.

"Wow! New jacks!" he said.

"That's really your main present," Angie explained. "I have something else to give you later on at the party. But this is for now, 'cause I know this is what you really want."

Billy understood why Angie was giving him the jacks in private. She realized that his father didn't like him to play jacks. In fact, he didn't much like Billy being with Angie and her girl playmates at all, even though she was his best friend.

Once when he was younger, he had wanted to show Alan how he could jump rope. Alan had watched him do some fancy steps, including a side swing, a scissors and a double skip. Then he said, "Why are you playing jump rope? That's a girl's game."

"But Daddy, I saw a picture of Joe Louis jumping rope," Billy replied.

"That's different. That's for exercise, not for fun. It's different."

So Billy had started to be careful about the games he played, at least where he played them and when. He became mindful in the late afternoon to avoid hopscotch with the girls or fancy rope jumps with them on the sidewalks. He didn't stop playing altogether, but he made sure Alan wouldn't see him as he arrived home from work.

Billy picked up the jacks from the attic floor. "Thanks, Angie. These are swell. But where did you get the rubber ball?"

"Well, the ball isn't new. The jacks are, they're real metal or something like that. I forget. But I had to...borrow an extra ball my cousin had, if you know what I mean." Billy didn't ask what Angie meant, but he knew that she had visited her cousin in Hartford last week.

"We'll play tomorrow after school," said Angie. "Hey, want to go get an ice cream? I think Sal said the variety store is open this afternoon. They had ice cream yesterday, just vanilla."

They stopped in the kitchen on their way down the stairs. "Ma, can I have a nickel for an ice cream cone?" Billy asked.

"I don't know about that, it's awful close to dinnertime." Laura paused and then said, "Oh, just a minute." She reached into the jar on the top of the refrigerator. "Boy, these new pennies with no copper look just like dimes," she said, handing him a real dime and five pennies, two that were silver-colored and three the usual bronze. "For you and Angie, and for Gary if you'll take him. Would you? He's in the yard."

"C'mon, Gary," Angie said as they walked down the steps of the porch. The game of catch was over, and Gary was playing in the driveway with a small scooter that had belonged to Billy. "Want to come with us to get a cone?"

Angie took Gary's hand, and they started off, Lucille picking up the rear. Often when they went up the street Gary had trouble keeping up with the two older kids. "Wait up!" he'd cry. "Wait up for me!" Angie always slowed down, but sometimes Billy didn't.

They strolled up to State Street. Most of the stores were closed, but lots of American flags, more than usual, were flying out in front or taped inside the windows. As they paused on a corner for a car to pass, they saw two nuns waiting to cross on the other side.

"Yikes, it's Sister Michael," Angie said. Billy knew that Sister Michael was one of Angie's teachers at Holy Family School. "I don't know the other one."

"Maybe she's visiting from somewhere," Billy said.

"Nah, they never go anywhere. She must be one who never leaves the convent, but they let her out today."

Angie and Sal and all the Mazzarellas were Catholic. Billy's family was Protestant, even though they hardly ever went to church. Still, Nan always lowered her voice when she talked about the Mazzarellas' religion. "If Angie comes for dinner Friday, we'll have to be sure and have fish," she'd say, raising one eyebrow, as though being Catholic meant believing or doing things that were best left unsaid.

There were two religious pictures on the wall in Angie's living room, a big one of Jesus with a yellow halo around his head and a sad expression on his face, and another of a pale lady with a pointed chin.

"Who's that?" Billy once asked. "She looks kind of sick."

"Saint Clara worked with Saint Francis, but not so much with animals the way he did. Yeah, all the lady saints look real bad. They died when they were young. That's because they prayed so much they forgot to eat."

The traffic cleared and they began to cross the street. As they passed the nuns, Angie said, "Hello, Sister."

"Good afternoon, Angelina," replied Sister Michael. The other nun smiled.

"They're not so bad," said Billy.

"Nah, she's OK," replied Angie.

"Are nuns really bald? Did Jesus make them have bald heads?" asked Gary.

"Yep, I think they're all bald," Angie said. "Once my cousin saw a nun sick in the hospital. She was definitely bald. Hey, want me to ask them?" She turned and cupped her hand to her mouth. "Hey, Sister Michael," she whispered at their retreating figures. "Does Jesus like your big shiny noggin?"

Lucille barked.

❧❧

After they returned from the store, the boys went to wash up and get ready for dinner. Gary had vanilla ice cream all over his striped polo shirt. Billy changed into gabardine pants that didn't itch like his woolen ones, a plaid shirt, and his good Buster Brown shoes. Standing in front of the bathroom mirror, he rubbed a dab of his father's Wildroot into his hair and carefully arranged a part with a black comb that Sal had given him.

As they sat down at the dining room table—Billy, Gary, Alan, Laura and Nan—Billy discovered his presents stacked under his chair. He knew they'd be there, but you couldn't open them until dessert, sometimes not even until afterwards. He and Gary piled them up on the big mahogany sideboard, next to the cut glass bowl with the fake fruit that looked like one of the hats Carmen Miranda always wore in her movies.

They went ahead with the meal without waiting for Belle. "That's OK, Belle told me she might be late," Billy said. He knew she'd be there for the presents, and so would Sal and Angie.

Nan insisted on helping Laura serve dinner. She just couldn't sit still. "It's my nature," she always said, by way of explanation for that and lots of other things that people told her not to do. "What can you say to that?" said Belle. "It's hopeless!"

"Gary, elbows off the table," said Alan. Both boys knew they had to be on their best behavior at meals, and that meant finishing whatever was put before them. Everyone loved spaghetti and meatballs, but on other nights, it wasn't unusual for Billy to sit at the table long after everyone had left because he hadn't finished his vegetables. Lima beans and beets he could sneak under the table, hiding pieces on a ledge he'd discovered, but summer squash and spinach were more of a challenge.

Once when Laura was moving the table to clean, all sorts of discolored and moldy bits of food fell to the floor. She'd mentioned her discovery to Billy, and he'd begged her not to tell his father.

Just as the last of the dinner plates was being cleared, Belle walked in. "Cripes, what a day," she said. "I thought it was going to be easy, but some poor old guy had a heart attack or something in the middle of the cartoon and we had to stop everything. Police, ambulance, the lights up, the whole schedule off, what a mess."

Sal and Angie arrived just as Laura and Gary were fixing the cake in the kitchen. Angie was wearing a blue pinafore dress with short puffy sleeves. Even Sal had changed from his usual t-shirt and jeans to slacks and a loose Hawaiian shirt with brightly colored parrots and big jungle leaves.

"Ready!" yelled Laura from the kitchen. Alan switched off the overhead light and the room became dim. Gary walked through the door, the cake gingerly balanced on a plate held between his clenched hands. Laura followed closely behind. The light from the ten birthday candles reflected the sparkle of her rhinestone earrings and the glimmer of her silky green dress. Billy thought she looked especially pretty.

Everyone sang "Happy Birthday," Nan's wobbly falsetto voice louder than anyone's. Billy noticed that she was crying a little bit, the way she always did at birthdays, but even more so today because of the Memorial Day holiday. She called it Decoration Day.

Gary stood next to Billy as he prepared to blow out the candles. Billy glanced at his brother and said, "Gary, you have to count and help me blow them out, OK?"

"OK," said Gary. "ONETWOTHREE!"

Everyone had a piece of cake and a small serving of ice cream from a pint that Nan had gotten at Jimmy's Market up the street. "It's lovely strawberry," she said. "No coffee or chocolate or butterscotch in stock."

"Let's open the presents now," said Alan. "Everyone finished? Ready, Billy?"

"Yes!" said Gary. He retrieved the packages and handed the first one to Billy. It was Mrs. Brown's gift, two books from the *Childhood of Famous Americans* series. Billy had read all the older titles, but not these two, one about Clara Barton and the other, the composer Stephen Foster. Next came Superman and Batman comics from Gary—"I picked those out!" he said—and more books from Belle, *Bomba the Jungle Boy in the Swamp of Death* and a Smilin' Jack adventure.

Angie's other gift was a pack of Bicycle playing cards. "I knew you really wanted those," she said sweetly. Laura and Alan's present was just what Billy hoped it would be, a shiny brown Viewmaster camera, along with three slides, "Garden of the Gods," "Mexican Bullfight" and "Scenes from Hawaii."

As Gary handed Billy the last package, he said "Here comes the Roy Rogers shirt from Nan!" Then he said, "Oops!"

"Oh what a scamp!" said Nan. "He helped me wrap it up."

"Wow, all my presents are great," Billy said, holding up the shirt, gold and green with white fringe, for everyone to see. "Thank you. Thanks a lot."

"Wait, one more," said Sal. "You got to look out the window."

It was almost dark by now, and it was hard to see much of anything from the second floor. "What, Sal?...All I can see is your bike." Sal's big, shiny black Columbia bicycle was propped up against his porch.

"Yep, that's it," said Sal, smiling. "It's yours now. I won't be riding it much and it's no good just sitting in the garage."

"Oh, Sal, that's too kind of you," said Laura.

"Hey, like I said, I want someone to use it, and why not Billy?"

"Gee, thanks. I'll take good care of it," Billy said. Sal's bike. He didn't know what else to say. Sal was getting kind of embarrassed, he could tell, so he didn't add anything more.

"Laura, would you play some songs, dear?" asked Nan.

They moved to the living room, gathered around the piano and sang some tunes they knew Nan loved, like "I'm Forever Blowing Bubbles" and "After the Ball Is Over." Then Laura sang a couple of the new songs on the Hit Parade, including the one she had just learned, "I Had the Craziest Dream."

Then Sal said, "Hey Laura, play "Anchors Aweigh."

"Sure, OK," she said. They didn't know all the words, but they managed to stumble through and finish with a flourish.

"I like that one," Gary said. That's the sailor's song, 'Anchors Aweigh.'"

"Yes, honey, it is," said Laura slowly "It's what sailors sing."

"Then that's what Daddy will be singing soon."

Everyone looked at Gary and then at Alan.

"What do you mean, Gary?" Alan asked, laughing. Billy saw him glance quickly at Laura.

"I heard you and Mommy last night. You said you were going into the Navy."

No one spoke. Billy stared at his mother. *Was it true?* But he could tell from her expression that it was. Everyone except him must have known, even Gary.

Nan said, "Wait. What is it? I don't understand." Sometimes she didn't hear everything that was being said, but she could tell by the silence that something was wrong.

Belle said, "It's OK, Nan. I think Alan has something that he needs to say. Alan, tell us."

Alan cleared his throat. Laura got up from the piano and took his arm. "Well, I enlisted in the Navy this week. That's it. I'll be hearing in a couple of weeks, maybe before. I passed my physical."

"Oh dear," said Nan and began to cry. "Oh dear." She fumbled in her pocket for her handkerchief.

Billy looked at his mother. She was trying not to cry, too. He looked over at Sal, who was half-smiling. "Gosh, you beat me to it," he said.

"Hush," Nan said. "You don't know what that means, going to war and all. Alan, why? What made you do it now?"

"Mother, you know I'll be drafted sooner or later. It's coming. This way I'll have my choice. I want to be in the Navy."

"Nan, Alan and I have...well, we've talked about this. We have. And I think he's right," said Laura. "He wants to do what he thinks is best. And I think we all need to stand behind him."

There was more silence in the room. Then Belle jumped up and said, "For Christ's sake, everyone, it's not the end of the world. The war will be over soon. Look, he...Alan, you probably won't even get sent overseas before it's all over. And you're going to look pretty handsome in those sailor whites.

"Come on Laura," she urged. "Play something else. Play "Roamin' in the Gloamin'." Belle knew all the old Scottish songs, which she performed with an exaggerated burr. Her voice wasn't so good, though it wasn't as bad as Nan's.

Belle sang "Roamin' in the Gloamin" and another Harry Lauder song, "I Love a Lassie." Then she said, "Come on Nan, haven't you and Billy been practicing a song?"

Nan motioned with her handkerchief that she didn't want to sing, but Belle grabbed her arm and then Billy's. "Laura, scoot over so Billy can sit and play. Come on, Billy, let's hear you and Nan. It'll cheer her up. Us, too."

Billy didn't feel like singing any more than Nan did. Mainly he didn't want Alan to see that he was upset that he hadn't known and Gary had. And he didn't want anyone to see him cry. Especially Sal. He was about to shake his head "no," when he caught Angie's eye. She had a stern look on her face as she mouthed the word "yes" and pointed over to the piano.

"OK," he said. "Come on, Nan." As he sat down to play, Billy realized with a sinking feeling that it was another sailor song they'd been learning, but it was too late to stop now.

Nan wiped her eyes and tucked her handkerchief back in her pocket.

"Well, dearies, what's to be is to be," she said. "We just have to make the best of it." She kissed Alan and patted Laura's arm and then, without waiting for Billy to start playing, began to sing: *"Bell bottom trousers, coat of Navy blue, she loves a sailor and he loves her, too."*

Billy concentrated on the keyboard. He could only play this song with one finger, but even so it was hard to think of the next note because Nan's voice was so off-pitch and loud. Somehow they got through the chorus and the one verse that Nan had memorized, and everyone applauded.

"That's more like it," said Belle. "Happy Birthday, Billy, and many more."

"Happy Birthday, Billy," said Alan, coming up behind him and placing his hands on Billy's shoulders. "You'll be the man of the family soon." Billy turned and smiled halfheartedly at his father, but his shoulders had stiffened and he knew his face had gotten all red. He was relieved when Alan moved away and went over to talk to Sal.

Laura moved closer to Billy on the piano stool and put her arm around him. Nan came up and gave him a big kiss on the cheek, and Belle leaned down and whispered in his ear. "It'll be OK, sweetie," she said. "We'll all be fine. You'll see."

Chapter 7: Alan

Alan woke very early the morning after Billy's party. He slid silently out of bed and turned off the alarm on the night table next to Laura. He'd make his own breakfast and buy lunch at the plant.

Lighting a cigarette, he gathered his clothes together, quietly shut the bedroom door, and went into the bathroom to wash and shave. As he lathered up, he was surprised at how good he felt. He thought he might be unsettled or jumpy after last night. Instead, he was relieved, maybe even happy, now that the news was out.

Considering that Gary had spilled the beans, things had gone pretty well. He still needed to have a conversation with Nan. Although she'd hugged him and patted his face when she went downstairs with Belle, there were tears in her eyes. Billy, he knew, was angry, but at what he wasn't sure. He certainly must have realized that Gary hadn't been told anything deliberately. Alan knew Billy felt that he favored Gary, but that couldn't be the cause this time. Maybe he was hiding something else by acting angry.

Alan had given up trying to figure out his older son. Nothing involving the two of them ever seemed to go right, so there was really no point trying to analyze Billy's behavior this time. Maybe it was just an awkward age for him. Maybe their not being around each other for a while would be for the best.

Alan finished shaving and splashed some Old Spice on his face. Buttoning his stiffly starched shirt and fixing his tie, he checked himself in the mirror. Despite the jokes from the guys, he liked getting dressed up in the morning. It made him feel good about himself. Whistling softly under his breath, he decided he needed to talk to Billy after all. Nan and Billy. The others were OK.

Lucille, shaking the sleep away and wagging her pointy tail, appeared in the hallway. He walked her downstairs the back way, let her out and left the porch door open. In her younger days she'd have been jumping all over him, but now she was content with a pat on the head before she went out to do her business. In a few minutes she'd be clumping back up the steps, looking for breakfast.

He set out a bowl of Red Heart, adding water to the dry, unsavory clump of flakes. Even dogs had to make do these days, but Lucille had adjusted surprisingly well to the new dehydrated chow.

"Hi, Daddy." Gary stood in the doorway, barefoot and still in his pajamas.

"Hiya, Gary, what are you doing up so early? Go get dressed and we'll have breakfast. But don't make any noise."

"OK," he said, racing back down the hallway.

Alan opened a new box of cereal Laura had left on the table. He sampled one of the tiny doughnut-like bits. Not bad. CheeriOats it was called. On the cover, the Lone Ranger held a silver bullet, offering one just like it for only ten cents. Alan carefully tore away part of the box top and placed it, along with a dime, on the table.

"For Billy," he explained to Gary as they sat eating their cereal. "Tell him when he gets up, all right?"

"Can I get one, too?"

"Next time. This one's for your big brother." Billy was still a faithful follower of the masked man's radio adventures. Alan recalled the Halloween a few years ago when Billy had dressed up in a white hat and gloves, light blue shirt and black mask. Gary was just a baby, but they had stuck a feather in his hat and called him "Little Tonto" as they made their rounds of the neighborhood. Despite the cold, Billy had refused to spoil his outfit by putting on a jacket, and nobody could make him change his mind. Later that night he had one of his first asthma attacks.

Alan grabbed his wallet, cigarettes, and glen plaid sports jacket. Gary was playing with a truck on the kitchen floor, Lucille curled up beside him, her breakfast already wolfed down. "Did you say something, Gary?" Alan asked.

"Nope," he replied. Then he giggled and said, "*I'm not talking while the flavor lasts. Beechnut gum!*"

"Oh, boy, you know 'em all," Alan said. "See you later."

Laura would be awake soon, he knew, probably sorry that she'd overslept. He thought he heard Billy stirring in his room. It was nearly time for him to be getting up for school. He considered walking down the hall, but it was late. He slipped out the front door and down the stairs.

It was Joe's week to drive, and he was already waiting at the curb in his Ford woody. Alan's '38 Packard was sitting out in the garage. He wondered if he'd be driving it to work again before he left. Maybe Laura would want to keep it running after he was gone.

"Sorry I'm late, guys, got stuck making breakfast." He joined Joe in the front seat. He was the last to be picked up. Fred and Clarence were already sitting in the back.

"Yeah, sure, it just takes you longer to get dressed these days, that's all," said Fred, leaning forward and tugging at Alan's shirt collar. Enough time had gone by since Alan's promotion to allow them to joke about the "big shot."

They headed across town, past the low, sprawling Smith and Wesson arms plant, set far back from the road and surrounded by a series of high fences. Even at this early hour, the streets were full of cars and public buses converging from all parts of the city, transporting workers to and from the first and third shifts. Most of the big factories were running on a 24-hour schedule.

As they approached Westinghouse, Alan said, "Well, guys, this may be my last week. You know last Friday? I didn't go home early because I was sick. I went down to the recruiting station. I'm in the Navy."

"Holy shit!" Fred smacked Alan on the back of the head. Like Alan, he was a young married father and was also expecting to be drafted any day. Clarence and Joe were both over 50. "Wow, so you picked the Navy!"

"Hey no fair, Alan, it's your turn to drive next week," said Joe, laughing.

Clarence, ever serious, asked, "What about your job? Will they hold it?"

"So they say. But who knows? Anyway, who cares? You guys know I'm not happy with it. I should have stayed where I was."

They reached the main gate of the plant, flashed their security badges at the guard, parked and went their separate ways. Alan's small glass-enclosed office was in the shipping and receiving area, where he headed part of the expediting operation—the receiving of parts and equipment and the shipping out of the finished products. He took off his jacket and began to review the manifest and pick-up schedule for the day.

Later in the morning he met with his boss, Walter Green. "What's up, Alan?" Walter asked, gesturing for him to sit.

"It's all taken care of," he replied. Alan had already told him his intentions last Friday morning. Green was a veteran of the First World War and an active member of the local Veterans of Foreign Wars. Years ago, he'd known Alan's father when they worked together at the nearby Indian Motorcycle factory.

"Well, I'm sorry to lose you," Green said. "But you won't regret it. And you've chosen the branch you want. Good luck, Alan."

The two men shook hands. "You know your job will be waiting for you," Green said. They agreed that Alan would stay on until he got his call-up orders. Then he'd terminate immediately so that he could have a few free days before he reported for duty.

By lunchtime word had spread throughout Alan's area. His assistant, Bob, would be the likely candidate to replace him.

"Jeez, Alan, I'm sorry you'll be leaving," he said. Then he added, "How soon do ya think it'll be? Any idea?" Alan knew he was concerned about what he'd need to learn.

"You mean, before you can take over?" He smiled at Bob.

"Nah, I didn't mean that."

"No, that's fine. I've already recommended you to Mr. Green. Stick close to me the next few days and we'll go over everything. You'll be all set."

Alan left work directly at the end of the shift but declined Joe's offer to stop off at the High Life. "Thanks, Joe, but I'm going straight home. I'll catch the bus. See you all tomorrow."

He got off the cross-town near the multi-acre sprawl of the Armory, its workforce of thousands turning out weapon after weapon every hour of every day since the war began. Walking briskly up State Street, coat slung over his shoulder, Alan felt good, not tense the way he usually was at the end of a hectic work day. Passing two bars where he often stopped off, he picked up a pint of ice cream from the fountain at Doc's drugstore.

He approached the small campus of the college, the neat brick buildings with their white columns and wide steps an oasis on the busy thoroughfare. He imagined himself enrolling after the war on one of the scholarship deals that were being talked about for veterans.

Arriving home earlier than usual, he put the ice cream in the refrigerator, changed his clothes and went back downstairs. Laura and the boys weren't home yet from wherever they'd gone.

"Hello," he called, knocking and opening the door at the back landing. "Mother?"

A meat stew simmered on the stove. Potatoes lay peeled and waiting on the counter, next to an unopened glass jar of canned peas, one of many that Nan and Laura had preserved from last year's garden. The victory garden...he probably wouldn't be around to help plant it this time.

He sat down at the kitchen table, moving aside a half-finished cup of tea. After eating a couple of the Ritz crackers that were sitting on a plate next to a small mound of strawberry jam, he began to wonder where Nan was. He walked down the hallway, past the open bathroom door, and continued on to her room.

She was sitting on her bed with her back to the door. Although he couldn't be certain, he was pretty sure she was kneading her hands, "fussing," as she called it, something she did when she was nervous and upset.

Alan moved quietly into the room. "Mother?" He sat down next to her at the edge of the bed.

"Oh, my dear, you surprised me," she said, instinctively adjusting loose strands of hair under her hairnet and wiping her eyes. She reached over and kissed Alan on the cheek.

"Leg bothering you?" Nan was always having trouble with the veins in one of her legs.

"No, it's fine since Belle got me that lovely new bandage."

"Everything's going to be all right you know," Alan said, taking her hand. "It'll be over before you know it. I might not even get sent anywhere."

"I know, dear, I know," she replied. "It's just with Donny Hathaway and all..." Donny had gone to high school with Alan. Belle had told him at the party last night that the gold star was already up in the Hathaways' window.

"But Donny was a pilot, right in the thick of things. I won't be doing anything that dangerous." He laughed. "More likely than not, I'll be stuck on some old ship in dry-dock in Norfolk or San Diego."

"Well, you know I worry. And I just hope that you'll be safe and take care of yourself. You know." She made a motion of raising a glass to her mouth.

"Mother, don't worry about that. I know when to stop."

"Well, I hope that's true, dear. It's a powerful urge, I know that."

"Please, don't worry." Alan patted her hand.

"And then I think about my dear brother," Nan said, her gaze moving to the photos that crowded the top of her high bureau dresser.

One gold leaf frame held a brown tinted print of a young soldier, Nan's kid brother, Harry. Harry had dark wavy hair and deep melancholy eyes. He stood alone in the photo, his left hand resting on a high-backed bench, one foot extended in front, probably just the way the photographer had instructed him to pose. He was dressed in a short, tight-fitting coat with brass buttons, jodhpurs, and high leather boots. In his right hand he held a riding crop.

Harry was a member of a horse brigade when he first went off to the Great War. Nan said he had loved the little pony on their small farm in Scotland. But he died in the muddy trenches of the Somme and was buried in a military cemetery somewhere in France. Alan noticed, not for the first time that Billy had Harry's eyes and hair.

"Looks like our Billy, doesn't he, dear," she remarked, as if reading Alan's thoughts.

"Yeah, he does, a bit, now that Billy's growing up," Alan replied. "Listen, Mother, no one's going to die. We're all going to be fine. I promise...All of us, me included." He put his arm around her shoulder and they sat quietly together on the bed. The only sound was the ticking of Nan's wind-up alarm clock on the round end table. It sat on a lace doily she'd tatted, next to a picture of Billy in a diaper, laughing and shaking a rattle.

"Hey, Nan," Alan said after a moment. "I forgot. Something was getting kind of hot out in the kitchen. Maybe you'd better check on it."

"Oh my, no, the stew! How did it get to be this hour? And me with dinner to finish and Belle getting home any minute."

Nan stood up, smoothed her apron and kissed Alan again. "You run on upstairs. I'm perfectly all right now. And thank you, dear, for stopping to check on your silly old mother."

She laughed and patted her son's arm. "Come along now," she said, giving him a poke in the back as she steered him out of the bedroom and down the hallway. "Off with you." She walked so fast that Alan had trouble keeping ahead of her.

Chapter 8: Laura

Laura carefully placed the receiver back on the hook. "Darn it all!" she muttered, tapping her nails impatiently on the maple telephone table in the hallway. She'd been trying to make a call for the past twenty minutes, but Mildred Sludge across the street was having a morning conversation with her daughter Suzy. Suzy was a new mother, and the two seemed to be on the phone day and night. "It's like no one ever had a baby before," Laura said to Nan one day.

"Well, dear, Suzy was always a bit slow, you know. Remember once when she was a little girl she pasted two paper wings on her shoulders and jumped off the second floor porch? Landed right in that fir tree." Nan pointed to a large tree across the street. "Hmm... It was much smaller back then. But look, you can still see how it's curved funny. Took several branches off. Maybe Mildred thinks of things like that when she imagines Suzy raising little Elmer."

Resisting the temptation to interrupt the Sludges' chitchat, Laura decided to make out her grocery list. If she was able to get an interview at the Mutual today, she'd stop at the supermarket on the walk home.

She grabbed the ration coupons from the top of the fridge and sat down at the kitchen table. The government had issued official books for each family member, with red stamps for some items and blue for others. There were also little colored tokens given as change, to be saved and used with regular money. You also had to be mindful of expiration dates, as well as any number of other rules and regulations.

It had been so complicated at the beginning, even with the detailed pamphlets issued by the Office of Price Administration. Figuring it all out was still a tedious affair, and there was never a guarantee of getting what you wanted or needed. All the red stamps in the world were useless if no beef was available this week or no cheese the next. You just never knew.

Laura perused the A&P ad in the morning *Union*. No meat except chicken listed, but that didn't mean much. There might have been an unexpected shipment overnight, and sometimes you didn't even know what they'd have from one hour to the next. She could stop off at the butcher shop further down the block, but Mr. Simka always gave her a creepy feeling if there was no one else in the store. That dark mustache and those piercing eyes. She'd heard stories about him. Maybe she'd just wait and buy fish on Friday from Perry's at the corner.

Coffee, thank goodness, was back in plentiful supply. The big ad proclaimed, *"Now you can drink all the Eight O' Clock you want!"* It had gone way up—51 cents for two pounds—but she'd buy it anyway. Cabbage and spinach were also on sale. Not the kids' favorites, but she still had a lot of homegrown canned beans and peas and corn from last year for them. She clipped the grocery list to the ration books and returned to the hallway.

The phone line was free, finally. She dialed the number Billy had copied on the message he'd taken, careful not to break her nail in the little holes encircling each digit on the base of the phone.

"Massachusetts Mutual Life Insurance Company, how may I help you?" asked the operator.

"Mr. Blackwood's office, please," Laura said. He was the personnel officer she'd spoken to a few weeks ago. She knew he'd been impressed by the experience she had from her work at Travelers Insurance in Hartford, even though that had been a few years back. He'd told her to get back to them early in June, when they were scheduled to ease their policy against hiring married women. Today was only June 1, so he must be interested to have called back so soon.

She was in luck—they'd see her early this afternoon. She walked quickly down the hall to Gary's room. "Honey, how would you like to spend some time downstairs with Nan?" she asked.

Gary was playing with a big pile of Tinker Toys. An oddly shaped contraption, spokes and extensions shooting off in every direction, was rising precariously in the middle of the room. Nearby, Lucille lay basking in a patch of morning sun, dead center in the path of the thing's collapse, which seemed imminent.

They hustled down the stairs to Nan's. Laura knew she'd be happy to watch Gary. "I'm about to grind some meat and you can be a big help. Would you like that?" Nan asked. Gary nodded his head vigorously. He liked working with Nan in the kitchen. "And then I have some oleomargarine to fix. You can squeeze the color in and mix it up for me. That would be grand. And then, lunch!"

Laura went back upstairs. She picked her outfit, checked her nylons for runs and, while the iron was heating, switched a few items from her white pocketbook to a small monogrammed strapless bag

Realizing she had forgotten all about her own lunch, she wolfed down an apple and a glass of milk as she carefully applied her makeup and fixed her hair. Then she changed her clothes, gave a final look in the mirror, remembered to pick up the grocery list and ration books on the kitchen table, and was off.

She could have walked to her appointment, but she was running late and, besides, the pumps she was wearing weren't her most comfortable. She spotted a bus making its way up past the college on the other side of the street, so she quickly crossed and flagged it down.

The home office of the Massachusetts Mutual Life Insurance Company was a huge colonial style brick pile, easily the biggest building in this part of the city, its clock tower visible from halfway downtown. Laura got off the bus after her short ride—she felt a bit guilty about not walking—and turned into the semi-circular drive that led to the impressive main entrance. Massive bushes, immaculately trimmed, bordered the sidewalk, and tall elms and oaks dotted the wide expanse of green lawn.

The front facade was supported by huge columns that rose several stories above the broad stairs leading to the entrance way. As she pushed through the smoothly revolving glass door, Laura was again struck by the splendor of the interior rotunda, a cavernous, dimly lit space encircled by gleaming pillars of speckled, rust-colored marble and oversized flags. The effect was one of opulence, power, and permanence, much like the interiors of the big banks downtown on Main Street.

She stopped at the reception desk and was given directions to the personnel office by an elderly gentleman in a guard's uniform. He spoke in a hushed voice that reverberated softly in the vast expanse. "Thank you," Laura replied in a near-whisper. Clutching her bag, she walked down one of the wide hallways leading from the rotunda, her heels tapping loudly on the highly polished marble floor.

She was ushered into Mr. Blackwood's office by a middle-aged woman who made no eye contact whatsoever and whose face was devoid of any expression of warmth or encouragement. *She'd be a great guard in the rotunda*, Laura thought. No one would get past her.

"I'm pleased to see you again, Mrs. Stewart," Mr. Blackwood said, motioning her to a chair in front of his massive dark mahogany desk. "Just a few questions. Not about your qualifications and experience," he said, waving the form she'd filled out from her first visit, along with the aptitude and typing tests she'd taken.

"As you know, we've recently reviewed our policy relating to the hiring of married women such as yourself." He folded his hands and paused. "I see you have two children. Boys, is that correct?"

"Yes, one who's nine—no, ten—and the other is five."

"Both in good health, I take it?" Laura nodded. "And the five year old. In school?"

"No, not until the fall. My mother-in-law will take care of him and Billy—my other son—when they come home from school. She lives downstairs from us."

"Ah, good. And your husband?"

"He's a manager at Westinghouse. But he's being called up, that is, he enlisted. In the Navy. That's why I'm getting back to you so soon, actually."

"Ah yes, I understand. And I hope you appreciate why we need to ask these questions. We must be sure that you'll be able to maintain a regular schedule just like our unmarried employees...our unmarried women employees."

"I do understand, Mr. Blackwood," replied Laura, "and I assure you that it won't be a problem."

"I'm sure it won't." He unclasped his hands and slapped them together. "So! I told you a bit about the job earlier, I believe. You'll be in the tabulating department. Your supervisor will be Mr. Sloan. He's not here today, but you'll meet him when you begin. I believe he may be planning keypunch work for you because of your earlier experience at Travelers. It's a good opportunity, Mrs. Stewart...Any questions?"

"No, I think I'm all set. Well, yes. Would you remind me again about the wages and the hours?"

"Of course. Twenty-five dollars a week to begin. We'll explain more about benefits when you start. Work is from 8:30 to 4:45 with a 50-minute lunch. We have a lovely dining room. The food is quite good, and the prices most reasonable. When might you begin?"

Laura thought for a moment and then said, "As soon as you like."

"Wonderful! This week's nearly over. Shall we say first thing Monday morning? Report here, and Miss Boyle will get you started." He stood up and reached his hand over the desk. "Welcome...I'm delighted you'll be joining us."

"Monday is perfect. And thank you so much, Mr. Blackwood. You...the company...won't be disappointed." They shook hands, and Laura walked out of the office.

"I'll see you first thing Monday morning, Miss Boyle," she said, smiling. "Bye for now!"

Laura felt like singing as she walked down the hallway,. She nodded hello at two men in suits who were standing by an open doorway. They smiled back, and one tipped his water cup in greeting as she passed. Laura sensed they were still watching her as she continued down the long passageway. It felt good to be dressed up and looking her best.

Heading back down State Street, she was so eager to get home to tell everyone her good news that she forgot about her groceries until she was nearly in front of the A&P. Entering the store, she noticed a line down by the meat department, as well as another crowd gathered in one of the middle aisles. She sighed. This was going to take a while. Knowing she could pick up a number at the butcher's counter, she grabbed a cart and raced over to the glass-covered cases to see what was available.

"What's in?" she asked a customer in front of her.

"Don't know, but I hope it's beef," the woman replied. "If I give 'em chicken one more time, my family will disown me. Ever had chicken pancakes?"

As Laura feared, there were about 30 numbers ahead of hers. She walked over to the aisle where the other crowd had gathered, but it was already dispersing. "They're out, goddamn it," a man muttered, as he pushed past her.

"Evaporated milk," a girl next to her explained when Laura questioned her. "But I think we should wait a minute. The clerk winked at me. I think he'll be back."

Sure enough, the stock boy returned with a big carton. "It's not evaporated, folks," he said. "Condensed milk."

Ugh. Condensed milk was really more like syrup, but Nan actually liked to spoon it right out of the can. She'd probably been giving Billy and Gary some, too, all along. Great for their teeth, but what the heck. Laura placed two cans in her cart.

She selected a few more items. A new supply of soap flakes had apparently just arrived, so she picked up a large Duz for 23 cents, as well as a Jane Parker orange cream layer cake on sale for a quarter. She was low on red points, so she passed on the butter. Twenty-four points for a pound. No wonder they were calling it "yellow gold." Surprisingly, jars of dried beef were in good supply. She splurged on two and also gingerly picked out a jar of lamb tongues, sliced and packed together lengthwise in cloudy brine, for Nan. In the same aisle, she grabbed two boxes of macaroni and cheese and returned to the meat counter.

She waited several minutes, watching the roasts disappear and then the sirloins and finally the last of the cube steaks, sold to the lady who had run out of chicken recipes. But she was able to buy a pound of hamburg for 19 cents, a couple of nice roasting chickens, and a large fowl. She'd need to use 12 meat points for the beef, but that would still leave nearly 100 for the rest of the month. When she got to the checkout counter, she realized she'd forgotten her sturdy mesh shopping satchel, but she pleaded with the young cashier and he produced a wrinkled paper bag.

Carrying the big bag in her arms was more difficult than Laura had anticipated. As she approached the Maynard Street block, she saw two familiar figures turn the corner. Billy waved to her first and then Angie. Billy looked older in his long pants and sweater, she noticed, and he seemed to be parting his hair differently. She wondered how he'd feel this summer about wearing his shorts and polo shirts. He was so self-conscious about being skinny.

"Hello, kids," Laura said as they approached. "Here, give me a hand." She put the bag on the sidewalk and took out the packages of meat. "Billy, can you carry these? That makes it a lot lighter. Angie, would you grab my purse?"

"Well, I've got some news," she continued as they began to walk. "You have to keep it a secret, at least until I've had a chance to tell everyone tonight. All right?"

"OK," they said in unison.

"I'm starting work at the Mutual next week. I've got a job."

"Wow," said Billy. "No one else knows?"

"Gee, Mrs. Stewart," Angie said. "That's swell."

"Thanks, Angie. Nope," she said to Billy. "You two are the very first to know."

She stopped downstairs to pick up Gary and tell Nan the news. Nan appeared happy for her, but Laura knew that she was still all upset about Alan's enlisting. This development probably only added to her fears. As resilient as she was, Nan didn't like change, Laura knew that. Still, she suspected that Nan was happy not only to take care of Gary, but also at the prospect of having Billy with her every day after school.

As she was putting away the groceries, she showed Gary the two chickens and the fowl lined up on the counter.

"Mommy, what's a fowl? It looks just like a chicken to me."

"Well, it is, honey, it's just an old chicken. I'll use it to make soup and to chop it up in something."

"So it's like you and Belle and Nan. Two girl chickens and an old lady fowl!"

Laura laughed. "Gary, you're the limit! Well, kind of like that, I guess, except you know what? I like a nice soup made with the old fowl better than any other kind of chicken."

Alan was home again early, for the second night in a row. He greeted her news with some relief, she thought, but he was quiet during dinner. After the kids left the table and they were having a second cup of coffee, she asked him if anything was wrong.

"No, not wrong. Can't say that. I'm really glad you got the job. I don't know, I just feel funny, you having to go to work and all."

"Alan, don't say that," she replied. "Me and a few million other women. It'll be fun. I'm honestly looking forward to it."

"I know," he replied. "A lot's happening so fast, I guess. What do you think your parents are going to say?"

"About my working? They won't like it. But you know I stopped worrying about that a long time ago." She reached over and stroked his cheek. "Anyway, the last time I talked to my sister, she was thinking about getting a job, too. And if Ceil's working, that'll change things in their eyes."

What did bother Laura more than anything was leaving Gary. Alan would be gone anyway, and Billy would be fine—off at school most of the day and in the summer out from morning to night with Angie and his other friends. But Gary was used to being with her most of the day.

That night, when he was taking his bath, she stuck her head in the door. "OK in there?" she said. The tub was full of his toys—rubber animals, play boats, balls. She was reminded of how young he still was.

"Yup," he replied. "Mommy, come here."

She went in and sat on the knitted toilet seat cover and leaned over the tub. "What is it, dear?"

"Mommy, will you be gone just during the day? What time will you come home?"

"Honey, I'll be home every night to make your dinner. And you'll be with Nan and Lucille all day, and then Billy will be home at his usual time. And then you'll be at school in the fall, at least in the morning. Won't that be exciting? And you know what I heard? They have a big, big Christmas party at the Mutual for all the kids. I hear you get a whole big bag of presents. Won't that be fun?"

"Yeah, I wonder what I'll get. I'll be almost six by then." He was right. Laura counted the months; Christmas was still over half a year away. She prayed that everything would go well 'til then, for Alan, for the family and for Sal next door too, wherever he ended up. She hated the war.

Gary took the big bar of soap from the dish on the side of the tub and dropped it in the water. "*Ivory soap,*" he said solemnly. "*Ninety-nine and forty-four one hundredths per cent pure. It floats!*" And sure enough, the white bar had bobbed to the surface and was bouncing off the brightly colored rubber Donald Duck and a sleek little Navy boat painted battleship gray.

Chapter 9: Belle

"Gee, Laura, I'm kind of jealous," Belle said. "How're you fixed for clothes?" They were sitting in the upstairs kitchen having a Saturday morning coffee and discussing Laura's new job.

"OK for now, but I'm going to have to take up a few skirts and dresses," Laura replied. Because of the shortage of fabrics, all the fashion ads were featuring above-the-knee hems. "But I guess I want to get a better sense of what the other girls are wearing these days. I don't know, I feel so behind the times. It's been a while since I was at Forbes." When Billy was a toddler Laura had worked one night and Saturday at the cosmetics and perfume counter of one of the big downtown department stores.

"Don't worry about it," Belle said. "With your looks you could get away with a potato sack. Pour me another coffee."

She lit a Chesterfield from the one she was finishing. "I was thinking of taking Billy and Gary downtown today. Maybe to the museum and then a bite to eat. I don't go in until six tonight." Both boys appeared to be fine with the big changes happening, but still... it had to be an adjustment for them, too.

"Would you, Belle? That would be swell. Nan said she'd watch the boys tonight. Alan wants to take me out. You know, a kind of farewell dinner."

"Where are you going? I heard the Highland is running a special on lobsters."

"I saw that in the paper, too," Laura said. "Maybe there, or The Student Prince. You know how he loves veal. But if they even have it, it's probably sky-high."

"Hey, this is a special occasion. Splurge. How about if you send the kids down at noon or so?"

Billy and Gary arrived downstairs a few hours later, dressed and ready for the outing.

"Hi, Belle!" Gary said. When Billy was little Belle had encouraged him to forget about "Aunt Belle"—that sounded so stuffy, despite what Nan said—and Gary had pretty much done the same when he started to talk.

"Well, hi yourself, sweetie," she replied. Belle recognized the short pants and striped polo he was wearing as an outfit she had given Billy. She'd have to remember to buy Gary a couple of shirts of his own. Billy had never been hard on clothes, and Belle wondered if there were any of his little knickers suits still packed away somewhere. Kids didn't wear those anymore, so Gary would probably be spared having them dragged out of mothballs in the fall.

"And how's my other best buddy?" she asked. For some reason, Billy was looking more grown-up these days. Maybe it was his slicked-down hair.

"Hair looks good, kiddo."

"Thanks, Belle." He appeared to be embarrassed that she'd noticed, but she knew he liked getting compliments from her.

They didn't have long to wait for the bus. Belle and Billy shared a double seat and Gary had one to himself in front of them. The bus headed down the hill, zigzagging noisily around potholes and stopping frequently to pick up shoppers heading to the busy downtown stores, movie theaters, and restaurants.

After a particularly big bump that made everyone bounce, Belle noticed that Gary was staring behind them, toward the rear of the bus. She looked around and met the eyes of a big colored man sitting on the long seat that spanned the back, always warm from the engine. He was tall, very heavy, and jet-black.

"Gary, stop," she said in a low voice. "Don't stare."

"Boy, he's fat!" he replied in an exaggerated whisper.

"Shh, be quiet," Billy said, looking at Belle nervously. Belle remembered that when Billy was little he had been afraid of the coal man who came to the house during the winter, hiding under the table in the dining room when he knocked on the back door, the bill receipt in his big gloved hand. There were no Negro families in their immediate neighborhood and very few colored kids at the local grammar school.

Gary continued to stare at the man. The next time Belle pretended to look back casually, she could see that he was definitely scowling in their direction. *Oh boy*, she thought.

"OK, kids, time to get off," she said with relief as they pulled up to the hill leading to the museum quadrangle. "Gary, want to ring the bell? Billy, give him a hand."

Billy helped Gary stand on the seat so he could reach up and pull the heavy wire cord. As the bus slowed down, Belle got up and walked toward the back, guiding Gary by the shoulders. She was relieved when the man nodded to her; she smiled in return. As they stepped down the stairs, Gary turned and yelled, "Bye now!"

As they began the steep walk past the city library and up to the quad, Billy asked, "Belle, why do they call colored people 'colored'?"

"Well, because they are, I guess. They're colored."

"But we are, too. We're just a different color."

"Well, we're not so colored, and it's a way we can describe who they are."

"But why?" Billy asked.

"Well, I guess because some people think that they're different."

"But do they call themselves colored? Do they call us colored, too?"

"No, I think they call us what we call ourselves. White."

"Why?" asked Gary this time.

"Oh, kids, I don't know. But it doesn't matter. Colored people are just like you and me underneath. You know Mr. Jones in the fish market. Isn't he nice? And what about our coal man? Remember you used to be afraid of him, Billy? Wasn't that silly?"

"He's a nigger," Gary said.

"Who told you that?" asked Belle.

"My friend Jimmy. He said that's what they are."

"OK, boys, stop right here." They paused and looked up at Belle. "Now listen, you must never use that word. The proper name for colored people is Negroes. It's fine to call them that. But not the other word. Do you understand that? That's a bad word. You tell your friend Jimmy that, next time he says it."

"Yes, Belle," said Gary. When she looked at Billy, he nodded, too.

Reaching the top of the incline, they passed by the imposing, larger-than-life statue of the Puritan, cloak extended on either side of his outstretched arms, peaked hat splattered with pigeon droppings.

"Yuk, that's all covered in poop and green icky stuff," Gary said.

"Yeah, what a mess," said Belle. "I wonder why don't they clean it?"

"Well, they could clean the poop but not the green stuff," said Billy. "Mrs. Brown said that's what happens when bronze statues get old. It's called patina, and you should never remove it." He added, "This statue was made by the sculptor Saint-Gaudens. He's American."

"Well, what do you know!" Belle answered. "See Gary, your big brother is smarter than me. So you came here with Mrs. Brown already?"

"Yes, last summer." He paused and said, "But it wasn't so much fun. We went to the art museum. This is better today. With you, I mean."

Belle smiled and gave him a kiss on the cheek. "Now don't get all embarrassed on me," she said, laughing, as Billy blushed. Gary giggled, so she kissed him, too.

They cut across the lawn to the large gray concrete building that housed the Museum of Natural History. Belle was ready to pay for Billy and her—Gary would be free—but the man in the blue uniform smiled and said, "No admission charge today."

"Hey, that means an extra dessert at lunch," Belle said, dropping her purse. "Aw shit," she said under her breath as she bent to pick it up.

"Oooo, now you said a bad word Belle!" Gary was laughing and pointing at Belle.

"Yep, you got me there, all right. But that's not as bad as the other one. Anyway, don't tell your mother on me, hear?" Laura was finicky about swearing.

They walked through the spacious foyer and made their way down a wide hallway lined with stuffed birds in glass cages. The birds were colorful but kind of boring, so they continued on. Ahead of them was a huge room with big floor-to-ceiling display panels, like the department store windows at Forbes & Wallace, except these enclosed life-sized animals that looked very much alive

"These are dioramas," Billy said. "They show animals in their natural habitats."

They paused in front of a huge buffalo grazing on the plains. The grass and bushes appeared real, as though they were blowing in the hot prairie wind. At the buffalo's feet was a large, coiled rattlesnake.

"Look at the snake!" yelled Gary. Belle knew Billy didn't like snakes, so she kept them moving along.

They approached a window that held a ferocious big beast, with huge tusks. A mastodon, said the small sign to the left of the window.

"Wow," said Belle, "that's a real monster."

Gary grasped Belle's hand and moved close to her. "Let's go faster," he urged. "I don't like him."

"Gary's scared," said Billy.

"No sir! He's just too big for my eyes!"

By the time they were ready for lunch, Belle's feet were killing her, even though she had worn her most comfortable shoes. "OK, kids, let's head down to Main. How about burgers at the Waldorf? I could eat a horse." Lately she wondered if it *was* horse meat she'd been served at a couple of the local joints. There were rumors.

They got home in plenty of time for Belle to help Nan finish up some of the spring cleaning she insisted on doing every year, for weeks at a time it seemed. Today it was the rugs. When she first came from the old country, Nan had worked as a housekeeper. She still was a stickler for cleanliness.

"Nan, let it go, nobody's going to notice if you don't pull the house apart today," Belle would sometimes admonish her.

But she always knew what to expect as a reply, and so she'd roll her eyes and join in when Nan began the familiar refrain, "Now, dear, you know it's my nature…"

❧

When Belle arrived for work a few hours later, she had time to meet briefly with the other assistant theater manager, Jack Jackson, who'd been on duty during the late morning and afternoon. "Good-sized crowd today," he said, loosening his tie and taking off his maroon jacket. "Had to kick a drunk out, then he threw up all over the sidewalk. Bobby wasn't crazy about cleaning that up, poor kid. The new girl, her name is Sandra, remember? She's doing OK. I put her up in the balcony. She's on 'til 8."

"Oh yeah," Jack added, "the boss is here and I think he's around tonight, too. Must've been another fight at home." Belle inwardly groaned. Simpson would be looking for sympathy and sometimes that meant he'd try to cozy up and get fresh. She wasn't in the mood.

After checking the box office to make sure Lorraine had enough cash and the ticket dispenser machine wasn't acting up again, Belle walked back into the theater and up the winding stairs to the balcony. The sounds of voices and then a gunshot were audible from inside the theater, and she could see flashes of Alan Ladd in a trench coat on the black and white screen as she walked past the aisle entrances in the upper lobby.

"Hiya, Sandra, everything going all right?"

"Hello, Miss Stewart...Belle...Yes, fine." Sandra hesitated and, gesturing with her flashlight, added, "But maybe you could check over in the back of the row at the end? A couple."

"Sure," Belle replied. "Let me have the light. Forgot mine. Follow along behind me." They walked to the end of the lobby and entered the theater. The steeply inclined rows at the top were nearly empty, but she could faintly see the outline of two people in the next-to-last row. She quietly made her way across the aisle. As she got closer it became apparent that they were putting on a pretty good show of their own.

She flashed the light directly on them. There was a flurry of activity as the girl pulled down her blouse. The boy quickly covered his lap, but not before Belle caught a glimpse of his erection bobbing between his trouser legs.

She quickly extinguished the light. "This is a theater, folks, not a hotel," she said in her best stern voice. "Cut it out. Right now."

She returned to the lobby with Sandra. "Usually all you have to do is flash the light. That scares 'em." She smiled and patted Sandra on the shoulder. "I'm grouchy today, so I gave 'em a bit more. Don't worry, it's usually not that bad." She wondered if Sandra had seen the boy. By the dazed look on her face, she guessed she had.

Belle talked to Simpson briefly in his office later on when she delivered some big bills and got more change for Lorraine. He liked to keep a close eye on the cash when he was there, counting the money as soon as she set it in front of him, so she slipped out easily.

The rest of the night was uneventful. Belle stayed in the public areas, monitoring the ushers, checking on the concessions and helping patrons. At the end of the evening, she hung up her jacket in the ladies staff lounge. Heading out, she knocked on Simpson's door and walked in.

"All set, Mr. Simpson," she said. He was sitting behind his desk, reading the paper, a half-finished sandwich—corned beef, from the smell—and cup of coffee on the tattered blotter in front of him. The cigar he was chomping on made the big mole next to his nose move up and down like it had a life of its own. Belle couldn't stand that mole and wondered why his wife didn't at least trim the bristly hairs that stuck out from the middle of it.

"Ah, Belle, come in," he said. "How are you?"

"Just fine," she answered. She knew this was her cue, but she didn't respond.

"Ah, I wish I could say the same," he replied, sighing. "But you don't need to know my troubles." *No, I definitely do not*, she thought, hoping he would stay where he was.

"And how did tonight go?"

"All right. The new girl, Sandra, she's going to work out. We had a little incident in the balcony, but she was fine."

"Oh, and what was that?"

"A couple fooling around. Older teenagers."

Simpson sat up and rummaged around for a pencil. "Tell me about it. I'll need to write that up." Belle knew he didn't have to write anything up in this case—she had handled it—but she was too tired to argue.

"Well, we—I—took care of it. They were, you know, petting."

"Petting, like clothes mussed up?"

"Yes," she replied. "Like that."

"Anything exposed?" He had stopped writing.

"Well, you know...the girl's blouse was up and the boy..."

"The boy...what?"

"Oh, for heaven' sake, Mr. Simpson, the boy's thing was out, if you have to know." She got up to leave.

Mr. Simpson wheeled his chair back away from the desk and leaned back. "Like this, Belle?" he asked. Belle looked down at Simpson's lap. His fly was unzipped, and a stubby purple nub protruded from the opening in his white underpants.

"Jesus Christ!" Belle yelled. Without thinking, she reached across his desk, picked up the cup of coffee and flung the contents directly at his crotch.

He squealed and tried to blot himself with his shirtsleeve. "I'm burned! You've burned me!"

"Don't give me that crap, you dirty old man, it was lukewarm!"

"You're fired!"

"Good!" Belle's heart was pounding. "Good! And don't you dare give me any trouble with my pay. I'm sure Mrs. Simpson would be interested to know what happened tonight. And about Maureen. Remember Maureen, Mr. Simpson? Remember why she quit?"

"Get out!" He was waving his cigar, which was now smoldering—the coffee must have doused it as well. Good.

As she walked out, Belle turned. "You pathetic old fart! Hey, you know what? I feel sorry for your wife if that's what she's got to look at every night!" She slammed the door behind her. Then she opened it again. "Yuck!" she added, this time closing the door firmly with all the dignity she could muster.

By the time she got on the bus, she'd calmed down considerably. Getting another job wasn't going to be a problem. She'd call her friend Flo tomorrow. Flo's boyfriend, Tommy, worked at Milton Bradley, and she knew there were openings there. It wasn't quite what she'd planned on right now, but the pay would be a hell of a lot better.

As the bus lumbered up the hill, nearly devoid of traffic at this hour, Belle felt satisfied at how she'd handled Simpson. She'd have to find a way to let everyone else at the theater know she wasn't coming back. They'd probably figure out why. Poor Sandra, she'd probably wonder what she'd gotten herself into and hightail it out of there by next weekend.

Belle started laughing to herself. She couldn't wait to tell Flo what happened. It really *was* pretty funny—two unzipped flies in one night. Simpson was disgusting, but the sight of the guy in the back row made her realize that she hadn't had a real boyfriend in a long time, not since Dan. Daniel Patrick Flaherty.

Nan had almost fainted when she told her Dan's name. "Irish? He's *Irish?* Oh, my." But, not surprisingly, Nan had grown to like Dan. They had even sung Irish and Scottish songs together. That was almost three years ago. She'd heard months back that he was married with a new baby. Just what he'd wanted. He'd been fair and always told her that, right from the beginning. She just wished he'd also told her about his new girlfriend before she'd discovered he was running around with someone else. She wondered if he'd be drafted with the change in the regulations concerning fathers.

Walking down the dark street from the bus stop, Belle was already imagining how things would be at the Milton Bradley plant. An easy ride downtown, good pay, maybe a discount on games and school stuff for the kids. And—if they weren't already married or engaged or in the service—a few single men around. That wouldn't be bad at all.

Chapter 10: Billy

"Ma, my book and quarter!" Billy paused at the door, out of breath from racing back up the stairs. He was halfway down the street when he realized that he'd forgotten his war bonds booklet and stamp money. A few more stamps and he'd be able to exchange his book, worth $18.75, for a bond that would someday pay back $25.

"Here," said Laura, "Now, take your time, don't run. You don't want to get all wheezy."

He walked as fast as he dared up the street, crossed State, and headed down Homer to his school at the end of the short block. He slipped into his chair just as Mrs. Lawler began leading the class in the daily recitation of "The Lord's Prayer." Then everyone, hands over hearts, rose and droned "The Pledge of Allegiance," eyes raised dutifully to the flag hanging above the blackboard in the front of the classroom.

As they finished, the door opened and Mrs. Bowles, the school principal, entered. She smiled at Mrs. Lawler and said, "Good morning, boys and girls."

"Good morning, Mrs. Bowles!" they yelled back, well aware that she would settle for nothing less than an all-out, ear-splitting response. Some of the boys competed with each other to see who could shout the loudest, but that seemed to make her smile all the more.

"I'm here this morning, boys and girls, because I want to make sure that you are all aware of the drive we are having this weekend. You know we are counting on you and every last boy and girl here at Homer Street School to collect as much as possible to help our fighting forces. Cans, tins, foil, rubber, all are desperately needed. So, fourth graders, are you ready to do your duty?"

"Yes, Mrs. Bowles!"

"Good for you! Remember, you are all citizen soldiers, each and every one of you. Let's add a special prayer this glorious spring morning for all those in service." Mrs. Bowles bowed her head. Everyone knew she had two sons in the war, one in the Navy and the other a Marine. Billy's teacher's husband, Mr. Lawler, was serving, too, in the Army in Europe.

After Mrs. Bowles left the room, Mrs. Lawler said, "Class, who can tell me where Tunisia is?" She liked to keep everyone up-to-date on what was happening in the war. Today Billy knew she was going to talk about the recent Allied victory. He was hoping someone else would raise a hand this time, but when no one did and Mrs. Lawler looked at him, he slowly raised his.

"Ah, Billy will tell us, everyone."

"It's in North Africa, and the Germans have surrendered there."

"That's absolutely correct!" replied Mrs. Lawler.

"Rommel was the German commander."

"That's right."

"And General Montgomery is the British leader."

"Right again, Billy. Thank..."

"Along with our General Eisenhower."

"Thank you, Billy. You certainly know your current events!"

He knew that some of the kids got mad at him for knowing all the answers, for being the "brain" in the class. Sometimes it bothered him to be singled out by the teacher, but he also sensed that most of his classmates respected, however grudgingly, the fact that he was probably smarter than any of them. Still, he wanted all the kids to like him. He wished he could fit in better, especially with the boys who were good at sports.

It had always been that way. Billy knew how to read and write even before kindergarten. When his first grade teacher tried to make him hold his left hand in a funny position so that the penmanship book would face the same way as the other kids', he resisted. "But this is the way I write, Miss Shea," he told her. "I'm left-handed. I learned to write when I was four, all by myself. It's how I do it." She eventually gave up.

From that incident, Billy knew that as a smart kid he had a certain influence over his teachers. And if you were *really* smart, no matter how different you might feel from the others, no matter how you might not like the way you looked, you were viewed in a way nobody else was. Even if you weren't chosen for team games or weren't good at telling a funny joke in the playground, you still had a certain reputation. But it came at a price. You were different from the others.

Later in the morning, the class trooped down to Miss Laramee's art room. Today they were sketching models of airplanes and ships from pictures in magazines and newspapers and on Wheaties cereal boxes. Most of the kids were already familiar with some of the planes because of the air traffic from Westover Field. Often the sky was black with the swarms of B-17s heading to Europe or up north, to places like Newfoundland and Labrador and Iceland.

Billy had chosen to draw the USS Arizona, one of the battleships sunk at Pearl Harbor, from a photo he'd found in an old issue of *Life*. "I'm going to write 'In Memoriam' on my picture," he explained when Miss Laramee asked why he had chosen a ship that had been totally destroyed. The weekly art class was one of his favorites, and before long it was time for lunch.

When Billy arrived home at noon, Nan and Gary met him on the porch.

"Hello, dear, your mother went downtown to buy some new clothes for her job," Nan said. "Come in, I'm fixing you a nice hard-boiled egg and toast." As they ate, the three of them listened to Kate Smith's mid-day program. After Kate trilled a hearty goodbye to everyone, a familiar sign-in signaled the start of *The Romance of Helen Trent*.

"*Romance can live on at thirty-five...and beyond,*" Gary intoned, along with the announcer, as the program began. "Nan, are you thirty-five?" he asked.

"Beyond, dearie, quite beyond. Now be a good boy, and let's listen. I think Helen's in too far over her head this time."

Billy returned to school and joined the kids in the playground, some finishing up the lunches they'd brought from home. Several lived too far to walk to their houses at noontime, while others, their mothers now working, had no one waiting for them. A few of the sixth graders were playing a game of stickball against the brick wall, and he ducked as the ball went sailing over his head. He tried to catch it once and throw it back, but it bounced away.

In the afternoon, Mrs. Lawler passed out the newest issue of *My Weekly Reader* and instructed the class to read a story about whales and then answer questions at the end. As usual, Billy finished before the allotted time, and so he felt around in the storage space under the writing surface of his desk and pulled out the sixth grade history reader that Mrs. Lawler had loaned him. This book was a collection of essays about great and mysterious ancient places.

He had already devoured several of the chapters, stories about King Tut's Tomb, Stonehenge, and Easter Island. Today he turned to the essay on Pompeii. Billy loved learning about the past, especially about places whose secrets were only partially revealed.

As he read about the eruption of Vesuvius, he was transported back to that terrible day when hot lava rained down and destroyed the ancient city. He read and re-read the description of the skeletal remains of a dog found lying atop a child. Was that dog trying to protect the boy? What were their names? Did the boy's parents escape, or were they killed, too?

The jarring ring of the afternoon bell brought the school day to a close. "Turn in your *Readers*, class," said Mrs. Lawler, "and be sure your name is clearly written on the top. I'll see you bright and early tomorrow. Melvin Sludge, no pushing!" Melvin was really dumb and not even good at sports. No one talked to him much, not even Billy, even though he and his parents lived just across the street from the Stewarts.

Gary was riding his tricycle down the driveway as Billy walked into the yard. Lucille came bounding toward him, wagging her tail. He leaned down and let her give him a series of sloppy wet kisses, scratching a favorite spot underneath her left ear.

"Mommy's still downtown shopping," Gary said. "She told me she'd bring a surprise."

Billy walked into Nan's kitchen, where she was bustling about, teakettle whistling, table set with crackers and cookies.

"Hello, Billy dear," she said, giving him a hearty hug. "Mrs. Brown is coming over for a wee cup of tea. Go wash up, and you can join us if you like."

As he returned from the bathroom, Mrs. Brown was knocking at the door. "Come in!" cried Nan.

When she talked loud like this or when she was calling the boys from the porch, Nan raised her voice to a high, singsong pitch. She sounded like the opera singers that Mrs. Brown listened to on Saturday afternoon. When Billy mentioned this once to her, Mrs. Brown laughed and said, "Well, yes, I can see the comparison, but I don't think our Nan would be singing at the Met. She does have the proper volume and gusto, though, that's a fact!"

"Good afternoon, Mrs. Stewart, and hello, Billy!" Mrs. Brown said. She sat at her usual chair next to the window, crossing her legs so that her gold ankle bracelet caught the light as she tapped the toe of one of her high heels on the linoleum floor. Nan's shoes were different, black and square, with laces and chunky heels.

"Thanks a lot for my books, Mrs. Brown. They're really keen."

"You're more than welcome, my dear," she answered. "It gives me pleasure to know you'll be reading them."

They settled down for their afternoon snack. Billy was allowed to have tea, and sometimes his mother even let him have a cup of coffee on a Saturday morning. He liked his tea with lots of milk and sugar, just like Nan, but he had learned to do with less because of the rationing. Nan hadn't cut down much, so neighbors sometimes gave her extra sugar stamps.

After he finished his tea and Ritz crackers with grape jelly, Billy excused himself and went into the dining room, where he sat at the table and looked at the morning paper and the latest issue of *Life*. He wanted to be close enough to hear Mrs. Brown and Nan, and he knew by leaving the room there was a better chance they would forget about him and say something interesting.

"Big changes, Mrs. Brown, big changes," Nan said, sighing loudly. Billy once asked his mother why two grown-up old friends like Mrs. Brown and his grandmother would address each other this way. She'd explained that some older ladies—"of their generation," she said—preferred to be very polite when they visited. "But that doesn't mean they're not good friends."

"Tell me about Belle," Mrs. Brown said.

"Well..." began Nan. "She hopes to have an interview at the Milton Bradley factory downtown any day. She says she just decided to quit on the spur of the moment, but I have my thoughts. You know about that boss..." Then she said something that Billy couldn't hear.

"Now, now, I'm sure Belle handled it well. She's a strong girl, you know, Mrs. Stewart." Billy wondered what she had handled well, but then they began to talk about his father.

"And now Alan will be leaving us," Nan said. "Dear, oh dear." It sounded like she had begun to cry.

"I just know Alan will come out of this with flying colors," said Mrs. Brown. "Besides, he loves Billy and Gary so much he'll be sure to return home safely for them. And this might be the best thing for him to be doing just now, with his...well, you know what I mean."

Billy suspected that Mrs. Brown might be referring to his father's coming home late a lot, but he wasn't sure. He was surprised at what Mrs. Brown had said about Gary and him. Maybe he wouldn't want to leave Gary, but Billy hadn't thought of his father missing him.

Before she went home, Mrs. Brown mentioned that she'd heard there would be an air raid drill that night. "Mrs. Crocker told me that her husband got a telephone call to be ready." Mr. Crocker, who lived down the street, was the local warden. They'd seen him regularly during the first year of the war, but there hadn't been a real air raid drill in a long time.

❧

Billy was glad no warning whistle sounded while he was in his bedroom later on listening to his before-dinner programs. *Terry and the Pirates* came on at 5, followed by *Superman* at 5:15, and then *House of Mystery*. After Gabriel Heatter and the news at 6, the family sat down to eat. Still no alert.

"Oh, I think that was just a rumor," Laura said as she served Gary a helping of macaroni and cheese. "You know how Mrs. Crocker likes to spread stories."

About an hour after dinner, however, the siren began to wail. The noise was loud and piercing, since it came from speakers located at Billy's school less than half a mile away. Lucille stumbled up from the kitchen floor and raced into Billy's bedroom, where she always scooted under the bed.

"OK, everyone, let's get all the curtains pulled and the shades down," Alan ordered. "Billy, make sure the bedroom lights are out." There were additional black shades in the kitchen and living and dining rooms, so the lamps could be left on there. "Remember to open a window in each room just a bit. Gary, go help your brother."

When everything was in place, the boys walked down the stairs to the door at the bottom of the darkened front hallway and peeked out. In the moonlight, they could faintly make out the shape of a car at the curb, where an obedient driver had apparently pulled over when the siren sounded.

"Look, a light," Gary said. "There's a light in the car."

"That man is still smoking," replied Billy, recognizing the orange glow of a cigarette.

Just as he spoke, someone approached the vehicle and the light was extinguished. Then the shadowy figure turned and began walking up their driveway.

"Daddy, someone's coming!" yelled Gary. He and Billy ran back upstairs in the dark, shutting the living room door behind them.

Alan came running just as the bell rang and went out onto the landing, the boys following behind. It was Mr. Crocker trudging up the stairs.

"Come on in, Oscar," Alan said.

Encumbered by his warden's regalia, Mr. Crocker clumsily made his way into the living room. He was wearing a white helmet and heavy rubber raincoat with a red, white and blue armband. At his side hung a gas mask and over his shoulder a small fire extinguisher, pick, and ax. He carried a special tinted flashlight in his gloved hand.

"Anything wrong?" asked Alan.

"'Fraid there is, Alan. There's a light on, and I bet I know which one."

"It was the bathroom light, Mr. Crocker," Laura called from the hall. "I just noticed it. It's off now."

"Yep, figures. That's the most common light that folks leave on. Don't know why. Need to see what they're doing, I guess. Hee hee." They all laughed, Alan apologized, and Mr. Crocker trudged back down the stairs, his pick banging against the banister.

"OK, who left the light on?" Alan looked at both boys and then at Laura. "No one here? Then I guess it must have been Lucille. Guess she's not as smart as I thought."

"Can I go to my room and listen to the radio?" asked Billy.

"Sure, go ahead," Alan replied.

Gary followed Billy to his darkened bedroom, and they waited for the little Emerson to warm up. It was exactly 8 p.m., and soon a low voice slowly said in a menacing tone, "*It...is...later... than... you... think*." A tolling bell followed these words. "*Welcome to 'Lights Out',*" the voice continued.

"You can listen, Gary, but you have to keep quiet," Billy said.

"I will," Gary whispered.

The story was about a family who had recently moved into a house where they'd begun to hear strange noises. When they called the police, they were told that the house was haunted because it was built next to a cemetery. "There's really nothing we can do, ma'am," the police sergeant said. "You have to make the best of it, as those before you did, bless their souls. And good luck to you"

During the commercial, Billy hissed to Gary, "Do you know that our house is built right on *top* of a cemetery?"

"No sir!" Gary whispered.

"Yes, it's true, and sometimes the ghosts come right up here. I saw one the other night outside the linen closet."

"No sir!...What did it look like?"

"Well, it was all slimy and green and..." Just then there was a noise under the bed, followed by a scuffling and a thumping against the door. Both boys screamed.

Billy jumped up and opened the door, nearly falling over Lucille, who bounded out of the room and down the hall.

Laura came running. *"What is going on here?"*

Gary was crying hysterically. "Billy told me there are ghosts coming up from the cemetery!"

"What cemetery?"

"The one under our house!"

"William Stewart, what are you saying to your brother? And what are you letting him listen to that crazy program for?" She marched over and turned off the radio. "Honestly, I'm surprised at you! Really, I am!"

Laura took Gary on her knee. "Everything's fine. Your brother is just being funny, except that he's not funny at all!" She turned to Billy. "It's a good thing your father is downstairs with Nan, mister, or you'd be in big trouble! Tell him you're sorry and that it's all a big story!"

"I'm sorry, Gary, I just made it up," Billy said. He was still kind of shaken up, too. Maybe listening to *Lights Out* hadn't been such a good idea.

Later that night, as he lay in bed, Billy wondered how the story about the house next to the cemetery ended. Maybe Angie had heard it. He'd ask her tomorrow.

He could hear the steady drone of planes flying overhead out of Westover. Did they already have American bombs in them, or were those put in after they landed at one of the airfields in England?

Lucille jumped up next to him, and he was reminded of the dog and the boy buried under the lava from Vesuvius. He fell asleep wondering what Lucille would do if a bomb accidentally fell from the sky. Would she jump up and scoot under the bed? No, he decided, Lucille would throw herself on top of him and do her best to save them both, just like the dog at Pompeii.

Chapter 11: Alan

A few days after his swearing-in, Alan received the official notice to report for active duty. He was to be at the main post office on Monday morning of the following week. He'd then take a night train from Union Station, just across the street, to a military facility where he'd begin his service in the United States Navy.

Although the destination wasn't specified, he suspected it would be Sampson, the big new naval training station in upstate New York. That's where Sammy down the street had gone to boot camp, and he remembered that the whole Ferris family had taken the bus downtown after dinner to see him off on the train. That had been last fall, just after the facility opened. Sammy had complained when he came home on leave about the bitterly cold winds that blew in from Lake Seneca. At least June wouldn't be so bad.

Laura was upset when she heard the date on which Alan had to report. "I wish I didn't have to work that morning, Alan," she told him, " but I promised. I'd feel so funny calling in on my first day."

"It's fine. I have to be down there early anyway. You'll be home in plenty of time to see me off on the train. You can drive everyone down in the car," Alan said. "You want to keep it on the road while I'm gone?"

"I don't know. What do you think?"

"It's not in bad shape—the tires are good and there are still the spares." He had moved the covered side-mounted spares on the Packard down to the basement after thefts of good tires had begun to be reported in the newspapers. "You can get by easily with the rationing. You wouldn't be using it that much. If you change your mind later on, talk to Joe or Fred or one of the other guys I work with. They'll get it up on blocks in the garage. Or Sal, if he's still around."

There were a lot of things to be taken care of, repairs around the house that he'd been putting off for months. The yard and lawn work was something else he was concerned about, but that would probably work out. Nan loved the garden, and Billy would be able to mow some this summer. And he was sure Sal's father and grandfather next door would help out. The elderly Mr. Mazzarella really liked Nan. He called her "the signora from Scozia" and always encouraged her to sing her Scottish songs at parties in the backyard.

Down in the basement the other night, he'd noticed the storm windows. Someone would have to be hired to put those in when the cold weather came. And the furnace. Belle was used to its eccentricities, but Laura had never gotten the hang of it. Belle would have to show her how to bank it with just the right amount of coal to last the night. It was good they'd all be together while he was away.

By the end of the weekend, Alan was set to go. He quit working the day his notice came, as agreed, and visited a few old friends around the city. He also stopped in at the High Life and said goodbye to the bartenders and the regulars. "Nah, have one for me next week instead," he said, when they kept offering to buy him another shot and beer. "Picture me doing push-ups and marching around some parade ground. That's probably when I'll be thinking of you guys."

Laura had talked about driving to Connecticut so that Alan could see her parents before he left, but it wasn't going to work out. That was all right with him. He knew they preferred the occasional visits Laura made by train with the boys.

"I'm really sorry that you won't at least get to see my sister," Laura said as they sat at the table after Saturday's lunch. He was, too. He liked Ceil, and they had hit it off right from the moment they met, years earlier. Even now, watching Lucille romp around the backyard sometimes made him think of that day.

Alan and Lucille, a frisky and badly behaved puppy at the time, had driven down to meet Laura's family in West Hartford. When they walked into the backyard, Lucille scampered about looking for a place to squat. Alan called to her, but it was no use.

"This little doggie who just peed in Dad's zinnia bed is called Lucille?" asked the pretty young woman who rose from a lawn chair to greet him. "Please tell me that was before you knew your girlfriend here had a big sister with that lovely name! Does he know that was also our grandmother's name, Laura?" she asked, turning to her sister and laughing.

"Actually, I hated my name," she confided to Alan as they were playing croquet later on the Reynolds' spacious lawn. "That's why I still make everyone call me Ceil. When you got out of the car and shouted 'Lucille!' I couldn't figure out what the heck was going on. Was this some bratty kid from my wretched nursery school past? No one calls me Lucille anymore."

Later, she said, "Well, Alan, I think it's safe to say we're going to be seeing each other again. Quite a bit, if I read my sister correctly. Just promise me one thing. Don't ever call that little ball of fur Ceil. Is that a deal?" Nodding in the direction of her parents, she added, "And don't mind Eunice and Horace over there—the Prince of Wales wouldn't be good enough for their daughters." She'd been right about that.

He was roused from his daydreaming by Laura's voice. "Alan, hello, did you hear me?" she said, picking up their coffee and dessert plates. "We were talking about Ceil. Why don't you at least give Bill and her a call before Monday?"

"Sorry," he replied. "I'm in a fog. That's a good idea, I will." He gave one last thought to that summer afternoon in West Hartford. That was also the day he'd first realized how different Laura's life was going to be with him. No country club, no summer beach cottage at Black Point, and certainly no maid coming in every week to clean the house.

Alan wondered if Laura would start having more contact with her parents in the coming months. For a moment he had the wild thought that as soon as he was gone she'd up and move with the boys back to Connecticut. Then he remembered that she'd once told him that she had grown closer to Nan than to her own mother. She was tied to his family now.

"Nan wants us down for dinner tomorrow," Laura said. "I thought that would be nice. I think she's going to make your favorite."

"Gee, when was the last time we had pot roast? I wonder if she can get any."

"If anyone can get it out of Mr. Simka, Nan can."

"It's funny, she never seems to mind going there. I wonder if he ever made a pass at her."

"Nan? Come on, that would be like flirting with your own mother. Anyway, if he did, she'd just tell him to be a good boy and

behave himself. Then she'd have a good laugh about it. Your mother's amazing, Alan." Laura paused. "Have you talked to her? I mean,
about your going?"

"Yeah, we had a little conversation the day after the party.
She'll be OK."

"I don't know. She always seems so strong, but... You know
how she can hardly talk about your father without crying. After all
these years."

"I know. But I don't think that's just sadness. When she does
that she's thinking about the good times, too. One time she told
Belle and me that she'd never even consider getting married again.
She was that happy."

"She's a lucky woman, then, to have been so sure," Laura
replied. "Say, you know what? Not to change the subject, but I think
I'll keep the Packard running after all. Can you go over a few things
for me? Let's have Billy listen, too. You know him, he remembers
everything."

❧

At Sunday dinner the next day, the adults all maintained a
determined cheeriness. Gary had the sniffles and was grouchy, and
Billy was his normal quiet self, though Alan sensed he was a bit
more pensive than usual. Lucille had been keeping close to Alan the
past few days and was curled up under the table at his feet.

"So, Nan, how did you manage the pot roast?" asked Laura.
"They told me at the A&P that there wasn't any this week."

"Oh, Mr. Simka brought one out for me. He's so
accommodating."

"Yeah, I heard that," Belle said. "Very accommodating."

"Now, Belle, be nice. He's a lovely man," Nan replied.

"Umm, heard that, too," said Belle, laughing.

Laura caught Belle's eye and gestured at Billy, who quickly
looked down at his food.

"Nan, what's for dessert?" Gary asked.

"Well, it's your daddy's favorite, lemon meringue pie. But, I
don't know, that dinner plate needs some cleaning up, young man."

"It's OK," said Alan. "Just for today, Gary."

After dinner they all moved to the living room to listen to Jack
Benny and then the Quiz Kids.

"I always tell everyone our own smart Billy should be on this program," Nan said as a commercial for Alka-Seltzer began.

"Aw, Nan," Billy said.

"Can I be on, too?" Gary asked.

"Why, yes, I'm sure you can someday, too," Nan replied.

"When your tablets get down to four...That's the time to buy some more. Fizzzzzz."

"What did you say, Gary?" Nan asked.

"Nothing, Nan," said Alan. "Gary's just reciting the Alka-Seltzer jingle. Boy, you'll have a whole lot of new ones for me, won't you?" He looked around the table and smiled broadly. "I mean, by the time I get back." Everyone nodded. "OK, school day tomorrow for Billy, and a big day for all of us, I guess." He got up and hugged Nan and Belle. "I'll see you two in the morning."

"Good luck tomorrow at the new job, Laura," Belle said. "I guess I'm next. Looks like I'll be making games at Milton Bradley in a few days."

"That's swell, Belle," Laura said. "And thanks, Nan, for the delicious meal. Come on, boys, off we go. You too, Lucille." They all kissed Belle and Nan goodnight and followed Alan up the stairs.

After the boys were in bed, Alan and Laura listened to Gabriel Heatter and Walter Winchell for any news of the war. Most reports these days were focusing on the European campaign. There was wide speculation as to where the big mainland invasion would begin. Sicily and Italy, close to the new Allied stronghold in North Africa, were likely targets.

On the other side of the world, it was another story. After the hard-won victory at Guadalcanal last February—a long six months after the assault the previous summer—there had been slow progress. Distances in the Pacific were vast, thousands of miles separating the tiny islands, most of whose names Americans on the home front were hearing for the first time. Tonight it was startling to listen to news of a place called Attu.

"I can't believe the fighting is so far to the north," said Laura. "They're talking about Alaska." She looked at Alan. "That's not where you think you'll be, is it?"

He shook his head. "No, it's got to focus again further south. That's where all the Jap strength is." But secretly he wondered just where he was headed. Maybe it wouldn't even be either ocean. He had heard of a local guy whose ship was patrolling the Gulf side of the Panama Canal, day and night.

After Laura went into the bedroom to get her clothes ready for the next day, Alan turned off the lights and, Lucille at his heels, slowly walked down the hallway. He stopped at each boy's room. Gary was clearly asleep, his breathing ragged and noisy from his head cold. There was silence across the hall. Was Billy still awake? After several seconds of gazing into the dark bedroom, Alan moved on. Lucille started to follow him, paused, and then turned and went into Billy's room.

Alan was already in bed when Laura returned from the bathroom, closing the bedroom door behind her. Her lavender silk nightgown shimmered in the dim bed stand light as she stood by the dresser brushing her long hair. She applied some perfume behind her ears and got into bed.

"I love that nightgown," Alan said.

"Yes, I know," she replied. She moved against him. The silk felt cool against his naked body. He was so tall that even with her head buried in his shoulder she could never reach his toes to wiggle them with hers.

"Alan, you'll take care of yourself. You promise?"

"Yes, I promise. I will."

"And be good."

"Of course. Don't even ask that. You know better."

"I don't mean with other girls. Well, that, too, I guess, but what I mean is, be careful when you're out. Drinking and all."

"I know. I will, promise." After a few seconds he asked, "You know this afternoon when I was talking about Nan and how she loved my father?"

"Yes, what?"

"What did you mean when you said that she was a lucky woman to have been so sure?"

"Oh. Well..." she began. "I guess I meant that it's hard nowadays to be sure, to be certain, about anything. You know, you wonder. I don't mean about me loving you and you loving me, I know we do." She kissed his shoulder. "It's just that it's hard to know right now what's going to happen. When you'll be back. Where we'll be in a few years. Things like that. Life seems more complicated, that's all."

Alan stroked her hair. "Well, I know one thing for sure. I want to have a better life after this is over. I want to make a good life for you and the kids."

"I know. Me, too."

"Hey, and I know something else."

"What?"

"I'm suddenly getting pretty warm with all this purple silk between you and me."

"I think we can take care of that," she whispered, reaching over and turning off the light. Alan could see her outline and hear the rustle of the silk as she sat on the edge of the bed, raised her arms, and removed the nightgown. "Better?" she asked, lying down on top of him.

"Umm, much better," he replied.

ॐ◌

The next morning Alan woke at dawn, well before the alarm went off. He lay on his back in the stillness of the room, listening to the sound of birds in the fir trees just outside the window. This is it, he thought. I wonder when I'll sleep in this bed again. Or if. The idea that he might be killed, or even wounded, had somehow not really occurred to him until recently. Thinking about it now, and his leaving today, he was seized with a sudden panic that wrenched his insides. He eased himself out of bed and raced to the bathroom.

By the time Billy and Laura left the house, Alan had calmed down. Everyone's arrangements were clear about meeting at the station later on, so no one was saying goodbye just yet.

Alan gave Gary his juice and cereal and waited for him to get dressed. Then they walked out into the backyard and played a game of catch. Lucille was soon drenched from chasing after the ball in the wet grass, though already the sun felt warm.

Alan wondered how different the weather would be in north-western New York. He was reminded of how big the state was when he'd looked at the map the other night for the town of Geneva. It was 'way up there, not far from Lake Ontario.

He stopped in downstairs and had a cup of coffee with his mother and Belle. Nan insisted on making him a scrambled egg and toast, which he ate only to please her. She was bustling about at a pace even faster than usual, but a cautionary wave from Belle stopped him from scolding her.

"OK, I'm going to go up and get my stuff together, I guess," he said. "I'll be back. Gary, you stay here with Nan and Aunt Belle."

He'd already decided what he was going to wear. He wasn't clear as to how often he'd be in civilian dress, if at all. Even though the letter had said to bring along two changes of clothes, he picked out slacks and shirts that he wouldn't mind throwing out later on. Those and a few toiletries and photos and writing paper and a few pocket novels—Erle Stanley Gardner mysteries and the Studs Lonigan books by James T. Farrell.

He wasn't sure what else to pack, but he also knew he could pick up other things he needed at the training camp, or ask Laura to mail him stuff he hadn't thought of. Everything fit into a canvas bag he'd used for baseball games at the plant.

He took a final look around, grabbed his old beige gabardine windbreaker and went back downstairs. As he placed the bag on the back porch, Mary Mazzarella and Sal walked across the driveway.

"You take good care, Alan, you hear?" Mary pulled him down toward her and gave him a big hug. *"Dio ti benedica!"*

Sal shook Alan's hand. "I hope everything goes OK. I'll watch out for Billy, that is, until I go in myself. I graduate in a few days." Alan knew how much Billy thought of Sal. Sometimes he'd even found himself a little jealous of that, since Billy seemed to be so much more at ease with Sal. But Sal was a nice kid. Not a kid anymore, Alan noted. His grip was firm, and he'd turned into a handsome guy.

"Thanks, Sal. You take care, too. I guess I'll be hearing from the family about you. Be good. And thanks for keeping an eye on things in the meantime."

"All set," he said, going back into the house, where his mother and Belle were waiting. "I won't say goodbye now. I'll see you before seven at the station."

"All right, dear, we'll be there," Nan said, drying her hands on her apron. He could tell she was doing her best not to cry. They all kissed and walked out the back door onto the porch, where Lucille was waiting to come in. When she spotted Alan's bag at the entrance, she begin to whine.

"It's OK. You take care of everyone now, old girl, you hear?" he said. Alan rubbed the back of her ears and for a moment held his cheek against the wet of her nose. "Hold onto her, Belle, I don't want her following me." He didn't look back until he was at the end of the drive. Then he waved quickly and walked down the street to the corner bus stop.

The rest of the afternoon passed quickly. He filled out endless forms at the Post Office, stood in line with a hundred other men for a quick second physical, and was finally handed a packet with a ticket that read "Geneva, N.Y." So it would be Sampson after all. If he were lucky he'd be able to come home on leave before being shipped out.

"That's it, young fella," the middle-aged processing clerk told him. "Your train leaves in a couple of hours. Take my advice and board early—you'll have a chance at a berth. Meantime, there's a USO on the second floor of the station. Just show them your papers if they ask. And good luck to you."

Alan crossed the street and entered the wide main corridor of Union Station. The last time he'd been here was a couple of years ago when he and Laura spent a weekend in New York City for their anniversary. Today it was mobbed with other men leaving for their tours of duty. Lots of them were Army, he suspected, on their way to Fort Devens over in the eastern end of the state.

He walked past the stairways on both sides of the hall that led up to the outside tracks. A constantly echoing barrage of announcements about arrivals and departures for Worcester, Boston, Hartford, New Haven, New York and parts beyond reverberated throughout the station. toward the rear was the big, high-ceilinged waiting room, as well as a newsstand and candy counter, restaurant and florist. Several shoeshine stands lined the wall next to the barbershop.

After finishing a grilled cheese sandwich, coffee and dough-nut in the spacious USO reception lounge upstairs, Alan returned to the waiting room. He felt too fidgety to read, so he went back outside and walked a while up and down Main Street. He got back just in time to see the familiar olive-green Packard pulling into a parking spot nearby.

"It's Sampson," he said as he reached the car. "I'll be in New York State."

As they all walked into the waiting room, he said, "The train's already on the track upstairs. Don't have much time." He held onto Gary's hand. Laura, Billy, Nan, and Belle followed. "They said I'd get a better seat or berth—sounded maybe like a Pullman—if I got on early."

"Do you have enough money with you?" Laura asked. He had given her most of his cash that morning.

"I guess. Don't think I'll need much."

"Here," said Belle. "Italian cookies from Mary. She ran out when she saw us leaving."

"And here's some sandwiches, dear," said Nan. "And shortbread."

"Mother, you must have used all your rations for the butter and sugar."

"Hers and a few of the neighbors'," said Belle.

"How did the day go?" Alan asked Laura. He'd almost forgotten that she'd started her new job that morning.

"It was fine. I think I'm going to like it. I'll write you all about it."

"Here, this is how you all get in touch with me." He handed her a slip of paper.

"That's not such a big identification number after all," Laura said.

"I think that's just temporary, like a post office box or something."

Just then over the loudspeaker came the muffled boarding announcement: *"All military personnel...Sampson Naval Training Station, Geneva, New York...may board now...Track 6...military personnel only on the track at this time."*

"That's me," Alan said. They all rushed to the entrance to the stairway that led upstairs to the outdoor platform. "I think we have to say goodbye here," he said.

"That's right, son," said the conductor standing at the open doorway. "Your missus here can go up with you, though."

They moved off to the side, and Alan embraced his mother and Belle. He reached down and picked up Gary and kissed him. Then he leaned down and awkwardly hugged Billy. "You're the man of the family, now, Billy. Take care of everyone for me."

"OK," Billy said. By now Belle and Nan and Laura were all crying.

"What's the matter, Mommy? Why are you and Nan and Belle so sad?" Gary asked, and then he burst into tears. Billy looked away.

Alan and Laura were swept up the stairs in the rush of the other early arrivals eager to board the train. As they reached the top and moved outside to the track, Alan looked back and raised his hand one more time. Nan, Gary in her arms, had taken off her gloves and was waving them wildly in the air. Belle was smiling and blowing kisses. Her other arm cradled Billy, his face half-hidden, sobbing at her side.

Chapter 12: Billy

Billy walked slowly up the street, taking care to avoid the puddles that had formed after last night's rain. Since his father's departure a few days earlier, it had turned damp and chilly, the kind of weather he had learned to be wary of. So far this week he'd avoided a bad asthma attack, but Laura had insisted on running the vaporizer in his room at night.

"Ma, I hate that smell," he said when she walked into his room carrying the rectangular white enamel container filled with water and a blob of sweet-scented gunk. "Even Lucille doesn't like it." It was true that last year she left the room when the thick steam started swirling out of the open top, but she had eventually gotten used to it.

"Too bad," Laura replied. "You don't want to be sitting up all night." The damp weather hadn't changed, and so the vaporizer stayed.

"Nan, make sure Billy wears his raincoat and rubbers, would you?" Laura asked when they walked downstairs earlier that morning. "I need to be in early for a training thing. You know where Gary's stuff is if he wants to go out later. He's upstairs playing. Billy, don't be running around today."

As he approached the schoolyard, Billy took off his black raincoat and rain hat. He was wearing a sweater underneath, and he hated getting sweaty from the rubber of the coat. Besides, he knew some of the kids would laugh at the get-up. "The fire's down the street," an older boy from the sixth grade had yelled to him one day after the sun had unexpectedly come out.

At recess he joined in a game of soccer baseball and then felt himself getting out of breath. As he moved away to sit on one of the swings, he noticed two of the girls in his class looking at him and laughing. One of them, a tomboy whose real name was Florence but whom everybody called Pinky, once asked him why he was so skinny. "My kid sister's wrists are bigger than yours," she said scornfully.

When he mentioned this encounter to Angie, she said, "Tell me if we ever see that girl on the street so I can give her a good smack."

Later in the morning, while the rest of the kids were finishing up a reading exercise, Mrs. Lawler called Billy to her desk.

"You're a bit on the quiet side, today, Billy. Is everything all right?"

"I'm OK, Mrs. Lawler. I'm kind of wheezy, though, with my asthma."

"Yes, it's that sort of weather today that bothers you, I know. Billy, I heard your dad is off to serve."

"Yes, he left for boot camp in the Navy on Monday."

"Well, you should be very proud of him. Tell you what. Why don't you mention to your mother at lunch that I thought perhaps you should stay home for the afternoon? We're reviewing some arithmetic that I know you've mastered. And I'm sure you'll be fine by tomorrow."

"All right. Except it isn't my mother. She's working now, so Nan...my grandmother...is taking care of my brother and me."

"Oh...oh, I didn't know that. Well, you couldn't ask for anyone better than that lady, now, could you?" Billy knew that Mrs. Lawler's mother was a friend of Nan's. "Have her make you a cup of tea," she said, smiling.

"Thanks, Mrs. Lawler."

When Billy got home, Nan insisted on taking his temperature, shaking the thermometer with determined vigor before sticking it in his mouth. "See, I told you I wasn't sick," he said, after she squinted and fiddled with the glass tube, finally asking him to help her read it.

"Never you mind, better safe than sorry. Now, I'm going marketing. Gary, you come with me. Lucille will stay here with Billy." Nan took off her apron and fixed her hairnet. "Your Aunt Belle should be home soon. She's down making arrangements for her new job. If you're upstairs when we get back, I'll call you when tea is ready."

After Nan and Gary left for the grocery store, Billy wandered for a while through the house. Lucille lay asleep on the rug in the kitchen. There was silence except for the vibrating of Nan's old Kelvinator refrigerator with its enamel claw legs, and the faint ticking of Belle's alarm clock. In her bedroom he squeezed the atomizer on a fancy new bottle labeled "Shalimar," sneezing as the perfume's heavy scent filled the air and misted the small mirror above the crowded vanity.

As he passed Nan's bedroom, Billy noticed two pictures lying on her bed. One was a photo of Nan and his father, his arm around her shoulder, taken last Christmas in front of the tree. Next to it was a faded newspaper clipping of a school baseball team, one face in the back row circled with red ink. Again, his father, almost unrecognizable except for his height and a certain familiar tilt to his head. Billy looked at the image for a while and then hurried from the room.

"Come on, Lucille," he said as he walked through the kitchen and out onto the back porch. The Mazzarella house looked empty. Maybe Mrs. Brown was home. He didn't want to go back in the house just yet.

"Why, it's Billy," Mrs. Brown said as she opened the door. "I didn't realize it was that late in the afternoon. Come in. Hello, Lucille." She was wearing her fancy Navajo shawl, the one Billy knew came from New Mexico, where Mrs. Brown used to live a long time ago.

"Hi Mrs. Brown," he replied. "I didn't go back to school after lunch. I wanted to, but my teacher said I should stay home."

They walked past the kitchen and into the den, where Mrs. Brown kept all her books. There was no door to this room. Instead, strands of glass beads in various shades of yellow and amber hung from the narrow arched opening. Billy liked the tinkling sound the curtain made as it parted, but Lucille always flattened her tiny frame as she scooted under the swaying beads.

Ashkii, Mrs. Brown's big black cat, was dozing on the floor in the middle of an oversized fringed pillow. Ashkii's name meant "son" in Navajo. He opened his green eyes and purred when Billy leaned down and petted him. Lucille sniffed near his tail, but he ignored her and went back to sleep.

"I'm sorry to hear you're not feeling well," Mrs. Brown said. "I'd offer you something to eat or drink, but your Nan invited me over for tea. In just a little while, in fact."

"I'm better now, thank you," Billy replied. "It wasn't just my asthma, but I'm OK now."

"Oh?" Moving a small green book from the seat, Mrs. Brown sat down in her chair. "I was reading when you knocked, Billy. One of my favorite poets, Emily Dickinson."

"The one who lived up in Amherst?" Billy said.

"Yes, indeed, the poet I've told you about. When I visited my friend Grace the other day I was saddened to learn that her neighbor, Madame Martha Bianchi, died just a few weeks ago. She was Emily Dickinson's niece, imagine that."

Billy nodded, and then Mrs. Brown said, "So, tell what the 'it just wasn't my asthma' is all about."

Mrs. Brown made it so easy to talk that Billy never had trouble confiding in her. Today, as he explained to her how the kids sometimes teased him, she listened and nodded.

"I don't like it when they talk about me. I want them to like me."

"It's very natural, Billy, not to want to be laughed at. And wouldn't it be lovely to be somebody that everyone likes or notices—that is, notices in a nice way? But I think the other boys and girls do admire you because of your scholastic achievements. They do, don't you think?"

"Yeah, I guess, but they never tell me that, and I know they don't like me in other ways."

"Maybe it's because they don't understand you." She reached over and picked up the Emily Dickinson book she'd been reading. She leafed through a few pages. "Listen to these words, Billy," she said.

I'm nobody! Who are you?
Are you nobody too?
Then there's a pair of us – don't tell
They'd banish us you know.

How dreary to be somebody!
How public like a frog
To tell your name the livelong day
To an admiring bog!

"That's funny, about the frog and the bog," Billy said.

"Yes, it's very clever, and perceptive, too. Emily Dickinson went her own way, Billy. It's hard to be what she calls a 'nobody,' because sometimes that means you'll be alone. And it also means you're a bit different in some ways." She smiled, "But who wants to be one of the croaking frogs? Dreary, indeed!"

Mrs. Brown closed the book and stood up. "We'll talk more about Emily Dickinson another day. She was a fascinating woman. But I think right now we'd better be getting across the yard or Nan will wonder where you've disappeared to." Billy held the back door as Lucille darted out, followed by Mrs. Brown, who tossed her Indian shawl over her shoulders as she nimbly descended the steps.

えつ

That night all the Stewarts were invited over to the Mazzarellas' for a small get-together after Sal's graduation. Billy had hoped to attend the actual ceremony, but only families were allowed because of the number of seats. "Anyway, it'll be real boring," Sal said. "A bunch of dumb speeches and then we all march up on the stage one by one and shake the mayor's hand. I wish I could skip it."

Before heading downtown with his family, Sal, cap and gown in hand, came over at dinnertime to remind them about the party. He had on a white shirt, maroon tie and black slacks.

"My, aren't you a handsome sight," said Nan. "Now be a good sport and show us how you look with your robe on."

"Aw jeez, Nan..." Sal replied. But he dutifully slipped it around his shoulders, placed the cap on his head, and, smiling uncomfortably, stood somewhat rigidly at attention.

"Hey, relax, you're not in the Army yet," Belle said. "And don't hide those curls under the hat."

"Yeah, I guess I won't have these much longer." He laughed and pushed the cap back a bit.

"So you're really leaving us, too, Sal?" Laura asked.

"Yep, I'm all set. Passed my physical and everything. Should hear any day." Nan got up from the table and hugged him. Sal awkwardly patted her on the back. "It'll be good," he said. He folded his gown and took off his cap. "So, guess I'll see you all later," he said, backing out the door.

Everyone gathered a few hours later next door for dessert and wine and grape punch. Mary had made a cake that read "*Buona*

Fortuna, Salvatore, 6-17-43." Sal's grandfather, Nonno, who spoke mostly Italian and kept to himself in his small apartment upstairs, was seated in a tall corner chair, his short legs firmly planted on the shiny wood floor. His snow-white hair was neatly parted on the side, and he was wearing a blue sweater vest.

"I don't know those words, Angie," Gary said, his face a few inches away from the cake. Like his older brother, Gary had already learned to read, even though he hadn't yet begun kindergarten.

"That's all right, Gary, I bet Billy doesn't know them either," she replied. "It's Italian for 'Good Luck, Salvatore.'" She pronounced Sal's name with an exaggerated accent and elaborate flourish. "That's his real name."

"I know," Gary said, giggling. "*Salvatore,*" he repeated, perfectly mimicking Angie's inflection.

"Hey, come out into the backyard in a minute or so," Sal whispered to Billy in the living room. "I got something to tell you."

When Billy went outside, he could see the light from Sal's cigarette down by the bench in the arbor. He walked through the damp grass and sat next to him.

"Listen, Billy, remember when I said over at your house that I'd be leaving pretty soon?"

"Yes, you said you'd be hearing any day."

"Yeah, well, I heard. A telegram came today. I'm going tomorrow, late tomorrow afternoon. Got to report to the train station and then from there to Fort Devens."

"Tomorrow, you're leaving tomorrow?" Billy felt the coldness of the concrete bench as he shifted closer to Sal.

"Yeah. Listen, I want to ask you a favor. I have some stuff I can't take with me. Like, personal stuff. I have it here." He reached under the bench and pulled out a battered suitcase.

Billy recognized the case. Once when he had walked into Sal's bedroom, Sal was bent over it, putting something away.

"Be with you in a second," he'd said, locking the suitcase and pocketing the key. Billy had wanted to ask Sal what was inside, but he never did.

"Anyway, I don't want to leave that suitcase in my room when I'm gone. Even locked. Do you think we could hide it up in your room? I'll give you the key to hold."

"Sure, Sal," Billy said. "I can do that. I'll hide it at the top of my closet, in the back. But you don't have to give me the key."

"Nah, I don't want to be carrying that around. If anything happens to me, you can just throw away the suitcase, OK?"

"Yes, and I won't open it."

"Thanks," Sal said. Then he looked at Billy. "Hey, if something happens to me, you can open it. I mean it. It won't matter. But that's not gonna happen. Let's take it over now." They walked quickly up to Billy's room, where Sal hoisted the suitcase behind a stack of old games on an upper shelf in the closet. He unfastened the key from his chain and gave it to Billy, and they returned to the party.

❧

The next afternoon Billy ran home from school as fast as he could. As he turned into the yard, he could see Angie pacing back and forth on her back porch. When she saw him, she rushed down the driveway.

"Listen," she said, clutching his arm. "Sal already left."

Billy's heart sank. "He's gone? But he told me..." He was gasping for breath.

"Yeah, he said he wasn't going until later today. But Ma just told me that he already took the bus downtown about an hour ago. She's lying down. He didn't want anyone to go with him."

Angie grabbed Billy's arm again. "Come on, we're going down to see him off. You said you did that with your pop."

"Yeah, but I don't know if we'll find him. And I don't think we can go up on the track. Anyway, Nan probably won't let me."

"Never mind all that. Here's the plan: You go tell Nan you're going to be at my house and Ma wants you to stay and keep us company for dinner. We'll find him all right, but hurry up!"

Running to the corner, they caught a bus that was just starting to pull away from the stop. When it finally turned off busy Main Street and headed down toward Union Station, Billy could see that the terminal entrance was even more crowded than the other day.

They pushed their way through the big door into the main corridor, rushing down the hall to the rear of the station. The place was teeming with young men carrying bags and small suitcases, family members crowded around them. Just as they spotted the track location written on the big black board above the information kiosk, the boarding call for the special train to Fort Devens was announced.

"Come on," yelled Angie, running back down the crowded corridor. They pushed as close as they could to the door leading up to the platform and waited. Eventually, the crowd began to thin out as the departure time drew closer.

"Angie, he must be on the train already," Billy said.

"He's not, I just know it," she replied. "Here, help me a minute." She leaned on his shoulder and climbed up on one of the long polished wooden seats set against the wall.

"I see him! I see him!" she cried. "He's running this way with some other guys." Angie grabbed Billy's hand, and they moved to the center of the corridor.

Sal almost bumped into them before he realized they were there. "Hey, I'll catch up with you in minute," he said to his friends, who raced ahead up the stairs. He scooted down in front of Billy and Angie, bag at his side. "How the heck did you kids get down here?"

"On the bus, same as you," Angie replied.

"Does Ma know? Never mind. I can't stop. Train's leaving. Come with me to the door."

"Here, Sal, take this. It's the three of us." Angie thrust a photograph in Sal's hand. When he looked at it, he squeezed his eyes shut and for a moment turned away. Then he said in a funny voice, "Thanks for coming down. Thanks, I really mean it." He leaned down and gave each of them a hug and a kiss on the cheek. "Take care of each other, hear?"

Sal handed the conductor his ticket and waved back at them before he started up the staircase. He was holding a Hershey bar in his hand. Billy wished he had brought him another as a going-away present. They waved as Sal reached the top of the stairs, but he didn't look back at them again.

As they walked out into the late afternoon sunlight, Billy asked Angie what photo she had given Sal. "Remember that day we went to the beach at Joyland and we all had ice cream on our faces and your Ma took a picture of the three of us? I gave him that," she said, wiping her eyes, "so he'll remember us wherever he is." They slowly crossed the street and got on the waiting uptown bus.

As they rode up the hill, Billy thought of his father's leaving, and now Sal's. He was glad they'd been able to see Sal off and he knew Sal had been glad, too, by the way he hugged and kissed them. Sal never did stuff like that.

Billy and Angie decided not to let anyone know about their trip downtown, though Billy was tempted to confide in Nan as he was helping her set the table late the next afternoon. She'd offered to start making dinner for everyone while Alan was away. "It's something I like to do, and it makes things easier for you, Laura," she explained.

"Say, what's in this stew?" Belle asked. "I can see the ham-burg—I think. What else?"

"Well, just about everything we've had this week and then some," Nan replied. "It doesn't do to throw anything out anymore."

"It's delicious, Nan," said Laura. "And look how Gary is clean-ing up his plate." As far as Billy could tell, all Gary was doing was mashing his potatoes around in the stew, but he didn't say anything.

"I think we need some cheering up," said Belle as they were finishing their dessert of canned peaches and cookies. "It's Friday and I feel like a movie. What about you, Laura?"

"All right, but my treat. I'll be getting paid next week."

"How about if a certain young man goes as our escort?" Belle asked. "No school tomorrow, and there's an Alice Faye musical at the Strand, *The Gang's All Here*."

"Nan, do you mind staying with Gary?" Laura asked.

"Do I mind staying with this good little boy? Of course I don't. We'll read some stories together."

Billy and Belle and Laura walked in the chill early summer dusk to Winchester Square, then down past the junior high school to the neighborhood movie theater. There was a sign outside the entrance to the Strand that read "BONUS DISH NIGHT!"

"Good, Nan's collecting this set," said Laura. "Let's see what we can pick up."

Billy didn't much like the first movie, *Moonlight in Hawaii*, about some crooked pineapple juice manufacturers. There weren't many scenes of the island, but it did have a good song and dance number called "Hawaiian War Chant" that reminded him of the Viewmaster slide he'd gotten for his birthday. Billy wondered if his father would sail into Pearl Harbor. Maybe he'd send a souvenir from Honolulu.

Everyone laughed a lot at the Donald Duck cartoon called *Der Fuehrer's Face*. Donald dreamed that he was in Nazi Germany, and a funny tune kept playing in which everyone made a bad noise when they sang, "*Vee heil (phhht!) heil (phhht!) right in der Fuehrer's face!*" Spike Jones' version of the song had become a big hit on the radio and in the jukeboxes.

Billy returned from the candy counter with a big box of chocolate Non-Pareils just as the main feature was beginning. When Alice Faye sang a sad song called "No Love, No Nothin' Until My Baby Comes Home," he peeked at his mother, but he couldn't see her face too clearly in the dark. Carmen Miranda was in the movie, too, wearing the biggest fruit headdress you could imagine. She sang a song called "The Lady in the Tutti-Frutti Hat" with a lot of girls who were holding gigantic bananas. It made everyone laugh.

During the movie, three people dropped their free dishes on the floor. Each time there was a crash, the audience applauded. Billy was afraid they'd drop theirs, but Belle said, "I've got them in my bag, Billy. Don't worry."

Later, as they walked home along State Street, Belle said, "Cheer up, Laura. I bet you'll be hearing from Alan any time now. He probably didn't have a chance to write the first couple of days. They run them pretty hard in boot camp, I've heard."

"I know. It's just that everything's so changed with him gone."

"And Sal," said Billy.

"Yes, Sal away, too," Laura replied. "Nan said he didn't come over to say goodbye when he left yesterday. That's Sal. Deep and kind of to himself, isn't he? Boy, it's going to be different in the yard this summer."

"So what about the movie, Billy? Like it?" Belle asked after a while.

"It was good! The musical numbers were keen."

"I knew you'd think so," she replied. "Say, Laura, remember the one Carmen Miranda did with all those bananas that kept growing? Didn't you think there was something kind of, you know, funny about that?"

"Yeah, they were so big," said Billy. "It was really funny."

"Didn't mean that kind of funny. Never mind."

They walked past the college, the dorm rooms in darkness now that spring term had ended. Belle started to laugh. "I'm thinking about that song. It's even wackier in the movie than when Spike Jones does it. OK, now let's all sing. Billy, you do the you-know-what part."

"The what part?" asked Billy.

"It's what's called a raspberry," said Laura.

"Otherwise known as a fart," said Belle. "Billy, you do the fart part. Like this...*phht.*" She demonstrated loudly, tongue sticking out between her pursed lips, just as a woman passed by. She gave Belle a startled look, and they all began to laugh.

"Oh, Belle," Laura said. "You're a ticket."

Belle grabbed Billy and Laura and arranged them on either side of her. "All right," she commanded in her best drill sergeant's voice, "You sorry recruits, attention! Billy Stewart, give us some nice loud sound effects. Now, one, two, three, forward march!"

And so they goose-stepped arm in arm up the darkened street.

PART II

Summer-Fall 1943

*Lt. John F. Kennedy's PT boat is sunk by
a Japanese cruiser in the Solomon Islands

*The "zoot suit" riots involving military personnel
and Mexican-Americans erupt in Los Angeles

The number #1 song on the Billboard charts
is "You'll Never Know" (Dick Haymes)

*Mass production of penicillin, Alexander
Fleming's "miracle drug," begins

*Roosevelt, Churchill, and Stalin meet
at the Tehran Conference in Iran

*Citizens of Naples free the city from Nazi
occupation ("The Four Days of Naples")

Chapter 13: Laura

Laura was feeling logy as she poured herself a glass of milk and put a slice of bread in the toaster. She'd forgotten what it was like to get up early every morning to go off to work. Even though she'd made Alan his breakfast and always got Billy ready for school, there was usually the option of lingering over a second cup of coffee or going back to bed for another hour if Gary was still asleep. All that had changed.

She was discovering that late in the evening, after the kids had gone to bed, was the only time she could relax and set her own pace. She liked to take a long bath most nights, when the only sound in the house was the radio broadcasting a concert recital or a band remote from one of the New York or Chicago ballrooms. After rinsing out her stockings and choosing her outfit for the next day, she'd get into bed, write a note to Alan, and then pick up a book. The employee library at the Mutual was stocked with the latest bestsellers, and she'd rediscovered how much she liked to read.

Often it was midnight by the time she finally turned out the light. She was rarely already awake when the alarm went off the next morning. After oversleeping one day, she knew to get out of bed right after reaching over and stopping the clock's infernal clanging. She was tired most of the time.

"Getting old, I think that's what it is," Laura said to Belle one night after dinner. "I don't remember feeling like this when I worked at the Travelers back in my Hartford days."

"Yeah, but you didn't have two kids to keep you busy then either," Belle replied. "You're doing fine. Bet you're turning a head or two. I mean it. You look pretty snazzy lately."

"Well, I don't know about that," Laura said, laughing. She did, in fact, enjoy getting herself fixed up every day. She'd been surprised at how well the other girls dressed, but with some alterations and a few new outfits she'd had no trouble making herself more than presentable.

Laura popped the toast out before it burned. The toaster was pretty well shot, but it would have to do. She couldn't afford a new one and, besides, they weren't making many these days. She wondered what in the world toaster factories had been converted to for the war effort. Probably making some military part she wouldn't have the foggiest understanding of.

Opening a new jar of Peter Pan, she stirred the standing oil into the thick mass, careful not to splash any on her hands or clothes. She spread the smooth, pungent mix on her toast and took a big bite. She was crazy about peanut butter.

By the time she'd fed the boys, checked to see that Billy had taken care of Lucille's food and water, fixed Billy's lunch, made her bed and Gary's, and gotten herself dressed and made up, Laura felt as if she'd been on the go for hours. She checked to make sure the gas burners were turned off and the appliances unplugged, then dropped Gary and Lucille off at Nan's on her way out.

"Nan, I don't know what I'd do without you," Laura often said when she'd come home and find the laundry done and the house tidied. "Really, watching the boys and making us dinner is more than enough."

"It's the least I can do, dear. It's my effort for the war, that's all. Besides, just picture me at loose ends all day, lounging around in my housecoat," she said one night at dinner. It was true that the thought of Nan whiling away the afternoon in an easy chair reading magazines and eating chocolates was impossible to imagine.

"Not quite our Nan, that picture, is it?" said Belle. "Now me, it'd be another story. Add cigarettes and a few cups of coffee and Bing or Perry singing on the Victrola and I'd be set for the day."

After saying goodbye to Nan and the boys, Laura began the short walk up busy State Street to her job. Half a mile away, the colonial tower of the Massachusetts Mutual home office was visible against the morning sky. The day was mild and sunny, a good omen for the coming week, and Laura felt invigorated as she entered the building fifteen minutes later.

Although she was early, she found Mae Holt already assembling work for the other keypunch operators. Mr. Sloan was the official head of the Tabulating Department, but Mae, as senior clerk, oversaw the distribution of data for electronic input.

"Hi, Laura," Mae said. "How are the boys? And did you hear from Alan?"

"Nothing since last week. All I know so far is that he's safe and sound at Sampson."

"Don't worry. I hardly heard from Tim the first few weeks. They're kept pretty busy." Mae's husband had enlisted in the Seabees shortly after the beginning of the war. He was in the Pacific, building airfields, hangers, barracks, and whatever else needed to be constructed and maintained after an island was stormed and occupied.

"Gary and Billy are fine," Laura said. "Say, that reminds me. I've been meaning to ask you this. Did anyone ever tell you you're the spitting image of Claudette Colbert? Your voice, everything."

"All the time." Mae laughed. "I tell them that my wallet sure as heck doesn't resemble Claudette's. I think it's the bangs," she said, pointing to her forehead. "But what's that got to do with the kids?"

"Oh, it's funny," Laura replied. "Billy is crazy about the movies and he's always giving people he knows the names of movie stars, especially when there's a resemblance. I can hardly wait until he sees you."

"Well, I'm looking forward to meeting him and the rest of the family." In the week since Laura had begun work, she and Mae had already become friends. Laura knew Mae had welcomed her as an experienced keypuncher and a responsible married woman with children, unlike several of the younger girls who talked about their boyfriends all the time and had to be gently and frequently reminded to get back to work. The fact that both their husbands were serving in the Navy was another bond. She and Mae also both seemed to laugh at the same things. Laura sensed the beginning of a real friendship.

It hadn't taken her more than a few days to familiarize herself again with the keypunch machine. Laura remembered her old boss, Mr. Perkins, telling her that the future of the insurance business was in electronic computing. "If you learn how to operate this machine," he advised, "you'll always have a job."

Here at the Mutual, Mr. Sloan felt the same way. On her first day at work, he said to her, "You're in the right department, Laura. Everything is changing. If I were a younger man, I'd be in the military. They're designing computing machines that'll revolutionize the insurance business once this damned war is over." She didn't see him often during the day. He was either fiddling with the larger tabulating machines at the other end of the department or off at some conference.

Laura's job was to input policy information using a keyboard similar to that of a large calculator. The data was recorded on rectangular Hollerith cards, named after the turn-of-the-century American engineer whose company later became IBM. Another operator then verified, or proof-read, the punched information on the cards before the batch was submitted to the electronic accounting machines.

After a few days of training with Mae, Laura began working in tandem with Helen Dorsey, a single woman who'd been with the Mutual a dozen years, ever since she'd graduated from high school. Helen and Mae often had lunch together, and they'd asked Laura to join them the previous week.

"Hey, you're a whiz," Helen said to Laura after a few days. "Can't hardly keep up with you." Laura was amazed Helen could keypunch at all. She had exceptionally long fingernails, carefully painted the same shade of bright red as her lipstick.

"'Fatal Apple'," Helen told her. "Revlon. And it works." She curved her fingers in front of her as though pouncing on a dazzled victim.

Like Mae, Helen was a sharp dresser. Laura hadn't quite decided whom Helen resembled, though Billy had already asked her. Rosalind Russell, maybe. Or Eve Arden. That type.

Sometimes the repetition of her job bored her, but she was happy to have two new friends. Except for Belle and her sister Ceil, she hadn't really spent much time with women her own age for years.

❧

When Laura got home late in the afternoon, she was happy to find a letter from Alan. "I received a short note, too, dear," said Nan, producing a postcard with tinted images of the naval station embedded in block letters that said '*GREETINGS FROM SAMPSON.*' "He's fine, but he misses us all, poor thing. He said you'll have more news in your letter."

"We'll all share it later, Nan," Laura said, intending to read it alone first as soon as she got upstairs. "Say, why don't you rest up tonight?" She knew Nan's bad leg had been bothering her. "I'll make dinner for us."

"Thank you, dear, but Belle is staying downtown and eating out with one of her new friends. I'll be fine. I have some vegetable soup I just made today. You and the boys go ahead, and I'll come up later."

When she and Gary went upstairs, Gary joined Billy to listen to the before-dinner radio shows. Although he rarely lasted through *Jack Armstrong* and *Captain Midnight*, Gary sometimes became engrossed in *Terry and the Pirates* and *Superman* during the first half-hour.

Dinner wasn't ready until nearly seven. Laura really hadn't planned on cooking, but with some ground beef, peas, carrots and potatoes she made a deep-dish hamburg pie the boys liked.

"How did your day go, Billy?" she asked. Billy had been worried about an oral report he had to deliver. He hated to get up in front of the other kids.

"It was OK. I said it all without looking at my paper one time. Phyllis Mertz was the only other kid who did that, but hers was real short and she talked too fast."

"And what did you do today, Gary?" she asked.

"Nothin'."

"Come on, nothing? I know you."

"Well, I played with my Tinker Toys. Then I played in the yard with Lucille. Then we went to the store. Then I helped Nan take in some wash, and she let me sprinkle the clothes so she can iron them later. Then...then, I played war outside but that wasn't fun."

"Why not?" asked Laura.

"'Cause the other kids always make me be a Nazi or a Jap and then they shoot me. And today I had to be a nurse 'cause there weren't any girls." Gary made a face.

"That's because you play with kids who are older," said Billy. "Know what? Ask them if you can be a wounded soldier or sailor. Then they can carry you around and you get a free ride."

"There you go. Good idea, Billy," said Laura. "Time for dessert. I still have some jars of that applesauce I made last year." Laura had a folder of wartime recipes that began to appear early in 1942, when shortages were already evident and rationing just beginning.

Her 'Patriotic Applesauce' used honey and cinnamon instead of sugar.

"Gary, run down like a good boy and tell Nan to come up for some dessert and we'll read Daddy's letter."

After fixing Nan a cup of tea with her usual three heaping teaspoons of precious sugar, Laura took Alan's letter out of a plain white envelope. He had written the word "free" in the space where the postage stamp would be.

"I already took a peek," she explained. "OK, listen."

Dear Laura, Billy, Gary, Nan and Belle:

Well, here I am at Sampson. I'm sorry I haven't written sooner but you don't get much free time here, I can tell you.

The ride from Springfield was a long one. We stopped a lot to pick up more fellows. I got a berth but it was crowded and smoky and I might as well have been sitting up in one of the regular seats for all the sleep I got.

My civilian clothes should be arriving home any day now. They took away everything except our shaving gear and watches and other personal stuff. We put those in what they call a 'ditty' bag. We were issued all new Navy clothes, with leggings that tie up the side like boots. I feel like a kid wearing them. That's where the name boot camp comes from.

We had shots for typhus and tetanus and a lot more. Most of the guys were sick, but not me. In fact I feel good. The food is fine—big breakfasts and dinners. All you can eat but if you don't finish they make you go back and clean your plate. So Gary and Billy what do you think of that?

Mail is delivered 2 times a day, so I'll be looking for letters. In case you can't read the address on the envelope it's Alan Stewart, USNTC Co. 333, Sampson NY.

I have a short haircut now. Everybody does. I wonder what they do with all the hair that ends up on the barbershop floor.

We do drills and exercises all day. Then we're in classes where the officers tell us about compasses and charts and knowing all the ranks and Navy lingo.

Yesterday they had a whole bunch of us make a formation like an anchor on the parade grounds and they took pictures from a plane. They said it'll be on a newsreel, so watch for it at the movies.

Did Sal make it through his enlistment? Have you heard where he is?

It's very pretty here, tho cooler than at home. I am writing this from a porch where I can see Lake Seneca. It's a big lake, 42 miles long, and I can hardly see across to the other side from here.

I passed my swimming test—in a big indoor pool, not the lake-- but you should've seen a lot of the guys. They couldn't even float. Some sailors!

I sleep in a big room in the bottom bed of a bunk. Laura..."

Laura paused and said, "This part's more for me. Daddy kind of forgot we'd all...Let's see..." She skimmed to the end of the letter.

"Mommy, read it all!" Gary cried.

"It's personal, Gary, just for Ma," said Billy. "Be quiet!"

"OK, here we go." Laura continued reading.

I'll end for now. I have guard duty until midnight. I miss you all, but I hope I'll be home on leave in a few weeks. Write soon.

Your loving husband, dad, son and brother (that covers it, I think!)

p.s. Give Lucille a scratch behind the ears for me.

They were all quiet for a few moments. Nan dabbed at her eyes with her handkerchief and sighed and fiddled with the buttons on her sweater. Gary leaned down and patted Lucille. "That's from Daddy in the Navy," he said, as she awoke, slowly wagged her tail, and licked his hand.

"Nan, tell Belle to come up tomorrow and we can read the letter again," Laura said as Nan finished her tea and rose to go downstairs.

"Don't bother to dry, Billy," Laura said later as he returned to the kitchen to help with the dishes. "It's too late tonight. They'll be all right on the counter till morning." She reached for the Jergens bottle and began rubbing the lotion into her hands.

"Working wives keep hands enchanting with Jergens," said Gary. "That's a new one. I heard it today."

Laura laughed. "Well, the only men I'm keeping these hands enchanting for nowadays are you two guys." She kissed both boys. "All right, Gary, bedtime. Billy, you can read or listen to the radio for a while. No scary shows. And in a minute this working wife is going to take a nice soak and get into bed herself."

As she walked down the hallway after her bath, Laura heard Billy's radio playing softly behind his half-closed door. She paused and listened to the familiar voice of Cecil B. DeMille introducing the *Lux Radio Theatre*. Nine o'clock already. Just as she was about to tell Billy to go to sleep, she heard the title of this week's movie dramatization: *Mrs. Miniver*, with Greer Garson and Walter Pidgeon. Billy had loved that film, so she decided to let things be and tiptoed into her room. One late night wouldn't hurt him.

She climbed into bed and picked up the bestseller she'd begun over the weekend, *A Tree Grows in Brooklyn*. She was enjoying it, but tonight she couldn't concentrate. Laura picked up Alan's letter and re-read the part she'd left out earlier.

I sleep in a big room in the bottom bed of a bunk. Laura, it's so strange to be sleeping alone. Well, not alone—there are 40 other guys talking and snoring and coughing and making other noises during the night. I miss you.

I found out that you and the boys will be getting an allowance in addition to my base pay. I'm not sure, I think it's about $100 a month altogether. Nan qualifies for something too. I also took out an insurance policy for $10,000—that's the highest they offer. Don't be upset at that—it makes sense.

Laura put the letter back on the bed table and turned out the light. She reached under Alan's pillow and took out a sweatshirt she'd found on the floor in the bedroom the night they all came back from the railroad station. He must have been wearing it that morning. She placed it next to her face, closed her eyes, and tried to fall asleep.

Chapter 14: Billy

"Hey, you kids be careful in here," said Mary Mazzarella. "Watch them noodles!" Angie's mother had been making pasta all afternoon, and the results were evident everywhere: long strands of spaghetti and linguine draped over chairs and on a laundry drying rack, macaroni and ziti covering the tops of the kitchen table and counters, wide strips of lasagna carefully laid out on towels on the floor in the corner. On a sunny day, she'd have used the backyard, but a late spring rain was keeping the noodles—and Billy and Angie—indoors.

"Ma, look, a postcard from Sal!" Angie zigzagged around the lasagna and waved the card in her mother's face.

"*Mamma mia! Madonna!*" Mrs. Mazzarella raised her arms in the air, sending flour swirling above her head. "Read it, Angelina. My hands!"

"It says, 'Hi to everyone'," replied Angie.

"And?" asked her mother.

"'Love, Sal,'" she replied.

"That's all? No more? *Che ragazzo!*"

"That means, 'What a boy'," explained Angie to Billy. "Ma, you know Sal. At least he got to the camp." She held up the picture side of the card, a tinted rendering of long rows of low hangar-like structures. "It says, '*Air View of Barracks at Fort Devens, Mass.*' I wonder which one is his?"

"Wow, look at all the buildings," Billy said. "There must be thousands of soldiers stationed there."

"Maybe he'll write again next week," said Angie. "Come on," she motioned to Billy. "Let's get some magazines and go read outside."

"*Attento!* Careful where you step!" Mrs. Mazzarella sighed deeply, picked up her rolling pin and began leveling more pasta dough. She always made more pasta than the family could eat, so Billy knew they'd be getting enough for several meals at his house, too.

Although the rain had eased to a fine mist, the seats of the worn metal porch chairs were filled with water. "Let's go sit in Sal's car," Angie said.

They walked back to the garage, swinging open one of its creaky wood doors. It closed behind them as they entered, leaving only a bit of light from the tiny, very dirty windows on either side of the small structure. The interior of the garage smelled of gasoline and an earthy mustiness. The car was backed in, so the winged hood ornament faced them, its chrome wings gleaming in the semi-darkness.

"Kind of funny to see Sal's car without him around, huh?" Angie asked.

"Yeah, I was thinking that, too," Billy replied. He was also feeling that it was too quiet and damp and kind of creepy. Once they had seen a garter snake slither out from under a wooden crate in the corner. "Let's prop open the doors so we have more light to read."

They sat in the front seat and began leafing through some of Angie's *Photoplay* magazines. "Hey," said Billy, showing Angie the cover of one, "my mother said her new friend at work looks just like Claudette Colbert."

"She's pretty but she always looks the same. Here's Esther Williams. See what I mean? She looks different in every one of these photos."

"That's 'cause her hair's all wet in some of them. She spends a lot of her time underwater."

"She looks like your Aunt Belle here."

"Yeah, you're right. That's who she'll be from now on." They'd already decided that Billy's mother was a look-alike for Linda Darnell or maybe Hedy Lamarr, without the foreign accent. His father was Gregory Peck with blond hair. Sal was easy: He was a dead-ringer for a young Perry Como.

Angie's parents were harder. They finally decided on Edward G. Robinson for her father and Maxine, one of the Andrews Sisters, for her mother. "Just the face, though," Angie said. "Ma can't sing and she's kinda heavier." *A lot heavier*, thought Billy, but he didn't say anything.

They'd had trouble figuring out a name for Nan. She looked a little bit like the mother in the Andy Hardy movies, but that actress wasn't famous enough. They finally decided they'd make an exception to the movie star rule and call her Eleanor, because Nan had an ugly fur wrap made from a real fox just like the President's wife. "Everyone likes Nan a lot, too, just like Mrs. Roosevelt," said Billy. "Nan's teeth aren't so big, though."

Angie agreed. "And her voice isn't so high and funny,"she added, "except when she sings."

They used these names as code words if they didn't want anyone to know what they were talking about. "Is Perry going out tonight?" Billy would ask. Once Angie reported, "Edward and Maxine had a big fight last night." Or, "Go ask Eleanor if it's OK to take Gary with us to the playground."

"Look at the ad for this new movie, *For Whom the Bell Tolls,*" Billy said, resting the magazine on the steering wheel of the car. Gary Cooper and Ingrid Bergman seemed to be lying in the same sleeping bag. *They clung together in the darkness before a thundering dawn!* the caption read.

"Wow, that looks good," said Angie. "How could they both fit in one bag?"

"Yeah," Billy said. "I don't know if my mother will let me see that one."

"We can sneak in or ask someone in line to say we're with them," she replied. "Don't worry about it."

"Hey, you in here, Angie?" They looked up to see Richie Reilly, Sal's best friend, standing in the open door.

"Hi Richie!" Angie stuck her head out the driver's seat window. "What's up?"

"I just came over to say goodbye to your mom and everyone. I'm heading out day after tomorrow. Got the OK at home to enlist."

"Congratulations," Angie said.

"Thanks. The Marines took me," he added proudly. "My old man was a Marine. He trained at Parris Island, too. Hey, Billy, heard your old man's in. Navy, huh?"

"Yes, he's at Sampson. That's in New York. Not New York City, 'way up near Canada."

"I know. It's a real big place. Angie, your mom said you got a postcard from Sal?"

"Yeah, want to see it?" Angie handed the card out the window.

"Wow, big place, Fort Devens." Richie turned the card over. "He don't say much." He laughed. "That's Sal for ya. A man of few words."

Richie ran his hand over the top of his head. "Well, gotta go. Tell Sal I'll let everyone know my address. Hey, who knows, maybe I'll see him in Berlin one of these days!"

"I bet my ma is all sad, seeing Richie now and thinking about Sal and everything," said Angie after he left.

"I know. Nan cries, too," said Billy. "I can tell sometimes when I get home from school. I wonder what time it is. I need to get Mrs. Herrmann's fish for her." Mrs. Herrmann, who lived on the upstairs floor of a neighboring house, often asked Billy to do errands.

"That old grouch," Angie said. Billy knew that one time old Mrs. Herrmann had complained to the police when the Mazzarellas were having a big party during the San Gennaro festival. But the cop who came to the house was Carlo DeFilippi, a family friend from down the street, so nothing happened.

"Aw, she's all right. She's real sad about the war. Nan said that some of the neighbors who don't know her thought she was Catholic 'cause she always gets fish on Friday, but she's not. She has some Jewish cousins trapped in the war."

"Sal liked her when he used to get her fish, too," Angie replied. "I guess she's OK. Well, I better go and help my mother with supper."

Billy cut through Mrs. Brown's yard into Mrs. Herrmann's. She waved to him from her second-floor kitchen window as he approached the back porch. Climbing up the dark stairway, he felt like holding his nose because of the smell, a combination of cabbage and fish and what Sal called "her sitting in that house forever." She was the oldest person Billy knew. She hardly ever went out, not even onto the porch. All her groceries were delivered, and she relied on a few kids in the neighborhood to do other chores.

"Ya, come," she said as he tapped on her door and entered. Mrs. Herrmann was sitting with her black shawl wrapped around her. The peaked woolen cap she wore winter and summer hugged her large head. A few strands of white hair, not much paler than the color of her skin, peeked out from beneath. Billy thought Mrs. Herrmann didn't have many teeth, but she rarely smiled, so it was hard to tell.

He took the dollar bill from the table where it was always waiting. "I'll be right back, Mrs. Herrmann," he said, as he turned to leave.

Something nudged his leg. "Oh, hi, Max." He reached down and patted Mrs. Herrmann's big black and white cat. Max was much friendlier than Ashkii, Mrs. Brown's cat. Sometimes Billy stayed a bit after he brought back the fish and played with him. Even though Max was pretty old, Billy suspected he got bored alone all the time with Mrs. Herrmann.

It was late in the afternoon, so Perry's Fish Market wasn't as mobbed as it would be just before dinnertime. Still, Billy had to wait a few minutes for his number to be called. Mrs. Herrmann always got one order of fish and chips, wrapped in newspaper and brown paper tied with string.

Billy watched the men at the steaming vats as they filled the steel baskets with fish and French fries. They immersed the containers in the bubbling fat and raised them back out at just the right moment. It was hard work, and even in the winter months the men usually stripped to their t-shirts. Today it was stifling in the store, the smell of fish wafting outside to the sidewalk and halfway down the block.

When he returned to Mrs. Herrmann's house and gave her the dinner and her change, she placed the customary nickel in his hand. "Here, Billy. You're a fine boy. It's good to see that in this bad world."

"Thanks, Mrs. Herrmann," he said. He noticed the morning *Union* open on the kitchen table, with Mrs. Herrmann's glasses lying on top.

"You know about what has happened in Warsaw, Billy? With the Jewish people in the ghetto?"

"They all had to leave. The Germans — the Nazis — came and got them."

"It's all right you say Germans. You are right. I never thought to see this happen. I am German, but I am Jewish, too. And some of my family members are there. Not in Poland. In Germany." She paused. "Or maybe somewhere else now."

Billy leaned down and scratched Max. He didn't know what to say.

"So I am here, and they are there. But I am sad because I do nothing. Too old." She looked down at her cat. "Maxie is not young, but not as old as me."

"You take care of him," Billy said. "That's doing something good."

"Ya, I do, but not for always." She patted Billy's hand.

Billy spoke about Mrs. Herrmann that night at dinner. "I don't think Mrs. Herrmann has any family here."

"She had a son but I think he lives in California," said Nan. "There was some trouble there, they didn't get along. Poor thing, and now with not knowing about her family in the old country. I think of our folks back in Scotland, but they're too far north to be bombed. They don't have a lot of food, though. Their rationing is worse than ours."

"One of the gals I worked with at the Paramount has family in Italy," said Belle. "She never said too much, but she told me she knew they didn't want the war with us. It was Mussolini. It's so bad there now, with the Germans still holding on. And if we invade..."

"Mommy, when will Daddy be home?" Gary asked.

"Well, we're hoping in a few weeks, if his training goes well," Laura replied. "For a few days, anyway. We're lucky he's not so far away. OK, guys, let's head upstairs. You too, Lucille. Thank you for dinner, Nan. The hash was really tasty. I don't know how you do it."

As Billy was getting ready for bed, his mother came to the door. "Billy, I'm sorry, I forgot to give you this before dinner. Look what came in the mail today. A postcard from Sal for you."

Billy took the card. It was similar to the one Sal had sent to his family, but the picture was of a lake set amidst pine trees. The caption read *Mirror Lake Bathing Beach, Fort Devens, Mass.* On the other side, Sal had written: *"Hi Billy: Remind you of Joyland? Sal."* When Billy was younger, Sal had often taken Angie and him on the Boston Road bus out to Joyland, a beach on Loon Pond. It was there he had learned to swim, jumping off Sal's shoulders into the shallow water before he could manage on his own.

That night Billy had a dream. He was with some people he didn't know in a big rowboat on a dark sea. Huge gray and white waves threatened to capsize them at any moment. At the head of the boat was the actress Greer Garson, who looked beyond him and said, "I am Mrs. Miniver and we are going to save our brave men from the Nazis." Billy turned around, and there in the middle of a group of soldiers and sailors sat his father and Sal.

Suddenly the boat overturned, and they were all thrown into the churning water. He heard his father say, "I'm OK, I passed my test," as he swam on by.

Sal's head bobbed in front of him, and he said, "Climb on my shoulders, Billy. Come on, remember? You can do it."

As he clung to Sal, Billy could hear someone's voice cry out. "Hey, you guys, I can't swim!" It was Richie. "Wait," he cried. "Hey, wait for me!" But the water propelled them along, and all Billy could hear was the roaring of the waves.

He awoke with a start. It was daylight, and the sun was already shining through the summer curtains his mother had put up a few days earlier.

Switching on his radio, he waited for it to warm up and tried to get the image of the angry ocean out of his mind. For a while he listened to John Gambling, broadcasting from a station in New York City. John Gambling talked a lot but he played good band music.

When the eight o'clock news came on, Billy threw back the covers and got out of bed. "Come on, Lucille," he whispered, "want to go out and do your business? Come on! It's Saturday. No school today!"

Chapter 15: Belle

"I had no idea the place was this big, Miss Clark," said Belle, stepping through another sliding green metal door at the Milton Bradley plant. They'd started off from the modern office area just inside the visitor entrance on downtown Park Street, but along the way she'd lost her sense of direction.

"Call me Grace, Belle, everyone else does. Makes us all kind of like family." Grace was a slim, middle-aged woman with a long pencil balanced behind her ear and reading glasses hanging from a chain around her neck. "Notice the heat here in this passageway. And it's only June." She fanned her face with the folder she was carrying. "Yes, this has become a pretty big operation, especially since the war. We have our president, Mr. Shea, to thank for that."

Belle knew from her friend Flo that the company was doing very well. "You'll get a job offer for sure," Flo had told her. In fact, she'd been pretty much given a choice of a couple of openings, and she hadn't even mentioned Flo's boyfriend Tommy's name. Anyway, she'd forgotten what department he worked in.

"Miss Stewart, you did quite well on the aptitude tests this morning," she'd been told earlier by Mr. Webster, the personnel man who'd interviewed her. "We're in a position to offer you work either here in the office or in one of the departments on the floor."

"Well, I hadn't thought about that. I guess I just assumed it'd be the factory. Isn't the pay better there?"

"Yes, that's correct. Wages can range from 35 to 40 dollars a week, depending. There's piecework, overtime, special contracts, things like that. In the office you'd start at around 25. Of course the working conditions are...well, nicer in the office." He smiled at Belle.

She immediately realized he'd been impressed and perhaps deceived by her appearance. She'd dressed carefully, perhaps too well, in her best gabardine suit But the combs holding her upswept hairdo in place were uncomfortably tight, her girdle was killing her, and her feet ached like hell.

"I guess I'm still leaning toward, what did you say, 'the floor'?" she replied.

"Tell you what," said Mr. Webster. "Miss Clark here—Grace— can take you on a tour of the place. Give you a sense of what's what." He added, "Grace, be sure to take Miss Stewart through one of Abe Sherman's departments."

The Milton Bradley factory had been part of the Springfield landscape for many years. What had begun as one modest building was now a labyrinth of inter-connected brick structures, some dating from the late nineteenth century. In the center of the complex was an interior courtyard, where even on the sunniest days the light was dim and the cracked pavement dank.

"This is a typical board game assembly room," Grace explained as they stopped near a long row of busy women sitting on stools next to a wide moving belt.

The process fascinated Belle. By the time a new cardboard box made its way to the end of the line, it had been fitted with various game parts and a shiny, freshly glued board. The last woman on the line placed the top cover on the container and stacked it on a large skid, where it was eventually wheeled away to be stored, packed, and shipped out to one of the 48 states. In peacetime, the destinations included many foreign countries as well.

"Looks like they're working on Pirate and Traveler today," Grace remarked. "That's been one of our big sellers for years."

Belle nodded at a few of the women who glanced up as she and Grace passed. Some smiled in return, others ignored her or looked away. Most looked bored. She paused briefly at the end of the line, noting how the women were dressed—generally in coveralls or jeans, though she spotted a few nice-looking slack suits. Most of the workers had their hair covered with bandannas, turbans or snoods.

Grace stopped at a small desk in the corner, where a young man was recording some data on a long sheet of paper. "Eddie, meet Miss Stewart, Belle Stewart," said Grace. "She's going to be starting soon, we hope. Don't know where yet."

Eddie stood up, wiping his hands on his pants leg. "Pleased to meet you, Miss Stewart," he said. He couldn't have been more than twenty, Belle thought. Good-looking guy. She wondered why he hadn't already been drafted. He looked too young to have kids.

"Hi Eddie, and it's Belle," she replied.

"Eddie will be leaving us, but we hope not for a few weeks," said Grace. "Navy."

"My brother just left for Sampson," Belle replied. "Alan Stewart. Say hi for me if you're headed that way. He's tall and blond and we haven't heard from him yet."

They all laughed. As they walked away, Grace said, "Eddie's the assistant in this department. Abe Sherman's the boss. Abe's the head of this one and a few others. He's at a meeting now, I think." As they passed through a narrow corridor that looked out onto the courtyard, she said, "Wait, here he comes now."

A tall man wearing a shirt and tie and dark slacks strode down the narrow passageway toward them. "Hiya, Grace," he said. "Looking for me or just out for a stroll?" He smiled at Belle. His eyes were blue and his hair a salt-and-pepper gray. He was big but in good shape. It was hard to guess his age. Fifty?

"Sure, just where I like to take my morning constitutional," Grace replied, fanning her face again. "It's already darned hot. Don't know if I could stand that anymore. I used to work on the floor," she explained to Belle. "A long time ago."

"Not so bad temperature-wise at the meeting I was just at. In fact, it was downright cold. Don't know as if I like that air-cooling machine they've installed up in the conference room. Or maybe it was the meeting." He gave them a rueful glance and stroked his chin.

"Abe, this is Belle Stewart. Miss Stewart, Mr. Sherman."

Belle noticed that Mr. Sherman was careful when he shook her hand not to squeeze too tightly. His own was warm and completely enveloped hers. Up close, he was at least as tall as Alan. "My pleasure, Miss Stewart. Funny, you look just like a good friend of my daughter's. In fact, thought it was her when I saw you from a distance a second ago." Belle noticed a wide wedding band on his ring finger.

"Miss Stewart—Belle—is going to be starting with us. Not sure what department, though." Belle noticed Grace look pointedly at Abe as she fiddled with her pencil. "Well, guess we'd better get on with it. We have a few more areas to cover."

"Good luck, Miss Stewart."

"Thanks, Mr. Sherman," Belle replied. "I'm looking forward to it."

"He's a prince, that man," Grace said, holding the heavy metal door for Belle as they entered a long room filled with noisy machines. "Everybody likes Abe. And he doesn't take any guff from anyone, big shots included. He lost his wife a couple of years ago. Sad. That daughter he mentioned, she's a firebrand. Women's labor causes. Maybe you've seen her name in the paper. Hannah Sherman?"

The din of the machines prevented her from explaining further. This department, whatever it was, resembled the kind of operation that Belle associated with places like the Armory and Smith & Wesson and some of the other big plants in the area. Women, and a few men, were working on individual machines, doing things with drills and cutters and lathes.

"OK, enough of that," said Grace as they closed the door behind them and entered another hallway. "That's one of the special areas. We have a couple of big government contracts. In there they're making what's called a universal joint. Something to do with landing gears on airplanes. Mr. Shea's invention. We also have a big gun stock department—for the carbine and Springfield rifles. I think they're making them for sub-machine guns now, too. Those departments go 24 hours—they never shut down. Pay's higher, too."

"Wow, I didn't realize that. I thought it was all games and toys."

"Well, it was, but everything's different now. In fact, our biggest game item is a kit for soldiers that we have on contract with Coca Cola. We ship thousands out every month.

"I'd show you the paint and crayon rooms, Belle, but I'm just too warm," Grace said. "We can peek in, though. Get ready." She opened a door and a blast of heat hit them, along with a sweet smell that Belle recognized instantly. Crayons. Inside, men were working over big vats attached to boilers that steamed and hissed. None of the workers had shirts on. Some were stripped to skivvies, others naked from the waist up, their bodies sweaty and gleaming in the dim light.

"The powder paint department is just beyond," said Grace. "You can tell at lunchtime what color they're working on. Skin, hair, everything, all covered in powder."

As they made their way back downstairs to the office area, they passed through another department in a newer building. "Educational division," explained Grace. "School supplies, paper products, stuff like that." The workers here were on their coffee break, most of them gathered around a small canteen wagon that Belle assumed was wheeled from area to area.

"On the floor you get two coffee breaks, ten minutes each, morning and afternoon. Half-hour for lunch. You can go down to Main Street if you rush, but most of the gals on the line bring a sandwich. Well, here we are." She sighed with obvious relief as they re-entered the office area, where large fans circulated air in each of the rooms.

"Administrative offices are up on the second floor," Grace said. "That's also where they develop the games and do the graphic work, things like that. You don't see much of those fellows, but you will see the big bosses walking around. Our Mr. Shea is a hands-on president." After a brief walk-through of the various accounting and filing areas, they returned to the personnel office.

"If you prefer the office, we have an opening as a file clerk," Mr. Webster explained. "As far as on the floor goes..." He paused and looked up at Belle.

"To tell the truth, Mr. Webster, I'm still thinking I'd like to try the floor."

He smiled and folded his hands. "Well, actually, I'm glad to hear you say that. Your work history does show some supervisory experience."

Belle had cited her position several years earlier at the big Diamond Match plant, where she'd managed several file clerks. She'd been careful in describing her job at the theater to list Jack Jackson, the other assistant manager, as her reference. She didn't trust Simpson, not even after her threat. But it didn't look at this point like they'd be doing any checking. Good. She shifted in her seat, trying unobtrusively to adjust her girdle. Maybe getting dressed to the nines had paid off.

"What I want to say is this," Mr. Webster continued. "We're losing several men to the service soon. Eddie Callahan, in one of Abe Sherman's departments, and a few others. I think you saw that floor?"

Belle nodded. "Yes, and I met them both."

"I can't promise anything, but we'd like you to float in several areas for a week or two. If things work out, you'd become an assistant to one of the managers. I'll have to work out the details regarding how your pay will be structured for the time being." He looked at Belle, smiled, and raised his eyebrows in a questioning glance.

"When do I start?" she asked.

❧❦

At dinner that night, Belle recounted her day to Nan and Laura and the boys. "You should've seen some of the rooms. Big vats with hot paint, crayons all over the place. They were making Pirate and Traveler in one department."

"We have that one!" Gary said. "But it's too hard for me."

"What about the jigsaw puzzles, Belle?" asked Billy. "Did you see how they make them?"

"Gee, no, that was one thing I didn't get to see. But I will, I'm sure. And I think I'll be able to bring some things home. Seconds, stuff that's good but the cover's smudged or something. Flo told me about that.

"Let's see," she continued, "what else? Oh, there were even these vats of glue where they paste the games together, and machines where they cut the cardboard. And they even make gun stocks now."

"Did you say guns, Belle?" asked Nan. "My oh my."

"Only the wooden part, sweetie, not the bullets or triggers or anything like that," Belle replied.

"So you picked the factory," Laura said. "I know the pay is good, but will you be all right? You hear stories about some of those tough girls. Then the men...you know."

"Look, if I could handle Simpson—well, OK, maybe he was a little too much even for me—I can handle anything. Since when have I been a shrinking violet myself, huh?"

"That's the truth, dear. You never were," said Nan.

They all laughed. "You're not afraid of anyone, Belle," Billy said.

"Besides, from what the personnel manager said, there's a good opportunity for getting ahead, maybe be in charge of the floor. I'll have to watch myself and be more refined." She patted her hair. "I'll be a lady, the floor lady."

"The way you were all dressed up today, Belle, that man would have hired you as vice-president," said Laura. "You looked swell."

"Yeah, well it was torture, let me tell you," Belle replied. "I was in agony. Either I've put on weight or that girdle's shrunk. Plus the tight skirt. And those shoes. Jesus, I couldn't sit down in the girdle and I couldn't stand up in the shoes!"

Chapter 16: Billy

"Ma, guess what! They had the anchor in the newsreel!" Billy burst into the kitchen, where Laura was preparing dinner.

Gary rushed in behind him. "I saw Daddy!"

"Well, we're not sure," said Billy, "but we think we did, 'cause he's so tall."

"Wait, kids, wait. What anchor?"

"You know, in his letter, when they made a big anchor and had the movie camera in the plane."

"Oh, yes! Tell me! Wait...Nan and Belle are on their way up for dinner. You can tell us all about it in a minute. Gee...you could see him?"

"What are we having, Ma?" asked Billy.

"Come on, what night is it? You know."

"I know! I know! Saturday! Hot dogs and beans!" yelled Gary.

"That's right. Hurry and go wash up."

Billy and Gary walked down the hallway to the bathroom, their hands still sticky from the root beer barrel candies they'd eaten earlier at the movies. Billy and Angie often went to the Saturday matinee at the Strand, and Gary always begged to go along. Today, Laura had agreed to let Gary join them when Billy told her that *Lassie, Come Home* was playing, but she made them promise to watch him carefully.

"We'll take real good care of him, honest, Mrs. Stewart," said Angie.

On the walk down State Street, they met two kids from Angie's school, Frankie and Mario. Billy knew Mario because he often came with his family to picnics in the Mazzarellas' backyard.

"Hey, Angie, want to get in free?" Frankie asked. "Here's how it works. You each give me five cents, then one of us—Mario today—pays the 25 cents to get in. Then right near the beginning, when the previews and stuff are on, he opens the door down near the front and you run in. It's easy."

Angie looked at Billy. "We'll be able to get more candy," she said.

"I don't know. What if we get caught, with Gary and everything?"

"We won't. Trust me," said Angie. She gave her nickel to Mario and nudged Billy. "OK, we'll do it."

Gary looked up at her with big eyes. "We'll stay together," she whispered to him. "Just stick with me."

They followed Frankie around to the side street in back of the theater. "It's this here door, down in the front on the left" he said. "Just wait, and be ready. Scatter as soon as you get in. The aisles on the side are best. Last guy in, slam the door shut. Fast."

"Remember, we'll stay together," Angie whispered to Gary. "Just watch me." They waited nervously.

After a few minutes, without warning, the door swung open. Frankie disappeared inside, followed by Angie, dragging Gary along behind her. Billy scooted in, closed the door and ran into the darkened theater. His heart was pounding as he followed Angie up a corner aisle. His eyes still hadn't adjusted from the brightness of the noonday sun, and he stumbled and fell as he struggled to keep up with her. As he got up, he turned around and saw a lady usher briefly open and then slam shut the door they had just come through. She turned and walked up the aisle on the other side of the theater.

"We made it!" Angie whispered to Billy as he joined her in the middle of an empty back row. A Bugs Bunny cartoon had just started. "Where's Gary?"

"What do you mean? With you," said Billy. Then he saw that the seat on her other side was empty.

"No, I had to let go 'cause he was too slow. I thought you had him. Oh, brother! He must be somewhere down in front!"

They waited a few minutes, but there was no sign of Gary in the aisle. The cartoon ended, and the coming attractions for *Thank Your Lucky Stars*, a new all-star Warner Brothers musical, began. Billy concentrated on watching the screen. He didn't want to miss the preview.

"Maybe he's in the back," he whispered after the preview was over. "I'll go look." Gary had to be inside the theater somewhere, but now Billy was scared. What would his mother say if she found out? And where *was* he?

The lobby was deserted except for a couple of kids buying popcorn.

"Excuse me, have you seen a little boy?" Billy asked the lady behind the counter.

"Sure, I seen a lot of little boys today." She laughed. "You mean alone or lost or something?"

"Yes, my brother. He's five."

"Nope, ain't seen him."

Billy peeked into the theater. The new *Dick Tracy* serial episode was already on. Billy didn't know what to do. He turned and walked toward an usher who was coming out the door on the other side. She looked like the same one he had seen closing the door.

"Excuse me, have you seen a little boy who's alone?"

"Would you be Billy, now?" asked the usher, a lady with a lot of gray-blue hair piled on top of her head. Billy knew that meant she shampooed with what was called a rinse, because once Nan tried it and her hair turned purple.

"We found your little brother walking up and down the aisle over here," the lady continued. "He said you had gone to the bathroom." She raised one eyebrow.

"Oh, yeah, I did, and...Where is he now?" asked Billy, afraid they'd already called the house.

"He's right inside, safe in the last row. He wanted to see the show. But you be careful not to lose him again, hear?"

"Hey, want some popcorn?" Gary yelled, as Billy tapped him on the shoulder. "The lady gave me some."

"Shh, be quiet. Just stay with me! Come on!" He dragged Gary out of his seat.

They sat down next to Angie just as the newsreel was beginning. The first story was about the people in the ghetto in Warsaw. Billy thought about Mrs. Herrmann and her relatives. He'd have to remember to tell her that he saw the pictures of the buildings, even though they looked pretty bombed out. Then he remembered that she'd said they weren't in Poland, but somewhere in Germany. Maybe they really were safer there.

Suddenly the words "SAMPSON NAVAL TRAINING STATION" flashed on the screen, followed by an overhead shot of a big anchor. The song "Anchors Aweigh" was playing in the background. The newsman said the anchor was made up of hundreds of enlisted men and women posing on the parade grounds of the base.

"That's what my father told us about in his letter!" Billy said to Angie. As the camera moved closer, they spotted a really tall sailor at the tip of the anchor.

"There he is!" shouted Gary. "Hey, Daddy!" A bunch of kids near them clapped and cheered. Then they all quieted down to watch Lassie find her way home in the feature movie.

"Ma, do you think that really could have been him?" Billy asked as they told their story at the dinner table.

"Well, we know he was there, he told us that. Yes, I do think it was," Laura replied.

"Imagine, your dad in the newsreel at the movies," said Nan. "Fancy that."

"Gary, did you enjoy the movies today?" Nan asked.

"Yes, Nan," he replied. "I had candy, two kinds. Popcorn, too." Even though he had warned him to say nothing, Billy was afraid Gary would tell them about his adventure. "A lot of popcorn," he added, smirking at Billy.

"Let me run downstairs and get the pineapple upside-down cake," Nan said. "I forgot to bring it up."

"I'm going down, too," said Belle. "Got a heavy date."

"Oh? You didn't mention that," replied Laura. "Well?"

"Just kidding. No date. It's a man from work, an older guy named Abe Sherman."

"Isn't he the one who was so nice to you when you started?"

"That's the one. I'm still in his department, but I think that's going to change if something else opens up."

"Hmm...I did kind of think you liked him," said Laura.

"I do like him...but that's it," replied Belle. "He's got a daughter not much younger than me, and, besides, we work together."

Like his mother, Billy wondered when Belle was going to get a new boyfriend. He remembered Dan Flaherty, who used to bring him books and take him along sometimes when he and Belle went to Riverside Park.

One fall when he was seven or eight they went to the Eastern States Exposition, where Billy got knocked over by a big cow when he tried to pet her calf. Last September, for the first time in many years, the Exposition was canceled because of the war. All the kids were really disappointed because it meant the public schools wouldn't close for a day so they could go for free. Billy wondered if they'd ever bring back the fair.

After dinner Billy picked up the two latest issues of *Life* from the magazine rack in the living room and walked out to the double glider near the new victory garden. A few lilac blossoms still clung to the huge bush that bordered Mrs. Brown's yard, their odor wafting sweetly in the mild evening breeze.

The cover of one of the magazines was a photograph of a flag-draped stretcher being carried by six tired-looking soldiers on some muddy foreign field. The other cover was a picture of a smiling Roy Rogers mounted on Trigger, rearing against a Western image of valley, mountains, and sky. Billy picked up that one and leafed through until he found the article about Roy, titled "King of the Cowboys."

He looked up when he heard the slamming of the Mazzarellas' porch door. Angie and her grandfather were walking slowly down the flagstone path, their arms entwined. Billy knew Angie and Sal really loved their Nonno. They even insisted on practicing Italian with him, despite their mother's wanting them to speak only English.

Once Billy heard Angie say, "Ma, if I don't talk to Nonno in Italian he won't ever get to say that much to anyone. It's not fair. He's too old to learn English as good as you."

"Hi Mr. Mazzarella," said Billy. "How are you?"

"Good, Billy, good, except leg. *Malata*, bad."

Mr. Mazzarella climbed into the glider seat with some difficulty and sat opposite Billy. "Angelina here has, how you say, *cresima*, tomorrow."

"He means my confirmation," replied Angie. Billy knew that she'd been going to catechism lessons for months. He remembered when she had her first communion a few years ago. Billy still had a picture of the two them together taken in the arbor, Angie in her white dress and veil and bouquet. He was wearing his brown suit with short pants and suspenders and a red woolen tie.

"I have to choose a middle name as my confirmation name," Angie had told him. "There's a ton of saints and you pick one. I looked up the patron saint of cats and stuff, but her name is Gertrude." She made a face. "And, besides, she's the patron saint of nuns, too."

Then one day, she announced, "I decided on my name. I'm going to be Elizabeth. That's Elizabeth of Portugal. She's the patron saint of peace. I'm picking her name 'cause Sal's in the Army. And for your dad and everyone else who is. *Angelina Elizabeth Mazzarella.*"

"That's a pretty name," Billy replied. But he thought to himself that if Angie ever became a movie star they'd make her change it. He had read about movie stars whose real names didn't work. Angie's name was too long, and Mazzarella was kind of hard to say and made you think of the Italian cheese, except that Angie pronounced it different.

"*Buona notte, Signora!*" said Mr. Mazzarella as Nan walked across the lawn and joined them. Billy jumped up and held the glider so that Nan could have a seat across from Angie's grandfather.

"Good evening, Mr. Mazzarella. How are you?"

"Good, good, except leg." He pointed to his foot.

"Well, I'm afraid that makes the two of us. It's no fun to get old," said Nan. She was actually somewhat younger than Angie's grandfather, but to Billy anyone who was over fifty seemed to be the same age.

"My, the scent of the lilac is still with us," said Nan. Lilacs were her favorite flower. "I wish they didn't die so early in the summer. It's a shame that something so lovely doesn't last."

Gary came running from the house, Lucille trotting behind him. He was carrying a covered glass jar.

"I'm going to catch fireflies," he said.

"Did you make holes in the top, dear?" asked Nan. "We don't want the fireflies to suffocate."

"Ma did," said Gary. "Come on, Lucille." He raced toward the far end of the yard, near the forsythia, no longer yellow but still bushy and green. Glimmers of light darted here and there in the gathering dusk.

I wonder what your dad is doing right now, 'way up near Canada," said Nan. Billy thought of the view of the lake his father had described from the window of the library. Maybe he was sitting there now, writing them a letter. "And Sal, too," Nan added, reaching over and patting Mr. Mazzarella on the arm.

"*Si,* Salvatore. Bad, war is bad. Mussolini bad." Mr. Mazzarella put his hands to the side of his face. "*Che pasticchio!*" he said. Then he pretended to bite his hand. "*Idioto!*"

"That means 'what a mess' and 'idiot,'" explained Angie.

"Well, we know Mussolini isn't all the Italian people," Nan said. "We know that."

"No, *grazie*, thank you," Mr. Mazzarella replied.

"Gary! Gary! Come in soon." Laura's face appeared in the kitchen window. "Five minutes!"

Billy had planned to hear *Inner Sanctum*, but it was so nice outside he decided to wait until *Your Hit Parade* came on at 9. Gary would be in bed by then, and he knew his mother would want to listen, too.

After another fifteen minutes, Gary slowly walked up to where the others were sitting. Lights flickered inside the jar he was carrying as the little bugs flew frantically from one side to the other. As Gary set the jar on the ground next to the glider, Lucille stationed herself next to it, intently watching the darting fireflies.

"Ah, *la lucciola!*" murmured Mr. Mazzarella. Softly, he began to sing, *"Lucciola lucciola, gialla gialla..."*

Angie joined in, her thin, high voice contrasting with the roughness of her grandfather's. When they were finished she said, "I know how it goes in English, too. Let's see: *"Firefly, firefly, yellow and bright, rein up the pony under your light. The son of the king is ready to ride, firefly, firefly, fly by my side."*

"That's an old song Nonno used to sing to me when I was little," Angie explained, holding her grandfather's hand.

"It's a lovely song, dear," said Nan. "The little fireflies...Do you know what they're called when they're babies? Glow worms. Gary, be a good boy and set them free before you go inside. They need to be heading home now, too."

"OK, Nan." Gary unscrewed the top and raised the jar over his head. "Go home, fireflies, go home!" he cried as the sparks of light scattered in the air. Billy watched one until it circled above the lilacs, around and around, and then vanished in the darkness of the night.

Chapter 17: Alan

Alan had hinted in a letter that he might be able to be home for at least a weekend when boot camp ended. As it turned out, the leave came earlier than expected.

A few weeks into training, he was given the news that he'd be staying on at Sampson. He'd been selected to attend Signalman School for a period of several weeks. He'd be learning semaphore, the use of flags for signaling, and Morse code, which involved the operation of high-powered lights.

More training for a permanent assignment might follow this schooling, but in the meantime he'd been granted a short leave. He'd be free to leave the grounds for 72 hours.

"Jeez, we'll miss you on the friggin' parade grounds tomorrow," said Buzz, a strapping kid of 18 from Nebraska who occupied the bunk above Alan's. "I don't get why we have this drill every friggin' day. How much walking is there on a friggin' ship, anyway? Shit!"

Alan smiled, wondering how Buzz's mother back in Nebraska would react to the new vocabulary her son had picked up. Everyone knew the joke about the Southern Baptist recruit who went home on leave and at the Sunday dinner table asked, "Hey, Sis, pass the fuckin' salt, will ya?" The change in Buzz had been funny to watch. Except for his language, he was still an overgrown farm boy.

"Wish you could come with me, Buzz, and sample some home cooking. I'll bring something back." Actually the food at Sampson wasn't all that bad, but he knew Buzz missed the family he'd left in the Mid-West. So many of the guys in Alan's class were just kids, really, hardly out of high school.

Catching an early Friday train from Geneva, Alan arrived in Springfield in the late afternoon. He boarded an uptown bus in front of Union Station and began the familiar ride along Main Street and up the hill. Sea bag slung over his shoulder, he walked into the yard as Gary and Lucille were heading down the drive.

"Daddy!" yelled Gary, dropping his scooter and racing up to his father. Lucille began to bark frantically. Nan appeared on the porch and almost fell as she ran down the steps.

"Oh my, where's Billy? And wait until Laura sees you! And Belle!" Nan kept patting Alan on the arm.

They both looked up as Billy came through the gate from Ada Brown's house. He began to run when he saw Alan, then slowed down a bit as he got closer.

"Look who's turned up like a bad penny, Billy, just like that!" said Nan.

"Hi, Dad," said Billy, blushing as Alan leaned down and hugged him. "Did Ma know you were coming?"

"No, no one knew, not even me until late last night. I've got only until Sunday." Lucille was sniffing at the sea bag that Alan had set on the ground. "Nothing there for you, old girl."

"When does your mother get home these days, Billy?" Alan asked, straightening up and adjusting his cap.

"About now. We...or you...could walk up and meet her on the way. She usually walks home."

"Come on, guys, let's go." He hoisted his bag onto the porch. "Mother, leave that there for now. It's heavy. We're going to meet Laura."

Lucille kept running ahead and circling back and nudging Alan's leg as they all walked up the street. His sailor cap stood at a jaunty peak atop the big shadow he and the boys cast on the sidewalk. The late afternoon sun felt warm on his back, and it seemed good to be walking on concrete again.

"I see her!" Gary yelled. "She's with her friend!"

Sure enough, a block away, near the A & P, Alan spotted Laura walking toward them. She was with another woman, taller—that would probably be the Helen she had told him about—and they seemed to be engaged in lively conversation. Laura was wearing a brown and white striped dress Alan didn't recognize.

As they got closer, she looked up, saw them, and began waving with both hands. She said something to Helen and started to run toward them.

"Goodness, Alan! What a surprise!" They kissed, and then Laura stepped back. She was still out of breath. "What happened? Are you all right?"

"I got the boot from boot camp. They don't want me."

"No sir!" She started to laugh as she realized from their expressions that everything was fine.

Laura introduced Alan as Helen approached. "Heard a lot about you, Alan," she said. "They'd better be treating you fine up at Sampson, or they'll be getting what-for from Mrs. Stewart here. Have a wonderful... weekend, is it? Here's where I turn off." She waved and started up her block. "Bye, kids!" she yelled back to Gary and Billy.

"What?" asked Alan, smiling, when he noticed Laura looking up at him. "Nothing...well, everything, I guess. Your uniform, it's so white. And your haircut..."

He'd taken off his cap, and she reached up and ran her hand over the top of his head. "You even have a tan. And I think you've put on a few pounds."

It was true that he was feeling better than he had in years. Less smoking, very little drinking, and the constant regime of exercise and drills had done him good. The weight he'd gained was more muscle than fat.

But Laura looked different, too, dressier and even more carefully groomed than he'd remembered. He did recognize her jewelry—a silver bracelet and earring set he'd given her years ago—and the brown and white shoes she liked to wear in the summer. Still, all dressed up, she looked changed, like she'd added more than just a new dress. *Well, she has changed,* he thought. *And I have, too.* Even the boys looked a little older. Only Nan and Lucille seemed just the same.

At dinner that night, Alan handed out presents he'd brought for everyone: pins and earrings in the shape of anchors and shells for Laura, Belle, and Nan; a painted wooden model of a battleship for Gary; and for Billy a book called *An Illustrated History of the United States Navy.*

"Is this the kind of ship you'll be on?" asked Billy, pointing to a destroyer on the book's jacket.

"Don't know. It could be this one or even a big aircraft carrier or one of the smaller ships that transport troops and equipment. Some of those are called LSTs—landing ship tanks. There are a lot of 'em."

"Daddy, what else is in your sack?" asked Gary.

"This is called a sea bag," Alan explained. "I've got some dirty clothes. You know, we have to wash all our own stuff."

"They don't have ladies around to do that?" Gary looked at Nan and Laura.

"Nope," said Alan.

"Well, I bet this weekend you'll find a few ladies willing to help out," Belle said.

"Hey, never mind, I can peel potatoes now, too," Alan said. "We all have mess duty."

"Is that what they call KP?" asked Nan.

"Yeah, like that," said Alan.

"What does KP mean?" asked Gary.

"Kitchen Police. But that's really Army lingo, KP," he replied. "We call it mess detail.

"Let's see, what else?" he said, rummaging through the bag. "This here is a ditty bag," he said, pulling out a smaller canvas sack. "We keep stuff like toothbrushes and razors in here. No regular bathrooms to store them in. There'd have to be 40 toothbrushes lined up!"

"What's this?" asked Billy, noticing a big blue book.

"That's *The Bluejackets' Manual*. It has our rules, all the rules of the Navy. I was reading it on the train. We have to study from it."

"Wow, it's over eleven hundred pages," said Billy. "It's like the Bible."

"Well, it is, in a way. It's sort of the bible of the Navy."

"Daddy, what's a bluejacket?" Gary asked.

"That's the name for all enlisted sailors," replied Alan.

"OK, kids, enough questions," said Laura. "Your dad's probably tired out from the ride."

"No, that's all right, I don't mind." Actually, Alan enjoyed talking about Sampson. "You know what? Everything is like we're on board a ship. The walls are called bulkheads, the stairs are ladders. When we first got there, they said 'Come aboard.' Guess what they call the floor?"

"I know!" said Gary. "The deck!"

"Very good, Gary!" said Laura.

"And what do they say to us first thing in the morning?"

"'Hit the deck!'" replied Billy. "I saw that in a movie with John Wayne."

"They say a few other things, too," said Alan, looking at Laura and Belle. "Wow, the language is pretty rich."

"I'll bet. Hundreds of guys cooped up in one place. And with no girls around," said Belle.

"Well, there are Navy nurses being trained, but we see them mostly on the parade grounds. Everyone is so tired at night there's not much socializing."

"No entertainment?" Belle asked.

"Well, yeah, we have movies, and there's a USO unit that brings in people. And the other day they came from *The Amateur Hour* to audition guys for a talent show."

"Wow, was Major Bowes there?" asked Billy.

"No, Ted Mack came instead," said Alan. "He's his assistant. We wanted to send one of the guys in the barracks. He has a special talent." He laughed.

"What is that, dear?" asked Nan. "Does he sing? You're a good singer, too, you know."

"No, what he does is at the other end. A special musical talent. He farts. Keeps us up at night."

"Oh, my," said Nan. "Poor thing."

"He farts!" yelled Gary. "That's funny!"

"They could recruit that guy for the Navy band," said Belle. "He'd be perfect if they played "Der Fuehrer's Face.""

Gary began to sing, *"Beans, beans the musical fruit, the more you eat the more you toot."*

"So, what will we do tomorrow?" asked Laura, giving Gary a look.

"Clam chowder makes 'em louder!" he yelled.

"That will do!" she said. "Gary, honestly!"

"Tell you what," said Belle. "Tomorrow in the morning, how about if we work in the garden and go for a walk, kids? That'll give your mom and dad a chance to have some time together."

"Then we could all go over to Forest Park and have a picnic in the afternoon," Alan added. "Have you had the car out?" he asked Laura.

"Just that once that I told you about," she replied. "When we all went to see the Mutual softball team play. But I felt kind of funny, driving and using gas. There's still half a tank, I think."

"I'll have my whites on. Nothing wrong with a sailor taking his family out to the park," said Alan. "Say, I wonder if Mary could whip up some meatballs and sauce for tomorrow night. We had spaghetti last week and all I could think of was her sauce."

Before anyone even had a chance to ask, Mary brought over a big pan early in the evening. "For your dinner tomorrow," she said, giving Alan a big hug. "I got noodles comin' later. Sal, he said in a card that he misses my noodles and gravy, so I thought, *I bet Alan does, too.*"

At Forest Park the next afternoon, they fed the ducks in Porter Lake and picnicked in the shady grove near the ball field. Later they walked to the rose garden, where the pink and scarlet and white blooms were at their peak. Laura took a snapshot of Alan and the boys, Gary saluting in his new sailor's suit with a navy blue tie and short white pants, a present from Belle. Alan's cap was perched awkwardly on Billy's head as the three of them smiled at the camera.

Laura asked a man walking a terrier puppy to take a picture of everyone. They all gathered under an arbor loaded with dark red briar roses and squinted into the bright July sunlight. Lucille and the little Scottie tentatively sniffed each other, their stubby tails quivering wildly.

"Lucille, behave yourself. He's too young for you," said Belle.

Alan laughed along with the rest, but there was a forced quality to everyone's good humor that didn't feel quite right. After the occasional joke or funny remark, there was silence until someone thought of something else to say or something else to do.

"Car sounds good," he remarked as they drove home. "Take it out again, now and then. There's enough gas and more coupons in the dresser drawer."

"Aye, aye, sir," Laura said, laughing. "Anything else, sir?"

Awake in bed on Sunday morning, Alan was surprised to find that he was thinking of the guys at camp. Though he wasn't looking forward to the long train ride later on in the day, he'd be glad in a way to get back. There would probably be further information about his new assignment. The truth was, the weekend was ending up feeling strangely flat.

He couldn't quite pinpoint his discontent. There had been some awkwardness when he first arrived home on Friday, but dinner and the family conversation that followed were, on the surface, just as before. The outing to the park had gone well enough, but not without a certain feeling he sensed that everyone was trying too hard.

He and Laura had gotten on OK. With the heightened sexual tension at camp—constant conversations and jokes, as well as detailed descriptions of real or made-up conquests by the single guys returning from weekend jaunts into Geneva and Rochester—Alan had been looking forward to being with his wife. They'd never been separated for so long.

"I guess we're still a good fit, huh?" Laura had said to him early Saturday morning as they lay entwined in bed. They were alone in the house.

He didn't answer, but he stroked her long black hair and held her tight. Their night together had been fine, but, still, it was hard to pretend everything was normal when he might be 6,000 miles away by August. And there was Laura's new job. He could tell that she was really enjoying it, but she wasn't saying much. Why? She did show him, with obvious pride, how much she'd already saved in the company credit union.

"And that's besides what I had to buy for clothes," she said. "Here, let me show you a few of my new outfits." She was clearly happy to be in style again. He'd bet she was the best-looking girl in the office. He was glad she'd become so friendly with Mae, older than her other new friend, Helen, and with a husband in the service, too.

"You know, they have a talent show every year, and I was thinking of singing. You remember Ray Jardine's band around town? Well, he works daytime at the Mutual and runs the talent show. He's playing weekends down at the Bridgeway now."

"Why don't you do it? Try out. Sounds like fun and the other girls would get to hear how good you are."

"I think you can pretty much just appear in the show. But Helen heard he's looking for a singer, too."

"You mean to sing with the band and get paid?"

"Well, yes. Like I did before we were married."

"Oh. Well, just don't take on too much." He was going to say more but instead turned and walked out of the bedroom.

He wanted to take the bus to the station on Sunday noon, but Laura insisted that they all drive down in the car. Nan brought up his clean clothes, neatly folded. He had cookies from Mary

Mazzarella and even a box of fudge from Ada Brown. "Made with love, Alan. Share it with the other boys in the barracks," she said to him, standing on the tips of her high-heeled shoes for a hug and kiss in the yard.

"Thanks, Mrs. Brown. Ada. And for all you do for Billy."

When they got to the station, there were no parking spots along Lyman Street. In a way, Alan was relieved. The train was due to leave in a few minutes, so he double-parked at the curb. Laura scooted over Gary into the driver's seat, her knees bumping the big shiny knob at the top of the floor clutch.

Alan retrieved his bag from the trunk and kissed every-one goodbye. "Keep writing. I look forward to everyone's letters. Especially all the ones you send, Belle." He smiled at his sister. Belle wasn't the most faithful of correspondents.

"I'll do better, Alan. Promise." He hadn't had a chance to talk to Belle much about her new job. There just hadn't been time. He'd have to ask her more in his next letter.

Alan leaned through the window and gave Laura one more kiss, patted Nan's arm, waved again to everyone, and entered the station. This parting, sure to be a longer one than when he'd left for camp, seemed so different from the noisy and teary goodbye of six weeks ago.

Surprisingly, the train wasn't crowded, so he spread out on both seats next to a grimy window that, for once, opened fairly easily. He read the Sunday *New York Daily Mirror* that he'd bought at the station, and then leafed again through sections of *The Bluejackets' Manual*. The amount of information was overwhelming. He con-centrated on aspects of flagging and codes that he figured he'd be studying in Signalman School.

After a while, he tried to doze, though he didn't want to be so awake later on that he couldn't fall sleep back in the barracks. Stretching out his long legs in the cramped space under the seat ahead, he tried to figure out why he was feeling a letdown from the past couple of days.

Gary, Nan and Belle had been fine. Billy...well, his contact with him had been, as usual, tentative and uncomfortable, though Alan had sensed when he arrived that Billy was really glad to see him. That was good. He made a promise to himself to write some letters just to him. Maybe they could establish a better relationship that way, before the war was over. Letters might work.

As for Laura...Things seemed different. Not when they were in bed. If anything, their lovemaking had been more intense than ever. But he sensed more of an independence, a self-sufficiency that she didn't seem to bother to hide. In fact, everyone—but especially Laura—seemed to be doing just fine without him.

He began to get a headache, so he forced himself to concentrate on the drone of the wheels as the train made its way across the Catskills and through the farmland of the Mohawk Valley. He picked up the *Mirror* again and read an article about Amelia Earhart, whose plane had gone down somewhere in the South Pacific back in 1937. No one knew exactly what had happened, but now there was a new theory: *"Japs Murdered Amelia Earhart!"* the headline blazed. There was a map showing the vast distances between the islands on her route, and Alan wondered if he'd end up anywhere near them in the coming months.

When he got back to his barracks later that night, other sailors on his floor were returning from a Sunday afternoon away from camp. His unit had won the Rooster Award again for cleanest barracks, which meant an unexpected leave to Geneva or, if they had transportation, as far as a six-hour pass could take them. A lot of the men had spent their time in the local bars.

"Aw, I don't feel so hot," Buzz replied when Alan asked him how the weekend had been.

"Didn't you go into town?"

"Yeah, but I don't remember too much. My friggin' head still hurts."

A low-watt bulb, lighted when cigarettes were allowed, was still on. Alan went to grab a smoke at the far end of the barracks, near the head and showers.

Walter Johnson, one of the petty officers whose room was at the other end of the building, approached Alan. "Stewart?"

"Sir?"

"Glad you're back. I have news for you. There's been a change. You've been assigned to radar training. You'll be leaving for Virginia Beach this week."

"Yes, sir." Alan was stunned. "Uh, what happens after that? Sir?"

"Fair question." Johnson smiled. "Took you by surprise, I know. But that's the Navy. Actually, I'm sorry to lose you." As one of the older recruits, Alan had been treated well by all the officers. He realized that Johnson had probably welcomed having a few men nearer his own age in the barracks.

"Thank you, sir," Alan replied. "I appreciate the leadership you've given me...us."

The officer nodded. "I'd guess—now, mind you, this is all a guess—I'd guess that you did well enough on your tests that they want to put you into specialized training right away. Radar likely means you'll be on active duty on a ship."

"That would definitely be at sea?"

"Yes, probably in the Pacific at this point, but that's not for certain. Not sure what's going to happen with the situation in Europe. But at sea somewhere, yes. There are several special ship schools down in Virginia—a big LST set-up at Bradford, in Norfolk—where you could also be sent later for more training." Johnson laughed. "Then again you could end up on a patrol boat in the Mississippi. You never can tell."

"Thanks for letting me know, sir."

"Good luck to you."

Alan returned to his bunk to tell Buzz. Then he sat down to write a quick note to Laura. Now he knew he wouldn't be going home again for a good long while, maybe not even before he shipped out from Virginia. He'd deal with that when the time came. Except for the suddenness of the news, he was surprised at how little it seemed to bother him.

Chapter 18: Belle

After a couple of weeks on the job, Belle knew more about the workings of a game factory than she'd ever imagined. Initially, she substituted for sick workers and kept an eye on the temporary summer kids who supplied the women on the assembly belt with game parts. Soon she was helping manage one of the lines.

The operation had a certain hypnotic appeal. Once the electrical switch was turned on, a seemingly endless procession of shallow cardboard boxes made its way down the conveyer. The women tossed dice, tiddlywinks, checkers, chess pieces over and over again into the compartments of the open boxes as they moved along the narrow belt.

Lately Belle had been shadowing Eddie as he coordinated the stacks of finished games that mounted, hour after hour, on skids at the end of the line. A different run would begin the next day, to be followed by another game, and still another the day after that.

"Honest to God," Belle said to Eddie, as they sat drinking coffee during a morning break. "I didn't think there were this many kids in the entire 48 states. Is it like this all the time?"

"Yeah, well, partly it's the war," replied Eddie. "These games aren't just for the kiddie market. Families stay at home more now, except for going out to the movies. And a lot of them play games."

That made sense to Belle, since Billy and Gary sometimes got the grown-ups to join in their board games. She recognized the box covers of several that made up the basic Milton Bradley catalog: Uncle Wiggly, Chutes and Ladders, Game of the States, Parcheesi.

"Belle, see if you can get me some Big Ben puzzles, OK?" Billy asked her one night. "I don't care if the picture on the cover is ripped or anything like that." Gary wanted crayons and finger paint. So far she'd brought home a few games with slightly damaged boards or punctured boxes—standards like Jolly Time Dominoes and Royal Jack Straws—that had been tossed aside during the packing process.

It didn't take long for the girls on the line to figure out that Belle was being trained to become a floor supervisor. At first she was afraid that this would cause some resentment, so she was a bit nervous one day when Joanie, a stocky middle-aged redhead, called her over to her bench.

"Hey, Belle, got you a present." She handed her a paper bag.

"Gee, should I open it now?"

"Sure." They still had about five more minutes before the warning whistle that would signal the end of the lunch break. Boxes of Pirate and Traveler waited in various stages of completion along the fifty feet of belt, motionless and silent until Eddie or Belle yelled the alert and turned on the switch.

Inside the bag were two snoods, one red and the other green. "Figured you're going to need something else besides those bandannas and turbans." She paused and looked up at Belle. "Especially at meetings with the big shots."

"Thanks a lot, Joanie. You know, I'm still not sure just what the hell I should be wearing. The other day I felt kind of funny in that denim jumpsuit number when Mr. Ryan came through and I had to talk to him."

"Don't worry about that, you always look good. You know, it's a big step that they're givin' us some responsibility. Even if it's not one of us older gals who's been here awhile. And even if it's just because of the war. Elaine's the only other woman really in charge of anything, at least in the factory." She was referring to a longtime worker in another department who had taken the place of a man who'd been drafted into the Army. "Course, she's not getting as much money as the guys make," she added.

"Do you think I'm resented because I'm new?" Belle asked.

"Nah, but only because you're like us, except you got a little more class, know what I mean? Me, I'm glad you're getting the job. You made a good impression right from the get-go. And we all like Abe, and we can tell he likes you. When Eddie goes we want someone who's not a pain in the ass."

"I know, it's lucky for us that Abe's our boss," Belle replied. "I like him, too. He seems like a good guy. Fair. I just hope Eddie makes out all right." They had just heard that morning that the husband of a woman in the next department was missing in action in North Africa.

Her conversation with Joanie pleased Belle. They often chatted during the morning and afternoon breaks, but it made her feel good to know that she was developing relationships, especially with her impending job change. She'd been concerned about that. She didn't want to feel isolated from everyone, especially if they became aware of any after-hours relationship with Abe.

What Belle didn't tell Joanie was that she was having dinner with Abe that very night. Several days ago, when it was definite that she'd be taking Eddie's place, Abe had said, "This calls for a celebration. How about dinner someplace downtown? Hannah's been wanting to meet you, so we can take the bus to my house later, and I'll drive you home from there."

The rest of the afternoon passed quickly. By the time she changed into a dress and met Abe in his office, the floor was deserted. It was still too early for the next shift. Just as well, she thought.

"You're looking awfully nice, if I may say so," said Abe.

"Thanks," replied Belle. "You're pretty spiffy yourself." He was wearing a different shirt, pale blue, with a wide rust and white flowered silk tie.

They headed down Park Street, and then turned right onto Main, toward the center of downtown and the Student Prince restaurant. As they walked along the busy street, Belle asked herself, *Am I having a date with this man?*

They had hit it off right from the start. Belle was intent on learning the ropes and grateful that her new boss was the exact opposite of that creep Simpson. It had seemed perfectly natural that they might celebrate by having dinner, especially since it was directly after work and on a weekday.

But then she thought, *Why had he mentioned meeting his daughter?* Belle recalled Laura's telling her that it was obvious she liked Abe. Had she talked more about him at home than she realized? He was older than anyone she'd ever even considered dating. But in Abe's case, she didn't even think of him in terms of his age, except perhaps regarding his experience and a certain ease and authority he conveyed.

Belle smiled and nodded as Abe commented on the balmy summer weather. As he raised his arm to shield her from a car turning onto Main from the Memorial Bridge, she noticed the size and strength of his hand and the thickness of his wrist. She decided to concentrate on the famous red cabbage and German potatoes served at the restaurant. And she hoped they had veal tonight.

"So, what'll it be?" Abe asked a few minutes later as they studied the well-worn menus. They were seated in one of the small dark pine booths near the bar. Dozens of fancy beer steins lined a high shelf encircling the room, and fancy plates of all sizes dotted the walls.

"Weiner schnitzel for me, with all the trimmings," Belle replied. "Makes me think of my brother. It's his favorite meal."

"Tell me more about him. He's younger than you, right?"

"Yeah, by three years. Let's see. Well, he was—is—the family favorite. Or I should say, my mother's favorite. Neither of us remembers our father very well. But my mother doted on Alan. Still does. You know, a boy and all.

"Don't get me wrong," she added. "Nan is wonderful. You'll—everyone loves her. Everybody. Sometimes I feel I have to share her with the world, you know?"

"It's easy to dote on your kids. I'd do anything for Hannah," Abe said. "Though she can be a handful," he added, laughing.

"Anyway, my mother had it tough," Belle said. "And Alan never really had a chance to go to school. I mean, beyond high school. But he's done well. He's a foreman at Westinghouse. He's had his problems, but who hasn't?" she said, raising her glass. *Funny*, she thought as she sipped her wine, *I can take a drink or leave it.* She was glad Alan had said he was feeling so healthy and fit up at Sampson. Maybe things would change for the better.

"You're close to his children, aren't you?" Abe asked.

"I sure am, and I like his wife—Laura—a lot, too. Gary's the little one, and Billy, who's ten, well, he was special from the day he was born. They've always lived with us, upstairs. We have a big house on the hill past Winchester Square."

"It's good to have family," Abe said. "I was an only child, and my parents are gone. All my other relatives are in Austria, but I've lost touch with them." He half-smiled. "Kind of funny to be here. In a German restaurant, I mean. Now that I think about it."

"Oh, it's been here for years. It's not like they're, you know, Nazis or anything."

"No, of course not. Still, it's easy to imagine this place in Berlin or Hamburg. I wouldn't be exactly welcome."

"Why?" Belle asked. Then she said, "Oh, I didn't realize..."

"That I'm Jewish?" He smiled.

"I guess it didn't occur to me. I usually don't think of stuff like that."

"That's good. I wouldn't want that to be an issue."

"Hey, are you kidding? I had a..." Belle paused. She realized she was blushing.

"What?"

"I was going to say, I used to have a...friend. He was Irish. Now *that* was a problem with my mother. Not really, but you know, the Scots and the Irish."

"Cheers," Abe said, holding out his glass. She raised hers and smiled. Well, that was that. *If I wasn't on a date before, I am now*, she thought.

After dinner they caught the bus to Abe's house, a large Spanish-style stucco on a quiet, tree-lined street across the city, near Forest Park.

"Nice place," Belle said as they walked to a side terrace paved with flagstones.

"Thanks," replied Abe. "Been here a long time. Let me see if Hannah's in. What can I get you? Coffee sound good?" He disappeared into the house.

Belle settled into a worn green Adirondack chair and rummaged in her bag for a cigarette and matches. She was curious to meet Abe's daughter. What had Eunice Clark called her that day when she'd taken Belle around the plant? A firebrand?

"Here, have one of mine." Belle started and looked up at the young woman standing before her holding out a pack of Camels. "You must be Belle."

"And you're Hannah. Thanks, I've got my own, but I'll take a light."

Hannah was tall, like her father, and thin. She was dressed in khaki slacks and a plain white cotton blouse. Her black hair was an unruly mop of thick curls, and she wore huge gold hoops on her pierced ears. It was hard to tell how old she was, but Belle guessed about 25.

"Wow, Pop was right," said Hannah. "You *are* just like Charlotte. Amazing."

"Yeah, he did mention I looked like a friend of yours the first day I met him at the plant."

"Well, judge for yourself." Hannah laughed heartily. "This is Charlotte." The pretty woman standing behind her looked to be in her early forties. Except for her pageboy hairstyle, she could have been Belle's older sister.

"Wow, I think I'm seeing my double," Belle said. "Jeez, if I didn't know better, I'd wonder what my father had been up to. Whoops, sorry!"

Hannah hooted, and Charlotte started laughing. "Don't apologize," Hannah said. "I'm thinking the same goes for Charlotte's dad." Can you imagine old Edgar?" she asked, rolling her eyes at Charlotte. "But you never know."

"That's a fact," Belle said, as Abe appeared, carrying a tray with cups and a pot of coffee. "Of course, present male company excluded," She added.

"Don't be so sure!" Hannah laughed.

"What did I miss?"

"Nothing, Pop, we're just talking about the foibles of men."

"Oh, boy, I guess I'm in for it in that case."

"Abe, you're a gentleman, believe me," Belle said.

"Well, sure, compared to that former boss of yours." One day at lunch Belle had told Abe about the incident that ended her job at the Paramount.

"You had a bad experience?" Hannah asked. She looked at Belle with interest and concern.

"Well, yeah, but it's funny now when I think about it." Belle proceeded to describe her last encounter with Simpson. "The capper was when I tossed the coffee across the desk. I swear, he just about disappeared from sight. All of him." The three women laughed uproariously.

"OK, ladies, OK, I'm embarrassed," Abe said. "We're not all that…"

"Well, Abe, you brought it up," Charlotte said sweetly. "Belle was just pointing out that gentleman's…shortcomings."

Hannah guffawed. "Of course, it's not really funny," she added. "You should have had that pig arrested."

"Believe me," replied Belle, "I thought of taking it further. But, to be honest, I was glad to get out of there. And he has grown kids. And I feel sorry for his wife."

"Yeah, and he knows that. But I guess I can see what you mean."

"So, how about you two? Where do you work?" Belle asked.

"I'm at Johnson's Bookstore. I do their accounts and book ordering," Hannah replied. "Charlotte's a nurse at Springfield Hospital. But I think she missed her calling. She's always getting me to order new titles at the store. I swear, I never saw anyone read so much."

"We're also involved in labor work," said Charlotte. "Are you familiar with the Women's Bureau?"

"The office in the Labor Department? I've heard them mentioned at work." Belle replied.

"That's it," said Hannah. "We do some investigative work for them. And also the League of Women Voters."

Charlotte learned forward in her chair. "The Bureau was instrumental in getting women included in the Fair Labor Standards Act," she said. "That was just five years ago. Minimum wages, work hours."

"You know, my sister-in-law just got hired at the Mutual," Belle replied. "They weren't taking married women with children before."

"I know. Can you imagine?" Hannah began pacing up and down the flagstone terrace. "And it's not over. Wait 'til the end of the war. 'Thank you, ladies. Now back to your kitchens'."

"Do you think so?" Belle asked. "Won't we have proved something?"

"You know that, and I know that, and Charlotte, and Pop, too. Maybe things won't be quite as bad as before, but I'm telling you, it's not over."

They continued talking on the terrace. Crickets chirped in the spacious backyard, and a light breeze rustled the large white oak that towered over the house.

Belle suddenly realized it had become quite dark "Hey, I'd better be going," she said. "Can't be late for work tomorrow. My boss doesn't go for that." She stood up. "You don't need to drive me, Abe. I'll be fine on the bus."

"Don't be silly. Gives me an excuse to take the car out. I hardly use up my coupons."

"Belle, it was a pleasure meeting you. Hope to see you again." Charlotte rose and put out her hand.

"Same here, Charlotte. You too, Hannah."

"Hey, any chance you can come to an exhibit this Friday night?" asked Hannah. "There's an opening of some paintings by Georgia O'Keeffe at a gallery a friend of Charlotte's has downtown."

"Well, sure, I guess." Belle had never been to an art exhibit, much less an opening, and she had no idea who Georgia O'Keeffe was. She looked at Abe.

"What do you say?" asked Abe. "I'm free if you are. OK if I come along, Hannah? Or is it by invitation?"

"You're officially invited, *both* of you," said Charlotte. "Say, you don't happen to know Ada Brown, do you? She lives over your way, I think. She'll be there."

"Ada Brown? Sure, she's our neighbor. In fact, our backyards adjoin. She'll be there?"

"Ada's very involved in our women's group. And she even knows Georgia O'Keeffe. She spent time out West. She's had quite a life. Do you know about her?"

"Yeah, she did tell my nephew that she lived in...what, Arizona or New Mexico? I'll be darned. She and my mother are great friends. And she's very good to Billy. Teaches him stuff. He's real smart. But I guess I already told you that!"

They drove across town in Abe's car, an old gray Desoto sedan. Belle settled back in the roomy plush seat, its pile worn and smooth and pleasantly warm in the chill night air. "I enjoyed meeting your daughter, Abe," she said. "She's nice. And I like her spirit."

"She liked you, too, I could tell. And I think she'd say the same thing."

After they stopped in the driveway, Abe got out and opened the door for Belle. They stood in the darkness next to the car.

"So, I'll see you tomorrow," Abe said. "Thank you. I had a great time." He leaned over and kissed Belle on the cheek.

"Same here, Abe. Thank you." She gave him a quick hug.

Nan was sitting up in bed, a magazine propped on her lap. Often Belle found her asleep with the light on, reading glasses still perched on the bridge of her nose.

"Whatcha reading, sweetie?"

Nan held up a *Ladies Home Journal*. "A nice article about Mrs. Roosevelt. I don't know how that woman has enough hours in her day," she said. "She does so much. And she still has time to answer all her letters and help everyone out. Do you know, I just discovered we're the same age. My!"

Belle told Nan about her about her evening, including the mention of Ada Brown.

"Why don't you sleep a while in the morning, Mother?" she asked, knowing the suggestion was pointless. Then she kissed Nan goodnight and walked down the hall to get ready for bed.

As Belle pinned up her hair, she thought about the evening. So, Abe was Jewish. That surprised her, but only because she'd never dated anyone who wasn't Protestant or Catholic. And it was a bit strange to realize she was going out with a man whose daughter could be her kid sister. On the other hand, Charlotte was in her forties, and she and Hannah seemed to be good friends.

Belle smiled at the notion that she'd be going to an art gallery opening. *La de da*. Mrs. Brown wouldn't be expecting to see her there, that's for sure. They'd never quite hit it off for some reason. Maybe she'd always been a bit intimidated by Ada Brown.

And what exactly *was* Mrs. Brown's story? She wondered if Charlotte was referring to something in particular when she asked if Belle "knew about" her. Knew what? Belle had never really heard much about Mrs. Brown's earlier life. She'd have to remember to ask Nan more tomorrow. If there was a story, she bet Nan knew it. People told her everything.

Chapter 19: Laura

"I don't know," said Laura. "Maybe this wasn't such a good idea."

"Don't be silly," replied Helen. "I've heard you singing at your desk. You're better than the one who just sang, that's for sure. Priscilla Klooper, she's from Policy Issue. Performs every year, and she's always bad."

Laura and Helen were sitting with a sizable number of other staff in the big auditorium of the high school across the street from the Mutual. Anyone interested in appearing in the annual company talent revue had been asked to show up directly after work for a cursory audition.

"It's not like it's a real tryout or anything," Helen explained. "Well, I guess if someone was really bad...but, believe me, I've heard some doozies. And you've sung professionally. It'll be fun. And it'll give Ray Jardine a chance to hear you."

"Oh, Helen, come on. I couldn't even consider joining his band." In fact, however, when Helen pointed out Jardine in the cafeteria and told Laura he was looking for a vocalist, she'd spent that afternoon thinking about her earlier singing days. Alan's reaction hadn't been exactly enthusiastic when she'd mentioned it to him over the weekend. That had bothered her at the time, but he was probably right. Where *would* she find the time?

Ray Jardine was at the old upright piano on the auditorium stage, a big pile of music on the seat next to him. He was talking to a short, stocky woman Laura recognized from the cafeteria.

"That's Aggie Krapinski, Mail Room. Last year she did an imitation of Sophie Tucker. She was pretty good, actually. Loud, anyway. Sometimes he'll ask you to sing something, but he already knows Aggie's OK. I think he had Priscilla run through something 'cause he was hoping she's gotten better since last year's show. Hah!"

"I think I'm next," Laura said just as Jardine looked at a list and called out, "Laura Stewart!"

She made her way down the aisle and climbed the narrow staircase to the left of the stage.

"Miss Stewart?" Jardine smiled broadly in a way that reminded Laura of the photo that occasionally appeared in the paper advertising his band downtown at the Hotel Bridgeway. His hair was dark and slicked back, his eyebrows, up close, bushy and black.

"It's Mrs. Stewart, but Laura's fine."

"So, you sing?" He smiled and looked up from the sign-in sheet.

"Yes. Shall I do something now?"

"If you don't mind, since I haven't had the pleasure. What will it be?"

"'Stardust'."

He smiled again. "I think I know that one." He played a few bars. "That OK?"

"Yes, C is fine."

"Ah, you do sing. Professionally?"

"A long time ago."

"All right, Laura, just begin. I'll come in." He hit a note.

Laura paused for a moment, took a deep breath, and started to sing. "Stardust" was her favorite song. She could sing it backwards, in her sleep, anywhere, anytime. She never failed to be moved by its beautiful melody and bittersweet lyrics, especially the last line: *Though I dream in vain, in my heart it will remain my stardust melody, a memory of love's refrain.* As the song ended, she was startled at the applause that came from the assembled audience. She turned and looked at Jardine.

"Yes, ma'am, you do sing. That was great." He shook his head. "Beautiful. So where have you been hiding?"

"Down in the Tabulating Department." Laura laughed. "Well, I just started last month. And I've been raising a family. Two boys."

"Ah," said Jardine. "Let's do that one for the show. We'll have a run-through Saturday afternoon. I'll have my band. But I'd also like to hear you down at the hotel. I'm looking for a girl singer. Interested?

"Gee, I don't know," said Laura. "I mean..."

"It's just on weekends. Tell you what, next Thursday night we'll be rehearsing. I'd like to have all the guys hear you. Can you stop down?"

"Well..."

"Bring your husband."

"Can't do that, I'm afraid. He's in the service."

"Bring a friend then. Please. Thursday, anytime after six"

Laura glanced out in the audience at Helen, who was smiling broadly at her. "OK, it's a deal. But I'm not sure about going back to singing, Mr. Jardine."

"Next Thursday. And it's Ray."

Laura made her way down the stairs and back up the aisle. Helen was already standing waiting for her. "My God, you were fabulous! I had no idea! What did he say?"

"He wants me to go down to the hotel and have the band hear me."

"See, I told you!"

"Oh, Helen, I don't know..."

By the time they reached the corner of Helen's street, they'd decided what Laura would wear the night of the company talent show and where they'd both have dinner on Thursday after Laura tried out for the band.

"I don't know what I'll sing," she said over dinner at home. "Something new. They'll know whatever is popular right now. Or maybe I'll just do "Stardust" again."

"Mommy, are you going to be a singer?" asked Gary. "Like on the radio? Like Kate Smith?"

They all laughed. Belle said, "More like Dinah Shore or Jo Stafford, wouldn't you say, Laura?"

"Ma, will you get paid and everything?" Billy asked.

"Whoa," said Laura. "I haven't been hired yet, and I don't know if I'd take the job. And even if I do get hired, I'd have to talk it over with your dad. But, yes, I'd get paid."

"I remember when we saw your mother perform down at the shore," said Nan. "She was so pretty and sounded so lovely. Do you still have that purple dress, Laura?"

"I do. It's in the back of the closet. In fact, I was thinking of wearing it for the show. I'll get us all tickets."

"Me too, Mommy?" asked Gary.

"Of course you, too."

"Can Angie come?"

"Sure, if she wants to, Billy," Laura said. "OK, enough about me. So, boys, what did you do today?"

❦

Laura was a big hit at the Mutual Merrymakers Revue later in the week. The whole family took the bus up to the high school auditorium, Laura's purple silk dress carefully wrapped in a cloth garment bag. "It's just like new," declared Nan, who had taken charge of airing it on the line for several days to get rid of the smell of mothballs.

"I don't know," said Laura. "I kind of feel like I've been brought out of storage myself." She wasn't as nervous about performing in the talent show as she was about the upcoming tryout with the band, although the brief run-through earlier in the afternoon had gone well. She noticed a couple of the musicians smiling at her. But she knew it would be different when she was being auditioned as the girl singer. A weak performer made everyone look and sound bad.

Laura's number in the talent show wasn't until the second act, between a tap-dancing secretary and four maintenance men who sang barbershop, so she was able to sit in the audience with Gary, Nan, and Belle. Billy asked if he and Angie could find seats by themselves.

"Break a leg, Ma!" Billy said as they left Laura in the school hallway at the end of the intermission.

"Mommy, why did he say that to you?" asked Gary.

"That's what they say in show business," Billy replied. "Just before the person goes on to perform."

"Billy's right, it really means 'good luck'," said Laura.

As they entered the auditorium, Gary turned back and yelled, "Good luck, and break your leg. Your two legs!"

After the show, they rejoined Laura in the corridor. "Ma, you got the most applause of anyone!" Billy said.

"Yeah, Mrs. Stewart, you did," said Angie. "Gee, and you looked just beautiful."

"Thanks." Laura hugged everyone. She was flushed, and she felt happy. "Let's walk home, and I'll treat everyone to ice cream cones at the Double Dip."

As they strolled in the warm June air down State Street, Belle walked ahead with Laura, who was still wearing her purple dress. "You were swell. I'd forgotten how good you are. And you really looked happy up there."

"I was. But I'm nervous about next week."

"Hey, don't be. You'll do just fine. It'll be good for you. And you deserve it."

"Well, I'm just concerned about the time away from the kids. You know, working during the day and all. They've just gotten used to that, and now I'd be gone even more."

As it happened, when Laura got home from work the following Wednesday night, she discovered that Billy had developed a fever and sore throat.

"I was afraid of that. It's your tonsils again. I'll make an appointment with Dr. Cahill. I'm sure he'll see us at his home office after I get home from work tomorrow. And if you don't feel better, he'll come here instead."

"But Ma, that's when you're going to have your band tryout. Nan can take me."

"That can wait, Billy. I want to go with you."

The next day at work, Laura walked over to Ray Jardine's department. "Mr. Jardine, Ray, I'm afraid I can't be there tonight. Billy, my older boy, has tonsillitis and I've made a doctor's appointment. Didn't want to do it during the day. I hope you understand."

"Sorry to hear that. About Billy, too." He thought a moment. "OK, here's what we'll do. The fellows were impressed with you at the show. They know a real singer when they hear one. Why don't you come down to the hotel on Saturday night? You could just do "Stardust." It would really help me out, I only have Danny DeCarlo at the mike. This way you'd get a sense of the place."

"You mean, sing the number during regular hours?"

"Yeah, you know it cold. I'll reserve a table for you. Plan on singing at the end of the first set, say around 8?"

Laura returned to her desk. She turned to Helen and said, "Hope you're free on Saturday night. We have a date at the Bridgeway."

By the weekend, Billy's fever had subsided, though it looked liked he'd need to have his tonsils and adenoids removed. "It will help his asthma as well," the doctor promised. "It's not an emergency, but let's set a date in the next month or so. Before September."

"Ma, remember the beach," Billy said. Sal was scheduled to be home on leave for a week after his basic training, and Billy had been asked to join the Mazzarella family at a cousin's cottage near New London for a few days. "Please, Ma, can it wait 'til after?"

"OK, as long as you're well enough to go to the shore," Laura said.

She'd agreed to meet Helen at the bus stop around seven on Saturday night. She left the boys and Lucille downstairs with Nan, ran back upstairs to get a handkerchief, checked her stocking seams in the hall mirror, and walked back down to the first floor landing. The heels of her ankle strap stilettos clicked on the wooden slats of the front porch as she hurried down the steps, white gloves and narrow bag clutched under her arm.

"Say, I'm glad Ray plays at the Bridgeway. That's where the officers go," Helen said as the bus clattered down the hill.

"Oh?"

"Yeah, you know, all the Westover crowd. Officers go to the Bridgeway, enlisted men to the Worthy. It's some kind of class thing. That base has gotten huge. Thousands of guys there, girls, too. Mostly nurses in training, I think. My brother-in-law works in one of the repair shops."

"Well, you can certainly hear the planes. I swear, there's a steady stream some nights, it seems for hours."

"I know. Those are B-17s and B-24s heading over to Europe. Did you know they also have patrols that go out and look for U-Boats off the coast? Scary, huh?"

"It is," replied Laura. "What does your brother-in-law know about the Germans there at the base? The prisoners of war? You never hear much about them."

"Well, they don't tell him much, except there are several hundred, about five hundred, I think. Anyway, might as well meet some officers tonight while we're at it."

"Well, you, maybe." Laura laughed. "You don't think my ring will drive them away?"

"Hey, you're wearing it, not me. Why? Do you want to dance?" Helen glanced at Laura.

"No, no, I was thinking more of you."

They could hear the sound of the band as they crossed the hotel lobby and entered the dining room. "I think we have a reservation," Laura told the maître d'. "Stewart? Mr. Jardine arranged it."

As soon as they were seated at a tiny table near the dance floor, a waiter brought over two drinks. "Oh, we didn't order yet," said Helen.

"Compliments of Mr. Jardine," said the waiter. They glanced up and smiled as Ray waved and nodded.

"Hey, this is pretty good," said Helen. "Looks like a Tom Collins. That OK with you?"

"Yes, except I think I'll wait until after my number."

Helen offered Laura a Chesterfield. "No thanks. Maybe later." She occasionally smoked, but she preferred filtered brands like Kools or Viceroy. She hated it when the tobacco on unfiltered cigarettes came off on her lips and tongue, and she didn't like the way it looked when women flicked away a stray piece with their finger.

"Oops, can't find my matches," Helen said, fumbling in her purse. The band had just finished playing "Jersey Bounce."

A serviceman at the next table reached over to light her cigarette with his Zippo. Laura couldn't tell his rank, but he was wearing a couple of bars. She was sure he was an officer.

"Thanks," said Helen.

"My pleasure."

"Here comes a lieutenant," Helen murmured as a young man in uniform approached their table. "Sure, love to," she replied as he asked her to dance. As she got up, Helen whispered, "The one who lit my cigarette is at least a captain." In a louder voice, she said, "I'll leave my bag here, Laura."

"Sure, I'm not going anyplace." She wondered when Ray would announce her number.

"Would you care to dance, Laura, or does not going anyplace mean just that?" The man-who-was-at-least-a-captain grinned. He had a nice smile.

"Gee, thanks, but no. Actually, I'm kind of here on business." She blushed when he raised his eyebrows and they both laughed. "What I mean is, I'm going to sing in a bit. With the band."

"Oh, you're the new singer?"

"Well, no, not yet, but I used to sing."

"Well, maybe after you sing—a dance?"

"Uh, actually, I'm married."

"Yes, I noticed," he replied casually.

"Oh."

Laura concentrated on watching the band, crowded onto a raised platform between the dance floor and the rear wall. The singer's mike was in the center, in front of the clarinet player. She counted nine musicians, plus Ray. The male vocalist—had Ray said his name was Danny?—was seated in a small chair on the far left. Suddenly Ray caught her eye and raised his finger. She must be on next.

As Helen returned with the lieutenant and sat down, Ray walked over to the mike. "Ladies and gentlemen, thank you. We have a special guest tonight. This young lady sang with us earlier in the week, and I want to tell you: She's sensational. You're in for a special treat. Miss Laura Stewart!"

Laura rose, patted Helen's arm and made her way across the dance floor and up to the center of the tiny stage. Normally, the vocalist wouldn't come in until at least the second chorus of the song, but she knew Ray was using the same arrangement they'd agreed on the other night. That meant she'd be the featured performer. She wished she'd had a chance to test the mike.

As soon as the audience recognized the song, several couples got up to dance. A few bars into the verse, Laura knew she was doing fine. She stopped worrying about remembering the lyrics and concentrated on projecting them. She noticed that a few of the couples had stopped dancing and were watching her instead. Eddie O'Shea, whose band she'd sung with in Hartford, used to say, "When they do that, kid, it either means you're so bad they can't believe it or you're so good they just want to listen."

The other night at the company show had been OK, but she knew she was even better here. When the applause ended, Ray said to the audience, "Didn't I tell you? And I have something else to say. If I can twist this gal's arm, you'll be hearing a lot more from her in the weeks to come. How about it, Laura?"

Everyone started clapping again, and when they finished, Laura said, "Well, what can I say? I guess...I guess you've got yourself a new girl singer."

"How about if you come in on one more song? Folks, we haven't rehearsed anything, but if it's one the fellows know, we'll just follow along. What'll it be?"

"Well...I could do 'I Had the Craziest Dream.' On the slow side?"

"You've got it, little lady. I'll even try a bit of Harry James trumpet."

As the intro began, Laura glanced across the floor. Helen and the captain appeared to be deep in conversation. She wondered for a moment what that was all about. Then she focused on the music and the tempo and waited for Ray to give her a cue.

Chapter 20: Billy

"How lovely that you'll be at the shore with Angie," said Mrs. Brown.

"Sal, too," replied Billy. "He's coming home on leave."

"Oh, that's right, before he...before he gets his further orders. How long will he be home?"

"About a week, he thinks. We're going tomorrow, just for the weekend. His aunt and uncle have a cottage, but they won't be there."

Billy and Mrs. Brown were sitting in her living room having lemonade. Ashkii was curled up asleep on his pillow in the corner. Spread out on Mrs. Brown's coffee table were a card and two photographs.

"Did you get a birthday card, Mrs. Brown?"

"I did indeed. But you mustn't tell anyone it's my birthday, Billy. Especially your dear grandmother. I don't like a fuss made. I'm like Jack Benny, you know. I'm 39 years old."

Billy laughed. He knew Mrs. Brown was even older than Nan, and his grandmother had already lived over half a century. "Thank you, dearie, for pointing that fact out," Nan had told him once when he'd reminded her. "And in such an interesting way."

Mrs. Brown picked up the pictures and held them for Billy to see. They looked like postcards, except they were cracked and yellowish-brown, like the pictures in Nan's bedroom. One was a photo of a solemn little girl in pigtails. The other was the same girl sitting in a wagon next to a boy dressed in a funny suit with a big, floppy bow tie.

"Who do you think this little child is?"

"Gee, Mrs. Brown, is it you?"

"Right you are, though I'm afraid she bears scant resemblance to the person sitting before you today."

"Who's the boy?"

"That's my dear friend, Marsden. Marsden Hartley. He's become quite famous, Billy. Look what else he has sent me." She pointed to a small painting propped up near the fireplace of a man in a bathing suit. He had big shoulders and arms and dark eyebrows that came together. The eyebrows gave his face a serious look, like Sal's.

"Do you think he looks like…"

"Like?"

"Well, like Sal," Billy said.

"Why, I believe you're right," Mrs. Brown said "You have a good eye, Billy. Yes, this young man does look like Sal. Maybe Sal's not quite so…oversized, but the eyes and face…Expressive and quite handsome, yes." She smiled at Billy. "Like Sal."

"Marsden also painted that desert scene," she said, glancing at the wall. "We've talked about that one, I believe."

"Yes, you said it's from when you lived in New Mexico. Mrs. Brown, was your other cat Marsden named after this Marsden?

"Ah, you remember my speaking of him. Marsden was already an old fellow when I came back East to New England. Before that, I had Lawrence, who was named after another of our friends, D.H. Lawrence. He's considered a great writer now, and I'll give you some books he wrote, but not quite yet. We all lived in New Mexico. Taos."

"Is that where the lady whose paintings you went to see the other night lived, too?"

"Indeed. Georgia O'Keeffe. I expect your Aunt Belle mentioned my being there? At the gallery? What a surprise to see her."

"She was with her new boss, Mr. Sherman."

"Ah, that would be Hannah's father, Abe. A lovely man. Yes, Hannah and her friend Charlotte were there, too. They're fine young women, and they're going to make a difference in this world. We attend meetings together, Billy, for women and their rights."

"Oh," Billy replied. He wasn't sure what that meant, but maybe it had something to do with money. He'd heard his mother and Belle talking about women and what they got paid at the insurance company and the factory compared to the men.

"The shore will be lovely, Billy. Marsden—Mr. Hartley—and I spent wonderful summers at the seashore in Maine, when we were just about your age. Of course, the water is colder down in Maine." She laughed. "I know, Maine is *up*, but we always say *down*."

She studied the photo of the girl in pigtails. "Shall I tell you something, Billy? Inside my body there lives a little girl who still wonders what she wants to be when she grows up." She looked sideways at him, cocking her head and smiling. "Does that surprise you?"

"Well, sometimes I think I'll never grow up either," Billy replied.

"Ah, but you will. And when you get to be as old as I am, you'll wonder where all those years went. The years go, but time doesn't move quite as fast inside." Mrs. Brown pointed to her head and then to her heart.

"I don't think of you as so old, Mrs. Brown."

"Well, thank you, dear, I don't either, I must say—most of the time." Mrs. Brown gave her red hair a pat. "Remember one day when we were looking at some pictures by the Spanish artist Pablo Picasso?" Billy did, because some of the ladies and men didn't look like real people, but Mrs. Brown had shown him that they did, if you looked more closely.

"Well, he had a friend named Gertrude Stein, a writer," Mrs. Brown continued. "She loved all the artists. Do you know what she once said? Gertrude Stein said, 'Inside we are always the same age.' She was right. Think about that, Billy. Always try to remain true to the person you know to be your own real self. You'll change as you grow older, but there's always a part of you that will be as you are now. And it will keep you young in spirit."

Just then they heard Lucille begin to bark loudly somewhere in the backyard. Ashkii yawned and stretched and meandered out of the room to investigate.

"Maybe that's Sal getting home for his leave," Billy said, leaning forward in his chair.

"Then you'll want to rush right over and be part of his homecoming. Take your glass of lemonade with you. I'll follow along. Hurry!" Mrs. Brown made a shooing motion with her hand.

Billy raced out the back door, just in time to see Mrs. Mazzarella and Angie hugging Sal. Lucille was racing frantically around him, yipping and making little spins in the air.

"Hey, I didn't realize Lucille missed me so much," Sal shouted, laughing and waving as Billy approached.

"How you doing, Billy?" he asked.

"Good, Sal." He was a bit out of breath.

"Still coming with us to the shore?" He reached out and tousled Billy's hair.

"*Si*, yes, sure he is!" said Mrs. Mazzarella. "Salvatore, you look good. *Robusto. Buona salute.* Healthy!"

It was true. In the few weeks since his departure, Sal appeared more fit, even a bit taller, in his neatly pressed khakis. At the same time, his nearly shaved head, shorn of its black curls, gave his face a more youthful appearance.

"Hey Sal, you do look a lot different," Angie said. "I don't mean bad. Ma's right."

"It's all that food and exercise. Wait'll I tell you about all the drills and stuff. Hey, is Nonno upstairs? And where's Nan?"

"Sal!" Nan half-ran down the steps, wiping her apron, just as Mrs. Brown arrived with an extra glass of lemonade. They all stood in the yard for a while, chattering about Sal's changed appearance and admiring his soldier's uniform.

❧

Early the next morning, Billy joined the Mazzarellas as they set off for the shore. Sal's father and Nonno were staying home. "Too much to do in garden," Mr. Mazzarella explained, though Billy knew he rarely went with them on any family outings. Nonno also preferred to stay around the house, especially when a trip to the ocean was involved. Angie told Billy that no one ever remembered him going into the water during all the summers they'd stayed at the shore.

Sal was in a talkative mood as they drove out of the local Mobil station, the gas tank filled with the last of his ration coupons, oil and tires checked, and windshield carefully cleaned by the attendant, Woody, Richie Reilly's younger brother. Richie was finishing up his basic training at Parris Island and Camp Lejeune in the Carolinas, Woody told them. He wasn't sure if he'd be home before shipping out.

"So old Richie made it as a Marine," Sal said as they headed past the tobacco fields on route 5. It would take them a couple of hours to get to the cottage near New London—if the tires held out.

"I don't know, that right rear one looks as thin as a balloon," Sal said. "Ma, say a prayer or two."

"Sal, is it OK that we're using the car? With the war on and all?" Billy asked.

"Yeah, we've got a full load, and I have my Army ID. It'll be fine."

"Your *Zia* Lucretia, she says she sees soldiers on beach," said Mrs. Mazzarella after a bit. "Dogs, too. And airplanes always going back and forth and sometimes ships in the water *a perdita d'occhio*."

"That means, 'as far as your eyes can see'," said Angie.

"Ah, Billy, I forget sometimes," said Mrs. Mazzarella.

"That's OK," said Billy. "I like to hear Italian. I like the sound."

"With the base next door at Groton they need to be real careful," said Sal. "And German U-boats are offshore. You know there's more of that than we read about in the newspaper."

"*Santa Maria*," said Mrs. Mazzarella, dabbing at her face with her white lace handkerchief. Although all the windows of the Ford were open, the sun was blazing and the breeze hot.

"OK, listen to this," said Sal. "The other day in the line-up the sergeant yells, 'Anyone with any musical talent?' Guys are always looking to get out of KP or other stuff, so a bunch of them raised their hands. Like maybe they were looking for a chorus to put on a show. Know what he said? 'OK, get over here, we got a piano that needs to be moved across the field.'" Angie and Billy laughed.

"Then, one day he says, 'OK, who has college experience?' Same thing happens, some guys raise their hands. So he says, 'Right, you smart guys go over there and begin to dig that hole. The rest of you men watch them and learn something'.'"

"Did anything like that happen to you, Sal?" Billy asked.

"Nah, not really. Well, one day I had to clean out all the latrines—those are the toilets—when it wasn't my shift. I was smoking in the barracks when I wasn't supposed to and they found the butt under my bunk."

They arrived at the cottage, opened all the windows, unpacked, and changed into their bathing suits. Angie and Mrs. Mazzarella had the bed in the big bedroom, and Billy and Sal were to sleep in cots in the smaller back room.

"They still haven't replaced everything from the hurricane," Sal remarked. Still, his aunt and uncle had been lucky. Several of their neighbors' houses had been blown right out to sea or damaged beyond repair in '38.

"Jeez, I forgot how this wool itches," said Sal, tugging at his dark blue bathing suit. "At the base we don't wear nothing when we go to the lake. Unless the nurses are around."

"That's what my dad wrote about the pool at Sampson, too," said Billy. "When they had their swimming tests."

"Ugh!" said Angie.

"Hey, let's do that here," said Sal. "We can start a new craze. Whatta ya say, Billy?" Sal pretended to unbuckle the belt of his trunks.

"Salvatore! *Basta!*" Mrs. Mazzarella hit him over the head with the fly swatter. "This army giving you bad ideas!" But she laughed, and Billy could tell she was glad that Sal was in such a good mood.

From the back porch, they walked gingerly in their bare feet down the narrow splintery steps to the water. In the distance, toward the base at Groton, barbed wire fencing blocked access to the dirt road extension. Wading along the shore in the other direction, the three of them reached the wide public beach a couple of hundred yards away. Mrs. Mazzarella stayed behind to tidy up the cottage and make sandwiches for lunch.

Billy recognized the lifeguard perched on his rickety wooden chair, a high school kid who came with his family from the Boston area every summer. Tall and blond, he was wearing a black bathing suit with an attached athletic top that showed off his muscles and deep tan.

"Hiya, Warren," Angie said. Billy remembered that Sal used to tease her about the crush she had on Warren.

"Hey," Warren said. "It's swell to see you. I thought maybe you'd be in by now, Sal."

"I am. Just finishing basic at Devens."

"Wow, no kidding. My older brother Jim just shipped out to Italy. Well, we think that's where he is." He and Sal began to talk about the Army, but not before he warned Billy and Angie about the sun. "A scorcher today, kids. Be careful, you're still real white."

"Kids," whispered Angie to Billy. "What does he mean? I'm almost twelve." She flipped back her braids. "Anyway," she said in a louder voice, "why does everyone have to go on about the war and stuff?" But Sal and Warren ignored her and kept on talking.

After a late lunch at the cottage they returned to the beach, now dotted brightly with big canvas umbrellas and blankets, even though the parking lot didn't have as many cars as in years past. By the time they returned to the house late in the day, Billy and Angie could feel their backs burning.

After dinner, Sal fell asleep on the sofa and Angie and Mrs. Mazzarella set off for the little general store near the shore road. Billy decided to take a walk along the beach. The sky had become overcast, and a breeze rustled the high grass that bordered the dunes down near the more deserted stretches of sand.

It was low tide, and in the distance Billy could see a few people digging for clams, their bent figures moving slowly in the shallow water. Further out, against the horizon, barrels and other floating barriers bobbed up and down. Overhead, an olive-colored plane with a white star roared past, flying low in a straight line along the beach.

Billy shivered. He wished he'd brought along the plaid flannel shirt his mother had insisted on packing. He turned away from the water, toward a series of wooden planks he knew led up to the narrow dirt road that ran parallel to the beach.

Suddenly there was movement in the grass and the sound of a deep-throated growl. From behind a dune an enormous German shepherd dog appeared, panting and straining at a short leash held by a sailor carrying a rifle.

"Prince! Heel!" The dog reluctantly obeyed, nervously sitting upright on the crushed grass and alternately looking at Billy and nudging the rough beige leggings worn by his master.

"Gee, I'm sorry," Billy said. "I'm just here for the weekend. From Springfield. In Massachusetts."

The sailor laughed. "That's good to hear. Don't look like you just washed up on shore. But Prince here doesn't know that, do you, boy?" He turned back to Billy. "Curfew is soon. Can't be out here after dusk, you know."

"That's OK, I'm going back now anyway." Billy headed up toward the road. "Bye. 'Bye, Prince." The dog gave a tentative wag of his tail, then a growl that was less threatening than his earlier snarls. As he walked back to the cottage, Billy wondered if Prince had once lived with a regular family. He tried to imagine Lucille in the Coast Guard.

As they were getting ready for bed that night, Billy remembered something he'd wanted to ask Sal. "You know your suitcase that I have in my room? Do you need that while you're home?"

Sal was making up his cot after fixing Billy's. "Nah, I don't. But thanks for thinking about it." He picked up his toothbrush and headed out the door.

When Sal got back from the bathroom, Billy was already in bed, a sheet and light blanket tucked up to his chin. His tonsils hurt and he was feeling a little wheezy. He hoped he wasn't going to have an asthma attack.

The rust-colored shade of the pin-up lamp on the table between the cots cast an amber glow in the tiny room. Billy wondered if Sal would wear his underwear to bed, as he had. He opened his eyes just a crack as Sal took off his t-shirt and jeans. Then he realized that Sal wasn't wearing any shorts.

Billy had seen Sal a couple of times in the locker room at Joyland, but he was always shy about looking at the older boys. Now he watched as Sal turned and threw his clothes in a corner. His body was framed against the shadowy light, and the whiteness of his middle section contrasted with the tan of his stomach and legs. Sal's thing was big, with a lot of hair around it. The cross around his neck swayed back and forth, the gold gleaming in the soft light against the dark mat of his chest.

Sal yawned, scratched his stomach and carefully picked a piece of wool from his belly button. Then he climbed into his cot, reached over and turned off the light.

"Hey, Billy," Sal asked in a low voice. "You still awake?"

"Yes," Billy whispered.

"We're having a good time, huh? I'm glad you could come down with us."

"Yeah, me too."

"That was pretty funny, Angie winning every game of rummy tonight. She's real brainy. Always was. Smartest one in the family. But don't tell my old man."

"When Angie and I play cards alone, sometimes I win."

"Yeah, well, you're pretty smart, too, you know. You two quiz kids." There was silence, and then Sal said, "Sleep tight, see you tomorrow."

"OK, you too. Night, Sal."

But it took Billy a long time to fall asleep. He could hear the rhythmic sound of the small waves lapping against the shore a few yards away. The sky had cleared again, and there was a full moon visible through the small open window. It was a bomber's moon—he heard it called that in an English war movie—a moon giving off the kind of pale light that illuminates the entire landscape far below.

Billy thought about Prince and the sailor on the beach. He wondered if they patrolled all night, and if they had ever captured any Germans. Were U-boats really lurking somewhere out in the Sound?

The rise and fall of Sal's shadowy form a couple of feet away gradually changed into the slow movement of deep sleep. Billy thought of Sal, Sal with his new short hair, and the way he yawned and stretched in the pale light between the cots.

As he lay on his side, head propped up on the pillow and legs bent, he realized that his own labored breathing had eased. Billy relaxed and turned over on his back, knowing he'd be all right for the night.

Chapter 21: Alan

USN Training Station
Sampson, NY

July 11, 1943

Dear Laura:

Just a short note before lights out.

The train ride back today was okay. I didn't sleep much but that's probably better—don't want to lie awake until reveille at 5:30.

It was swell to see you this weekend.

I just heard that I'm being sent to radar school in Virginia. Guess that means I won't be home again for a while. It's a better opportunity, but a big surprise. That's the Navy for you. Even our CPO (Chief Petty Officer) Johnson didn't know.

With the good reports about the invasion of Sicily maybe everything will be over soon. At least in Europe. Then we can concentrate on the Japs. That's all the guys are talking about here tonight. I guess you've been hearing about it on the radio too.

I'll tell you more when I know where I'll be. But you can write to Sampson and they will forward my mail.

Love to you and the boys. Tell Nan and Belle I'll write them this week.

Alan

p.s. I'm glad you like the job and the gals at the Mutual, but I'll be happier when you don't have to work.

☙❧

July 14, 1943

Dear Billy:
 This postcard shows the big hall here at Sampson where we have shows and movies. Last night I saw a good musical, Star Spangled Rhythm. You'll like it when it shows downtown.
 Leaving here soon.
 Are you holding down the fort?
 Love, Dad

USN Fleet School
Cavalier Hotel
Virginia Beach, VA
    July 20, 1943

Dear Mother:
 Well, here I am learning radar in very fancy surroundings.
 Talk about a different atmosphere from Sampson! This place is a big resort hotel that was taken over by the Navy. There are tennis courts, a sunken garden, and a private beach. There's a stable, but that's been converted to sleeping quarters, and the swimming pool is now drained. It would cost a pretty penny to stay here, that's for sure.
 The train ride down from Sampson was long and hot. I fell asleep, and when I woke up it was dark, and I thought something was funny. Turned out we were on a boat crossing Chesapeake Bay, train and all!
 The food is wonderful, tho I miss your hamburg and kidney stew. A lot of the hotel people, including the cooks, are the same ones who were here before the war.
 I hope you are doing well and not tiring yourself out. Ha! I guess that's like talking the man in the moon! Just be careful and don't fall again.
 You asked about radar. It stands for "radio detecting and ranging." Think of it like an echo. The radio wave we send out bounces back, and we can tell the distance and the kind of object it's made contact with. It's a pretty amazing invention, and it's essential for the war effort, so I'm glad I was picked for the training.

Tell Belle I will write her soon. Is she shaping everyone up at Milton Bradley?!

Your loving son, Alan

৵৵

USN Fleet School
Cavalier Hotel
Virginia Beach, VA

July 23, 1943

Dear Laura:

I got two letters at once that you had sent to boot camp and the latest one, which came directly here. The mail service is better than I thought it would be. We get our mail twice a day, just like at Sampson.

This still feels like a country club, though they push us hard in the classes. Not as much drill as boot camp, tho.

I get to play baseball a bit, but there aren't teams like at Sampson. There isn't enough time, and men come and go. Remember the young guy Buzz I mentioned to you at Sampson? He just got sent here too, so at least I have one friend, but who knows where we'll end up.

I was able to get over to Norfolk the other day. You never saw so many sailors. In the bus station there are separate waiting rooms and toilets with signs "Colored Only." Separate water fountains too. That was a shock to see. I feel bad for the enlisted Negro troops I saw on the streets who are from up north and not used to seeing those words written down on signs.

How are Helen and Mae?

Any more news about your singing? Maybe you decided it would be too much to do.

How are the boys? What about Billy's tonsils? Maybe he should have them out if it would help with his asthma and colds in the winter.

Lights out any minute.

Love, Alan

p.s. xxx for you and Gary and Billy.

p.p.s. Tell Belle I'll write her soon. But remind her she can write too!

৵৵

July 28, 1943

Dear Angie:
Tell your mother thanks for the cookies! They arrived with only two broken. Everyone liked them and one of my buddies, Mario, said they were just like the kind his grandmother makes.

This is a postcard of the kind of ship I'll be on. An LST—Landing Ship, Tank.

Hi to everyone—and Sal too. Billy said he had a swell time with all of you at the shore.

Mr. Stewart

ঔ৵ও

LST Amphibious Training Base
Camp Bradford
Norfolk, Va.

August 7, 1943

Dear Mother:
Thank you for your ever-welcome letters.

Just a short note to let you know that things are going well in my new location.

We have begun our ship training in earnest here at Bradford. They even have a replica of an LST called the "USS Neversail," except that it's made out of wood, not steel. Some of our trainers are men who have been sent back from the Mediterranean. But that doesn't mean I'll be heading across the Atlantic. It's just that they have recent experience with the landings.

The LST is about 300 feet long and flat-bottomed. That's so we can land right on the beach. You've seen pictures of the big doors that open to unload tanks and troops and supplies down a ramp. It's pretty amazing.

I'll be up on the top deck in the radio shack, near the bridge and wheelhouse.

Well, Mother, I'll close for now.
Your loving son, Alan
p.s. Belle, I got your letter! I'll be writing.

ঔ৵ও

LST ATB *Camp Bradford*
Norfolk, Va

August 18, 1943

Dear Belle:

Finally your long-lost brother is answering you, tho I know you see my other letters.

Things are winding down here, and I think we'll be heading north over to Chicago and then to meet up with our ship—a new LST that hasn't even been launched yet. I hope I get some time in the Windy City. Then I think we head down the Mississippi.

I'm glad you like your job. Say, that's swell about your promotion. Suits your bossy nature—ha ha.

What's the story with this Abe fellow that Laura tells me about? She says he's real nice—a gentleman. Older, huh?

Thanks for all the games you bring home for the kids, Belle, and for all that you do for Laura. I don't have to mention Mother—what would she do without you?

Love, Alan

&<&

LST Crew 47100
Navy Pier
Chicago, Ill.

August 26, 1943

Dear Laura:

The train ride to Chicago wasn't too bad, but it was pretty crowded and sooty and hot. We arrived in Union Station early in the morning, even so the place was bustling.

Chicago is BIG! We're situated out on Navy Pier. I have a top bunk on an old ship that serves as a barracks.

The weather is warm but there is always a breeze from the lake. Now I know why it's called the Windy City. It must be awful cold in the winter here.

Next we'll be going up to the Great Lakes Naval Training Station for more practice. Then we'll board the ship at the shipyard in a town called Seneca.

We saw Bob Hope on the Pier. He was real funny. Also Carmen Cavallero at the Aragon Ballroom. I thought of you when the girl singer came on. She was OK, but not as good as you.

Speaking of which, I finally got your letter with the news about your weekend job. At least the Bridgeway Hotel draws a nicer class of people. I suppose Billy wants to go down and hear you! Do they still serve that lobster special on Fridays? Where do you sit when you're not at the bandstand?

I was sorry you weren't at home when I called on Thursday, but I know it was a good opportunity to earn extra pay at the Knights of Columbus dance.

Love to you and the boys, Alan

p.s. For you—I love you and miss you and think of you every night before I go to sleep. Keep putting that perfume on your letters.

ॐ∾⧈

Seneca, Ill.

Sept. 3, 1943

Dear Billy and Gary:

Here is a picture of the mighty Mississippi River. It's much bigger than the Connecticut.

We'll pass through St. Louis, Memphis and New Orleans on our way south.

Love, Dad xxxxx

ॐ∾⧈

USS LST 1717
c/o FPO
New York, NY

Sept. 13, 1943

Dear Mother:

I expect you may find some of this letter blacked out, or cut out. We've been told that from now on our letters will pass through the censor.

I'm sure Laura has given you this address. Send mail there until I tell you different. FPO stands for "Fleet Post Office."

We left Seneca on our spanking new ship and sailed down the Illinois River and then met the Mississippi north of St. Louis. Boy, they don't call it the "Big Muddy" for nothing. It's huge and brown and in places the widest river you can imagine. Sometimes when we passed close to shore people waved to us.

We sailed over to _____ and had what is called our shake-down cruise in _____.

Tell Belle I saw Louis Armstrong play. Was he great! I was so close to him that I could see the sweat pouring off him. He put on a swell show.

The news about the Allied landing in Italy is encouraging. I guess it was expected after Sicily, but it came fast.

I expect you've been doing a lot of canning from the garden. That was good of Mr. Mazzarella and the grandfather to help out so much.

Take care, Mother.

Your loving son, Alan

p.s. If you don't hear from me for awhile it's because I'm somewhere on the high seas.

৯৵৶৻

USS LST 1717
c/o FPO
New York, NY

September 15, 1943

Dear Laura:

I got letters from you, Nan, Billy and Belle before we shipped out from _____.

The trip through the Panama Canal was something I wouldn't have missed. It took us a whole day. It's an engineering wonder. It was hotter than Hades on deck, but most of us stayed up there anyway. Even with the bugs and the hot sun it was cooler there than below, where the temp. was 120.

Conductors along the canal in little locomotives worked with colored men who came on deck to help guide us through the different locks. They spoke Portuguese. Some of the natives close to us on shore had water jugs and stacks of bananas balanced on their heads. We had to wait in _____ to begin our passage through.

I'm pretty used to the ship now, tho it took some time to get my sea legs. The LST is different from other craft because of its flat bottom. There's an awful lot of rolling. Something called "slamming" happens when you ride a wave. It's hard to describe, but believe me, you know when you've crested one and then slide down the swell. Shudders and creaking and then a big slam onto the sea. It's worse at night because it's strongest in the aft (back) where our bunks are.

Billy, we have movie equipment on board and a lot of new Hollywood films. So I guess I'll still be seeing the same ones you have back in Springfield.

Well, I'll sign off. When I can, I'll let you know where we are. If you don't hear from me for a while, don't worry.

Love, Alan

p.s. Boys, be good to your mother and do what she says. Pay attention to Nan and Belle, too. Gary, that goes double for you. I heard you've been getting a little bit fresh with Nan--but I'm sure that can't be true.

p.p.s. Laura, I miss you and hope you feel the same way, even with all your new activities. It will be good when things are back to normal. I love you.

Chapter 22: Belle

Belle was settling nicely into the daily routine at the factory. After Eddie left for the service, she'd been officially promoted, and the women seemed to accept their new boss. She sensed they appreciated the time she'd taken to listen to their concerns during her training, and she was determined to be fair.

Still, there was no dearth of complaints, usually filtered through union channels. Gert, the steward, who worked in a neighboring department, often showed up during break time.

"Belle, you gotta talk to that new kid you just hired," Gert had told her yesterday. "Her flying fingers are messing up the quota. Loretta's fit to be tied."

Belle knew exactly what she was talking about. Some of the smaller games or educational kits were assembled off-line by individual workers. This meant that they controlled their own level of productivity. Every summer brought in a few high school and college students. Determined to make as much money as possible, they worked at an unusually fast clip—at least for the first few weeks of their short-term employment.

"That would be Susan," Belle said to Gert. "I'll talk to her."

Later in the day, while one of the stock boys was setting up a short run of Chutes and Ladders, Belle called the girl over to her desk.

"Hi, Susan," she said. "Just wanted to tell you that you've been doing swell. I was looking at the figures from a couple of days ago. How are you holding up?"

"Oh, I was tired at night after I started working alone," Susan replied. "But I did a real lot of games. I even..." She hesitated.

"Even what?" asked Belle.

"Well, I was going to say, I even did more than Loretta, I think. But don't get me wrong, I like her."

"Yeah, well, in fact I did want to mention that. What will happen now is that *my* boss, the big boss, Abe Sherman, will start to look at those figures and think, 'Hmm, wonder why that's happening?' Let me ask you a question. Next time you work on that dominoes game, say in a few weeks, think you can keep up that pace?"

"Gee, I hope so. Anyway, I won't have to do it all the time."

"No, you won't, but our Loretta over there will. Let me put it this way. This is a pretty good summer job. Better than selling *Colliers* or *The Saturday Evening Post* door-to-door, right?"

"Oh my gosh, yes. Those kids don't make that much."

"And a hell...a heck...of a lot better than picking tobacco, right?"

"Well, those kids make out OK, but it's really hard and you get so yucky by the end of the day. Ugh!"

"Well, then. You can still do pretty good by taking it a bit easier. I don't mean really slowing down. But do you want to spend the rest of the summer at that pace? 'Cause that will end up being what management will expect."

"Really?"

"Yeah, think about it. If that becomes the quota rate, guess what that means for Loretta here? She's probably been doing that job since she was younger than you are right now, and she's a good, reliable worker. But you can't keep up that pace all the time, and she's getting on in years, too."

"I know. Gee, she's kind of like my grandmother. Wow, she's been here all that time? I hadn't thought about it like that."

"No, of course not, and I understand. I'd have done the same. Anyway, you're doing real good."

"Thanks, Belle," Susan said. "Say, can I ask you something?"

"Sure, what?"

"Where did you get those wedgies? I was telling my mother about your outfits."

"These? Thanks. Bought 'em at Forbes & Wallace. I love their shoes. But try the basement. That's where I picked these up."

⁓

That night during dinner, Belle made an announcement. "Listen, I was thinking of inviting my friend Abe over to dinner."

That would be nice, dear," said Nan. "What night were you planning?"

"Well, how about Tuesday?"

"Tuesday! You mean, this Tuesday? That's tomorrow!"

"Yep. We were going to go out to dinner, and I thought, why not have him over instead?"

"But tomorrow I was planning on macaroni and cheese. You know what President Roosevelt said about no meat on Tuesdays."

"Sure, I know. And that's just fine. I didn't tell you ahead of time because I don't want you to plan anything special. Abe loves macaroni and cheese, and yours is the best. He's very easy to please."

"So, we're going to get to meet Abe." Laura smiled and winked at Billy.

"Is that your best boyfriend, Belle?" Gary asked.

"Well, it's not like he's one of a crowd of boyfriends, sweetie," Belle replied. "Yes, I guess you could call him that now."

"Oh, I'll have to do a thorough cleaning tomorrow," said Nan.

"Mother, you do a thorough cleaning every day. Relax."

"Nan, the house is spotless," Laura said. "We'll bring dessert."

"There's something I have to tell you, though," said Belle. She coughed nervously.

"What, Belle?" Billy asked.

"He's a...Well, he's a Yankees fan."

"What!" Laura gasped.

Even Billy, who didn't care much who won or lost, was shocked.

"Boo! Boo! He likes the Yankees! I'll tell Daddy!" Gary yelled.

"Look, I didn't even know until our second date. I said something about Ted Williams being a pilot in the Navy, and he said, 'Yeah, well Joe DiMaggio is in the Army,' and then it came out."

"Yes, but Ted is going into combat and DiMaggio is playing baseball on some service team," Laura said.

"Yeah, I know, but look, just don't hold it against him tomorrow, all right?"

Gary jumped up from the table and ran out to the hallway. They could hear him open the door of the front closet. Pretty soon he re-appeared, wearing his father's Red Sox warm-up jacket, sleeves dragging along the floor.

"I'm going to wear this the whole time he's here!"

"Good for you!" said Laura.

"Well, Abe sounds like a lovely man just the same," Nan said. "Yankees or no."

৯৯৫

Belle arrived at work the next morning to find the early birds buzzing about an accident that had happened during the night, late into the third shift. The man who operated the board cutter machine had lost a finger.

"Jesus, how did it happen?" asked Belle.

"Well, he's new," said Joanie. "None of us really know him that good. Remember when he was being trained? Little guy with glasses? Stan."

"Yeah, I know who he is," said Belle. "Not much of a talker. He takes care of his sick parents."

"That's him," said Joanie. "Anyway, you know how they've been rolling out those checkers and chess games one after the other? They needed a lot more boards, so they stuck him on the third shift, maybe before he should've been alone, I don't know. Anyway, next thing you know, I guess he lets out a yell and there's blood all over. They rushed him over to Springfield Hospital."

Belle walked over to Abe, who was already talking to Margaret, the experienced daytime operator. They were inspecting the shiny guillotine blade suspended a few inches above the black metal surface of the big cutter.

"For that to happen, he would've had to lean over and stick his hand in there," Margaret said. "The equipment's in good shape. I think he just got careless. Stan's a good guy, but kind of impatient in a quiet way, you know? He wanted to learn fast." There was no trace of any of the blood. In fact, the machine looked cleaner than usual, as though it had been thoroughly wiped down.

"Well, be careful," Abe said. He turned to Belle. "I'll let every-one know when I hear how he is."

"OK," Belle replied. In a quieter voice, she said, "Everything's set for dinner tonight."

At the morning break, some of the older workers recounted tales of past accidents, like when Walter Stokowski's leg was scalded by a spilled pail of hot glue. Another time, a stock boy named Carlisle was run over by a trucker backing up at the loading dock, and a few years back Mary Ryan stepped out of the freight elevator and broke her leg.

"Yeah, but that's 'cause she got plastered at the Christmas party," said Joanie. "And did anyone ever tell you what she was doing in that elevator? Ask Harry Slater. Then another year she walked into a glass partition down in the office. Drunk as a skunk. Cut her nose real bad. We said to her, 'Mary, next year stay home before you get yourself killed.'"

By lunchtime, things had settled back to normal. Belle raced down to Liggett's drugstore on Main Street and picked up a couple of cartons of Chesterfields, a bottle of Breck shampoo, and a new elastic bandage for Nan's bad leg. They'd been in short supply for the past year because of the overseas shipments to the troops, but the pharmacist, who knew Abe, had been able to get one on special order.

Back in the department, Belle sat in front of the fan near her desk and wolfed down a tuna sandwich and grape Kool-Aid. As the whistle signaled 12:40, she took a bite of her powdered donut left from the morning break and walked over to check the line. As the last girl sat down, Belle switched on the power.

Suddenly, there was a piercing scream from the direction of the cutting machine. *Oh my God*, Belle thought as she rushed over to Margaret. *She's hurt herself.* Margaret was sitting on her high bench, one hand cupped over her mouth, the other pointing a few feet away to the big tray on her machine just below the guillotine. On top of a new pile of Uncle Wiggly board papers lay a severed finger. The machine was still running, and the finger jiggled slightly with the vibration. A small line of blood from the neatly sliced end trickled down along the surface of the shiny paper.

"Margaret, what happened? Let me see your hands!" Belle cried.

"It's not me," Margaret managed to squawk. "It fell right out when I turned the switch back on. It's Stan's. It's Stan's finger."

Belle leaned over and looked at the finger. Now she could see that it was definitely a man's: A tuft of black hair was clearly visible on the second joint, and there was dirt under the nail.

"Holy shit!" said Joanie, who had rushed over, along with most of the others on the line. The three summer student workers clustered in the back, their faces white.

"Jesus," Belle muttered to Joanie. "Why didn't they tell us they hadn't found it?" She turned to Margaret. "Margaret, it's OK. Somebody take Margaret to the john. And somebody call the nurse."

Just then Abe rushed up. "What?...Oh, God. I just assumed they'd recovered it," he said when he spotted the finger.

"Yeah, me too," Belle replied. She shuddered. "Is it...well...too late to do anything with it?"

"I'm sure it is. I don't think they can attach something like that anyway, but it would be too late now for sure." He took out his handkerchief, leaned over, and placed it over the finger.

"Oh boy," said Belle. She turned around and said in a firm voice. "Margaret's all right. She just discovered Stan's finger. Not a pretty sight, poor Stan." She paused. "So. Everyone take a few minutes and don't worry about the lost time; we'll figure something out. OK, kids, let's break it up."

Later, as they waited for the uptown bus after work, Belle asked Abe what he'd done with the finger. "I gave it to Gladys, the nurse. But she said it was no use. I didn't think they could do that kind of thing. But I'll bet they'll be able to after the war. Hell of a lot of guys losing fingers, hands..."

"Funny you should say that. Today made me think of the war, too," Belle said. "I mean, it was just a finger, but imagine seeing that kind of thing every day? Guys blown up, body parts. I have a friend whose brother is out at Westover. He says you should see the planeloads of guys who come in from overseas. No legs, no arms, a lot of them blind, lost their hearing. They ship 'em off to hospitals all over the country."

"We're pretty insulated," Abe replied. "Makes complaining about gas rationing kind of ridiculous, doesn't it?" He patted her arm. "So, what is your Scots mother making for us tonight?"

Belle laughed. "Laddie," she said with a brogue, "that good old dish from the Highlands, macaroni and cheese. She's taking meat-less Tuesday real serious. But it'll be the best macaroni and cheese you ever had, I guarantee that."

They'd managed to leave the factory shortly after the whistle sounded. The breeze from the open windows felt good as the green and yellow city bus made its way up the long hill, passing the blocks of Armory buildings. "God, they never close," Belle said. "I wonder how many guns have come out of there since the war started?"

"Plenty. They have about 18,000 workers now. Round the clock. And more women than men."

As they walked down the driveway at home, she could see that everyone was down in the backyard. "Our victory garden," she explained to Abe. "Come on. They've been dying to meet you." She took Abe's arm as they strolled across the lawn toward the grape arbor.

"Hello," said Belle to the two Mazzarella men, who were doing something to reinforce the vines that now encircled the trellises, heavy with green grapes. "Abe, meet Salvatore Mazzarella and his dad...is it Giuseppe? We all call him Nonno. Abe Sherman."

They shook hands, Nonno carefully wiping his hands first on his pants. Then Abe and Mr. Mazzarella laughed. "We're already acquainted," Abe said. "Mr. Mazzarella here did some work on my house last year. Good job, too. Your son was with you, I believe."

"Yes, also Salvatore. He's in Army now."

"Ah," said Abe. "A nice fellow. Good-looking boy, too. Well, I guess I shouldn't say 'boy'."

"Yeah, Abe, you should," said Belle. "He's still a boy. A lot of them are. God damn boys, that's all." She gave a rueful laugh. "Sorry, folks. I guess I'm kind of worked up or something. So, Salvatore, how are the ladies doing with our garden?"

"Good, good. Comin' good." He followed Abe and Belle as they continued down to the back of the deep yard.

"Here he is, everyone," announced Belle. "Mr. Abe Sherman in person. Abe, this is my family. My mother...Laura, my sister-in-law...and these two guys here, Billy and Gary. I've already told you about *them*! And the guard dog frantically wagging her tail at you is Lucille."

Abe let Lucille sniff his fingers. "I've heard a lot about Billy," he said, shaking Billy's hand. "Gary, too." He enveloped Gary's little hand with his own. "And Laura." He shook her hand, appreciatively, Belle noticed. Laura was wearing a pretty yellow halter dress she'd bought the week before, and her long black hair shone in the last rays of the late afternoon sun.

"And it's a pleasure to meet you, Mrs. Stewart," Abe said, turning to Nan, who had been weeding the string beans. "Or is it Nan? I've heard that's what everyone calls you."

"Aye, Mr. Sherman, that's what they call me to my face," Nan replied. "The Lord knows what else I'm called behind my back!" Most of the time, Belle didn't even notice her mother's Scots burr, but she was always conscious of it when she heard her talk with a stranger. Funny, it always disconcerted her, as though Nan had suddenly become someone she didn't know.

"Say, some of those are vegetables I don't think I've ever seen," Abe said, pointing to the Mazzarella patch. Salvatore smiled and guided him over to look at his much larger garden. "Guess I'm getting a tour," Abe said over his shoulder. "Be right back."

"Well, you didn't tell us he was *that* nice-looking," Laura said to Belle in a low voice. "And what did you mean. 'old'? I was expecting some geezer." She studied Belle. "Are you feeling OK? You seem a bit preoccupied."

"We had an accident at work. New guy got his finger chopped off last night. Kind of unnerved me, I guess."

"How awful," Laura said.

Belle realized Billy and Gary were staring wide-eyed at her. "He's OK now. Just his finger, kids," she added, waving her pinky. "A work accident, that's all."

Just then they heard the screen door slam. They turned to see Mary Mazzarella and Angie making their way slowly down the porch. Angie was holding on to her mother, who was crying.

"Something's happened," Laura said. "Oh no, Sal..."

Belle's eyes met Billy's. She glanced over at Salvatore, who had noticed his wife and daughter as well. He dropped the zucchini he was holding and walked quickly toward them. Mary said something to him, and he raised his hands.

"What is it, Mary? Angie?" Belle ran up to them. "Is there news about Sal?"

"No, no, not Sal, *grazie a Dio*. Richie, Salvatore's friend." Mary began sobbing.

"Richie died," said Angie. "He was killed. His brother just called us." Then she began to cry, too.

"*Richie Reilly?* But he can't even be overseas yet!" Belle cried. "How could he be killed?" She looked at Mr. Mazzarella. He spoke rapidly to his wife, who explained to him in Italian.

"Killed in airplane here," he told them. "In Carolina. At training. Crashed in the water."

"I'm sorry," Abe said. He looked at Belle and Laura. "Do you know his family well?"

"We know him mostly because he hung around here a lot with Sal, Angie's brother," said Laura.

"They were best friends," Angie sobbed.

"He came to tell us goodbye before he left," Billy said. His voice was shaking. Laura put her arm around his shoulder.

"I went to school with his oldest sister," said Belle. "They're a big family, a close family. God damn it!" She leaned against Abe and kicked at the ground. "It's not fair, it's just not fair. God damn this war!"

Nan wiped her eyes with her apron. "I'm going to go inside and get things ready. We'll be eating in a wee while. Mr. Sherman... Abe...you come on in whenever you want and wash up if you like." She turned to Mrs. Mazzarella. "Mary, you all come in, too. There's plenty for everyone. Or bring what you have over here and we'll all be together."

Nan took Gary by the hand. "Gary, come in with me and help me finish setting the table. That's a good boy." With Lucille trotting along behind, they walked up the porch and into the house, leaving the others standing in silence next to the victory garden.

Chapter 23: Laura

The insistent ringing of the telephone—one long, one short, their party line signal—startled Laura as she lay reading in bed. She put down Ben Ames Williams' latest bestseller, *Leave Her to Heaven*, and rushed out into the hallway. She couldn't imagine who'd be calling at this hour.

"Hi, kid!"

"Ceil!" Laura was somewhat relieved to hear her sister's voice. Still…"Anything wrong?"

"No, sorry, I should have said that right away. Hope I didn't get you out of bed. I thought if I waited long enough I wouldn't have the phone company on my tail." Customers were discouraged from using the telephone at night in case of a wartime emergency.

"I was thinking about Alan, but I couldn't imagine he'd be calling," Laura replied.

"Where is he now?"

"We think he's already left San Francisco. They went through the Canal and then up the West Coast. He's at sea, I'm sure."

"Gee, I didn't mean to upset you."

"No, no, it's good to hear from you. Wait, let me untangle this cord and take the phone into the other room. Don't want to wake Billy and Gary." Laura padded into the darkened kitchen. As she carefully made her way to a chair, she suddenly felt something sticky under her left foot.

"Ugh!"

"What happened?" asked Ceil.

"I just got tangled up in the flypaper. A strip must have fallen from the light fixture. Now it's stuck to my foot, probably with a bunch of dead flies. Anyway, how's everyone?"

"Well, Peter and the kids are OK. He's been kind of moody, though. I know it bothers him about his bum leg keeping him out of the service. You should see the cold looks we get sometimes, like when we're out in a restaurant. It's funny. After he gets up and limps off, they act ashamed and look the other way." Peter had been badly injured in a fall from a horse years ago, right after their marriage.

"I know. Everyone wonders about a few guys at the office."

"Actually, there is some news. Not too serious, I think, but Dad hasn't been feeling so hot. Mother called. It's his angina again. You might want to call or come on down for the day."

"I was thinking of that. It'd have to be on the weekend. Maybe we'll take the train. Don't think the tires will hold out on the car, plus the gas."

"I know, isn't it awful? We've got my little Studebaker on blocks and I hardly ever get to drive Peter's Buick. So, how's the job? Or, I guess I should say, jobs?"

"Isn't it something? I never thought I'd be singing again, at least while the kids were this young."

"And the guys in the band are behaving themselves? Remember that trumpet player?"

Laura laughed. "Oh, they're fine. I guess the difference is that I'm not single anymore."

"He wasn't either, as I recall, and that didn't stop anyone."

"And the job at the Mutual is all right," she continued, ignoring Ceil's remark. "Nice working conditions and I like the other girls and it's fun to get dressed up again. I didn't realize I'd missed that."

"And the kids?"

"Good, except Billy'll have to have his tonsils out one of these days. Probably before school starts. I need to get busy on that. He was upset today. We went to a funeral for one of the neighborhood boys."

"You took him to a funeral?"

"I know, Mother wouldn't approve. Actually, Billy's the only reason I went. You know how old he's always been for his age. He just understands things. Richie was a kid who used to hang around the yard with the fellow next door—Sal—who's always been close to Billy."

"Sal, he's the good-looking Italian kid?"

"Yes, he's in the Army now, probably on his way to Europe."

"Where was the friend killed?"

"Down off the coast from Parris Island. Not overseas or any-thing. He was being transported somewhere down South. He'd just finished basic training. He was from a family of Marines. Now his younger brother can hardly wait to enlist, and it'll probably kill his mother. It made me think of Gary and Billy and how I'd be with them in the service."

"Speaking of which, things OK with you and Alan?"

"Well, yes. I mean, we write and everything. He seemed kind of distant the one time he was home. Something was different. Maybe I was, too." She didn't add that in a way she was relieved when he left at the end of the weekend, and that she'd sensed he felt the same way. "I guess it's the war or something."

"He's OK?"

"He looked fine. He'd hardly been drinking before he left."

"That's good to hear. He really cares for you, you know."

"I know that," Laura replied. "So," she said. "Enough of me. How's things with you?"

They talked a while longer and made a tentative plan for the boys and her to spend the day in West Hartford the following weekend. After hanging up, Laura put the phone back in its cradle in the hallway and sat for a while. She was glad Ceil had called. They didn't have long talks anymore, but she could still say just about anything to her sister.

Wide awake, she returned to the kitchen for a glass of milk. It was a warm night, and she felt cooler sitting in the dark near the screened window. She thought again about the graveside service they'd attended earlier in the day.

Laura hadn't planned on going to Richie's funeral, but she'd sensed that Billy was more upset about his death than he was letting on. After they'd heard details about the airplane accident—Richie had died from drowning, not from the impact of the take-off crash—Billy had told her about a dream he'd had. "Ma, it was just like what happened. There was no airplane, but Richie was yelling for help in the water." Then he told her that Sal and Alan were in the dream as well.

"What about them?"

"Oh, they could swim."

"Were you in the dream, too?"

"Well, kind of. You know sometimes how when you dream you're sort of there but mostly watching?"

When he asked her if he could attend the service with Angie and her family, Laura reluctantly agreed. Then she decided she wanted to be with him. "Tell you what. If I can get extra time off before lunch, what if we just go to the cemetery after they've finished at the funeral parlor and church? You'll still get to see the military ceremony and all."

Laura and Billy and Nan arrived at the entrance to St. Michael's Cemetery just as the hearse was making its way through the main gate. Gary had been happy to stay at home in the backyard, bumping along with a watering can behind Nonno as he pruned and weeded the garden.

Even with Nan's slow pace—she'd told Laura she had a corn on her big toe—they kept up easily with the procession of cars that wound slowly around to a tented area among the newer section of graves. A large mound of fresh earth next to the open plot rose like a neat brown pyramid, in rich contrast to the emerald green of the lush grass surrounding it.

Laura had never been to a military funeral. She was surprised at the number of young men in uniform, none of whom she recognized as local boys. They were probably from the base at Westover. Six were serving as pallbearers, and seven took their places a short distance away, next to a carefully arranged stack of rifles. A serviceman stood at attention off to the side, a bugle in his white-gloved hand.

The service progressed, a military chaplain sharing words with a priest Laura recognized as none other than Bishop O'Leary himself, his presence, she supposed, evidence of the Reilly family's close connection to the Church. She remembered that one of the older girls had become a nun. probably one of the several young women in black habits standing in the back row, at the edge of the dark green canopy.

An initial rifle shot pierced the air, intensifying the incessant chatter of a flock of blue jays as they fled skywards from their perches in the stately oaks and elms. One of the young soldiers raised a trumpet to his lips.

As the plaintive notes of "Taps" began, Laura studied the faces of the mourners on the far side of Richie's flag-covered casket. Salvatore Mazzarella, his expression even more inscrutable than usual, looked uncomfortable but rather handsome and distinguished in his navy blue suit. Angie, holding one of her mother's flowered handkerchiefs, gave Laura a wan smile. Mary, fingering the large cross she always wore, sobbed quietly. The many members of the Reilly family bore expressions ranging from red-eyed grief to stoic acceptance. *Maybe their religion really sustains them*, Laura thought. She'd never quite understood that.

After two soldiers carefully folded the flag, the pallbearer nearest Richie's mother held it out in front of her and said loudly in a flat, boyish voice, "On behalf of the President of the United States, the Commandant of the Marine Corps, and a grateful nation, please accept this flag as a symbol of our appreciation for your loved one's service to Country and Corps."

Mrs. Reilly, her face expressionless, took the flag and, without looking sideways, passed it to her husband. He clutched it awkwardly in front of him and then smartly saluted the young soldier.

After a few final words from the two clergy, the bearers lifted the casket and slowly lowered it into the ground. Laura glanced down at Billy, who was staring at the gleaming mahogany top and biting his lip. Was he thinking of his father? She wondered. Sal? She stroked the back of his neck, then reached beyond him and patted Nan, brushing away a ladybug from her shoulder. Mrs. Reilly dropped a rose into the grave, then took her son Walt's arm and turned away. The service was over.

Now, sitting alone in the dark kitchen, Laura shivered and tried to put the funeral out of her mind. She finished her milk and carefully dropped the sticky wad of flypaper into the wastebasket under the sink.

Back in the bedroom, she picked up *Leave Her to Heaven* and tried to lose herself in the exploits of the novel's deranged main character. Much as she was enjoying reading about Ellen Berent's maniacal jealousy and wicked deeds, tonight her own life was interfering with evil Ellen's. She couldn't concentrate. She checked the setting on her alarm clock again and turned out the light.

Richie's senseless, unexpected death was making her think about Alan. Right now he was sailing further into the Pacific, somewhere, as the newscasters liked to say, "between the Aleutians and New Guinea." But, unlike poor Richie and his freak plane crash in Carolina, Alan would really be in harm's way, and soon—and who knew for how long?

President Roosevelt had a lot to say about Italy and the European operation in his Fireside Chat tonight--but not that much about what was happening on the other side of the world. How had he put it?...*We are still far from our objective in the war against Japan.*

What if Alan didn't return for years? She thought about the awkwardness she'd sensed when he was home a few weeks ago. Would the kids even remember him? Billy, yes, though Laura was all too aware how they already didn't get along. She was afraid that would only get worse as Billy got older. And Gary needed his father. She was already noticing some behavior problems. Or maybe he was just naturally fresh and sassy, the opposite of how she remembered Billy at that age. Billy had always been a serious little boy. She reminded herself not to compare her two sons.

It still felt muggy in the bedroom. She kicked off her sheet and thought about Ceil's trumpet player remark. Benny Jordan hadn't crossed her mind for years, not until recently, not until she'd heard Ray Jardine for the first time. Funny how they both played the trumpet. Even looked a bit alike, though Benny had been lots younger. She suddenly realized what she was thinking. *Why am I even putting those two names together? I'm not even attracted to Ray Jardine. Am I?* She nearly sat up in bed.

What she'd never told Ceil, or anyone, was that she'd have gotten serious with Benny in a minute, wife or not, if he'd been persistent. In fact, she almost did, one night when they had both stayed late to practice for a trumpet and vocal arrangement of the song *Sophisticated Lady*. But she hadn't really dated Benny, except for a sandwich or two, and that was that, despite what Ceil thought.

She fluffed her pillow and turned on her side. Then she found herself humming the Duke Ellington tune and thinking that it would work really well as a duet with Ray.

This time she did sit up. She got out of bed again, walked into the bathroom and turned on the bright light. She squinted and glanced at herself in the mirror, startled at the somewhat wild and scared face that stared back. She pulled at the skin under her eyes... Bags for sure if she didn't get some sleep.

Why did she always run and stare at herself in the mirror when she was upset? Now she was wide awake, too anxious to sleep. She washed her hands and splashed some cold water on her face.

Back in her room, she picked up her book again, but she still wasn't in the mood to read about other people's mixed-up lives.

Instead, she picked up the pretty, flowered stationery kit Belle had brought her last Friday as a payday present.

Dear Alan, she began, *It's hot as Hades here, and it's late, and I miss you, and I can't sleep...*"

Chapter 24: Alan

LST 1717 began its slow trek across the Pacific at sundown, sailing from Fort Mason in San Francisco Bay, past Alcatraz Island, and under the Golden Gate. Alan watched until the burnished silhouette of the bridge disappeared from view against the pale sky of early evening. Thoughts of the family back home in Springfield were tempered by the excitement he'd been feeling ever since they'd begun the long cruise down the Mississippi a few weeks earlier..

"Buzz, I can't believe all we've seen," he said one night as they waited in the crew chow line. Alan was glad his young friend had ended up on the same ship. He was a good kid and still moist behind his Mid-Western ears, despite his newly acquired vocabulary.

"Yeah, well that's what they promised, to see the friggin' world. 'Course it'd be nicer if there wasn't a good chance our asses'll be blown out of the water."

Ever since leaving San Francisco, they'd been aware of the possibility of an enemy attack. Everyone's fears were heightened by the strict shipboard rules, including a ban on all lights on deck after dark, even cigarettes. At this point in the war, however, the probability of a Japanese vessel this close to the American mainland had diminished. That would change the further they sailed into the Pacific.

During the shakedown cruise in the Gulf of Mexico, they were always on the lookout for German U-boats, where the threat, even near the Florida beaches, was still real. The little mock invasion they'd staged of a small island near Panama City, however, hadn't seemed real at all. It was a game, a dangerous one, perhaps, but not like actual combat.

"Hey, remember when we stormed that dummied-up beachhead in the Gulf?" Alan asked.

"Christ, that was friggin' pathetic," said Buzz. "The little kids in my hick town could have done better. I'll never forget Ryan screaming about the jellyfish that stung him. That jerk still swears they planted those in the water." He laughed. "And what about Petrone, knocking his own tooth out with his rifle? Shit!"

"Hey, give it a rest, Buzz! Quit talkin' up there, and move it!" yelled Malone, a radioman from Detroit.

"Aw, shove it where the sun don't shine, Malone!" Buzz gave him the finger and they all laughed.

Alan took his plate of ham croquettes, boiled potatoes and peas from the lackadaisical sailor dishing them out. Shuffling forward with the other men, he picked up a piece of apple pie and a container of milk and maneuvered his way carefully to the ladder leading below.

Navigating a full tray from the galley to the mess hall was still a challenge. In the calmest of seas, the LST was unpredictable, and this vessel, though brand new, was no exception. Alan had also learned to lower his head and bend his knees when he walked up and down the steep steps anywhere on the ship. Like his sleeping bunk, the passageways weren't meant for anyone over six feet tall.

Buzz, skinny and half a foot shorter, had already scrambled down the ladder with his dinner and staked out two places at one of the long narrow mess tables. "Wonder how long it'll take us to get to Honolulu?" he asked, moving aside so that Alan could squeeze onto the narrow bench.

"Don't know exactly. They don't tell us much, even up in the shack." The croquettes tasted pretty good, even if they were made from the baked ham they'd been served a few nights ago. "But that's not a sure destination anyway, is it?"

"No, but there's not much else between California and the fightin'," Buzz replied. "I figure wherever we end up, we gotta pass through Pearl. They say everybody does."

Pearl Harbor. Waikiki. Diamond Head. Alan had been thinking recently of the Viewmaster slides of Hawaii Billy had been so excited to get for his birthday a few months ago. He was surprised that a lot of the guys weren't interested in the places they were passing through or even the more exotic locales where they might eventually end up.

Alan felt lucky to catch a glimpse of whatever he could when he was topside manning the radar on the bridge. He loved being in the shack on the upper deck. The guys on the main deck were topside a lot, too, but they worked with the greasy guns. Those in the engineering section, known as "the black gang" because of the dirt and grime that covered their clothes and bodies, were always below in the engine rooms.

Though he'd made friends with several of the crew, he and Buzz pretty much stuck together. They both agreed that their leader, Lieutenant Commander Salisbury, was a good guy, stern but fair. The seven other officers were OK, too, except for a couple of CPOs who made it all too clear that their Chief Petty Officer status set them apart from the enlisted men. It was one thing that they ate and slept away from the crew, but Alan felt the ship was too small for some of the officers' virtual disregard of them except when orders were being given.

He wondered how things were on a really big ship, like the carrier Hornet. The LST was nearly as long as a football field, but a carrier was three times that length and four times as wide. And he'd heard the crew consisted of nearly 3,500 men.

"I pulled guard duty," Alan remarked as he took a forkful of apple pie.

"Nice night for it, if it's anything like yesterday," said the sailor next to him, a kid named Pete from Iowa City. "The sky was full of stars. Pretty. And the ocean was real calm. It's the first night no one up there puked."

Along with tons of supplies and a few jeeps and trucks, LST 1717 and the three other ships in the convoy were transporting a battalion of Marines fresh out of camp. Some bunked below on cots and bags in the large tank storage area, but it was hot down there. Most slept under a Landing Craft mounted on a timber platform on the crowded weather deck.

It was approaching dusk as Alan made his way to the bow of the ship. Several groups of Marines were getting in a few games of poker before the sun dropped into the Pacific. Others were writing letters that wouldn't get posted for days, maybe weeks. A few were engrossed in pocket novels, and one or two appeared to be making entries in diaries and journals.

This was Alan's favorite time of day. Ever since they'd sailed down the Mississippi, he'd felt a sense of peace and calmness as water and sky and air held still, suspended for just a brief time as darkness came on. This was the hour his mother called "the gloaming," but he'd never really understood the childhood memory of

Scotland that she described—the magical coming together of heather and moor and steely North Sea sky. Now he did.

Here in the vast Pacific, the sunsets were truly spectacular, bold swaths of purple and yellow and crimson against a vast grayness above the calm sea, itself a dazzling pattern of green, indigo, and black. Tonight, a deep pink hue, the color of the flamingos they'd seen on the shore of Lake Gatun in the Panama Canal, blanketed the horizon.

Alan watched one of the other LSTs a mile or so away turn from silver to gray and then disappear altogether from view. Far off he could see the lead ship in the small convoy outlined against the horizon, like one of Gary's little bathtub toys, before it too blended into the fast-approaching darkness.

Alan circled the supports of the big forward guns. He mounted the ladder to the 40mm twin placement and looked back down the length of the ship to make sure no lights were visible. The crew had been well trained in this regard. It was their passengers they had to worry about. They'd all been drilled about the likelihood of the transport troops trying to sneak a cigarette during the night.

As he began to make his way back down the port side, he noticed someone alone, hidden almost, against the starboard exhaust stack.

"Nice night," Alan remarked as he walked up to the crouching man. He was a Marine and, as Alan noted when he raised his head, very young. He seemed startled by Alan's presence.

"Yeah, I guess," he said in a low, flat voice.

"I wouldn't get too close to the edge there," Alan said. "We could have a sudden swell. Don't want to lose you, fella." He was about to say "soldier" before he remembered that the crew had been coached that a Marine was a Marine. Soldiers were in the Army.

The Marine glanced toward the water and shrugged. "Yeah," he said. Then he laughed.

"Are you OK?"

"Sure," he replied. He turned away and began to cry, quietly at first, then with convulsive sobs.

Alan knelt down. "Come on, take it easy. What's up?"

"Nothing, it's OK." The young Marine laughed loudly again, and wiped his eyes and nose. "Jeez, I feel embarrassed." He paused and then said in a barely audible voice, "I was just thinking that water don't look so bad."

"Get up and walk with me," Alan said. "I need to check the other side."

"That's OK, I'm OK."

"Come on, up." He took the boy by the arm. "You can't stay here."

They made their way down the port side. "Where are you from?" Alan asked.

"Hartford. Hartford, Connecticut."

"No fooling? Say, that's a coincidence. I'm from Springfield. Alan Stewart."

"Bill. Bill Jones."

"That's my son's name. We call him Billy."

"Well, yeah, that's what my family calls me, and..." He started to cry again. "I'm sorry."

"Don't apologize. What were you saying?"

"I was going to say 'That's what Carol, my wife, calls me.' Well, she's my family, too, but we haven't been married that long."

"You're missing her, is that it?"

"Well, kind of more than that. Guess she's not missing me. I got one of them letters." He patted the pocket of his shirt.

"Want to talk about it?"

"I got it just before we boarded. I didn't tell anybody. Nobody to tell." He paused and then began. "We both graduated from high school in the spring. We got married right away." Then he added, "Had to." He looked at Alan. "I was glad, 'cause I wanted to start a family but Carol, she wanted to work for a while." He took a deep breath. "Now she tells me she lost the baby and she started a new job. You know Pratt and Whitney? The Aircraft?" Alan nodded. He had friends who took the bus to East Hartford every day to work at the huge defense plant.

"I'm sorry," Alan said. "About the baby. But look, you're both young. There'll be more chances."

"Nah, it's not like that," Bill said. "Even before, something was wrong. I wasn't hearing from her when I was at Parris. Then when I went home before I got my orders it was, well, different."

Alan nodded. "Like, you weren't talking to each other the same? Not too much to say?"

"Yeah, like that. Anyways, the night before we came on board in San Francisco, I got this second letter. She met some guy, no one I know—so she says—but she don't say his name or nothing. She says she wants out."

They stopped under the deck house at the aft end of the ship and lowered their voices. Most of the Marines on deck had already settled down for the night. Alan wondered if it was still as hot down in the crew's berth area as it had been the past few days.

"It's that darned job she got. I knew this would happen. I knew it."

"Maybe it's the job, but maybe you didn't really know each other."

"Christ, we went through school together."

"I know, but people change. They change a lot right after high school, but sometimes they keep changing even after that."

"Yeah, but I had big plans. I want to get some schooling after this. You know, being a vet you can get government money. For her and the kid and all."

"Me, too. I do, too."

"You do?" Bill seemed surprised.

"Yes." Alan laughed. "I'm a lot older than you, but I didn't get past high school and I want to do something else when I get out, too."

"Like what?"

"I don't know. I was a boss, I guess you'd say, at Westinghouse, but, well, it's not that great. Don't know, really. But I'm looking forward to going to college now. Didn't think I'd want to go back to school. But you know what? Seeing all these new places, it's kind of made me want to learn more."

"Yeah, I know. When we came west on the train, I couldn't believe all the states we went through. The prairie, the Rockies. And then San Francisco. Man!" Bill's face had become animated. "Even places you never heard of had something.. Once we stopped at this little town in Nebraska, North Platte, where all these ladies served us food and stuff. I never knew there were that many people who cared about us."

"I've heard of North Platte. The canteen, right?"

"Yeah, it's famous, I guess, but I never heard of it before."

"Bill, look, I have to go up to the bridge and check stuff. Are you going to be OK?"

"Yeah, yeah, I am. Don't worry about back there. I mean it." He nodded toward the aft end. "But don't tell anyone, OK? I feel really dumb."

"I won't, don't worry. But we're going to talk again, right?"

"Yeah, I hope. Guess I needed to. Thanks...Alan. I'm OK."

"It was good to talk to you, Bill." Alan started up the bridge ladder. "Oh, hey, I know someone who just finished at Parris. A kid in our neighborhood. Richard Reilly. Everyone calls him Richie. Know him by any chance?"

"Nah, can't say I do, and I'd remember that name 'cause I have a friend named Reilly in Hartford. But that's a big place, Parris, you know?"

Before getting off duty at midnight, Alan did a final turn around the deck. The evening was clear and the stars were shining with a special brilliance. Had he just never noticed them back in Springfield, or was the sky really different on this side of the world? Everything seemed larger than life—brighter stars, bigger clouds, an oversized yellow moon that looked like a pasted backdrop against the blackness of the night sky. Billy would probably know the names of the constellations overhead. He'd been studying them in school last year.

Looking aft, Alan thought he could make out in the moonlight the dim shape of the fourth LST, the last one in the convoy. Small pockets of white foam rose and ebbed from the wake of his own ship, and there was an occasional sparkle of phosphorous from a larger wave as it splashed high in the air. He decided that he'd come back up with his pillow and sheet and sleep on deck for the rest of the night.

❧ ❦

In the days that followed, Alan talked to Bill Jones a few more times. He'd perked up considerably since their initial conversation. He no longer talked about getting a new letter from his wife that would indicate that everything was OK again. Maybe he was just trying to reconcile himself to the situation, but Alan sensed that their conversation had helped. He hoped so. Bill was a nice kid, too young to feel the way he did. There would be plenty of time for that later on.

Except for one afternoon patch of stormy weather that had most of the Marines and a few of the crew heaving again, the weather continued calm and sunny. Alan wrote a lot of letters. He wondered how many would be waiting for him when they reached port, though he'd stopped thinking of Laura and the boys and Nan and Belle as much as he had during boot camp. He became aware of this one day when it took him longer than usual to figure out what time it would be back in Springfield.

He did find himself wondering about Lucille, well up in years now. A lot of the guys, especially the really young ones, talked about the pets they'd left at home. He hoped she'd be waiting for him when it was all over.

From his regular shifts manning the radar equipment, adjacent to the radio shack and its incoming messages, he knew for sure now that they were heading to Honolulu. He was glad he'd bought an old travel book about the Hawaiian Islands in San Francisco, since it looked like they'd be at Pearl Harbor for at least a couple of weeks. There was something wrong with one of the guns, as well as engine work that needed to be taken care of.

Early one morning as he arrived on the bridge, the radar man on duty, Stan, said, "Take a look port side."

Far off on the horizon a tiny, shimmering dark mass was just visible. "Wow, is that it?" Alan asked. He felt like an explorer on the deck of an old sailing vessel. "You going to yell '*land ahoy,*' Stan?"

"Yeah, you got it. That'd go over big with our friendly CPO over there. By the way, what you're looking at is the island of Maui. Pearl's on Oahu." Suddenly, above them, two patrol planes, P-3 Orions, swooped past, their wings glinting in the sunlight.

"Hey, we're even getting the escort treatment," Stan said. "Glad they're ours."

Within an hour they could clearly make out the dark rise of the island. They sailed past Maui before entering the Kaiwi Channel, which separated yet another island, Molokai, from Oahu. Alan didn't expect to see so many mountains. They rose tall and densely green, with misty clouds shrouding the purple-hued peaks. This was a Hawaii he'd never seen in travel posters or at the movies.

Molokai, he'd read, was where Father Damien established the leper colony, still in operation, though on a smaller scale. Alan seemed to know more about the history of the islands than anyone else on the bridge, so he provided a fair amount of commentary as they made their way toward Honolulu.

By noon they had a clear view of Diamond Head on the starboard side. "Jeez, you'd know it anywhere!" Stan said. "It's like a scooped out mountain."

"It's a volcano. Extinct now," Alan explained.

As they made their way along the coast toward the entrance to Pearl Harbor, they passed, off in the distance, the pink shell of the Royal Hawaiian Hotel on Waikiki Beach.

"Hey, I heard they turned that into a military hotel," Stan said. "Think we can wangle a room?"

"Yeah, fat chance. Maybe the captain and the officers," Alan replied.

The water became choppy as they approached shore. They moored at Hickam Field to unload the Marines and the trucks and jeeps, the ship bumping and banging the dock as the two doors of the main exit were slowly cranked open and the ramp extended. Alan suddenly realized that he wouldn't be seeing Bill again.

"Stan, if I get the OK, could you cover for me while I go to the bow to see one of the guys off?"

By the time he walked the length of the ship, some of the Marines were already making their way down the wide ramp that spanned the entire width of the gaping bow of the ship. Bill, laden down with his gear, was looking over his shoulder as he tromped down the steel ramp.

"Bill! Bill Jones!" Alan cried.

Bill spotted Alan, who was waving from one of the gun turrets, and raised his fist in a thumbs-up salute. "Thanks, Alan," he yelled. "See ya back in New England!"

They pulled up anchor, heading toward Pearl Harbor a few miles away. As they approached the entrance, Alan noticed small tugs chugging toward both sides of the harbor. Chief Petty Officer Sloan, standing next to him on the bridge, remarked, "They're clearing the anti-sub nets for us. Those midget Jap babies squirm in anywhere."

As soon as the ship passed through the surprisingly narrow inlet into the protected bay, the water became totally calm. Ahead of them on the port side were the mooring docks of Ford Island, dubbed "battleship row." Several battered masts and funnels still rose at awkward angles above the water, a reminder of the devastation of 17 months ago.

CPO Sloan pointed and said, "That's where the Arizona lies. If we were just a bit closer, you could see it. It's only a few feet below the surface."

The air was warm and humid, though there was a breeze blowing across the deck. An announcement blared from the loudspeakers calling all men back to their posts to prepare to anchor in the Kewalo Basin.

Alan walked back inside the shack. It was hard for him to believe that he had just sailed into Pearl Harbor. This was where the war had begun, at least for America. He thought back to the moment they'd heard about the attack, just after dinner on a Sunday afternoon. Roosevelt's declaration of war came the next day.

As he sat down in his chair at the radar screen, Alan felt a sudden urge to talk to the family back in Springfield. He wanted to tell them all, but especially Billy, what it was like to sail past Battleship Row and the sunken Arizona and the site of all the explosions and fires they'd seen in the movie newsreels not so long ago. Pearl Harbor. For the first time, he understood how far from home he really was.

Chapter 25: Billy

"Yoo hoo! Yoo hoo!" Billy and Angie looked up from the movie magazines they were reading in the swing chairs down beyond the arbor. From the second floor porch, Nan, busy hanging clothes to dry, was yelling and pointing at the sky. "Kiddies, up there! The dirigible! Where's Gary?"

Above Mrs. Herrmann's house, high in the blue August sky, the silver Goodyear blimp hung in the air like a giant oblong balloon, its movement barely perceptible against the backdrop of puffy white clouds. A small box-like compartment was visible on the blimp's underside.

"Gary's over at that new kid's house," Billy yelled. "They'll see it from there."

"Gee, it's beautiful," Angie said. "I'd like to take a ride in one of those."

"Not me," said Billy. "My grandmother told me about one that crashed and burned just when it was landing. The Hindenburg. It was coming from Germany."

"Maybe they were spying or something."

"Maybe, but it was a long time before the war. Anyway, it happened in New Jersey. Why would anyone be spying in New Jersey?"

"'Cause it's on the coast. Remember last year when they caught those saboteurs down on Long Island?"

"Oh yeah, I forgot," Billy said. Secretly, Billy remembered that incident very well. He'd been scared at the time that German paratroopers were going to land next in Springfield and blow up the Armory and Westover Field. He'd thought of them again a few weeks ago at the beach, even with Sal sleeping right next to him.

"Anything good in that magazine?" he asked, changing the subject.

"This one has some pictures of Alan Ladd," Angie replied. "He's nice-looking but I read that he's really short, like about five feet tall or something. They make him stand on a box when he kisses the girl."

Billy moved over and sat next to Angie. Her issue of *Photoplay* was opened to a page with an ad captioned, *"For the girl with the small bust."* It showed a young woman in one picture woefully gazing down at her droopy blouse. In the next photo, after applying a special cream, she was smiling confidently at her happy boyfriend, her breasts full and perky under her angora sweater.

"Why do they say 'bust'"? Billy asked.

"I don't know exactly," Angie replied. "Maybe because if they're big you kind of bust through your clothes. My Aunt Rosa says I don't have to worry about being small because big ones run in the family."

Billy tended to agree with Angie. Mrs. Mazzarella's were very large, and they jiggled, especially early in the morning when she came out onto the porch in her housecoat.

"Hey, look at this here ad," Angie said. A sophisticated woman in a strapless evening dress was gazing provocatively over her shoulder. The caption under the illustration of a large bottle in the foreground read, *"She's Wearing 'Follow Me'...The New French Toilet Water."*

"That's funny...'toilet' water," said Billy.

"Yeah," replied Angie. "She should be saying, *"Don't follow me ...I just fell in the toilet and, boy, do I stink!"*

They watched as Nan continued to hang the wash, working the pulley until the line of drying clothes extended across the yard, all the way to the big oak tree on the other end of the rope. Billy glanced at Angie in embarrassment as a few pairs of his briefs, flapping in the breeze, slowly made their way high in the air to the center of the line.

"*I see London, I see France, I see Billy's underpants,*" Angie chanted in a singsong voice. "Hey, look at that," she said, pointing to a large pink corset with metal flaps that dwarfed Gary's Roy Rogers polo shirt hanging next to it.

"That's Nan's," Billy said. "She doesn't wear it every day. She says it pinches and makes her out of breath."

"Did you ever put on a jockstrap?" asked Angie.

Billy hesitated. "No, but my dad has one. Why?"

"Just wondering. Sal has one, too. One time I saw him wearing it. It looked real funny."

"It's for when you get older," Billy said. "The real name is athletic supporter. It holds everything up." He blushed, and then they both giggled.

Billy looked over at the grape arbor, where Nonno and his friend Mr. Gionfriddo were sitting at the card table playing Briscola, or Brisk for short. He wondered if they'd noticed his underwear and Nan's corset, too, but they seemed engrossed in their game. Angie had taught him Brisk last summer, using the special set of Italian cards with cups, batons, swords, and coins as the suit symbols. You could also play with a regular deck if you took out the joker and the eights, nines and tens.

"'Member when Nonno cut all the vines down last year?" Billy asked.

"Yeah, you thought they were all dead. Now look at 'em." The leaves were so plentiful you could hardly see between the thick vines that wound around the sturdy twine extending from the ground to the top of the arbor. The clumps of juicy purple grapes were almost ready for the fall harvest.

Angie turned the page of the magazine to an illustration of a perplexed-looking young woman standing next to her military husband. The caption of the ad read, "*How ignorance and false modesty may ruin a young wife's happiness. Use Zonite, the liquid solution for newer feminine hygiene.*"

"Is that some kind of perfume, too?" Billy asked.

"Well, kind of. It's for certain smells. Women have particular needs," Angie said cryptically. "My Aunt Rosa said she's going to tell me more about it if my mother doesn't."

"He's a Marine," Billy said, pointing to the man's uniform.

"I know. It makes me feel sad," Angie said.

"Richie, you mean?" She nodded. Billy paused and then asked, "What did he look like at the funeral parlor?" He hadn't questioned Angie before now, because he could tell she didn't want to talk about Richie. But he was curious.

"Well...Like Richie, but kind of funny, too. I mean, you could tell it was Richie but he looked, I don't know, waxy or something. Sort of like those mannequins in the windows at Forbes. And you know what? They had put some rouge on him. Ma said that's what they do to make you look more fresh and alive."

"Did you find out more about the accident?"

"Yeah, a little," Angie replied. "His mother told us that it wasn't the crash, that's why he looked OK. They weren't high up and the plane sort of plopped down in the ocean. He kept yelling that he was sinking. He was the only one who got drowned."

"I know, my mother said that, too." Then he told Angie about his dream where Richie was yelling for help in the water. "But you're sure that Sal and your dad were all right?" she asked.

"Yes, I know they were because my dad swam by and Sal had me on his back. Anyway, they're both good swimmers."

They swung slowly in the chair and watched Lucille sniffing under the lilac bush down near the picket fence. "She must see a rabbit. There's a whole family living in Mrs. Brown's yard," Angie said.

Suddenly they heard a clatter out in the front, near the street. A strong odor of rotting food wafted up the driveway and into the backyard. "Ugh, it's worse now that they're using those horses," Angie said. Since the war, the big gas-guzzling garbage vans had been replaced by open trucks led by pairs of old dobbins wearing blinders.

"Hey, I need to go in, " Angie said. "My mother wants me to help her make cookies. I'll have some later on for us, after dinner. You can come and watch now, if you want."

"Nah, that's OK, I need to get Mrs. Herrmann's fish in a little while."

After Angie left, Billy wandered down to the far end of the yard. The day before he had helped Gary make a little tent in the corner, using a big old sheet draped over the fence and bushes. They'd forgotten to take it down last night.

He raised an edge of the flowered sheet and crawled inside. A big green cotton blanket, donated by Mrs. Brown, served as a rug. One of her old brocaded pillows, also left out for the trash man, provided a nice cushion for his head.

Billy sprawled out and looked up at the sheet billowing gently in the slight breeze. He could see the blue sky through a circular hole cut out at the top. When he was little, Sal used to make secret places like this for him, and he'd spend hours devouring books. He'd taught himself to read. long before anyone expected him to know what the letters meant.

Now he lay back on Mrs. Brown's old pillow, enjoying the silence and the scent of the small briar roses twined around the fence. He hoped that Gary had forgotten all about the tent.

The sore throat he'd awakened with again that morning hadn't gone away. He coughed and swallowed a few times. He'd gotten used to his inflamed tonsils and avoided mentioning them to anyone, especially his mother. The new school year was beginning next week, the day after Labor Day, and so far he'd avoided another visit to the doctor. He didn't want to end up in the hospital.

Billy closed his eyes and thought about Sal and his father. They were probably on the ocean right now. He knew his father had already headed out into the Pacific. The last they'd heard from Sal was that he was leaving for New York to board a troop ship bound for Europe.

The moving sheet above his head made Billy think of waves on the ocean, maybe like the ones when Richie drowned. He tried to picture Richie in his casket, buried now under the dirt at St. Michael's. He wondered if worms had started to crawl over him the way they did over the corpses in *The Mummy's Tomb*. Billy felt something brush against his arm, a fuzzy gold and brown caterpillar that slowly crawled across the blanket, away from his elbow. He shivered and moved his hand up over his chest.

Suddenly, outside, there was a loud series of hisses, following by a few short barks from Lucille. Billy scrambled out of the tent, just as Lucille reluctantly backed away from Max. Mrs. Herrmann's cat, back arched, was crouched behind a small azalea bush.

"Max! What are you doing out?" Billy got to his feet. "Lucille, stop! Go home!" He moved between Max and the dog. "Come on, Lucille. Max, you wait here." He picked up Lucille, walked as fast as he could to the porch, and deposited her inside the screen door. "Nan, I'm going over to Mrs. Herrmann's to get the money for her dinner. Keep Lucille inside, OK? Max got out." He didn't wait for Nan's answer.

Max had followed him to the door, looking up at him and meowing loudly. He allowed Billy to pet him briefly. He was wet, the white of the fur on his back stained and reeking of coffee. Suddenly, he bounded away in the direction of his house. When Billy didn't immediately follow, Max turned and waited. As Billy got closer, the cat scurried ahead again.

"OK, Max, I'm coming!" Billy walked through Mrs. Brown's gate and cut across the next yard to Mrs. Herrmann's back porch. He looked up at her window, but he couldn't see if she was there because of the glare of the late afternoon sun.

Max was waiting for him on the porch. The back stairs door was open, as was Mrs. Herrmann's when he got to the second-floor landing. Sometimes she left her door ajar, especially if she knew he was coming. Max would always obey her and go back into the room if he began to sniff around the open door. Now he looked at Billy one more time and raced into the kitchen.

Mrs. Herrmann was sitting at her usual place, but she appeared to be sleeping. Billy often found her like this, but today he noticed right away that her cup had tipped and was balanced awkwardly near the edge of the table. Coffee was still dripping down the checked tablecloth, and there was a puddle on the floor. That would explain Max's wet coat. Billy hoped he hadn't gotten burned.

He walked quietly over to Mrs. Herrmann and cleared his throat. Usually if he made a noise or coughed she looked up. "Ach, Billy, caught me having a cat nap," she'd say in her guttural voice. But today she didn't move.

Max, agitated and meowing incessantly, jumped up on the table. He pattered over to Mrs. Herrmann, circling around the cup and spilled coffee, and began to lick her face. When she moved slightly, Billy thought she was waking up. Instead, she rolled sideways in her chair, her head falling back and her wool cap tilting at a funny angle. Her eyes were wide open.

"Mrs. Herrmann!" Billy shook her warm, plump arm, but her expression didn't change. He knew something was very wrong, but she didn't look the way Angie said Richie looked. Except for her eyes, she appeared to be asleep. "Mrs. Herrmann!" he yelled again. The coffee cup moved slightly and fell to the floor, shattering. Max jumped down and ran to a corner of the kitchen. Then everything was quiet.

Billy backed up and raced out the door. "Max, come on!" he cried. As he stumbled across the yard, he nearly knocked over Mrs. Brown, who was carefully closing her gate and heading in the direction of his house.

"Billy, my goodness! I was just on my way to visit Nan. What's wrong, dear?"

"It's Mrs. Herrmann! Something's happened to her. Her eyes are wide open, and she won't wake up. But she doesn't look like Angie said Richie looked at the funeral parlor."

Mrs. Brown put her hand on Billy's shoulder. "Billy, you continue straight on to your grandmother's house and wait for me. I'm going to see about Mrs. Herrmann. I'll be right over. You tell Nan to wait there with you." She noticed Max pacing near Billy. "Isn't that her cat? Max, is it?"

"Yes, I think Mrs. Herrmann's coffee spilled on him. Maybe he's burned."

Mrs. Brown quickly reached down and picked Max up. He struggled at first, but then he began to meow less frantically. "There, there, you big boy, it's all right." She parted his fur where he was all wet. "Billy, I don't think Max is hurt. His coat is so thick. Here, you take him with you. Don't set him down until you get inside. He's trembling."

When Billy got to Nan's screen door, his own heart was pounding. "Nan, Nan," he cried. "Put Lucille in the bedroom or somewhere and then let me in with Max."

Nan made Billy sit down at the table, and then he told her what happened. When he got to the part about Mrs. Herrmann's eyes, he began to cry. "Does that mean she's dead, Nan?"

"We'll just have to wait and see," said Nan, bending over and giving him a kiss on the cheek. She handed him her flowered handkerchief and said, "Perhaps I should go over, too."

"No, Mrs. Brown said for you to wait here with me." He didn't want Nan to leave. He patted Max, who was crouched at his feet. Lucille was barking frantically from somewhere down the hall.

Nan poured a saucer of milk for Max, who gingerly circled the plate and then began delicately to lap up the contents. He continued to drink as Mrs. Brown quietly entered the kitchen.

"Well," she said. She looked at Nan and shook her head. Then she said to Billy, "I'm afraid Mrs. Herrmann is gone, my dear."

Billy looked at Nan, who had raised her hand to her face. "Oh," he said. He knew that meant Mrs. Herrmann was dead.

"Mrs. Stewart, why don't I call the police? I think they're the proper ones to telephone. They'll probably bring an ambulance, though I'm sure that's not necessary. And why don't you finish up fixing us a nice cup of tea, and one for Billy, too. And then we'll take a look at our Max here."

"Mrs. Brown," Billy said in a shaky voice. "What will happen to Max?"

"Oh, don't you worry about Max. He's a lovely old boy. We won't let anything bad happen to Max. Now, I'll be right back." She smiled at Billy, nodded at Nan and walked out of the room.

"Here, Billy, you go and wash your hands," said Nan, leaning down and giving him another kiss on the forehead. "Then you can help me finish setting the table." She reached into the box of ginger snaps on the counter. "Here, give this biscuit to Lucille. She's being a perfect pest!"

Billy led Max to the door, tempting him with the cookie. He wondered if Mrs. Brown had tried to move Mrs. Herrmann, or if she was still staring straight up at the ceiling, her eyes and mouth wide open.

Chapter 26: Belle

"Good morning!" Belle said as she opened the upstairs back door. "Who'd like to go to Riverside?" It was early on a Saturday morning in late September, and Billy and Gary were having their breakfast at the kitchen table.

"Me! Me! I would!" Gary waved his hand in the air.

"Come on, you're just kidding, Belle," Billy said. "Riverside Park closed for the year right after Labor Day."

"Well, Mr. Smarty, that may be, but they've opened it just for today for some of the local factory workers. So there. Anyway, Abe and I are planning to take the trolley over."

"That would be swell," Laura said. "And with Abe going along, too."

Belle nodded. She and Abe had expected to spend the afternoon together at Forest Park and then have dinner at his house, but she knew the boys would like the outing to the amusement park. She'd noticed that Billy had been quiet, even occasionally sullen, the past couple of weeks. And she'd heard Gary acting fresh to Nan. She wondered if Alan's absence had anything to do with their behavior.

"Good. It's settled. I'll call Abe and tell him."

"We won't be able to take the trolley over to Riverside," Billy said. "That definitely stopped running. I know that for sure."

"Right," said Belle. She rolled her eyes at Laura. "Don't worry, Billy. They're running special ones today."

Half an hour later they got off the downtown bus, and, sure enough, several trolleys were lined up on the street that led to the Connecticut River.

"You're looking awfully pretty, Belle," Abe said as he walked up to greet them. She'd washed her hair last night, and it looked especially shiny. It felt good to be dressed up and even better to be told she looked nice.

"How are you doing, boys?" Abe said. They both greeted him politely, but as soon as the trolley bus started over Memorial Bridge, Gary jumped up and started toward the back.

"Gary, come back here!" Belle said.

"He's been that way lately. I don't know what we're going to do with that kid," Billy said in a querulous, adult voice. Belle hoped they weren't going to be like this all day.

As Gary turned around and started to walk past them toward the front, Abe said firmly, "Gary, guess you didn't hear your Aunt Belle. That's funny, the rest of us did."

Gary stopped and stared at Abe, and then at Belle, who raised her eyebrows meaningfully and looked away. "I forgot," he said. He sat back down in the seat next to Billy and stayed there for the rest of the trip.

"Wow, even the roller coaster's running today," said Belle as they entered the park grounds a few minutes later. In the distance they watched the chain of little cars approach the peak of the wooden track, the occupants' screams audible over the roar of the train as it swooped down out of sight.

"That's the Thunderbolt. What do you say, Billy? Shall you and I try it?" Abe asked.

"Nah," Billy said.

"I'll go!" Gary said. "Can I go?"

"I'm afraid you're too little, Gary. Maybe next year," said Belle. "But Billy...come on, go with Abe."

"Never mind, let's just walk around," Abe answered. "How 'bout if we head over to the midway?"

They stopped in front of a shooting gallery, where prizes ranging from huge Kewpie dolls to rabbit foot key chains were arranged on shelves. Along the wall in the back, puppet faces with yellow skin, slanting eyes, and buckteeth moved jerkily across a jungle landscape.

"Mow the Japs down!" shouted the barker, pointing to the bobbing cartoon figures. "Give 'em what for!"

"Think I'll try my luck here," said Abe. He handed the man a nickel.

"Half price today, ya get two rounds. Boys want to try?"

"Here, Billy, you can shoot with me," said Abe.

"Nah," said Billy.

"Well, I guess the gun is kind of big," said Abe.

"It's not that. I just don't feel like it," he said, turning away.

Belle inwardly groaned. Maybe they should have something to eat.

"Can I shoot?" asked Gary.

"OK, here I'll hoist you up." He lifted Gary onto the counter and let him hold the handle of the gun while he aimed and fired. Three Japanese soldiers bit the dust.

"Wow!" said Belle. "Good shooting, guys!"

"Ya get a prize," said the barker. "Anything on the two bottom rows except the Kewpie."

"Shall we let your Aunt Belle pick something she likes?" said Abe.

"Yeah! Belle, you get to choose!" Gary said. "Or we could get something for Nan," he added.

"There you go," said Belle. "You and Billy pick out something for her."

Billy suddenly turned around. "Hey, you know that lady's head that got broken?" he asked. Belle was glad he didn't remind everyone that Gary had knocked it off the kitchen table.

"Look, there's one of them down there, next to the monkey purse," he said. "Let's pick that one, Gary, OK?"

"OK. We pick that one," Gary said to the attendant. He pointed to a large white porcelain planter in the shape of a woman's head. The back of her pompadour hairdo was scooped out so you could plant something in it. Oblivious to her scalped condition, the lady glanced provocatively over the top of one shoulder, her eyelashes and full lips carefully outlined on the surface of the cheap pottery.

"Say, that looks like Betty Grable," said Abe.

"Yes, that's who it's meant to be," said Billy. "I read in a magazine that they've made thousands and thousands of those."

"Good choice! Nan'll love it," said Belle. "Now, how about some lunch? My treat."

After eating hotdogs served in little paper boats and orange-ade dispensed from a big glass vat with churning blades, they headed over to the giant Ferris wheel. "You guys go ahead," Belle said. "My stomach feels like that orangeade machine back at the snack bar. I wonder what kind of meat those dogs were made from?" She was really feeling OK, but she wanted to give the boys a chance to be with Abe.

She waved to them as their car, bars locked in place, rose slowly in the air, swinging gently as each group of succeeding passengers was unloaded and replaced by another. Soon the three of them were out of sight, suspended somewhere near the top.

"Belle!" She was still looking up at the wheel, but there was no mistaking the owner of that voice. She'd recognize it anywhere. She slowly turned around.

"Danny," she said. Dan Flaherty. He was holding the hand of a little girl about three or so. Next to him was a young woman, a pretty blonde younger than Belle, wheeling a toddler in a go-cart.

"Here with your nephews, Belle?" He smiled tentatively. Belle could tell that, behind his familiar bravado, Dan was a bit nervous as he rubbed his hand against the dark stubble of his cheek. He looked about the same, perhaps a bit scruffy. *Or maybe that's how he always looked*, she thought.

"Yeah, Billy and Gary are here," Belle answered. "Up there, with my friend." She smiled at the blonde.

"Oh, this is my wife, Patsy," Dan said. "Patsy, an old friend, Belle. Belle Stewart."

Patsy nodded. Belle got the feeling Patsy knew who she was.

"Hi," Belle said. "And this must be...your daughter?"

"Yes, Laurie," Patsy said. Laurie, a pigtail version of Patsy, smiled shyly. "And this is our Danny, junior." The baby opened his eyes sleepily.

They exchanged a few more words. Dan asked about Nan. He explained that he'd tried to enlist but his flat feet had disqualified him. Belle remembered how they'd always made a joke about his funny wide footprints in the sand, like a duck's.

"Your kids are just adorable," Belle said to Patsy, shaking her hand as they began to move away.

"Thanks...Belle," Patsy said. She smiled, relieved, perhaps, that the conversation was over.

Belle watched the four of them walk slowly through the crowd. Dan paused to slick back his black hair and tuck in his t-shirt. Fitting him a bit too snugly around the middle these days, Belle noticed. It occurred to her that she was looking particularly nice today, but she realized she didn't really care whether Dan had noticed that or not.

Well, he's got a family now, anyway, she thought. Then she laughed to herself. *I did all that crying for him? Was I nuts?* She looked up and gave Abe and the boys a big wave as they swung past her and into the air once again as the Ferris wheel made a final circle.

Later, strolling back to the front entrance and the waiting trolleys, Billy whispered, "I saw him."

"Yeah, I figured you did. Leave it to you. Dick Tracy. Know what?" She made a face. "He didn't look so good."

They both laughed. Belle put her arm around Billy and squeezed his shoulder.

As they passed the roller coaster, Abe said, "Well, I can't leave here without a ride on the Thunderbolt. It just wouldn't be right. Any takers this time?"

"Not me, I'd be too scared," said Belle.

Billy looked at her, and then turned to Abe. "Can I go, Abe?" he asked.

"Sure can! Gary, you take care of your Aunt Belle here. Keep her away from the hot dogs."

Later, when they'd taken the boys home, Nan invited Abe to stay for dinner. Laura was singing at the hotel, so Gary and Billy joined them downstairs, too. Nan knew by now that whatever she cooked would please Abe. Tonight she'd made beef and kidney stew.

"Nan, your mashed potatoes are the best I've ever tasted," Abe said.

"These beans are from our garden, and the others are Italian whatchamacallits from Mr. Mazzarella," she replied, smiling and ignoring Abe's compliment. Then she added, "I always like to see a man with a good appetite," plopping a huge second serving of potatoes on his plate.

Belle smiled and looked across the table at Billy, who gave her a knowing look. She knew he could tell Nan liked Abe, too.

At first Belle had worried if Abe's being Jewish would be a problem. Nan had wondered if Abe went to a temple and wore those little black caps, and once she'd asked him if there were any foods that he couldn't eat. "I'll eat anything you put in front of me, Nan," he replied.

Belle had also been concerned that her mother would think Abe was too old for her. But no, it seemed that Abe's maturity and gentlemanly ways more than made up in Nan's eyes for Dan's Irish charm. Besides, with Abe in her life, Belle wasn't staying out late anymore at dance clubs with her old friend Flo. She knew that Nan worried about stuff like that.

"OK, Billy, tell us a good show that's playing," said Belle as they finished dinner. "What would Abe and I like?"

"Well, let's see," said Billy. "It's all war movies this week, but I think there are two that would be good. There's Tyrone Power in *Crash Dive* at the Loew's Poli. That's about submarines. And then *Guadalcanal Diary* at the Paramount."

"What if we stroll down to the Strand?"

"Oh, they still have *Casablanca*. You saw that already."

When Belle and Abe left the house and started to walk up the street, she asked, "Do you really want to go to a show? I'd rather just take the bus over to your house. You said Hannah's away, right?"

∂∽∽

The leaves had already started to turn on Abe's tree-lined street. There was a chill in the fall air, so they decided not to sit on the patio. Abe made coffee, and they listened to a special war bonds program with Lowell Thomas and his guests, Kate Smith and Jimmy Durante. Then Drew Pearson reported on the war. There wasn't much news from the Pacific, but he spoke about the continued Allied progress since the invasion of Italy a few days earlier.

"I think Sal Mazzarella may be over there," said Belle. "He sailed a few weeks ago from New York. Turn it off, Abe. We can catch *Hit Parade* later."

Belle curled up on the sofa in the nook of Abe's arm. "That feels nice," she said. "You were awful good today, Abe, with the kids. I think they miss Alan, whether they realize it or not."

"Well, they're nice boys. It's been a while, but remember I had some practice with Hannah."

"It's funny," Belle said, "I forget about your whole life before, with your wife and Hannah as a little girl and all. I guess we tend to view people we know mostly in terms of our own time with them." She was reminded of Dan and how it had surprised her this afternoon that he seemed so different.

"True," he said. "But sometimes it's hard even for me to remember Hannah back when she needed to have her diapers changed and her bottle heated." He paused, then added, "Guess I won't be doing any of that as a grandpa."

Belle turned and faced him. "Yeah, I was wondering about that. You mean Charlotte? Hannah and Charlotte?"

He nodded. "Don't get me wrong. It's fine with me. She couldn't do better than Charlotte."

"I guess I've never known anyone for sure who...Well, you know, I *was* thinking about Gert at work. Doesn't she have a friend? Another woman?"

"Yep, you're right. How do you feel about all that?"

"How do I feel? I feel that what counts is how you are as a person. I don't know, it's confusing." She sat up. "Abe, can I ask you something? Did you ever notice anything, you know, different about Hannah when she was little? You know, like a clue or something?"

"When I think back now, yes. But no, I was a bit taken aback when she told me. And she told me when she was just starting college. I was so glad—honored, really--that she did that. Now it's like it's always been. Why do you ask?"

"I don't know," said Belle. "Well, yes. Sometimes I, well...I wonder about Billy. You know, he's kind of different from the other boys."

"What, smarter than most of them?" asked Abe. "Does what he wants? Plays more with his little friend Angie than with the other kids? Those kinds of awful things?"

"You're right." She laughed. "But he's also shy and, I don't know, withdrawn. I don't want him to be unhappy, that's what it is. I just don't want him to be unhappy. And he and Alan don't get along. Alan wants him to be what he isn't."

"That may change," replied Abe. "I hope it does, for their sakes."

"Me, too. Anyway, I guess it's hard enough no matter who you want to be with. It's not like I've exactly batted a thousand with men. Oh boy, there've been some real bozos."

Abe pulled Belle back down against him and nuzzled her neck. "What about this bozo?" he murmured.

"This bozo may just be the exception that proves the rule," she replied. She kissed him several times on his cheeks and forehead, and then for a long time on his mouth, hard.

"You know what?" she asked.

"What?"

"I had a dream the other night we were on some tropical island. We were swimming in a pool and you had a flower in your hair and when you came out of the water you were naked."

"*I* had a flower in my hair? Oh brother, that must have been a sight. And?"

"Well, it was hard for me to really imagine other things in that dream, seeing that I haven't had the pleasure."

Abe looked deeply into Belle's eyes. "Are you sure about this?"

"I'm a big girl."

"Not too big. Just right." He began to unbutton her blouse.

"You know what I mean, Mr. Sherman." She lay back further in Abe's arms. "What do you say we forget about listening to *Hit Parade*? I feel like another swim...in that tropical pool."

Chapter 27: Billy

Billy swung slowly back and forth in the garden rocker as he watched a cleaning lady in the distance shake a dust mop off Mrs. Herrmann's back porch. A big auction house truck had come and hauled away all her stuff. Soon someone new would be moving in.

He had wondered if Mrs. Herrmann would be on view at the funeral parlor, her face painted the way Angie said Richie's had been. In a way he was relieved when Mrs. Brown told them that Mrs. Herrmann's son had made arrangements for her to be cremated and her ashes flown to California for a service there.

"Well, she'll finally get to make that trip," Nan said, shaking her head. "Dear, oh dear. Once she told me he'd promised to move her out there. Now she's going in a...jar, poor thing."

"Will they put it on a seat just like she was a passenger?" asked Gary.

"No, no, dear, I'm sure she'll be in a special place in the airplane, not with the other people."

"Do they have to pay for you if you're dead?"

"Well, I suppose they do. Probably not as much as when you're, you know, all there," said Nan.

"What if the jar breaks and she spills all over?" asked Gary.

"I'm sure that won't happen. Now that's enough about our poor Mrs. Herrmann. Who wants lunch? I have some lovely ground sausage for patties."

Max, Mrs. Herrmann's cat, was spending a lot of time with the boys. At first he'd been reluctant to leave his yard for any length of time, but that had changed as he began to realize he had no one to go home to.

"I'll feed Max for now," Mrs. Brown told Billy. "He'll be fine outdoors for a good while yet. When the weather gets colder, we'll figure out what to do. I'm afraid Ashkii won't welcome him as a guest in our house, but perhaps Lucille will be more accommodating."

Right now Max was curled up next to Billy on the rocker, his fluffy tail swaying with the gentle swing of the chair. Lucille sat at Billy's feet, one eye occasionally opening a bit to let Max know she was watching him. But already they'd gotten pretty much used to each other.

School was well underway, and Billy liked his new teacher, Miss Stanton, but he still stopped in sometimes to see Mrs. Lawler, from his fourth grade class. When word spread one day that her husband was missing in action, Billy felt bad, but he was shy about talking to her.

One day as he arrived early and walked past her room, he saw her sitting alone at her desk. She glanced toward the doorway, smiled, and waved him in.

"How are you, Billy?" she asked. "It's been a while." She looked the way Nan did sometimes when he surprised her sitting on her bed, deep in thought, but he was glad when she smiled again. "How is the fifth grade?"

"It's fine. It's pretty easy so far," he replied. "I'm sorry about your husband...about Mr. Lawler."

"Thank you, Billy. Actually, we got a telegram just last night that he is being held in a prisoner of war camp, so that is good news. Very good news, in fact." She smiled again, but Billy could tell she was still worried. "That's very kind and thoughtful of you. And your dad?"

"He's OK. Well, he was in Hawaii the last time we heard from him. He sent us a record that he made in a store in Honolulu."

"My, isn't that something? Be sure to say hello to your grandmother for me."

Later that afternoon, Billy played Alan's recording for Angie. "It's not too clear, but you can tell it's him," he said. He slid the small disk from its cardboard envelope, placed the record on the turntable of the old Victrola and turned on the machine. Lifting the arm, he gingerly placed the needle at the edge of the spinning record. Pretty soon, after some loud static, Alan's voice came through, scratchy but recognizable.

"Hello, hi there everyone, guess who this is?" In the background, another voice yelled, *"Hey, Stewart, who do ya think they think it is?!"* and several other people laughed.

"Can it! Quiet! I'm trying to talk," Alan continued. Then someone else yelled, *"Tell 'em where ya are, Alan! Honolulu!"*

"Sounds like they're having a good time," Angie said.

Billy didn't say anything. Belle and his mother had exchanged glances as they listened, and he knew it was because they were probably wondering if there was a party going on with drinking and stuff. But his father sounded more serious than the others as he told them he was in downtown Honolulu and that things were going well. He mentioned everyone at home, even Lucille. Then he said he needed to go because the recording time was ending and, besides, he was going to find a place to eat some Chinese food.

"Oh, one more thing," he added. *"Billy, I wanted to..."* And then the needle reached the end of the disk with a loud, scratchy hiss.

"Gee, wonder what he wanted to tell you," said Angie.

"I know. Me, too." Billy had thought a lot about that ever since they'd all listened to the disk the night before. He put the record back in the envelope and showed Angie the cover. Under his father's name in the upper left corner the words *"Courtesy of Pepsi-Cola"* appeared in the familiar red, white and blue Pepsi script, along with the statement *"This is a recorded message from your man in service."*

"Wow, imagine this coming from Honolulu, Hawaii," Angie said. "Look, it only cost one and a half cents to mail it all the way from there."

She tapped her finger on the word "man" in the printed blurb. "Hey, you know what? See this? What if a WAVE or a WAC wanted to make a record and send it home? They're not men."

"That's what my aunt thought, too," Billy answered. "I said, 'Maybe they have special envelopes for them,' but Belle said she wouldn't bet on it."

That night Billy had trouble falling asleep. He was still awake when he heard his mother turn off the radio in her bedroom, and then the house was still. His throat was bothering him, but he didn't want to say anything to her.

Sometime during the night he was awakened by a loud noise. He'd been having a dream about Max, so he thought maybe it was a cat's crying that he'd heard. He felt hot and flushed, so he walked over to the window and carefully opened it, letting in a gust of late October air. Across the yard, there was a light coming from Nonno's third floor room. Billy sat for a while, looking at Sal's darkened bedroom window, its shade never pulled down anymore. The last they'd heard from Sal was a postcard from London, England. All he'd said was that he'd be "heading out" soon.

Suddenly Billy saw a blurry black and white ball dash up from the backyard. Max. Slipping on his moccasin slippers and his red plaid flannel bathrobe, he tiptoed into the hallway. He didn't want to rouse Lucille, who was sleeping in Gary's room these days. Her hearing wasn't so good lately, but you never knew when she was going to toddle down the hallway. Billy wondered if dogs ever had insomnia, too.

He walked quietly down the back stairs and out onto the porch, where Max greeted him with a loud meow. As Billy stroked the soft skin under his chin, he could feel the vibrations from Max's increasingly loud purrs. But when he tried to coax him into the house, the cat balked.

Billy wiped down the damp surface of a porch chair with a rag from the hallway and sat down. After a while, Max jumped up on his lap, and before long they were both asleep.

❧❧

"Billy! What in the world?!..." He opened his eyes to find his mother, still in her nightgown, standing in the doorway. It was light, and the chill of the fall morning made him shiver. Max jumped off Billy's lap and scampered away.

"Hi, Ma," Billy said. "I came out during the night because Max was crying." His throat was so sore he almost gagged.

"You look like you have a fever," his mother said. She felt his forehead. "Well, not bad. Still, get inside, right now. What about your throat?"

Billy couldn't pretend. "It hurts," he said, grimacing as he tried to swallow.

Dr. Cahill, who had delivered him at Mercy Hospital a decade earlier, made a house visit later that afternoon. While he was there, he called the hospital and arranged for Billy to have his tonsils removed in two days, if his slight fever went away.

The next night Angie came over to say goodbye and wish him good luck. "Those nuns down there at Mercy, they're real nurses, you know," she assured him. "They don't just sit around and pray." And Mrs. Brown promised she'd take special care of Max.

In the morning Billy and his mother drove into the hospital entrance way, which circled a carefully clipped lawn with beds of yellow and orange mums. A large stone statue of Jesus stood among the flowers. A nun came through the front entrance and down the concrete stairs, her black skirt sweeping the steps as she approached the car. Her hands were folded in the sleeves of her habit, so that only her round face was visible within the white wimple bound tightly under her chin.

"Is this young man our patient?" she asked, tilting her head and smiling as she peered in the passenger window. "You can come with me, my dear, while your mother parks your auto." She motioned to a spot next to a shiny black van that looked like the hearse that had carried Richie to the cemetery a couple of months ago.

Billy waited while his mother made the necessary arrangements at the reception desk. Then he said goodbye to her from the wheelchair in which he'd been told to sit.

"I'll see you tomorrow" said Laura. "Off to work for me now." Billy thought she looked especially nice this morning in her new red dress and high-heeled black shoes. As she bent down to kiss him, the scent of her perfume overcame the strong odor of disinfectant in the long, dark corridor they were facing.

"Maybe Nan and Gary'll ride down with me to get you. We'd come visit tonight, but they say you'll still be fast asleep by then." She kissed him again, then turned and walked away, the click of her heels on the polished marble floor echoing in the silence.

A different nun, older than the sister who'd greeted them but dressed in the same black robes, wheeled Billy down the hallway. The corridor was lined with religious paintings and lighted alcoves that held statues of saints. Some of them looked happy and peaceful, but others had agonized expressions on their faces, like they were being tortured. One resembled Jesus, except that he had little arrows sticking in his chest, with scarlet streaks of blood trickling down his bare stomach.

They stopped by a large open shaft enclosed by metal grill work. It wasn't until the nun picked out a large key from a big ring around her waist, turned it in a lock on the front, and slid the lattice sideways that Billy realized they were entering a large elevator.

"Hold on tight, now," she instructed as she wheeled him in, slammed the apparatus shut and began to fuss with a thick pulley against the elevator wall. She seemed even older than Nan, but she tugged the rope up on one side of the pulley and down on the other as they slowly ascended to an upper floor.

Billy was assigned a bed with sidebars in a large dormitory room already occupied by a few boys just waking up or already eating their breakfast. He changed into a long hospital shirt that wouldn't close properly in the back. He didn't have time to think about that before a man attendant with muscular arms picked him up, put him on a stretcher, and wheeled him to another part of the hospital, where blood was drawn and some needles stuck in his arm. Then it was off to surgery.

They entered a bright room with lots of fans that made the air seem very cold. The man with muscular arms lifted him from the stretcher onto a table and strapped him down. He quickly left the room.

A nun, this one dressed all in white, held a cone-like cup stuffed with gauze above his face. "We're going to put you to sleep now," she said in a pleasant voice, leaning down close to him. "When I place this little cloth over you, I'd like you to start to count slowly to ten. It's not a nice smell, but it won't last long, I promise. And then you'll wake up and find it's all over. Are we ready?"

Billy hardly had time to nod before the nun dressed all in white covered his mouth and nose and said, "Now, BEGIN...ONE... TWO...." A horrible, acrid odor exploded into his body, searing his throat and nostrils. "There we are...THREE...FOUR." He wanted to escape, but he was pulled into what seemed like a yellow and orange fire that roared louder and louder, obliterating the face of the nun and then the sound of her voice.

❧

Everything was dark and very quiet. Billy could still smell the awful fumes somewhere in his head, but not nearly as much as before. Slowly, he opened his eyes and looked around. It seemed to be nighttime, and he quickly realized he was back in the bed in the long room where he'd been taken in the morning. He could feel a big lump in his throat. Very carefully, he tried to swallow. As he feared, a pain that was even worse than before gripped him.

He turned and moved his legs so that the sheet was raised like a tent at the bottom of his bed. At the front of the room, near the door, a nun in white sat at a desk dimly lit by a lamp with a green glass shade. She must have noticed him stirring, because she rose immediately and walked down the aisle toward him.

"Now then," she whispered, touching his forehead. "Awake, are you? Would you like something cold?"

"Yes, please," Billy croaked. It hurt even to talk.

"Just let me take a look down your throat.." She held a flashlight up. "Say Aaahhh.... Very good. Now your temperature." He opened his mouth again, but instead she nudged him over on his side, flipped open his gown and stuck the thermometer in his bottom. It felt cold. "Don't move, now there's a good boy. I'll be right back."

"Do you know what time it is...Sister?" Billy whispered after the nun returned and he'd had a few sips of water.

"Oh, it's late. It's past midnight."

"The whole day went by? My tonsils are gone?"

"Yes, and your adenoids, too. You were asleep upstairs for a few hours, and the whole time since we moved you back here. That's good. Daylight will be coming next thing you know. Then, if the doctor says so, you'll be going home sometime soon after that. You've done just fine." She patted his arm. "See if you can sleep a bit more."

He awoke again several hours later when another nun came in to look at his throat. He didn't know if she was a nurse or a doctor, but she checked his heartbeat and looked at a chart at the foot of his bed.

After a breakfast of apple juice and milk, he was told to dress and get ready to go home. He said goodbye to the boy in the bed next to his whose name was Robert. Robert had a big cast on his arm and shoulder and told Billy he'd had a bad fall on his bike.

Nan and Gary were waiting in the car as Laura and Billy, escorted in his wheelchair by the same nun as yesterday, emerged from the hospital. There was a cold nip in the morning air. Leaves from a large maple swirled around their feet and caught in the spokes of the chair.

"How come you can't walk?" Gary asked.

"I can, they just do it this way 'cause you've had an operation," said Billy. "I'm recovering from surgery." It hurt him to speak.

"What was it like in the wheelchair?" asked Gary on the ride home. "Was it fun?"

"Kind of," Billy replied. "They don't push you very fast, though."

Even though it was still morning, they all had vanilla ice cream to celebrate Billy's return. Then he went to bed. Lucille curled up at the foot of his bed, and they both slept most of the afternoon and evening.

The next day Mrs. Brown came over to visit, carrying a bag filled with strips of green cloth, wire, and pieces of thick paper shaped like poppies. She spread them out on the table next to the sofa where Billy was lying in his bathrobe and pajamas.

"I'm helping my friend, Major Pierce," she explained. "He'll be selling these for Armistice Day in a couple of weeks. I thought we could make some while we visit."

As they wound the cloth around the wire and twisted and fastened the red blossoms at the top, Mrs. Brown said, "Do you know why we have poppies for this holiday, Billy?"

"Is it because they're kind of bright?"

"Well, you're right, they're awfully pretty and cheerful with their vivid color, aren't they? But in the last war—that was the Great War, the war to end all wars, at least that's what they told us—well, in that war, poppies sprouted up all over the battlefields. That's because poppies love lime, and lime was like dust everywhere because of all the buildings that were destroyed."

"But why do they sell them?"

"It's not so much for the money, dear—though that goes to help the Veterans of Foreign Wars—but it's more so we won't forget." Mrs. Brown laughed a sad laugh and sighed. "I'm not so sure we did a good job of that, did we?"

She held up a poppy. Billy noticed that the red of the paper flower matched the polish on her long fingernails. Mrs. Brown's hand trembled slightly. "There's a famous poem about the poppies, a sad poem, Billy. It begins, *'In Flanders Fields the poppies blow between the crosses, row on row, that mark our place; and in the sky the larks, still bravely singing, fly scarce heard amid the guns below'*...

"The poem talks about poppies, but it's really about the dead," Mrs. Brown said. She let the poppy fall on the sofa, its blossom crimson against the pale green of a satin pillow.

From the kitchen they heard Nan's voice as she arrived at the back door with some soup. She entered the room, her apron a splash of bright pink, red, and purple flowers. "Now *there's* a poppy who will cheer us up for certain!" Mrs. Brown said.

That evening after dinner Gary tried on his Halloween costume for everyone. This year he was dressing up as a sailor in summer whites and a jaunty cap. Because the weather was turning cold, Laura had added brass buttons to an old black jacket to serve as a pea coat.

"Do you mind not going trick or treating this year, Billy?" Laura asked the next night. She and Gary, big cloth bag in hand, were preparing to head out into the neighborhood. Lucille wagged her tail in anticipation of the unexpected walk.

"Nah, I don't mind, Ma," Billy said. "My throat's still kind of sore. Besides, I'm too old for that stuff anymore."

Chapter 28: Laura

"I think you're a bit down in the dumps, Laura," said Nan, finishing her cup of tea.

"No, not really, just a lot going on," Laura replied. "And we were busy at work today. I'm glad the weekend is almost here."

"Well, I know it's hard for you, with Alan so far away and all," Nan said, patting Laura on the arm.

"Yes, that's it," she replied. In fact, that wasn't it, at least not all of it, but there was no use in upsetting her mother-in-law. Nan had an understanding heart—the kindest Laura had ever known—but her unfailing optimism could be a bit hard to take at times. Sometimes it was difficult to make Nan acknowledge, much less accept, those gray patches that clouded everyone else's life now and then. Best to let Nan be Nan. Besides, what would they all do if Nan suddenly became the gloomy one?

"Tell you what, come on upstairs and hear the song I'm working on," Laura said. "The dishes can wait."

They sat together at the piano as Laura practiced a new tune she'd just learned, "You'd Be So Nice to Come Home To." She'd be singing it at the hotel on Friday night for the first time.

"It's lovely, dear," Nan said. "So romantic."

"Dinah Shore has the hit record," Laura said.

"Well, you sound just as good as Dinah Shore. You've got such a gift, Laura. Sometimes I wish I'd had something like that, you know, to keep me busy and make people feel good."

"You make us feel good just by being the way you are, believe me," Laura replied. "But I do enjoy my singing. I've even thought of continuing afterwards, after the war." She glanced sideways at Nan.

"Of course you should. Why not?" asked Nan.

"Oh, I don't know. Alan, I suppose."

"I'm sure when he sees how happy you are, he'll be tickled. You just wait and see. Now you stay up here and practice. I can manage the dishes," Nan said, rising and rubbing her right hip. That meant her leg was bothering her again, but it was no use saying anything.

Laura could hear her say goodnight to the boys, both listening to "Blondie" in Billy's bedroom, before she returned downstairs.

The next day at the office, Laura spent the morning verifying Helen's keypunch work from the previous afternoon. Helen was out sick today, and Laura was bored. Though she occasionally turned up an error, both women were so fast and accurate on their machines that Laura found her mind wandering.

She couldn't pin down her discontent, but Nan was right: She was definitely down in the dumps. She'd never felt so separated from Alan. Except for the scratchy greeting from Honolulu, she hadn't heard anything in weeks. She'd played that record over and over, trying to determine just how much he'd been celebrating. She didn't know why that was bothering her so much, other than the fact that he probably shouldn't be drinking at all.

Over the weekend she'd also overheard a conversation that disturbed her. Gary's new friend, Freddy, was playing with him in his bedroom, and she was down the hall cleaning the bathroom.

"My mom says your mom is in show business," Freddy said. Laura smiled as she sprinkled Dutch Cleanser over the surface of the tub. She hadn't realized she'd achieved that kind of notoriety in the neighborhood.

"That's at night," Gary replied. "But she works in the day, too."

"I know," Freddy said. "My mom told my dad that she's never home."

"She is, too," Gary said. "She's home right now."

"She said she must meet a lot of men when she sings."

"Yeah, I know," said Gary. "They all like her."

"My dad says he wouldn't let my mom work 'cause there'd be no one home with me and my sister."

"Yeah, but I have Nan. She's kind of like my mom, too."

Laura dried her hands and walked into the bedroom. "OK, boys, who's hungry? Freddy, you run home and ask your mother if you can eat here. Tell her Gary's mom is going to make her special grilled cheese sandwiches. And then you can have some brownies if you like." She added, "And tell her I made them myself."

Laura was shaken out of her thoughts about Freddy's and Gary's conversation when Mae leaned over her machine and tapped her on the shoulder. "Say, you really get engrossed in your work.

Didn't realize you find the punch holes in those cards so fascinating." She laughed. "How about lunch?"

As she ate her liver and bacon, one of the cafeteria specials she always looked forward to, Laura told Mae what she'd overheard. Neither Mae nor Helen had children, but she needed to mention it to someone.

"Look, maybe if Freddy's dad was in the service, he'd appreciate your working. It's easy for him to talk. And I'll bet you anything the mother wishes she were out singing in a fancy dress herself. Don't worry about it, Laura."

"Thanks for saying that, Mae," Laura said. "Still..."

"It's not just that that's bothering you, is it?"

"Well, no...I guess I'm worried about Alan, too." She told Mae about the Honolulu recording.

"Look, I know you've mentioned his drinking before. But didn't you say he'd been doing much better before he enlisted? Besides, what's a spree once in a while? What's he supposed to do on leave, and in Honolulu of all places? All those hula hula girls." She looked at Laura. "Whoops, maybe that's not what you wanted to hear."

"Well, I do think of that. What about Tim? Don't you ever worry that he might, you know...?"

"Listen, everyone thinks of that. But you know what? If anything happens, I know it's not me. It's the circumstances. Has nothing to do with me."

"I wish I had your confidence, Mae."

"I think you do. I think all this is more about you. How are you feeling yourself these days? A bit lonely?"

Laura blushed. "Can't fool you, can I? It's not that...well, yes, I guess I do get lonely. But there's something in the air. I don't know. The men seem more...forward, even when they know I'm married. I guess it's the war that's affected everyone."

"I know. Helen told me about the officer you met a few weeks ago. Look, you're very attractive and you're in an environment at the hotel that's pretty charged. Just enjoy your singing and be careful."

Laura had forgotten she'd promised to make dinner that night, so she decided to stop at the A&P on her way home and see what cuts of meat were available. It was Friday, but she was tired of fish and chips.

When she entered the supermarket, she saw that the line at the butcher's counter stretched all the way down a grocery aisle. Something scarce, maybe sirloin, must have come in. Laura's feet were tired and she didn't feel like waiting, so she walked around the corner to Simka's butcher shop.

When she entered the store, Mr. Simka was in the process of cutting up a big slab of beef. The blade of the thick cleaver chomped through the bone and fat and gristle with lightning speed.

Simka raised the knife again and brought it down with a *thwack. Like those wild bandits in Gary's Ali Baba and the Forty Thieves picture book*, Laura thought. Simka's fingers, thick and smeared with blood, were covered with dark tufts the same color as his slicked-back hair and mustache.

"Ah!" he said in recognition, setting down the cleaver and rubbing his hands on his stained apron. "How can I help you, Missus?" He wiped his brow with his heavily muscled forearm. Laura guessed he was around forty. Mr. Simka never smiled, but to Laura the intensity of his piercing gaze never seemed unfriendly—intimidating maybe, but not hostile. She wondered if the stories about his escapades with certain female customers in the back of the store were really true.

"Hello," said Laura. "Yes, I need something nice for dinner. A steak?" It appeared as though Mrs. Simka, a tiny woman who always had dark circles under her eyes, wasn't in the store today.

"Ya, I give you somethin'." He moved to the large doorway that led to the refrigerated storage room and turned around. "You want to come see?"

"Oh," said Laura. "That's all right. You choose a cut, Mr. Simka. For five people. That'll be fine."

He shrugged and raised an eyebrow in the slightest hint of a smile. As he propped open the door and disappeared into the room, his shoulder brushed against a long string of thick Czech *vursty* sausages suspended from the ceiling. They continued to sway as condensed air from the refrigerated space swirled into the counter area.

Laura shivered and waited. What was taking him so long? For a wild moment she had an image of a naked Mr. Simka, hairy and ready, waiting impatiently for her to change her mind and scurry in to join him.

She turned nervously, wishing someone else would enter the store. The slam of the metal door made her jump as Simka returned to the counter, a large sirloin balanced in his palm.

"That'll be fine," Laura said. "And a pound of ground chuck, if you can spare it. But I just realized I don't have my ration book. I wasn't planning on stopping by."

"Don't you worry, bring it next time." He weighed and wrapped the meat and, licking the tip of a small pencil he took from behind his ear, added the cost of the purchases on a small pad.

"Thank you, Mr. Simka," Laura said. "I do appreciate it. Really."

"A pleasure, Missus." He gave her that same, slightly mocking look. Then he suddenly smiled, revealing strong, even white teeth. "Anytime, Missus." Laura blushed. He was really quite handsome.

As she turned at the corner and began the walk down her street, Laura saw old Mr. Pringle in his yard up ahead. She gave him a big wave, which she knew would please him. Mrs. Pringle didn't seem to be outdoors tonight, so Laura wondered if she was in for some mild flirting. She wasn't in the mood, and Mr. Pringle could get a bit suggestive when his wife wasn't around.

"How are you Mr. Pringle?" Laura asked, determined not to stop.

"I'm just fine, Missy, and I can see you are, too."

"Now, why is that?" Laura asked.

"My, you just have a real glow tonight. Looking like...well, you're looking just like a summer rose in full bloom!"

"Aren't you the flatterer! See you!" she replied, continuing down the street. The encounter with Simka had made her feel flushed. Kind of jumpy. Maybe Mr. Pringle had noticed that, the old goat. She tidied her hair and hurried on, turning her thoughts to the dinner she was about to prepare.

❧❦

The next morning, Saturday, Laura decided to spend the day with the boys. Billy had already asked earlier in the week if they could all go downtown to a big bond rally that was being held on Main Street.

"Ma, they're bringing in that midget Jap submarine that was captured at Pearl Harbor. They've fixed it all up and everything, and it's touring the country."

"All right, if you'll let me do some shopping at the department store."

As they rode down State Street, Gary practiced reading the advertisements above the windows on either side of the bus.

"*No more hair with Nair!*" Gary recited loudly. "Hey, we have that at home!"

"Ma, can you get him to keep quiet?" Billy pleaded.

"Gary, that'll be enough, thank you," Laura said quickly, noticing that the next ad read, *"Ex-Lax, the Happy Medium Laxative."*

A crowd had already gathered at Court Square, where a large flatbed truck was parked. Atop it was a gray cigar-shaped vessel, long and tapering, unlike any boat Laura had ever seen. Nearby, an orderly line had already formed in front of the war bond booth.

"Wow, the sub's bigger than I thought!" said Billy. "And it's all sealed up, except for those little windows." As they got closer and read the information sign, they learned that the ship was 80 feet long and six feet wide at its middle point. Narrow openings, covered by Plexiglas, had been newly cut in the sides of the hull, and electric lights added to illuminate the interior.

"Mommy, I can't see to look in!" Gary said as they made their way down a platform lined with a wooden railing.

"Here, let me," said a male voice behind them.

"Gee, thanks," said Laura, as the man lifted Gary up to the narrow windows. He looked familiar, but it wasn't until she pictured him in his uniform that she recognized the officer she and Helen had met that first night at the hotel.

"Didn't know me dressed as a normal human being, did you?" He smiled. He was wearing dark gabardine trousers, a pale blue cotton shirt and a wool plaid sports jacket.

"I didn't at first, no," Laura said. "Now I remember." She put her hand on Billy's shoulder. "These are my boys," she said. "Billy and Gary, this is...I think it's Captain...?"

"Good memory. Lawrence. John Lawrence."

"I'm Laura Stewart."

"I know that. I've admired your picture down at the Bridgeway, the one in the lobby."

Laura didn't recall having seen him since that first night, but perhaps he'd been there when she wasn't singing.

"Actually, my friend Helen...Do you remember her? Helen mentioned you the other day. We happened to be talking about that night. My audition."

"Hey look," Gary yelled, pointing inside the little strip of window. "Japs are still in there! Dead!"

"Those are just mannequins," Billy said. "Dummies to show you that there were two crew members. Wow, it's so tiny in there."

"Are you in the Navy like my daddy?" Gary asked as the captain set him back down.

"No, the Army, the Army Air Force."

"Are you a pilot?" asked Billy.

"I am, Billy. On a B-17."

"The Flying Fortress," Billy said.

"That's the one."

"Do you ever fly over our house?" asked Gary.

"I'll bet I do. I fly nearly every day."

"Where?" asked Gary.

"Oh, here, there and everywhere in the wild blue yonder," Captain Lawrence said.

"Can we come to Westover to see where you live?"

"Gary, that'll do. Captain Lawrence is too busy for that," said Laura.

"Tell you what, Gary," Lawrence said, "I'll let your Mom know the next time we have visitors' day. I'll give you all a tour."

"Gee, that's awfully nice of you, Captain Lawrence," said Laura. "What do you think, boys?"

"Yes, yes!" yelled Gary.

"That would be fun," said Billy. "Can we go in those real big hangars?"

"Some of them, yes, if you're with me." Captain Lawrence glanced at his watch. "Got to run," he said to Laura. "I have Helen's telephone number. I'll be in touch. Or perhaps I'll see you with the band. Friday and Saturday nights, isn't it?" He raised his hand as though to tip a hat, then laughed. "Oh boy, I've been in uniform too long," he said, shaking her hand instead.

On the bus ride back up the hill, Laura thought about the Captain...John. She couldn't recall anything they'd talked about that night, but she clearly remembered him. He'd asked her to dance. More than one officer, and not a few civilian customers—usually businessman staying at the hotel—had tried to engage her in conversation and, occasionally, to dance. She never accepted.

Flashing her ring and making a witty remark about her marital status had become a standard and increasingly tedious routine. Sometimes she thought she'd be better off not wearing it and just saying "yes" or "no" depending on how she felt. Truth be told, she wouldn't mind a dance or two once in a while.

"Ma, come on, we have to get off the bus!" Billy had already helped Gary stand on the seat to pull the bell cord before Laura realized they were approaching their stop.

Walking with the boys from the corner, Laura noticed that nearly all the foliage had fallen from the maples and oaks. The bare branches of the tallest trees were outlined against the steely sky above the houses, a hint of the long winter months ahead. The familiar smell of burning leaves was in the air.

Across the street, a neighbor she didn't know well was tending the remnants of a small bonfire with his grandkids. He yelled hello, and Laura waved back. She was reminded of fall days back home, when she and Ceil helped her dad rake their big yard.

As they approached the house, Billy asked, "How come that Captain had Helen's telephone number, Ma?"

"Oh, we met him one time at the hotel. In fact, it was the night I went down and sang for the first time, remember? Helen went with me that night."

"Do you think he called her? Like for a date?"

"I have no idea." In fact, Helen hadn't mentioned that she'd given the Captain her number. Laura wondered why not.

"Maybe he will," Billy said. "Helen's really pretty. And Nan says she has a wonderful personality, too."

"Nan's right," said Laura. Had he called her? What was the story? She'd have to ask Helen at work on Monday. Or maybe she'd phone her before the end of the weekend if she had a chance.

Chapter 29: Alan

"It's the smells you're gonna notice first," said Buzz as he and Alan walked from the Naval base to the fleet landing at Pearl. They were looking for a liberty bus to take them into downtown Honolulu. "It sure ain't nothing like I ever smelled back on the farm. "Food cooking, stuff rotting away, and other smells you never smelled before. You'll see."

There were long lines of sailors and a few Marines waiting for the buses, so they hunted down a cab, convincing two other sailors to share the ride. It was already nearly noontime, and there was a 9 p.m. curfew. Still, the few hours in town would be a welcome respite from the monotony of the barracks.

It was obvious that everyone leaving the base for Honolulu today had recently passed inspection: shoes shined, whites spotless, hat at the proper angle. "Christ, they even make you check your fly to be sure all 13 buttons are fastened," muttered Buzz. "But wait 'til you see 'em staggering back later on. Like they been through a cyclone."

Because their LST was in dry dock, they'd been assigned to a barracks on base, so it was an easy walk over to the landing. Others had to take liberty boats from their ships anchored in the harbor, though the larger vessels had their own shore craft.

"You fella goin' to Hotel Street, Fort Street, some place around there, right?" asked the cabbie, a wizened old guy. Chinese, maybe. It was hard to tell, though he did look just like one of the waiters at the Canton, the only Chinese restaurant back in Springfield. That was pretty much the extent of Alan's exposure to anyone Oriental, except in the movies.

"Yep, the bars, buddy," replied Buzz. "You know where those are, I bet."

"How about the Y and the USO?" asked Alan.

"Yeah, yeah, same place, no problem. All close together," said the driver, nodding vigorously and removing both hands from the steering wheel as he formed a tight circle to show them what he meant. "Bar, girl, anything you want, all there. Good Chinese food at Wo Fat's, next to New Senator Hotel. You know New Senator Hotel?" he asked, turning around and grinning.

"Sure, that's where the girls are," said Buzz. "I been there, but where it is exactly I ain't sure."

"Lotsa girl at New Senator," said the cabbie. "All kind *wahine*: Chinese, Haole—that mean White—Filipino, all kind."

"Where you guys from?" Buzz asked the two sailors riding with them.

"The Shaw. Destroyer," said the kid sitting up in front. "Been in dry dock for repairs for a few weeks. Me and Chuck been all over the island."

"The Shaw was here on December 7," added Chuck. "Wally and I weren't in Hawaii then, but the ship was, right at the entrance to the channel. It got hit pretty bad that morning."

"So what happened this time?" asked Alan.

"We grounded on a reef in New Caledonia, down near Australia. Scraped the hell out of the bottom. Lost part of the boiler room. Took us six weeks to get back here."

"Anyone hurt?" asked Alan.

"Nah, not us, we been lucky," replied Wally. "Hey, you know who was on board the whole time? Guy who wrote *Tarzan*, Edgar Rice Burroughs. He's some kind of correspondent."

"No shit!" said Buzz. He gave a loud imitation of Tarzan's yell, and everyone laughed, including the Chinese cabdriver. Alan made a mental note to remember to tell Billy he'd met someone who knew the author of all the Tarzan books. He'd love that.

"Yeah," said Wally, "Never know who you're going to run into out here. Saw Bob Hope and Frances Langford at a show in Pago Pago. That's in Samoa. They were swell. We been everywhere."

The cab made its way into downtown Honolulu, stopping near Hotel Street on a corner across from the Army & Navy Y, where all the taxis seemed to be lined up. Alan paid, and they stood in the gutter figuring out the amount each owed.

It was a hot day. Already there had been a late-morning downpour, leaving a few puddles and an oppressive mugginess. Buzz was right: The air was ripe. The smell of sweat and smoke and aftershave lotion from the hundreds of military men swarming the narrow sidewalks of Hotel Street permeated the atmosphere. Mixed with the stench of rotting fruit and urine and the aroma of sizzling meats from the rickety carts of the vendors, the effect was overwhelming. The flowered leis and cheap perfume of the hula girls waiting to pose with customers at the many photo kiosks added yet another layer to the pungent mix.

The storefronts were topped with garish signs advertising tattoos, loans, palm readings, souvenirs. Small boys swarmed among the men, hawking restaurants, bars, and island tours. Others, carrying portable kits or stationed beside makeshift stands, tugged at passing elbows and arms. "Hi, Mac!" they cried. "Shoeshine?"

Alan could see that Buzz was itching to be on his way. "Bet I know where you're heading."

"Damn right," Buzz replied. "Everything's open, even in the morning, 'cause of the curfew. Now's when the girls do most of their business."

They agreed to meet in the same spot at 7 p.m. "If you change your mind, I'll be at the New Senator Hotel," said Buzz as he walked away. "Down that way, I think. You'll see the line of guys, or just ask anyone. If I'm not around the bar, that means I'm...uh, upstairs." He winked at Alan and the two sailors.

"Say," said Wally, glancing at Alan's wedding ring, "if you don't want to go to bars and places like that, they've got stuff to do at the Y and the USO. Or you can go to the Maluhia dance club. That's more like places back home."

"Yeah, and once we went to the Waikiki Theater," said Chuck. "That's a big movie palace, but they got palm trees on the walls inside and a goldfish pond in the lobby."

Alan walked across to the YMCA building, which also housed the central USO. The middle-aged lady behind the desk was kind and helpful as she told him about the library and music listening booths. There were also outings available to the historic Hawaiian royal residence, Iolani Palace, as well as scenic spots on the outskirts of Honolulu, such as the fabled overlook called the Pali.

Alan thanked her, but instead of heading to the tour reservation desk, he walked back out into the bright, steamy sunlight. Though he usually didn't mind being by himself, today he was feeling restless and a bit lonely. Conscious of his age and the ring on his finger, he was nevertheless drawn to the street teeming with young soldiers and sailors and Marines on the prowl.

Walking up Hotel, he was struck again by the size of the milling crowds—hundreds of people on the sidewalks, in the street, and at the various booths and open shops. Besides the ubiquitous American military, there were Chinese, Filipinos, Koreans, Japanese, and a variety of off-island Polynesians, like the tall and husky Samoans.

Alan wondered how many native Hawaiians were left among the population. He guessed their numbers had probably been decreased through disease and intermarriage. Did those left still speak their own language? How did all these groups get along? He realized there was more to Hawaii than Pearl Harbor, Diamond Head, and the tourist hotels on Waikiki Beach.

Making his way past the hawkers and food stands and photo kiosks, he became increasingly hot and sweaty and thirsty. He paused at the open entrance to a small bar, next to a huge floor fan in the doorway that was blowing air into the shaded interior.

Alan walked in, thinking something cold, a soda, would hit the spot. But when the bartender approached him, he impulsively said, "Give me one of those," pointing to the fancy drinks a pair of Marines and their dates were having at a table behind him. He'd heard everything was watered down anyway, so one pop wouldn't hurt.

"Mai-tai? You want mai-tai? Four drink limit," said the bartender, a skinny young guy—Filipino?—in a red and white flowered Hawaiian shirt.

"Yes, that's fine, I understand," Alan said, nodding.

He lit a cigarette and watched the throngs pass by the open door. The air from the fan felt good against his damp whites. When he turned back to the bar, he was surprised to find four ruby-red glasses lined up in front of him, each topped with a slice of pineapple and a cherry.

"Wait, excuse me," Alan said, but the bartender had already walked away.

"They do that," the private sitting next to him said. "Most guys order the limit so they give 'em to you all at once. That's why he asked you."

"But I'm only having the one," Alan said.

"Yeah," said the soldier. "You must be new in town. I'm George. George Anderson. What ship you on?"

The mai-tai was cold and sweet, like pineapple juice. By the time he'd finished his second, Alan was feeling friendly and relaxed. George was from St. Louis, so they talked about the upcoming World Series.

"Bet you're rooting for the Yankees," George said.

"Are you kidding? I hope like hell the Cardinals win," Alan replied. "Anyone but the Yankees. You're looking at a true Red Sox fan. From 'way back." He raised his glass, spilling some of the drink onto his hand. "'Way back," he said again in a loud voice.

Alan made his way out of the bar half an hour later, shielding his eyes from the mid-day sun. He leaned back against the wooden wall, momentarily regretting having ordered the drinks. Talking about the Red Sox had also made him homesick. As he resumed his shuffle along the crowded sidewalk, he was soon deep in woozy thoughts of the family back in Springfield.

He noticed a Pepsi sign in front of a military service center that read, *"Servicemen! Send Your Voice Back Home."* He strolled in, had a hamburger for a dime and a free soda and walked into a back room, where he spotted two of his shipmates in booths, busy recording their messages. A middle-aged lady wearing white gloves set him up in one of the vacant cubicles. When she signaled, he cleared his throat and began to speak.

"Hello, hi there everyone, guess who this is?" he said loudly, carefully articulating his words into the microphone.

"Hey, Stewart, who do ya think they think it is?!" yelled one of the guys who was now standing outside the half-closed glass door.

"Can it! Quiet! I'm trying to talk," he shouted.

He rambled on for a couple of minutes. Just as he was about to say a special hello to Billy and tell him about the ship's arrival in Pearl Harbor, there was a click. His time was up. He considered making a second record, but he was feeling fuzzy and couldn't think of much else to talk about.

Carefully addressing the cardboard envelope to Laura, he walked back onto Hotel Street. He'd developed a bad case of hiccups, so he decided he needed to drink something else to get rid of them. He spotted a bar whose neon sign was meant to read ALOHA. The glass of the last letter had shattered, so the word ALOH flashed on and off, its pink glow pale and incongruous in the blinding light.

Aloh to you, too, Alan said to himself as he walked through the swinging door.

He carefully took a seat at the long bar. "A bottle of beer," he said to the bartender. Back at the base they'd been advised to ask for bottled beer to be sure it hadn't been watered down or otherwise tampered with. The bartender opened the bottle in front of Alan, wiping off the counter as he set it down.

Despite its scruffy exterior, the Aloha was surprisingly spacious. There were a number of customers at the bar and sitting at small tables around a tiny dance floor.

A big jukebox glowed in one corner, with a set-up for a small combo on a raised stage in the center. They probably came in later in the afternoon, though he remembered reading that they weren't supposed to play past the 9 p.m. curfew either. Tommy Dorsey's "Hawaiian War Chant" blared from the box.

Most of the patrons were servicemen, in small groups or with dates. A couple of women were sitting at the bar, including a pretty brunette on the stool next to Alan's.

He reached into his pocket for a Camel. Before he could offer her a cigarette, she turned and said in a husky voice, "I have my own but I'll take a light."

She leaned toward him, red nails brushing his fingers as she cupped the lighter he was holding. The fragrance of her flowered perfume cut through the smoke as she exhaled and smiled at him. She was more than just pretty.

"My name's Alan," he said to her. "What's yours?"

PART III

Winter-Spring 1944

*Allied bombing destroys the monastery atop Monte Cassino, Italy

*The #1 fiction best-seller is *A Tree Grows In Brooklyn*, by Betty Smith. Non-fiction: *I Never Left Home*, by Bob Hope

*Merrill's Marauders begin an offensive ground campaign against the Japanese in Burma

*Chiquita becomes the first named banana brand to be marketed in the United States

* The #1 song on the Billboard charts is *Don't Fence Me In* (Bing Crosby & The Andrews Sisters)

*The Mark I computer is born at Harvard (Grace Murray Hopper --later Rear Admiral Hopper--is its principal programmer)

Chapter 30: Belle

"Flo's kind of nervous about moving away, so don't ask her too much about it," Belle instructed everyone as the doorbell rang. "'Course if *she* brings it up, that's different." Belle was a bit apprehensive about her friend's coming for dinner. You never knew what Flo might blurt out when things were running smooth in her life, let alone when she was having big problems, like now.

It had all started earlier in the week at work. Belle was counting a run of GI game kits piled high on a skid when Gert, the union steward, walked up to her. "Say, Belle," she said. "That guy, Tommy, in my department. Didn't you know him through his girlfriend?"

"Yeah, Flo's her name. We went to high school together. Why? Something happen?" Belle realized she hadn't talked to Flo in weeks, nor had she seen Tommy around the factory.

"Well, she was just down in the department lookin' for him. Came right up the back stairs, I guess. Seems kind of upset. Tommy left a couple of weeks ago. Enlisted, I think. Funny she didn't know that. I told her to wait down in personnel."

"Thanks, Gert. Keep an eye on things for me, will you, Joanna?" Belle asked one of the older, experienced women on the line.

Walking through several departments on her way to the offices in the newer section of the factory, she greeted a number of new friends. It already seemed like a long time ago that Grace Clark had taken her around the building. That was the day she'd first met Abe. She could still see him as he walked toward her that morning, calm, authoritative, gentlemanly.

"Flo! What is it? What's wrong?" Belle asked as she walked into the personnel waiting room. Flo was sitting in an armchair, her long legs carefully crossed, one foot arched in front of the other. Her face was a picture of pained yet stoic suffering. Flo was always one for the melodramatic gesture, but Belle could tell from her red eyes and the way she was twisting the handkerchief in her lap that something was really going on.

"Oh, Belle, I don't know what's gonna happen!" She carefully dabbed at her eyes, but her mascara was already streaked.

Belle noticed that the cherry-colored polish had chipped away on a couple of her long nails. Not like Flo.

"It's about Tommy?" Belle asked.

"Yeah, we broke up two weeks ago and I don't know where he is. And now they tell me he enlisted!"

"Can't you get in touch with his family and find out his address?"

"Yeah, but you know how they feel about me, and besides, it's more than that." She paused and gave Belle a mournful look and then lowered her eyes.

"More?" Belle looked at Flo. "Like...?"

"Yeah, you got it," Flo said, starting to bawl again. "I'm gonna have a baby. And he don't even know it!" she wailed. "And my father wants me to get out!" They both looked around, but the room was empty. The girls typing at desks behind the glass partition gave no indication if they'd overheard.

"Oh, Flo," Belle said, leaning forward and giving her a hug. "You're sure?"

"Yeah, I'm sure, all right. I even had to pretend to thank the doctor who said he had good news for me. That's 'cause I called myself Mrs. Flanagan." Flanagan was Tommy's last name.

"Do you want to marry him?"

"No, but now I gotta."

"Well, you could go away somewhere and then come back. You know, they have places where you go and then they find a home for the baby." Belle remembered back in high school when one of the fast girls, Joy Mercer, had disappeared for several months and then returned to school in the spring.

"You mean, like Joy What's-her-name from high school?" asked Flo. "She went away and had a baby, right? Remember my brother used to say 'We're goin' on a Joy ride'?"

"What if Tommy doesn't want to marry you?"

"He will. He thinks he's a big shot but once I talk to him it'll be different. He don't want no trouble."

That had been several days ago. Belle told Flo she'd try to find someone who knew a doctor, just in case. When she'd mentioned Flo's situation to Abe, he told her about a friend of Hannah's who'd gotten help from a young woman doctor in town.

"Maybe Flo would at least see her," Abe said. "This shouldn't determine how the two of them are going to spend the rest of their lives, especially if she doesn't want to marry him."

But just last night Flo had called Belle with good news. "Everything's settled!" she said excitedly. "It's all fixed up. Got my bus ticket. Tommy wants me to come out to Los Angeles where he's stationed. We're tying the knot as soon as I get there."

"Then what?" asked Belle. "Won't he be shipped out somewhere?"

"Once we're married, my folks said I can come back and stay with them. I don't know. I'll think about that later."

Belle needn't have worried about anyone asking Flo too many questions that night at dinner. "*California, here I come!*" she sang as she breezed through the doorway. "Like my new hat, everybody?" she said, twirling around in the front hallway.

"Are you going to be a cowgirl in California like Dale Evans?" asked Gary.

"Well, not exactly, but I wanted something kind of Western," Flo replied. She adjusted her hat, a wide-brimmed red felt with little tassels all around the rim. She was wearing a pleated flower skirt, a scooped sleeveless white cotton blouse, red high heels with straps, and big hoop earrings. "The new Mexican look," she explained.

"Flo, dear, aren't you a wee bit cold, dressed like that?" asked Nan, glancing at Flo's plunging neckline.

"Well, yeah, a bit, Mrs. Stewart, but Tommy said it's warm out in Los Angeles right now."

Belle had asked Nan to prepare Flo's favorite meal: ham, cabbage and boiled potatoes. She suspected her mother was glad enough to oblige, since she was sure Nan was happy that Flo was moving out West. Nan had never quite approved of Flo after she'd seen her smoking one day at the drugstore soda fountain.

"Ladies don't smoke on the street or in public places," Nan said. "You don't, do you, Belle?"

"Now, what do you think, Nan?" Nan didn't answer. "Anyway, why is it OK for Alan to smoke anywhere he wants to?"

"It just is, that's all. It's different."

Belle wondered if Nan had an inkling of the real reason for Flo's sudden decision to move. She'd already told Laura in confidence. "Poor kid," her sister-in law said. "Well, at least she'll get some Army money if they marry. Plus insurance. Tell her about the policy Alan was able to get."

"Mmm, I think I can smell my favorite meal," Flo said as they walked into the living room. She leaned down toward Gary, her blouse dipping dangerously low, and gave him a big kiss. "Now, where's my other boyfriend?" she asked. "Where's Billy?"

Belle knew that Billy was fascinated by Flo's flashy good looks, though he was always a bit shy around her. "Boy, she wears a lot of make-up, just like a real movie star!" he told his aunt after Flo had stopped by to pick up Belle for a ladies' dance night down at the Hotel Worthy.

"Hi, Flo," Billy said, putting down the *Life* magazine he was reading. He blushed as Flo bent over and planted a big kiss on his cheek.

"All right, everybody, don't get comfortable in there," Nan called from the dining room. "Dinner's ready."

"Say, what's that shade?" asked Laura, as they sat down at the table. "Your nails look swell."

"Thanks. It's 'Scarlet Passion,' answered Flo, spreading her fingers and waving her arms sinuously above her head.

"My," Nan said. "Potatoes?"

"Sure, thanks, Mrs. Stewart," said Flo. "Perfume's new, too. 'Endless Nights'."

"I'd be careful wearing that one, dear," said Nan.

"Hah, I don't need to worry about that!" Flo replied with a laugh. The she added quickly, "I mean...now that I'm getting married and all. Guess I'm out of circulation."

"Well, now," said Laura. "How long will the trip take, across country?"

"About a week," said Flo. "But I heard they can bump you and give your seat to a man in the service. So who knows? I just hope I get there before Tommy ships out."

"How can you sleep on the bus?" Gary asked.

"You just sleep sitting in your seat," said Flo.

"Wow, you don't even have to go to bed all that time if you don't want to!"

"And you eat in all kinds of restaurants and everything. That's keen," said Billy.

"It'll be an adventure all right," said Belle. "And before you know it, Flo will be a married lady in California."

"How long will you stay, Flo?" asked Nan.

"Gee, I don't know. At least until after..." She looked at Belle. "...Until after Tommy ships out. Maybe I'll stay out there and try to get into the movies. What do you think, Billy?" Flo put her hands on her hips, turned her head, pursed her lips and raised one eyebrow. "Betty Grable," she explained. "Have I got what it takes?"

"There's plenty of ham," said Nan. "Seconds, anyone?"

By the time Flo left, in a flurry of hugs and kisses, everyone was in a good mood. "You can't help but like that girl," Nan admitted grudgingly. "I hope things work out for her, poor thing."

"Why is Flo a poor thing, Nan?" asked Billy.

"Well...," Nan said. "What I mean is, she's going to catch her death of cold if she prances around the Greyhound bus terminal in that get-up!"

Laura glanced over at Belle, and they both rolled their eyes and laughed. Nan had figured it all out. "OK, boys, let's head upstairs. That was delicious, Nan."

ॐॐ

The next morning at work, Belle joined a crowd that had gathered around Joanna's bench. Joanna had begun working at the factory right out of high school, nearly twenty-five years ago.

"What's up?" Belle asked, hoping there wasn't any bad news. Joanna had a niece in the WACs somewhere in Italy, and a nephew on Guadalcanal.

"Joanna just got a letter from her boyfriend," said Gert.

"Oh stop, now, Gert," said Joanna, who was single and lived with her older married sister in the Polish section of town, called, for reasons no one remembered anymore, Indian Orchard. Belle had already heard about the pierogies Joanna always brought in for the girls during the holiday season.

"So, what's this about a boyfriend?" asked Belle.

"Oh, gee, it's nothing, Belle. I just put a, you know, a little note in one of them GI kits and I got an answer from a soldier. An Army medic."

"Wow, kind of like a message in a bottle," said Belle. "What does he say?"

"Yeah, come on Joanna, you brought in the letter. You gotta read it!" said Gert.

"Yes, all right," Joanna said, taking her reading glasses from her purse and tucking a stray lock of her blond hair into her kerchief. "It's dated *Sept. 23, 1943,* so it's already a couple of months old. Maybe it didn't get mailed right away, or something. He wrote the place name down but the censor cut it out. I think it's in Italy somewhere, from the number of his Division. I know they're supposed to be in Italy. Anyway...."

She began reading. "*Dear Joanna--I am taking the liberty of calling you Joanna because Miss Lachowski seems too formal after thinking about you as much as I have.*" Joanna paused and looked up. "Gee this is kinda embarrassing."

"No, no, just pretend like we're not here," said Belle.

She began to read again, slowly and with feeling. "*I can't tell you how much it meant to get your note inside the kit you assembled. You won't believe this, but I am from Stockbridge, up in the Berkshires, and I'm of Polish descent, also. My parents came from a small town near Warsaw. Yes, of course I know where Springfield is—that's where I enlisted—and I used to play Milton Bradley games when I was a boy, though that was a while ago.*

I am a medic with the 45th division. Right now things are kind of quiet, but we've seen our share of action. We hadn't gotten any mail or anything at all from home for quite some time, so it was a special treat to get the kits.

Just seeing the label 'Milton Bradley, Springfield' was a thrill, and then to find your letter inside. To think that someone would take the time to send a note, not knowing if anyone would ever read it. That's really something.

Thank you for telling me about yourself, Joanna. Yes, I would like to correspond.

Please mention to the ladies in your department how much we appreciate their work. Sometimes we wonder if we're remembered, but when a letter like yours comes, we know there is a reason we are here. Z poważaniem, your friend, Walter Wojciechowski."

There was silence after Joanna finished reading her letter. Then Belle said, "How about if we all say a silent prayer for Walter and all the boys—and gals—in Italy, and wherever else they are."

At lunchtime, as they ate their sandwiches in his office, Belle told Abe about Joanna and her letter from Walter. "It was so touching, Abe," Belle said. "But what really surprised me was Joanna writing to a stranger in the first place. She's so quiet and shy. Imagine smuggling the letter into the game kit! She wouldn't tell us what she said, but she must've suggested they get to know each other better or something."

"It's a nice story, all right," Abe said. "Gives *me* a lift, that's for sure. The war gets you down. It's so frustrating to sit here and think you're doing nothing. Better not say too much about her putting the letter in the kit, though. Might not go over with the big shots."

"Gee, I hadn't thought of that. Listen, I have news about my friend Flo, too," said Belle. She told Abe about Flo's dinner visit. "Abe, I know she's in a pickle, but marry him? I don't think she even likes this guy. You remember when he was here, kind of a troublemaker, right? And he even made a pass at me once, when they were going out. What kind of chance does Flo have?"

"But what can she do, Belle? She doesn't have much choice, does she? It sounds like her family'll disown her if she has the baby and doesn't get married. If she arranges not to have the baby, they'll still know what happened. Too bad she told anyone before she really decided."

"I don't know, I think this war's made everyone act kind of crazy."

"Well, different, yes. Crazy, I don't know," said Abe. "Know what I think it is?" He started to cut up his apple. "It's like everything is speeded up. When I was young, I thought I had all the time in the world." He whirled his knife in the air. "Time? Didn't mean anything to me. Remember how the school summer vacation seemed like forever when you were a kid?"

"Yeah, sure, and I see it with Billy and Gary."

"Well, now when I look in the mirror, Belle, I know that's not true. Nothing's forever, that's for damn sure. So you want to act on your feelings. You want to take advantage of the things that are good, or that even *may* be good in your life, before it's too late." He looked at her. "Like you, for instance, Belle."

"Thanks." She took his hand and held it tight. "So in a way that's what Joanna's doing with her message in the game kit, right?"

"Yeah, and why not? You'll understand even more what I mean in a few years."

"I think I'm beginning to now, Abe. I think I am. As least where you're concerned."

Belle leaned over and pecked Abe on the forehead, then picked up her lunch box and walked back into the department. They were beginning a big run of Uncle Wiggly that would probably extend into the next day. Hundreds and hundreds of boxes to be assembled, stacked, packaged, and ready to go.

Belle stretched and sighed at the prospect of another afternoon of watching the conveyer belt. The whistle blew as she walked over to flick the switch. At least there wouldn't be any of those damned slippery tiddly winks to contend with.

Chapter 31: Billy

Billy wiped away the moisture on the bedroom window with the sleeve of his pajama top. It was going to be a white Christmas after all. The storm must have begun in the early hours, and now there was already a small pile of snow on the sill. It was unusually cold in the room, even for early morning. Maybe the furnace had gone out during the night.

Hopping from one scatter rug to the other, he raced back to bed and nestled under the covers. He was soon warm again, but too excited to go back to sleep. With a mighty effort he jumped out of bed and gathered his clothes. Shivering, he dressed quickly, tugging on his red and brown wool reindeer sweater. Then he stripped his bed and headed toward the kitchen.

Gary, studying the back of the Wheaties box with its cutout model of an Army tank, was nearly finished with his cereal. Billy sat down at the table, just as his mother scooped his Saturday morning poached egg out of its shallow pan and onto a piece of toast. She'd remembered to trim the crusts. He was fussy that way.

"You boys can go out and play right after you finish the beds," Laura said, picking up the carpet sweeper and a dusting rag. Nan cleaned during the week, but everyone pitched in on Saturday.

"There'll be even more snow in an hour or so," she said as Gary started to complain. "Billy, go down and check the furnace first, would you? I had to add more coal earlier. I hope we don't run out before our delivery comes next week. Especially with the holiday on Monday."

"Are we still going to Hartford today, Ma?" Billy asked hopefully. They'd planned to take a trip to Connecticut to see his cousins Ralph and Sandra and his grandparents.

"No, I don't think so. If it keeps up, who knows about the buses and trains? Maybe tomorrow, if it's cleared."

By the time Billy and Gary were ready to change the sheets, the bedrooms--windows open and doors closed--were freezing. Laura always aired out the rooms on Saturday morning, whatever the weather. Billy knew she did it to get rid of the smell from his father's cigarettes, though she never complained. By now, though, the old smoke from Alan's Camels was evident only in the living room furniture, especially the overstuffed green chair he always sat in to read or listen to the radio.

Sometimes Belle helped them reverse the bedroom mattresses, a housekeeping routine passed on from Nan. "Makes them last longer," Nan explained. Turning the mattresses on the boys' single beds was something one person could do, but without Alan around it took another adult to help Laura raise the Sealy on the double bed and flip it over.

They discovered that one Saturday when she and Billy made the attempt. They lost control of the wobbling, vertical mattress, and it came tumbling down just at the crucial moment of turning, the casualties a fallen table lamp, smashed alarm clock, and spilled perfume. Lucille, who'd been sniffing around the pile of bedclothes on the floor, yelped, and raced out of the room. Belle had even come running upstairs to investigate the crash.

As Billy smoothed the sheets on his newly made bed, Gary stuck his hand out the window and scooped up a handful of snow from the sill. "It's like talcum powder, except freezing," he said. "We can't make a good snowman."

"Yeah, we can," said Billy. "You just sprinkle a little bit of water along the ground before you roll the snowball. Close the window now, it's too cold and anyway we're done. Come on, we'll do Ma's room." Gary followed him in to Laura's bedroom, and they began to make up the large bed, awkwardly snapping the double sheets into large billowing tents before tucking them tightly between the mattress and box spring.

"What does *'under penalty of the law'* mean, Billy?" Gary asked. He was holding a cloth tag with printing on it.

"It means you have to obey what it says or you get arrested," said Billy.

"*This tag is not to be removed under penalty of the law*," Gary read slowly.

"Uh oh. Did you tear that off Ma and Dad's bed?" Billy asked. "Oh, boy."

"Why?" Gary looked frightened. "What?"

"You're never supposed to take that off. *Ever*," Billy said. "Now something bad is going to happen."

"But how does anyone know?"

"They just do. Sometimes they come around to inspect, like the air raid warden. Boy, are you in trouble. You'd better get that back on."

Gary tried to make the tag stick to where he had ripped it off, but it was no use. "And you can't use Scotch tape, either," Billy said. "So don't even try that. It's forbidden."

"Billy, don't tell, OK?" Gary asked, sticking the tag under the mattress.

"Well, OK, but let's just hope no one finds out. Come on, help me tuck this blanket in, then we'll do yours."

As they were smoothing the worn Roy Rogers and Trigger spread on Gary's bed, there was a knock at the kitchen door. Someone asked Laura in a baby voice, "Can Billy and Gary come out and play?"

"Boys, some pretty little girl is looking for you!" Laura called out.

It was Belle, dressed in red slacks, sheepskin jacket and matching boots, a red serge kerchief, and white angora mittens. She was hopping up and down and clapping her hands together.

"Jesus," she said to Laura, "it's kind of nippy out there. But nice. Kids, ready for some playing in the snow?"

"That's some outfit, Belle," said Laura.

"Yeah, all I need is a few friendly reindeer and a sled," she replied. "I shoveled the front porch steps and figured I'd get some help from the men in the house for the sidewalk. Don't expect anyone'll be using the driveway, so we can skip that for now."

They trooped down the back steps, followed by Lucille, avidly sniffing the air and pawing the snow-covered ground. Earlier, Max had scratched at the door to be let out, but after taking one look at the small drift on the porch, he'd scooted back in the house. Though the snow wasn't very deep yet, Billy and Belle made a narrow path down the driveway to the street and cleared the sidewalk in front for the mailman.

Gary wasn't much help with his kid-sized shovel, but he was fun to watch. Hands hidden by oversized yellow mittens knitted by Nan, he flopped around in his metal-clasped gaiter boots, an old pair that belonged to Billy and were still a bit large for Gary's five-year-old feet. He was stuffed head to toe into a camel's hair one-piece snowsuit with a pointy elf hood, also a cast-off that Billy remembered wearing.

"Let's go in the backyard and see if there's enough snow to make a snowman," Billy said.

The three of them walked past the grape arbor, exposed and bare, its slats and gnarled vines dusted white in the still, wintry air. As they reached the garden area, Mrs. Brown appeared on her back porch and waved them over.

"Hi, Mrs. Brown," Billy said.

"Hello, Billy and Gary. How are you, Belle?"

"I'm fine, Ada," Belle replied. "Feeling like a kid today. Playing in the snow and all."

"That's the spirit. Don't I wish I could join you."

"You can, Mrs. Brown," said Gary. "You can play with us."

"My dear, I'm tempted, I can tell you. Actually, I got all dressed to go to a meeting of the Art Club at the museum. But I doubt I'm going downtown today. Too nasty." Mrs. Brown was wearing her fluffy silver fox coat, a purple turban and high-heeled boots with black fur trim.

"Do you want us to shovel, Mrs. Brown?" asked Billy.

"That would be lovely. You may have to do it later as well, but a good sweep of the front walk now would be grand. You could all come in for tea later if you like. I want to hear more about your visit to see Santa, Gary. Nan told me you went this week."

"We did!" Gary said. "He was going to pick me up on his lap but I was too big, so we just talked."

As the boys walked to the front of her house, Billy heard Mrs. Brown ask Belle, "How's Abe, and how did you like the meeting the other night?"

"How come Belle called Mrs. Brown 'Aidie'?" Gary asked as they began to shovel.

"Ada, it's Ada," replied Billy. "Because that's her first name."

"It is?" Gary giggled. "A-da, A-da. How come Nan doesn't call her that? They're friends."

"Well, sometimes older ladies are like that with each other. It's being polite. Like when we call her Mrs. Brown, but that's because she's older."

"Yeah, but she's not as old as Nan. She doesn't have gray hair."

Billy was going to tell Gary that Mrs. Brown really *was* older than Nan, and the reason her hair wasn't gray was because she put red color in it. But he decided that maybe she wouldn't like everyone to know that, and you never could tell when that kid would blurt out whatever you'd told him.

As he and Gary shoveled, Billy thought of their trip earlier in the week to see Santa Claus at the Forbes & Wallace department store. Nan and Gary, who'd already gotten home from kindergarten, were waiting for him when he returned from school in mid-afternoon.

"Hurry, Gary's been waiting since lunchtime. We want to be sure and see Santa before he goes home from the store."

"Does he go all the way back to the North Pole every night?" asked Gary.

"Oh my, no," replied Nan. "He stays around here somewhere, maybe with the relatives of one of his elves."

Billy remembered when Nan had told him the same thing. He'd figured out that it had to be at Tiny Pinket's house. Tiny was a little hunchbacked lady who lived with her elderly father in an old house near the school. The kids in the neighborhood were used to seeing Tiny in her long black dress with black stockings, eyes focused on the sidewalk, pushing her shopping cart down the street. No one ever talked to her.

"It's Tiny Pinket," Billy whispered to Gary. "He stays with *her*, but don't tell."

Gary looked up at Billy with wide eyes and nodded. "Wow! Tiny Pinket! OK, I won't," he promised.

They got off the downtown bus in front of the department store and waited on the corner for the policeman to direct them across the busy street. The cop was bundled in his greatcoat and earmuffs, his face scarlet and his breath frosty in the frigid air. When he blew his whistle and waved his arm, they hustled in front of the waiting traffic. As they passed the officer, he reached down and patted the top of Gary's head with a mittened hand.

The big display windows in front of the store were filled with images of an old-fashioned Christmas. In one scene, mannequin skaters glided on a pond to piped-in music, the women wearing long hoop skirts, the men dressed in top hats and long plaid scarves. Another window depicted a family decorating a tree in front of a fireplace whose real-looking flames shimmered in waves of soft orange. The father was conspicuously missing, but a large photograph on the mantel showed a blue-uniformed soldier with a mustache gazing solemnly at the festive scene.

"Now, mind the swinging thing!" Nan said as they approached one of the two big revolving doors that opened onto the street. Billy knew that she really didn't like entering this way. Sometimes she walked by herself through the small door off to the side, but today the crowd waiting to get in out of the cold had carried them all along.

"I'll take Gary, Nan!" Billy cried. "Go ahead!"

When he and Gary emerged on the other side, Nan was waiting safe inside, pocketbook dangling from her arm and feathered hat askew. "I don't know how I got in, but here I am!" she said. "Oh, my!"

Walking down the central aisle of the main floor, they were swept up in the bustle and excitement of the big store: the distinctive tinkling sound of the counter bells used to signal for assistance, perfectly coiffed saleswomen offering samples at the perfume counters, cash registers ringing up sale after sale. The bright red of the long carpet runners, as well as the green and silver tinsel around the massive central columns, added to the festive air. It was Christmastime, and the war seemed a long way off.

They headed over to the west wall of the store, where lots of elevators were loading and unloading holiday shoppers. "This way to the North Pole Express!" announced a lady dressed in an orange velvet outfit with a short skirt, green stockings and blue shoes with curved, pointy toes.

"Are her feet really like that?" Gary asked.

"No, she's the regular elevator lady dressed up," Billy said. "The *real* elves are upstairs with Santa."

After they crowded into the elevator, the operator, also in costume, closed the outer door, slammed shut the safety gate, and rotated the large steering lever at her side. They were off. The bells on the lady's floppy elf cap jingled as she announced, "Next stop: Santaland!"

"All right, kiddies," Nan said as they got off the elevator. "I'm going to let you stand over there while I go off and do some shopping of my own."

She pointed toward the long line that led into the North Pole cottage. A seated Santa was just visible behind the frosted front window. "Wait up here in the toy department if you finish before I get back. Billy, I know you'll do a good job watching Gary."

"I see him!" shouted Gary. "He's talking to a kid on his lap!"

It didn't take too long before they were near the front of the line. A mother led the little girl ahead of them up to Santa's big gold chair. As soon as he reached out to lift her onto his lap, she began screaming. Gary blocked his ears "Mary Ann, dear, that's Santa. He's your friend," said her mother. But Mary Ann screeched all the louder, so they finally carted her away.

"That's a dumb kid," Gary said.

"Well, now, who do we have here?" Santa looked somewhat relieved, Billy thought, when Gary walked right up to him. He made a brief attempt to lift Gary and then said, "My, you're a big, strapping boy. I think we'll just have our little chat like this. Santa's been busy all day, listening to lots of your friends here in Springfield."

"That's all right, Santa," Gary said. "I just want to ask you for two things."

"And what would those be?"

"Well, first, a Flexible Flyer sled."

"That seems to be a fair request. If you've been good, of course. And?"

"And a pair of ice skates."

"That sounds fine, too. Now, *have* you been a good boy?" asked Santa.

"Yes, I have," Gary replied. "Even Billy—he's my brother here—will tell you that."

"Well, fine, then. And I hope you have a very Merry Christmas. And what about you, young man?" Santa asked, shifting his gaze to Billy.

"Oh, no, that's OK," said Billy. He moved back. Now he was afraid someone he knew might have seen him and assumed he was in line for himself, too. He hadn't thought about that. "I'm just watching my little brother. Come on, Gary."

Gary ignored Billy. "Santa?" he asked.

"Yes?"

"Since you said I was good, I have another thing."

"And what is that?"

"Well, I'd like a scooter."

"We'll see what we can do."

"And...well, I just thought of something else. How about a Roy Rogers gun and holster?"

"I don't know. This is getting to be a pretty big list. Besides, I have to greet the young lady behind you."

"OK," said Gary. But as Billy grabbed his hand and pulled him away, he looked back over his shoulder. "I forgot! One more thing! A baseball glove! And not a kid's one!"

"Gary," Billy said sternly as they walked away. "You can't ask for everything."

"But you don't get to see him for another whole year! It's not fair!"

They walked over a few aisles and looked at all the Milton Bradley games, several of which they already had, thanks to Belle. Then they went to get a drink of water at the fountain near the stairwell. As they turned to walk back, they saw Santa heading toward them.

They raced back down an aisle filled with basketballs and other sports equipment and watched as Santa walked into the room marked MEN. He started to take off his red plush and white fur jacket as the door closed behind him.

"He went into the men's room!" Gary whispered.

"Yeah, so what?" said Billy.

"Santa's going to the bathroom!"

"Maybe he's just going to wash his hands."

"Let's wait and see when he comes out," said Gary. "Maybe he had to do something else, too!"

Sure enough, when Santa opened the door, he was still fumbling at his zipper. Then he stopped and took a puff of the cigarette dangling from his lips before he turned around and flipped it back into the bathroom. As he walked past them toward Santaland, he tugged at the back of his bunched trousers.

"See, you can tell!," Gary yelled. "He went to the bathroom! And he smokes!"

"Well, he's like regular people in some ways."

"*Santa?*" Gary asked in amazement.

When Nan returned, arms laden with packages, Gary ran up to her. "Nan, guess what?! We saw Santa going to the bathroom!"

"Oh, my," said Nan, looking at Billy with alarm. "What do you mean?"

"He went to the bathroom!"

"He doesn't mean that we saw him *going* to the bathroom," Billy said. "We just saw him going *into* the bathroom."

"Oh, well!" said Nan. "Of course, after all day he'd have to go, now, wouldn't he?"

"I never thought of Santa going to the bathroom! And he had a cigarette, too."

"I'll tell you something, dearies," Nan said. "One year, a long time ago, before you were born, Gary, and when Billy was younger than you are now, Santa came as usual on Christmas Eve. And do you know what? I know he went to the bathroom right in our house! I could hear the toilet flush, and *no one else had gotten up*. And he took a cigarette from your dad's pack of Camels. Your dad knew that happened, because he had only one left. So what do you think of that?"

"Wow!" said Gary. "Maybe he'll go to the bathroom again tomorrow night when he comes. I'm going to try to stay awake and listen."

"There you are!" said Nan. "But mind you, don't disturb him. Let him do his business in peace!"

Billy was startled out of his daydreaming by a gust of snowy wind and the scraping of Gary's toy shovel on Mrs. Brown's sidewalk. He looked up just as she came back out on her porch to meet the mailman, briskly walking up the freshly cleared path with his big leather mail pouch.

"Hi, Mr. Connors," Billy said, walking toward them.

"Hello, Billy," he replied. "Good job with the sidewalk!"

"Thanks. Any mail from my dad?"

"Well, now, I'm not sure." That meant there definitely wasn't, since everyone knew that Mr. Connors read everyone's postcards and noticed the return addresses on all the letters.

"Come on, Gary, let's run home and see," said Billy, starting toward their backyard. He hoped Mr. Connors was wrong, since he knew his mother was concerned that they hadn't heard anything for a while.

"Come back later, boys, and I'll give you a snack and a little something for your dandy shoveling," said Mrs. Brown.

"OK," Billy replied. "Oh, Mr. Connors, I forgot. Any mail from Sal next door?"

"Now, I'm not sure about that, either. I don't think so, though. Not to his house, or to you. Maybe next week."

"Billy, how come we didn't get a letter from Daddy or Sal?" Gary asked.

"It takes a long time. They're real far away."

"Maybe they got shot or something. Or maybe they're prisoners in one of those camps."

"That's not funny!" Billy replied. "And don't say that in front of Ma or Nan or Belle, or even Angie. Or anybody! Come on, I'll race you to the house. Let's check the mail, and then we'll build a snowman. And remember what I said!"

Chapter 32: Alan

As soon as he woke up, Alan knew something was different. The sheets felt cool and smooth against his bare skin. The pillow was fluffy and perfumed. And his legs weren't curled in the cramped position he'd gotten used to in his bunk on board ship

When he turned on his back and opened his eyes, he was hit by the sickening thud of a hangover headache. A familiar enough sensation, but one he hadn't experienced in some time. Alan closed his eyes and rubbed his fingers against his temples.

After a few seconds, he gingerly tried again, squinting as he looked around the semi-darkened room. Against the opposite wall, he grimaced at a dim reflection of himself in a vanity mirror surrounded by fancy spray bottles and other toiletries. Through the slats of Venetian blinds drawn against a small window, the sun cast thin strips of light onto the reed mat covering the floor.

He sat up with a start. What time was it? Whose room was this? He jumped out of bed, groaning and holding his head. He was naked, his clothes a tangled heap in the corner. Alan looked around for a clock and then spotted his watch and wallet and change on a small night table. Five o'clock...in the afternoon, apparently, so it must be the same day. He wasn't AWOL. His pass was good until nine that night. But where the hell was he?

He put on his shorts and pants and padded barefoot to the closed door. Opening it slowly, he looked into a bright and cheery living room furnished with a bamboo sofa and chairs and adorned with flowered pillows and throw rugs. At the far end of the room, a wide screened door opened onto a porch surrounded by palms and potted plants with purple and orange and red blossoms. He could smell coffee brewing, but there didn't seem to be anyone around.

He found the bathroom and raised the toilet seat, craning his neck as he stood so he could examine his face in the mirror. Same face, a bit white and strained, hair disheveled, but otherwise OK. He splashed his cheeks and forehead with cold water and drank from a glass with a painted rooster that reminded him of a set of tumblers back home.

Lying on a clothes hamper in the corner was a recent issue of the "Honolulu Star-Bulletin" with the bold headline "**MARINES READY FOR BOUGAINVILLE & TARAWA.**" A smaller picture showed a man spraying bushes with an insecticide gun. Its caption read, "Dengue Fever Outbreak Continues On Oahu."

Walking back into the living room, he nearly tripped over a low coffee table, on top of which were arranged several family pictures. Among them was the image of an exceptionally pretty, smiling young woman standing between an older couple. The brunette from the bar. In a flash, their meeting came back to him. He even remembered the red glow of her fingernails as she cupped the light he'd offered.

As he was trying to reconstruct what had happened next, the front screen door opened and she walked in. He recognized her tall, willowy figure and the purple flowered blouse she was wearing. She set down a satchel of groceries and ran her fingers through her hair in a gesture that also seemed vaguely familiar.

"That was a fast recovery," she said. "You OK?"

"Yeah, I guess so," Alan replied. "Headache, but it's not so bad. I'm sorry about...whatever happened. I must have passed out."

"Yeah, you did, but only about an hour ago," she said. "Remember my name?"

"If you give me a minute..." She really was a knockout, with shapely legs and beautiful skin. "It's Edie, isn't it?"

"Hey, not bad, considering. And don't worry about the time. I expect you need to be back at the liberty bus in a couple of hours, right?"

"Yes, will that be possible?"

"Sure, we're not that far from downtown. Actually, we walked here." She began to unpack the groceries. "So, Alan from Massachusetts, how about a quick snack?"

"You know, it's funny, I *am* hungry. I'm usually not...I mean, after drinking."

"You do this a lot?"

"I don't really...anymore, that is. I don't know what happened."

"I do. It was the crap that passes for booze in most bars here. Plus the afternoon sun. That can get you if you're not used to it. Not to mention the four drinks you slugged down, and I know those weren't the first of the day." She smiled at him and raised her eyebrow. "Am I right?"

"Yeah. It was just that it was so hot and I was thirsty and..."

"You don't need to explain to me. I'm not your wife...Laura, isn't it?"

"Jesus, yes. I was talking about her?"

"I'd say a bit, yes. You really did black out, didn't you?"

"What happened? Do you mind telling me? I feel really embarrassed."

"Sure. But first, go and finish putting your clothes on and I'll fix up something quick. Bathroom's over there if you didn't already find it."

When he returned to the kitchen, there was a steaming cup of coffee on the counter and two places neatly set at the small pink Formica and chrome table. "Scrambled eggs and toast all right?" asked Edie. "Here's some pineapple, too."

"Yes, fine, thank you," Alan replied. He wasn't quite sure what to say next.

"So," Edie said. "You're wondering how you ended up bare-assed in my bed. Right?"

He was startled to hear her speak so frankly. "Well, yeah, I am. It's a...new experience."

"No kidding." She gave a laugh that wasn't unkind but seemed worldly beyond her years. "That I could tell."

"You mean...things were...bad?"

"No, I don't mean that. You were a little wobbly by the time we got back here but, ah, standing at attention all the same."

"Oh," Alan replied. He thought he might be blushing.

"I embarrass you?" She laughed again. "I guess I'd embarrass a lot of the people I used to know, too, come to think of it. Shows you what happens after you're all grown up."

"No, I'm not embarrassed, not about you. Just foggy...I'm not sure how I feel."

"Don't mind me. Anyway, you made a pass at me at the bar and then we came back here. And then in bed you started talking more about Laura after I asked you who she was. You said her name a few times."

"Oh. I'm sorry. So...we still...?"

"Did the deed? No, you passed out. Your honor is saved." She took a sip of coffee and then said, "Sorry, I didn't mean that either. Actually, it was nice."

"Nice?"

"Nice that you felt that way. You must care for her a lot. That's what's nice."

"And what about you? Why did you let me come back here?"

"What, a girl can't be attracted to someone, too?" She paused and looked away. "You reminded me of someone."

"Oh?"

"More coffee?" she asked. "And then we've got to get you back to your ship. Feeling better now?"

"Yes," Alan replied. "My headache's almost gone." He reached over and stroked Edie's arm. "And you've been so...understanding."

She pulled away. "Yeah, well, we'd better get going."

"I didn't mean ... anything now. Just that it was good to talk to someone." He laughed sheepishly. "Even if I'm kind of vague about the conversation."

"Yeah, I know," she said. "I know." She leaned her hand on his shoulder as she got up. "Let me freshen up a bit and we'll be off."

They left the house and began walking along an unpaved residential street. Water dripped from the eaves and drainpipes of the small frame bungalows lining both sides of the narrow road. There were large puddles everywhere.

He must have slept through one of the frequent cloudbursts that came out of nowhere and departed just as fast. Now, sundown had brought a slight breeze. The smell of tuberose and jasmine in the tiny front yards they passed permeated the humid air.

"Where are we, exactly? Alan asked.

"Up there behind us is the Punchbowl. That's an old crater. A new military cemetery is supposed to open there sometime soon." She pointed to the left. "Waikiki is there. In fact, you can sort of see the outline of Diamond Head. And Pearl Harbor is off in the other direction." As she spoke, several planes swooped over them, low and loud.

"Wow, does that happen a lot here, too? We have it over at the base all the time."

"Yes, but you get used to it. And at least we know whose they are."

"Were you here on December 7?" Alan asked.

"Yes," she replied.

"You're lucky to have that nice little house."

"It's not mine. I wasn't living there then."

"You work in Honolulu?"

"Yes," she replied. "So, you're feeling OK now?"

Approaching the downtown area, they began to see more and more passersby, a few military personnel but mostly locals—again, the same mix of Chinese, Koreans, Hawaiians, Japanese, and Filipinos. Some of them wore non-Western dress.

Glancing at a woman in a long silk skirt, Edie remarked, "A lot of these are people who've moved here from the smaller towns inland. You see them gradually start to look like everyone else. It's kind of sad. The war's changed everything."

By the time they reached Fort Street they found themselves following scores of sailors converging on the YMCA square. Many of the men were obviously drunk, hats missing, uniforms stained and soiled. A few showed signs of a scuffle or two, their faces bruised and shirts bloodied.

Military police in pairs were everywhere, stationed on corners or slowly patrolling the crowded streets. One unruly sailor waving a bottle was the recipient of a painfully audible crack on the head from an MP carrying a large billy club. He sank to the ground, but was quickly helped up by his buddies as they all staggered off to join a ragged line forming near a slowly approaching bus.

"I'll leave you here," Edie said.

"Will I get to see you again?" Alan asked.

"I don't think so. I don't think that's a good idea."

"I'll behave, I promise," said Alan. "I mean, no drinking, and you can just show me around. Please. I'll only be here another week or two."

Edie started to shake her head. "Please?" Alan asked.

"All right," she finally replied. "You can get the number from the operator or the telephone book. It's under Crosby. Like in Bing. It's the only one."

"I can get a leave again in four days. Will you be working?"

She hesitated. "I can arrange something," she said. "I've got to go. I don't like this crowd."

Edie turned and walked away. "Bye," Alan called out. She looked back and ran her fingers through her hair. She didn't smile, but instead nodded and half-waved before she disappeared in the crowd.

❧

"So where *you* been?" Buzz, clearly feeling no pain, arrived at the bus stop a short while later and tugged at Alan's cap.

"Hey, Buzz. Oh, I was around. How about you?"

"The usual. A few bars and then, like I said, the New Senator. The Navy man's favorite home away from home." Buzz did a little jig and stumbled against Alan. "I even found the same gal again. Like a friggin' little doll. Half Chinese. Know what she calls herself? Lotus. That ain't her real name I bet. Most of 'em don't use their real names."

They moved up in the line. "Hey, watch the mess," said Alan, steering Buzz around a puddle of vomit.

"Yeah, yeah, I see it. Jesus, some of these guys got no class. Never mind. You didn't tell me where *she* came from." Buzz stumbled and waved his finger at Alan. "Hah, I saw the two of you talking. She didn't come from no New Senator!"

"I met her in a restaurant," Alan said. "She's a nice girl."

"She's sure nice all right. Real nice. What a knockout."

"Yeah, well, nothing happened."

"Don't worry, I won't tell anyone back in Springfield. Hell, I don't even know where Springfield is."

"No, I mean it. Nothing happened."

"Yeah, OK. Jesus, know what? I believe you."

They climbed aboard the next bus to arrive and grabbed two seats near the front. As the driver maneuvered slowly through the downtown area, Buzz fell asleep, snoring loudly, cap tilted over his forehead.

Some sailors in the back started to sing "Don't Sit Under the Apple Tree with Anyone Else but Me." A Marine across the aisle from Alan woke up and muttered, "Jesus Christ, they stink." He turned around and yelled, "Shut the fuck up! Ya ain't the Andrews Sisters!" One of the singers started to charge down the aisle, but his buddies stopped him.

Alan leaned back in his seat and closed his eyes. His headache had returned, dully lodged somewhere at the back of his skull. Otherwise he felt alert and wide-awake. He thought of the somber nod Edie had given him when she waved. Maybe she was just like that all the time, a serious person. At least he knew how to get in touch with her, if he wanted to. Right now, he did.

The bus reached the landing dock at Pearl and lined up behind several others as they slowly advanced to the unloading area. Most of the men were now asleep, snores replacing the loud conversations and raucous singing.

Alan thought back again on the last few hours. He really hadn't learned anything about Edie—how old she was, what she'd been doing in the bar, where she was from in the states. He assumed she hadn't been born in Hawaii, but, who knows, maybe she had. But if she hadn't been, why was she here? Was she married? She said she worked. Where?

Crosby, he thought. *Like in Bing*. Then he realized Crosby probably wasn't her last name. She'd said the house wasn't hers. All he knew for sure was that her first name was Edie and that she was beautiful and that he reminded her of someone she'd known. He wondered who that was.

He nudged Buzz. "Come on, buddy," he said. "Wake up."

Buzz groaned. "Go away, I was dreamin'."

"Lotus Blossom'll have to wait," Alan said, "Come on, Buzz. We're back at the base." He stood up, hitting his already sore head on an overhead rack, and slowly made his way up the aisle.

Chapter 33: Laura

"Ma, Bob Hope's on in a little while," Billy said. "Want to go down to the cellar now?"

Tending the heat in the house meant checking both furnaces in the basement several times a day. Belle had the responsibility one week, Laura the next. And Nan still persisted in running down to the basement during the day, even with her bad leg.

"I'll be right there. Just let me finish rinsing these out," Laura called from the open bathroom door. She hung her stockings on the shower rod and joined Billy in the kitchen, where Lucille was already waiting impatiently at the closed door. Max hovered under the table, seemingly uninterested, but ready to dash out ahead of everybody.

Laura was uncomfortable going down the winding back stairs to the dark, musty cellar, especially at night. She figured it had something to do with being frightened one winter evening as a kid when a strange man—a hobo who'd jumped from a train at a local crossing—wandered up their long driveway. She'd seen him from her bedroom window and waited upstairs, terrified, until her parents returned from a neighbor's house. She'd not forgotten that incident.

Though Laura never said anything to the kids, she sensed Billy felt her unease. Gary always liked the adventure of going downstairs, but tonight he was already in bed.

"Let me grab my sweater," Laura said, retrieving it from the kitchen coat rack and nearly tripping over Lucille and Max as they raced to the door. As soon as Billy opened it, Max disappeared, scooting past Lucille, who half-slid across the waxed floor, her nails clicking on the shiny linoleum. Sometimes Max had already caught a mouse by the time they arrived in the furnace room, always warm with a faint but unmistakable odor of coal gas.

The fires in both furnaces were burning steadily. After Laura shoveled powdery ashes into a trashcan, Billy retrieved fresh black hunks from the bin under the narrow window and threw them on top of the glowing orange-colored coal. They banked both fires to ensure an even burning throughout the night and then slammed the thick doors shut with the long, heavy poker.

Over the years the furnaces had been responsible for a few minor burns and the occasional singed article of clothing. Alan had ignited his hair and blistered his forehead one boozy winter night when he'd come home late. After that episode, the understanding was that if he hadn't arrived by a certain hour, one of the women would check the fire before bedtime.

"OK, guess we won't freeze before morning," Laura said, putting her arm around Billy. As they made their way over to the staircase, their reflections cast flickering shadows behind the light of the swinging bulb.

"Come on, Lucille. You too, Max," Billy said.

Both pets were always reluctant to leave the dark corners of the cellar, but as soon as Laura and Billy began to walk up the stairs, Lucille emerged from the shadows. She dashed on ahead, clumsily thumping the wall, then slowed down and soldiered on. Max silently scurried past everyone up the two flights and waited, licking his paws, outside the closed kitchen door.

Later, getting ready for bed, Laura thought about their plans for the rest of the holiday week. All in all, things were turning out better than she'd expected, and she was actually looking forward to New Year's Eve. It didn't seem possible it was almost 1944.

Christmas itself hadn't been half bad. They'd picked out a nice evergreen at Pete's fruit stand, which always re-opened for the holiday season, its deserted storefront temporarily brightened by the colored lights strung around the empty produce bins. The fragrance of the trees and wreaths stacked right up to the sidewalk reminded Laura of the taller fir trees in the spacious front yard back home in Connecticut.

She had no idea where Alan was—"somewhere at sea" was all they ever knew—but he'd sent Navy-themed Christmas cards to everyone. Hers was a wreath-trimmed anchor that spelled out "I Love You," and he'd written a sweet note inside. The boys' card showed a jolly Santa and his reindeer making a landing onto an aircraft carrier. Nan's and Belle's depicted a sailor lying on his bunk daydreaming about a motherly lady holding a cooked turkey. The last time they'd had real news from Alan was when he'd sent that phonograph record from Honolulu in the fall.

Laura was scheduled to sing on New Year's Eve, but she'd arranged to leave right after the midnight celebration. The next day she and the boys would take down the tree, and then they'd join the Mazzarellas for a yearly New Year's get-together.

She wondered if Captain John Lawrence would show up to hear her sing. Since she'd talked with him a few months ago at that Jap submarine exhibit, he'd come to the hotel a few times. There was no mistaking his interest in her. She probably shouldn't be joining him at his table between songs, but she'd been careful to make it clear that was as far as she'd go.

Ray encouraged members of the band to sit with friends and to mix with other customers. Though Laura had begun by turning down requests, she'd been on the dance floor with plenty of officers in recent weeks.

The night after they'd met John at the submarine exhibit, she'd telephoned Helen. "Yeah, the captain's called me a couple of times," Helen told her. "But it's you he's interested in, that's pretty obvious, so I've always said no."

"He said he might call you to get my phone number," said Laura.

"OK, thanks for the warning," Helen replied. "I'll think of some excuse."

"Well..."

"Unless you want me to give it to him?"

"It'd be all right. He offered to give us a tour of Westover."

"Oh, right," said Helen. Then she started singing, *"Off we go into the wild blue yonder..."*

"Now, stop!" Laura laughed. "It's not like that at all. The boys want to see the base."

"See you Monday at work," Helen replied. "Bye!"

That had all been weeks ago. Now, as she climbed into bed, Laura decided she'd invite Belle and Abe to come to the hotel, and Helen, too, if she didn't already have a date. That way John could join them at their table. Safety in numbers, and she was sure Abe and John would have a lot in common. John seemed older than his years, and Abe younger.

Laura thought about a conversation she and Belle had the night before.

"You really are getting serious with Abe, aren't you?" she'd asked.

"Yeah, I guess I am," Belle replied. "But it's kind of complicated."

"How so?"

"Well, his daughter still lives at home, plus there's my mother."

"I thought Nan was crazy about Abe."

"She is. I don't mean that. But I'd hate to leave her alone."

"Wow, you're *that* serious?"

"Hey, I want to settle down with someone eventually. Who doesn't?"

"Don't worry about Nan. You know we'd always take care of her here. Honestly, she's more like a mother to me than my own, you know that," Laura replied. "Even if we moved after the war, she could come with us. The kids would be lost without her."

"I know. Thanks, Laura," said Belle. "Well, anyway, nothing'll happen for a while."

As she drifted off to sleep, Laura thought more about her sister-in-law and Abe. She could understand Belle's attraction to him, since she herself had been drawn to more mature men. Even in high school, she'd dated older boys. And then there was Alan, the same age as she but always introspective and serious.

When she'd first met him, she thought he was in his late twenties, he was so quiet and reserved. Was it a father thing that attracted her? She thought about that for a minute, then decided there wasn't anything particularly appealing about her own father, except that he'd always been a good provider. Must be some other reason. Maybe she just wanted to be taken care of, though she'd been surprised at how much she was enjoying her independent life since Alan enlisted. Belle was right: It was all so complicated.

For her appearance in the Mayfair Room on New Year's Eve, Laura decided on a new gown she'd seen at Steiger's department store, a black, high-necked jersey, sleeveless, with a jagged row of silver sequins decorating the upper right bodice. She took special care with her hair, styling it in an elaborate upsweep fastened with delicate ivory combs that had belonged to her grandmother. She wore her best rhinestone earrings, dangling and glittery, and a matching bracelet Alan had given her years ago.

"Wow, Mommy, you look just like a movie star!" said Gary. Laura laughed and put her glossy black skunk coat over her shoulders, fastening the elaborate antique buckle at the top.

"Yeah, Ma, you do," Billy added. "Really glamorous!" Laura knew he'd have liked to go along and hear her sing, but at least she'd promised to be back shortly after midnight.

"OK, kids, let's go down to Nan's. I think Abe and Belle are waiting for me." Both boys had been given permission to stay up with Nan until Laura got home.

Abe drove Belle and Laura to Helen's house in his big Desoto sedan. When Helen joined them, resplendent in her Alpine lamb and fragrant with the scent of Arpège, Abe said, "Boy, I feel like we just made a raid on some fancy fur salon. Next to the three of you, I look pretty shabby in this old gabardine." Belle was wearing her red fox, which Laura knew had cost her a pretty penny a few years ago.

"You look pretty elegant to me," replied Helen. "Silk scarf, leather gloves and all."

"Now, let's see," Abe said. "We have a skunk, a fox, and a lamb. What is that telling me?"

"It's telling *me* that you're a pretty lucky rooster to be in the midst of such staggering beauty," said Belle. "Just watch the road there, mister, and don't get carried away." She leaned over and kissed Abe on the cheek.

"At least you didn't say 'old geezer,'" replied Abe.

"Now would I ever say anything fresh like that?" Belle turned around. "Don't answer that question, girls!"

As they reached Main Street and headed over to the Bridgeway Hotel, Helen said, "Oh, John Lawrence will be joining us. He's a captain in the Air Force. He flies out of Westover."

"You'll like him," Laura said to Abe and Belle. "He's a regular. Usually comes in alone. Billy and Gary met him the time we saw that touring Jap submarine at Court Square." She felt Helen give her a nudge with her shoe.

"Well, aren't you the sophisticated one," Belle remarked as they walked by a large placard at the hotel entrance advertising Ray Jardine's band. A glossy 8x10 of Laura was mounted in the center.

"Oh, that was kind of funny," Laura replied. "The photographer kept saying, 'Sultry, give me sultry,' so I really couldn't smile or anything like that."

"What are you singing tonight, Laura?" Helen asked after they were shown to a table near the dance floor.

"We're doing a couple of Jimmy Dorsey and Helen O'Connell numbers. And there's a new arrangement of "You'll Never Know." I'm doing that one with our new trumpet player, Buddy, who can sing, too."

"What about "Stardust"?" asked Abe. "That's always been one of my favorites."

"Everyone loves that. Yes, I think so. We always rehearse a few more songs than we actually do, just in case, so I'm not sure. Oh, and we're trying out a brand-new song, "Don't Fence Me In." It's by Cole Porter, but you'd never know it. It sounds more like a western song. I think it's in a new Roy Rogers movie. Everybody's recording it, Bing Crosby, even Kate Smith."

As she spoke, Laura watched as John Lawrence entered and crossed the room to their table. "Hello again," he said, smiling also at Abe and Belle. "Mind if I join you?" She noticed immediately that he'd grown a mustache since she'd last seen him. He was looking rather dashing in his uniform, and the mustache made him appear more British than American.

The evening went well. A good number of the crowd already knew Laura, but the place was packed, so some were hearing her for the first time. After she finished her first number, "Green Eyes," she was aware of the attention their table was getting after she returned to her seat.

As she'd expected, Abe and John carried on a lively conversation about the base at Westover and the war in general. Talk turned to how things were going in the Pacific, where the hopscotch invasions of Japanese-occupied islands seemed to be dragging on and on.

"That war won't end anytime soon," John said. "It's a whole different ballgame, not like in Europe. I'm not sure what it'll take for Japan to give up."

Laura and Belle exchanged glances. Laura wondered what Alan was doing right now. She tried to remember what time it would be in Hawaii, then realized he could be thousands of miles west of the islands, heading closer and closer to the Japanese homeland. The four short letters they'd received just yesterday had been a month old.

"Gentlemen, find your ladies, we're about to welcome in the New Year," announced Ray from the bandstand. Just before he started the countdown, Laura quickly rose and joined the regular male vocalist, Danny Davis, at the mike. As the band began to play "Auld Lang Syne", Laura, Danny, and Ray held hands close to the mike and swayed to the music. Behind them a red, white, and blue banner was lowered from the ceiling. It read, in sequined script, *"PEACE IN 1944."*

Laura returned to the table, where she hugged Belle and Helen, kissed Abe, and turned to John. "Happy New Year, Captain," she said.

"Happy New Year, Mrs. Stewart." He smiled and leaned toward her.

She realized she'd never been kissed before by a man with a mustache Her uncle Charles had a bushy, walrus-style one, but his pecks on the cheek didn't count.

"Well, I hate to break up the party, but I promised the boys I'd be home," she said, looking over at Abe and Belle.

"Look, you folks don't have to leave. You either, Helen. I can take you home," John said to Laura. "I've got a base car."

"No, that's all right," Laura said. She felt herself blushing. "Helen, you stay. You're all right with going now?" she asked, looking at Belle and Abe.

"Sure we are," Belle said, patting Laura's hand. "Wonder what Nan and the kids are up to? Wanna bet on whether Gary lasted 'til midnight?"

They drove slowly up State Street, along with a lot of other revelers tooting their car horns. People must have somehow gotten hold of extra gas rations at the last minute, since Laura suspected everyone wasn't as careful as Abe in planning ahead.

"Captain Lawrence there is a nice guy," Belle said. "Kind of reminds me of Errol Flynn. You know, the mustache and all."

"Yes, that's new," said Laura. Then she quickly added, "I think." She could still feel where it had tickled her upper lip when he kissed her.

☜∘☞

The next morning Billy kept Gary amused and Lucille quiet so that Laura could sleep a few hours later than usual. After breakfast, she telephoned her parents and Ceil to wish them a Happy New Year. Originally, they'd planned to come up to see her sing, but she was just as glad that hadn't worked out. There would have been disapproving looks from her mother regarding John, and questions on the side from her sister. Since there was clearly nothing to tell either one of them, it would have only irritated her.

Late in the afternoon everyone walked across the yard to the Mazzarella house. As Angie opened the heavy storm door, its glass steamy from all the cooking inside, the aroma of Mary's tomato sauce filled the back porch. Laura brought her wartime chocolate cake with no eggs, butter or milk. Nan made a Scottish shortbread that used so much sugar and butter it nearly wiped out both her own monthly rations and Laura's.

Abe contributed a gallon of cider and a bottle of Manischewitz Concord grape wine. "Not as good as yours, Salvatore," he said, as he handed it to Angie to put on the table. Several bottles of the Mazzarella homegrown variety were already neatly lined up on the checkered cloth.

Despite the ongoing shortages, Mary had outdone herself in the food department. The dining room table was laden with a huge plate of antipasto, two big pans of cheese lasagna, and a steaming pot of hearty lentil stew. On the sideboard, the chocolate cake and shortbread joined plates of Italian desserts—*panettone* filled with raisins and dates and apricots; *crostata*, made of pears, almonds, and chocolate; and lots of cookies in all shapes and sizes.

Laura noticed that Billy was examining the colored illustrations on the *torrone* containers, little pale yellow boxes that held individual nougats wrapped in rice paper.

"You were always fascinated by those pictures, even when you were little, before you could talk," Laura said to him. He was acting quiet today, and she wondered if he was thinking about Sal. Sometimes she forgot Alan wasn't the only one everyone was missing. Billy had been around Sal and Angie ever since he was a baby.

"The ladies and men in the pictures always look so dressed up," Billy said, holding one of the boxes. "And the old buildings are so different from Springfield." He showed her a painting of a man in a fancy feathered hat and a billowing shirt. On the opposite side of the miniature box was a drawing of the leaning tower of Pisa.

Laura turned to Nonno, who was sitting in a big overstuffed armchair. "Nonno," she said, "Have you been here? Pisa?" She pointed to the picture on the little container.

"I come from the south. *Bella*. Not Pisa. Too far up, near Firenze." He made a motion with his hand on his nose.

"That means he doesn't like the north," said Angie. "Gary, come here, you can take one of these little presents from the *ceppa*." Angie walked over to the small tree made out of triangles of wood that Nonno had built shortly after he came to America. On the lowest shelf of the tree was a nativity scene composed of figures that had been in the family for years.

Laura heard the doorbell ring and watched as Salvatore went to the front hallway. Suddenly there was a cry outside the living room. Laura glanced out the window near where she was sitting and saw a Western Union delivery boy walking slowly down the steps. She quickly got up just as Mr. Mazzarella appeared in the doorway. He was holding an open telegram in his hands.

"*La Santa Madre de Dios!*" Mary screamed.

"What is it, Papa?" cried Angie.

"It's good, it's good!" replied Salvatore. "From Sal. Happy New Year!"

"Ah, from Salvatore!" Mary clapped her hands. "Read, read!"

"Here, Angelina, you read to everyone," her father said.

"Sure." Angie jumped up and took the telegram. "It's in Italian, so I'll read and then translate. He says: *Buon Natale Felice Anno Nuovo* stop *Grazie per i presenti* stop *Abbraccio a tutti* stop *Ciao al Billy ed alla famiglia* stop *Sal.*'

"OK, he says: '*Merry Christmas and Happy New Year and thanks for the presents.*' And he gives us all a hug. Then he says hello to Billy and his family, too."

"Oh, the sweetheart," said Nan, wiping her eyes.

"I'll bet he's in Italy," Abe said. "I think he's giving us a hint, plus he's probably really used to Italian by now."

"Angie, maybe your grandfather could say something, give us a toast," said Laura.

Nonno nodded. "*Si*, I know." He rose slowly from his chair, paused and then raised his wine glass. "For Salvatore. *Alla sua vita lunga*." He slowly added in English, "To... his... long... life."

There was a noisy clinking and shuffling of chairs as everyone toasted Sal.

"That's like your life, Nonno" said Laura. "Like your own long life."

"*Si, mia graziosa*, my pretty one. Like me," Nonno replied, smiling. "*Con speranza*. I hope."

Chapter 34: Belle

"What do you talk about with the other ladies, Belle?" Billy asked as he helped clear the table for dessert. Belle, along with Ada Brown, was heading downtown after dinner to attend a meeting of a women's group she'd recently joined.

"Mostly stuff about how things can be changed for us in the workplace," Belle replied. "I think someone from out of town is speaking tonight."

"Can I go, too?" Gary asked.

"Nope, only us gals are allowed. Well, I suppose a man or boy *could* go if he wanted to. But so far the only one I've seen at a meeting was a guy from one of the unions. And he wasn't too popular."

"Why was that, Belle?" asked Laura.

"Well, he was trying to explain why the union wasn't in favor of day care centers at work," Belle explained. "Some bull about how it would give companies too much control over our lives. Trouble is, the unions are run by men, and they really don't understand how hard it is to work and make sure the kids are taken care of." Belle laughed sarcastically. "Jerks!"

"But we have Nan to take care of us," said Billy.

"That's right," said Laura. "I probably couldn't work otherwise, and then where would we be without your dad's regular paycheck? We're just lucky we have Nan. I think it's wonderful that you've gotten involved, Belle."

"How come you don't go, Ma?" asked Gary.

"Well, I would, but with working in the day and singing on the weekend...I want to be home with you and Billy when I can."

"That's right, your mother has enough to do," said Belle. "But she's helping 'cause she's a married lady who finally got hired by the Mutual. See?"

"How come Mrs. Brown goes to the meetings?" asked Billy. "She doesn't work."

"No, Ada—Mrs. Brown—doesn't work anymore, but you better believe she understands."

"Oh, I expect Mrs. Brown was a real troublemaker in her day!" said Nan. "Now, mind you, I don't mean a *bad* troublemaker." She glanced at Gary, who had broken a bottle of milk earlier when he was poking around in the refrigerator after school. "I think it's good to see the girls get ahead.

"When I think of how hard I had to work when I first came to this country…I have half a mind to go to this meeting with you! I didn't mind the long hours, it was the poor wages. And I don't think that girls today who clean houses are much better off. No sir!"

"Gee, Nan, you *should* go. You'd be a good speaker," said Billy.

"Nan's right. Things haven't changed much," said Belle. "See, so that's why we're meeting!"

The talk was being held in the small upstairs reception room at the art gallery where Belle had seen the Georgia O'Keeffe paintings. The owner, an old friend of Ada's, greeted them at the entrance way. Belle remembered her white hair, severely pulled back and fastened with a big amber clasp. Tonight she was wearing a long black dress with oversized silver and turquoise jewelry. She didn't look like she belonged in Springfield. *Well, neither does Ada*, Belle thought, as Mrs. Brown took off her silver fox and tucked a few loose strands of her hennaed hair under the green turban that covered her head.

Belle was sure Hannah would be in the crowd, and she looked forward to seeing her again. And Charlotte. She'd visited with them only a few times since that first night at Abe's, though he talked about his daughter all the time.

"Ada and Belle! Good to see you," Hannah said as they took a seat in the row behind her. "Charlotte's introducing our guest tonight, Leonora Abercrombie. She's from the WTUL."

It pleased Belle that she already knew this stood for the Women's Trade Union League. A few months ago she'd have wondered what in the world Hannah was talking about—and probably wouldn't have cared.

Mrs. Leonora Abercrombie was an older woman—Belle guessed she was pushing sixty—wearing a dark maroon wool suit and matching handbag and shoes. It was hard to tell if the lavender hue of her carefully coiffed hair was the result of a rinse or the effect of the soft pink light from the torchière set up next to the lectern. An impressively large diamond glinted on her ring finger.

Not the kind of person you'd expect to be talking about workers' rights, Belle thought.

When Mrs. Abercrombie began her remarks with a story about serving on a committee with Eleanor Roosevelt in New York, however, Belle was intrigued. "Wait 'til I tell Nan about her knowing Mrs. Roosevelt," she whispered to Mrs. Brown.

"Yes. Rather impressive, that, isn't it?" she replied.

Mrs. Abercrombie's brief talk focused on efforts to enact new legislation that would benefit women in the labor force. She'd been involved in lobbying for the Fair Labor Standards Act back in 1938, which set minimum wages and decent work hours for all. Now, with millions of women in wartime work, it was time again for action.

In the question-and-answer session that followed the speaker's remarks, Hannah was first to raise her hand. "Most of what has been accomplished by the League has focused on women in professional jobs," she began. "I'm not saying they're not discriminated against—they are, especially financially when they've taken the place of male managers.

"But what about the women on the front lines?" she continued. "I'm talking about factory workers, for example. A lot of them are young mothers who've been left alone with their kids. And what about Negro women?"

Mrs. Abercrombie cleared her throat. "Well, unfortunately you're right. I have to be frank with you about that. But it's a start. Look, what we need to do is work more with the War Manpower Commission and the National War Labor Board," she explained.

"But nearly all of them are men!" a women in the back said.

"Yes, true again. But at least they deal specifically with issues that have come up since the war began."

"What about *after* the war?" Belle asked. "What happens to us then?"

"That's a difficult issue," Mrs. Abercrombie replied. "We can't have the men going on the unemployment line, now, can we? And I do believe most women will be willing to give up their jobs and go back to their important work at home."

"Yeah, but what about those of us who have to work?" Belle asked.

"Well, I hope your employer would recognize the value of women who do want to remain at their jobs."

Mrs. Brown raised one eyebrow and smiled skeptically. "Don't hold your breath," she whispered to Belle.

After the talk, the four women—Belle, Ada, Charlotte and Hannah—decided to skip the reception and get a bite to eat at a downtown restaurant. As they headed up the side street toward Main, they passed the Loew's Poli Theater. Despite the chill of the early March wind, there was a crowd standing in line for the second show.

"*The White Cliffs of Dover*," said Belle. "That's supposed to be a real tearjerker."

"Get my dad to take you. He likes Irene Dunne," replied Hannah. "Yikes, it's freezing. Let's move it, girls."

Heads lowered against the wind coming up from the river, they crossed Main and hurried over to Broadway and the Honeymoon Hamburg restaurant. As they settled into a booth, Charlotte said, "So what did you two think about the meeting?"

Belle hesitated, but Mrs. Brown said, "I admire Mrs. Abercrombie for doing what she's doing. At least some things have changed since I was a young woman after the last war. And that's certainly because of groups like the WTUL. But I wonder if they're directing their efforts on behalf of all of us—all of us women, I mean."

"Well, Ada, that's exactly the problem," Hannah said. "Trouble with the WTUL, as I said at the meeting, is that they've focused a lot of their energy on women in upper level jobs. You know about the Lanham Act? Well..."

She paused as the waitress took their orders. "Anyway," she continued, "that act provides money for day care centers to be established so that women with kids don't have to worry what's happening when mommy's fitting gun barrels down at the Armory. Trouble is, unions aren't crazy about the idea, because they think that it's giving management too much direct access to government funding. And too much power. And even women's groups don't seem to be as concerned as they should."

"Plus," added Charlotte, "you can be very sure that this funding will end after the war. They've even *said* it's a temporary thing until the men are back in the workplace."

"But if the war goes on...," said Belle. "Right now, with us stuck at Anzio, it doesn't look like it's going to end any time soon, never mind the Japs over in the Pacific. If it goes on, won't it be harder for women to leave, the longer they're working?" Belle asked.

"Sure, it'll be harder for the *women* to leave, those who want to stay on. But who's going to argue against giving the men their jobs back? Somehow, we've got to work toward a situation where we can all manage together." She added, "And I don't think Anzio is anything more than a brief setback. You watch, there'll be a big invasion of the continent before you know it."

"Well, I hate to say it," added Charlotte, "but women being seen as equal to men—this so-called working together—is going to be hard when the government's not really on your side."

"What do you mean, Charlotte?" Mrs. Brown asked. "What about the Lanham Act that Hannah just mentioned?"

"All right, that *is* an example of their doing something positive," replied Charlotte. "But, remember, it was done only out of necessity and as a temporary measure. The Office of War Information, which is essentially a propaganda factory—and I'm not saying that's bad—is constantly portraying women as...I don't know...as *handmaidens* to men."

"Yeah," said Hannah. "I saw a short film on army nurses the other night that showed them checking their stocking seams and applying their makeup as much as doing anything else. It was ridiculous. The impression you get is that they're either vain little creatures or strictly in the service to snag a man."

"And what about the Children's Bureau!" said Charlotte. "They just came out with a report showing that child care without the mother leads to delinquency. Thank you, gentlemen," she said sarcastically, waving her coffee cup in the air and nearly spilling its contents.

"Maybe things haven't changed as much as I thought," Mrs. Brown said. "Thank heavens for young women like you two. And you and Laura, Belle," she added. "You're doing your share. Speaking of applying makeup, excuse me for a moment while I powder my nose."

While she was gone, Hannah said, "You know, Belle, it's so good to see how my dad is these days. It's like he's dropped ten years. You've been great for him."

"That's not hard, Hannah," said Belle. "He's one in a million. Younger men, phooey!"

"I'll second that," Hannah said. They all laughed and finished their coffee.

"Has he mentioned our plans to you?" Charlotte asked. "Our big adventure?"

"He said something about your wanting to go into business, that's all."

"Yes, well," began Hannah. "We're thinking of opening up a bookstore."

"Wow," said Belle. "You mean, like Johnson's?" Johnson's, on Main Street, was the place everyone thought of when the word "bookstore" was mentioned.

"Yes," said Charlotte. "Except that we'd just have books, not gifts and stationery. And we'd try to stock titles that are a bit out of the mainstream, too."

"Won't that take a lot of money?" asked Belle. "To start up and all?"

"I've been saving for this for years," replied Charlotte. "And Abe's offered to be an investor."

"Well, girls, if you ever need anyone in the store, keep me in mind," said Belle. "After our conversation tonight, I'm not so sure now how long I'll last at the factory!"

"Just might take you up on that. But you'll end up OK. Believe me, most working women are a heck of a lot worse off than you. Look, you're already a boss, kind of."

"Yeah, I know," Belle replied. "Still, sometimes I wish I'd continued someplace after high school. Not necessarily a regular college, but something extra."

"It's never too late for that, Belle," said Ada Brown, who'd returned to the booth, fresh lipstick and newly applied perfume evident as she sat down. "I had my real education out West, and I wasn't in my teens, I can tell you."

What is her story? Belle wondered. She'd meant to ask Nan more about Mrs. Brown's past. "Thanks, Ada. I may just do something. Actually, Abe's been after me to enroll in business school."

"There you go," said Hannah. "You could help clerk *and* do our books!"

After Charlotte and Hannah explained their bookstore plans to Ada, the four women left the hamburger joint and walked to the bus stop. Belle and Ada's State Street bus arrived first. As they boarded, Belle handed her a red ticket. "Here, put your dime away," she said. "I've got an extra."

As the bus trudged up the hill, the deep potholes wreaked havoc on the shocks, and the wind whistled through the loosened window frames. "I hope we don't puncture a tire," shouted Mrs. Brown, laughing. "They're probably worn straight through to the tube!" Although public utilities had first priority in the replacement of vehicle parts, rubber was still extremely scarce.

They reached a smoother stretch of road at the top of the rise, near the big High School of Commerce, Belle's alma mater. "How do you think Billy is faring during all this war business, Belle?" Mrs. Brown asked.

"All right, I think, though sometimes I do worry. With Sal away, it's like he's missing both his father *and* his big brother. I hate to think of...anything happening." She looked out at the window as the bus passed the hundreds of lighted windows of the Armory.

"Billy's so...well, to himself," Belle continued. "You never quite know what's going on in that mind of his. And it's a pretty sharp mind. Sometimes he makes me feel like I'm his kid sister or something, instead of his aunt."

"Isn't that true, though?" answered Ada. "I often forget that I'm talking to a little person who could be...well, not my son certainly, but my grandson. It's funny how we relate to people.

"You know how highly I think of your mother, Belle. Now, when it comes to her—promise you won't laugh—I often feel I'm with my mother. Imagine...I'm the older by several years. Sometimes when I come for tea in the afternoon, I can hardly wait for her to greet me at the door. It's like coming home to your family, or maybe to the one you never had."

"She affects a lot of people like that, Ada," replied Belle. "When I was a kid, it used to bother me. 'Hey, she's *our* mother!' Alan and I wanted to say. Now I feel I'm just lucky."

They rode in silence for a while. Then Mrs. Brown said, "Belle, do you have a sense from Alan or Laura of any plans they have for Billy after high school?"

"College, you mean? Gee, that seems like a long way off, but I guess it's not. No, I'm not sure. He'd be the first in the family to go. I guess if he got a scholarship it'd be possible. You know, Alan would have managed to go on to college—he was the one with the brains when we were kids — but he had to work to help Nan and me." She looked at Ada. "You think Billy definitely should go, I guess?"

"Oh my, yes. I've been thinking about it. He's an exceptional boy. We'll have to see what we can do."

Now what does she mean by that? Belle wondered. But their stop was fast approaching, and they both had all they could do to yank the cord and reach the back door without falling as the bus lumbered to a wheezy halt. "Brakes aren't in too good shape, either," Belle said as they stepped out onto the dark pavement.

"It's easier for me to go down my street here," said Mrs. Brown. "So I'll say goodnight. Thank you, Belle. I had a lovely evening."

"Me, too, Ada." On impulse, she reached over and gave the older woman a brief hug. "Goodnight."

The wind wasn't as strong as it had been downtown, but it was chilly enough as it whooshed against Belle's legs and up under her coat and skirt. She was sorry she'd decided against slacks, especially since half the women at the talk had been wearing them. She should have realized that would be the case.

Shivering as she turned the corner, Belle wondered if her mother would still be up, knitting or reading. If she'd already gone to bed, she'd probably be dozing by now, glasses askew and book open on her lap.

Belle quickened her pace, the sound of her heels on the cold pavement echoing down the darkened street. She was glad to see the living room lights still on as she walked up the path to the front porch. Belle thought of what Ada had mentioned about always feeling like she was coming home when she stopped over to visit Nan. Opening the unlocked door, she understood exactly what Ada meant.

Chapter 35: Alan

"Christ, I can hardly wait to get into town," said Buzz as the liberty bus pulled away from the fleet landing.

"Yeah, this hanging around is for the birds," replied Alan. They were heading into Honolulu again after several days of virtual inactivity at the base. Though their ship was still under repair, the crew was on normal call. They could be told at any time they were taking a trial run in the waters off the islands or ready to pull anchor for parts unknown.

"Sometimes it seems like the Japs aren't even out there," Alan said. Except for the swarms of military personnel and the stockpiles of *materiel* evident everywhere on Oahu, the only other concrete evidence he'd seen of the war was the devastation in the harbor along Battleship Row. These days the battles were being fought thousands of miles away in places like Bataan, Guadalcanal, the Coral Sea, and, most recently, Tarawa.

"So, you coming with me, or heading off by yourself?" Buzz asked.

"Oh, I think I'll just wander around," Alan said.

"Ha! You must be seeing that babe again!" Alan said nothing in reply, though he smiled slightly as he looked past Buzz out the window. He knew he could probably trust Buzz, but he wasn't even sure himself what was happening.

When he called Edie yesterday, she agreed to meet him in town, though he had to persuade her all over again. You couldn't blame her for that, he supposed. After all, he was a married man, a detail he'd apparently made her only too aware of during their first encounter.

What surprised Alan was that he himself wasn't especially bothered by this fact. Everything about his life now—Hawaii, the war, his shipmates—was so unlike anything he'd experienced before. Sometimes it felt like he was floating in slow motion through a new world, observing a stranger—himself—as much as watching all the others he was also encountering for the first time. It reminded him of the pleasant buzz he'd get after a few drinks, except that he'd been pretty much on the wagon for a long time, if you didn't count the recent afternoon with Edie. In any event, Laura and the boys seemed a million miles away. The war and Hawaii and Edie were here, and so was he..

Edie. He couldn't get her off his mind, and he was determined to see her again before he left the island. It was as simple as that.

"How about if we meet in the lobby of the Army-Navy Y?" Alan suggested to her on the telephone.

"The Y?" she asked, laughing.

"It's perfectly respectable. I was in the lobby the other day."

"Oh, it's more than respectable, I know that," Edie said. "It just struck me as funny, that's all."

As the bus lumbered into the central drop-off area near Chinatown, the scene was the same as Alan remembered from the week before. Hordes of enlisted men spilled into the square like randy jailbirds, the first-timers obvious as they gaped and took in the cacophony of sounds and smells. The second- and third-timers headed straightway for the bars, whorehouses, restaurants, and movie theaters that filled the surrounding streets.

Alan waited for some time in the large and comfortable sitting room of the Y, reading a copy of the *Star-Bulletin* the volunteer lady at the reception desk had offered. The war news was sobering. Though the Italian campaign was progressing, the advance up the mountainous boot was taking its toll. The Anzio landing had been especially brutal, and the beachhead still wasn't under firm control.

Alan wondered about Sal. In one of her letters a while back, Laura had mentioned that they'd heard he was somewhere in Italy. Not exactly the best way to see his ancestral home for the first time. Alan had a sudden craving for a plate of Mary Mazzarella's spaghetti.

"Anything good happening anywhere? Or is that a silly question?" He looked up with a start to find Edie standing a couple of feet away from him. He quickly folded the paper and stood up.

"Hey, I didn't hear you." He was momentarily flustered. "Well, the beach assault in that town in Italy, Anzio, was a killer. And now I'm reading that the casualties on Tarawa were worse than—"

"Whoa, I asked about *good* news," Edie replied, smiling. "Quick, give me a real friendly hug, and let's get out of here. This place makes me nervous."

As they walked away from the square, they passed the Black Cat, where the smells of steak and hamburgers and the sound of a swing band spilled out onto the narrow sidewalk. "Hungry?" Alan asked.

"No, let's eat later," Edie replied. "Somewhere, uh...different."

"I didn't mean there in particular." He realized he didn't really know whether that was a place you'd take a girl to or not. They didn't tell you about stuff like this in the Navy Blue Book.

"Say, what was that about, back there?" he asked, remembering Edie's rush to leave the Y.

"The hug business? Didn't want them to assume I was on the prowl for a lonely sailor." She ran her fingers through her hair in that half-casual, half-nervous way Alan remembered.

"Gee, that never crossed my mind," he replied. "Anyway, they wouldn't have thought that." Edie was wearing a pretty halter sundress, white with large red flowers, and high-heeled strap sandals that reminded him of the kind Laura liked. "You look swell."

"Yeah, well, Honolulu is full of swell-looking girls you wouldn't want to take home to mother." She laughed. "Believe me."

"Where are we headed?" Alan asked as they turned into a side street. Edie's loose skirt moved gracefully to the tap of her brisk steps on the sidewalk.

"Here we are," she replied. "Hop in."

"This is yours? Really?" They'd stopped in front of a lime-green Lincoln Zephyr convertible.

"Surprised? Yeah, I guess it *is* mine, sort of. Let's just say it was a nice present. "Want to drive?"

"No, that's OK," Alan replied. "Not used to these narrow streets. You do the honors." He examined the mahogany interior. "This is a pretty late model, isn't it? I don't think I've seen one like it."

"Yes, it's a '42. I don't think many more made it off the assembly line." Passenger car production in Detroit had come to a virtual standstill last year. "I get asked about it all the time."

They headed in the direction of the mountains that rose behind the sprawl of narrow residential streets on the outskirts of the downtown area. *"Uka,"* explained Edie. "That means 'inland'. I thought I'd take you to see the view from up there." She pointed toward the purple and green mountains ahead, their peaks shrouded in misty gray clouds. "The Pali. It's pretty spectacular."

Within minutes they were high above the city, cruising along the narrow Pali Road, the 12-cylinder engine of the Lincoln easily negotiating the steep climb into the Koolau Range. Except for the frequent hairpin turns, which she negotiated with care, Edie was not your usual lady driver.

"Hey, you don't have to make this boat live up to its name!" Alan yelled above the roar of the wind. He'd lowered himself in his seat so that his eyes were level with the silver and bronze ornament adorning the front of the hood. A sphere with a plumed spire, it resembled the helmet of a Roman centurion heading into battle.

"What do you mean?" she asked innocently. "I don't get the joke."

"Zephyr, wind. Jesus, I feel like I'm in a cyclone!" he replied, laughing.

"Oh, this breeze is nothing," Edie said, pretending not to understand. "Wait 'til we get out at the top. That's when you'll really feel the wind."

With a quick turn, Edie pulled off the road near the top of the pass and came to an abrupt halt. They were within a car's length of a sheer drop of several hundred feet. The scarlet burst of an occasional Royal Poinciana and the vivid golden hues of the rainbow shower tree underscored the lush green of the jungle valley far below.

"Alan, hand me my sweater from the back, would you?" shouted Edie, who'd already gotten out of the car. "And brace yourself!"

He stepped out and was nearly knocked over by the force of the wind. Though the weather had been clear and balmy as they ascended, now the clouds blocked out the rays of the sun, except for filtered ribbons here and there in the distance. The air felt about 40 degrees cooler.

"Come here, look at this!" Edie yelled as she faced the gusts blowing furiously through the pass.

The view was spectacular, an unbroken vista of green and brown plains and hills stretching to a distant semi-circular bay sparkling in the muted sunlight. A few military vessels, small silver slashes, were just visible near the horizon

"That doesn't look like Honolulu," Alan said, noting the sparseness of buildings and harbor activity.

"No, no, you're looking at the northeast coast, the windward side of the island," Edie said. "That's Kaneohe Bay. The wind is like this because it's all coming through the pass in the mountains. Just like the Jap planes on their way to Pearl Harbor. They came through right here that morning." She shivered.

"Cold?" Alan asked. He nuzzled Edie's neck and hugged her from behind, enveloping her with his arms and body. Her hair whipped around his face, and he could smell the flowered scent he remembered from her bedroom pillow. He found himself getting hard as he moved slowly against her.

She turned and kissed him, and for a long moment he forgot how close they were to the edge of the cliff. "Hey, we're going to end up on the top of one of those trees," he finally murmured.

"Wouldn't be a bad way to go," Edie whispered in his ear. "I can think of worse." But then she pulled away, took his hand, and led him to the car. "Let's head back," she said.

As they zigzagged more slowly down the Pali Road, the Zephyr in second gear, Edie said, "I love that spot. There's quite a history to it. A long time ago a lot of warriors hurled themselves over that cliff rather than surrender to King Kamehameha and his army."

Alan shuddered. "What's the matter? Cold, too?" she asked. "I warned you."

"No... I don't know...that story, plus the Jap planes and the shrieking wind. The view is something all right, but it's kind of a creepy place."

"Well, the part about the Japs, yeah, I guess," she replied. "And that wind is god-awful. But not the warriors. They knew what they had to do and they did it."

Alan glanced at Edie, her face in sharp profile as the wind buffeted her hair. She had to be young, that was pretty obvious, but you wouldn't think it from the way she spoke.

"I have to remember to tell my son that story," Alan said. "He's real interested in history and stuff like that." He instantly regretted mentioning his family, but he hadn't known what else to say.

"How old is he?" Edie asked.

"He'll be 11 his next birthday. My other boy is almost six."

They rode in silence for a while, and then Edie said, "How about a swim? You'll want to be able to say you were on the beach at Waikiki."

"Uh, OK," Alan replied. "If we have time." He wondered what else she had in mind. "I don't have a bathing suit or anything, though."

"Oh, you can get something at the hotel. They have special facilities for servicemen. And I have mine in the car. Always carry one just in case I get the urge. Even with the military restrictions, you can stop lots of places."

As they walked through the lobby of the Moana Hotel and headed toward the beach, Edie said, "This is where they broadcast 'Hawaii Calls,' out here in the courtyard." An enormous banyan spread its roots over half the terrace, threatening to invade both the interior of the hotel and the beach itself.

"Gee, we've...I've...listened to that show I don't know how many times," Alan replied. "I can't believe I'm really seeing the tree."

"Meet you back here in a couple of minutes," Edie said. As he walked over to a booth with a sign that read 'Welcome Military Personnel,' Alan was already imagining Edie in her bathing suit. It was still only mid-afternoon, time enough to spend a couple of hours on the beach and then, he hoped, a couple more at her house before curfew.

"Well, you're really going native!" Edie exclaimed as she approached Alan a few minutes later in the deep shade of the banyan. "Hubba hubba!"

"Hey, I'm supposed to be the one that says that," Alan replied. "All the trunks they had left in there were small. They told me other sailors were wearing these, so I guess it's OK." He felt the knot at his waist to make sure his skirt was fastened securely.

"That's called a lava-lava," Edie said. "It's the Samoan version of the sarong. Say, did you choose that particular number yourself?" Alan's lava-lava was a red print with big white flowers, the same colors as the dress she'd been wearing a moment ago.

"Nah, that's what they gave me," he laughed. "Maybe they saw us come in. Are you sure it looks all right?" He was admiring her two-piece purple suit, which showed off her slim figure. She reminded him of Laura—small-breasted with great legs.

"Sure, it's OK. I'll be the envy of every girl on the beach," Edie replied. "Just be sure you've got that tied right." She reached out and tugged at the knot.

"Hey, careful!" Alan yelled, laughing. "Just what I need—to be picked up by the shore patrol." They made their way across the hot, white sand to the edge of the water.

Behind them, to the left of the Moana, the Royal Hawaiian Hotel, a Spanish-Moorish palace, rose in fairytale splendor, its pink stucco walls and delicate bell tower in stunning contrast to the grim evidence of war everywhere. Heavy barbed wire ran along the entire shore as a barrier to enemy infiltration, and military police patrolled the beach in both directions.

Edie raced into the water and swam a good distance out beyond the breakers, in a strong, deliberate crawl. Alan, nervous about the possibility of a big wave making off with his lava-lava, waded closer to the shore.

Later, they relaxed on folding chairs supplied by an elderly Hawaiian beach boy and his helper, a smiling little kid with a missing front tooth who looked to be somewhere between Gary and Billy in age. Alan guessed that virtually all the other men sunning on the rather narrow strip of sand were military. Most were together in groups, though there were a few loners, as well as a handful of other couples, the women all young and good-looking.

"Here, roll over on your stomach and let me put some stuff on you," Edie said, shaking the wet strands of her long hair. "You're going to get broiled." She began smoothing baby oil over his shoulders and neck. He loved the touch of her fingers and hands as she moved lower down his back.

"So...we've got only about four more hours or so..." Alan said. "Umm...how about stopping off at your place in a little while?" He felt awkward and surprisingly shy in suggesting this, but he wanted to make up for last time. And he did want to be close to her—in bed.

Alan felt Edie's hand pause for a moment. Then she said, "Let me finish this up, and we'll talk." From the tone of her voice, Alan had a sudden sinking feeling that his plans might be taking an unexpected turn. He closed his eyes and tried to concentrate on the feeling of Edie's touch on his body.

"Done," she said matter-of-factly. She sat up and removed her sunglasses. "OK, here's what I want to say."

She turned halfway and gazed toward Diamond Head in the distance, and then looked at him directly. "I think it's better that we just stay friends," she said slowly and carefully. "You know, leave it at that."

"Oh," he replied. "Well...All right...What can I say? You have every right. But...why? Was it, you know, when I mentioned my sons?"

"Mmm, yes and no. I don't know, I've been thinking about it. Maybe I was feeling this way all along." She turned again and looked out to sea. On the horizon a seemingly endless convoy of ships was moving slowly toward Pearl Harbor.

"Ready for a long and not-so-pretty story?" she finally asked. She lay back, adjusting the beach towel so that the sand wouldn't get in her hair. He could feel her arm brushing against his. "I feel I owe you that."

"Yes, please," he replied, reaching out his hand and stroking her shoulder. "Thanks."

"OK. Well, first of all, haven't you wondered about my work? What I do for a living?"

"I did, the other day," he said. "Then I figured it was some boring job, and you just didn't want to talk about it. Or maybe couldn't because of security."

"Well, you're right on all counts, kind of" she said. "How do you think I can manage to have a nice little house and a big fancy car?"

"OK, you're right," he said. "I did wonder when I saw the Lincoln. And then when you said it was a gift."

"Well, the house is definitely not mine, not on paper. It belongs to a man...a man who, I guess you could say, employs me. Do you know what I mean?"

"Like...an old man?"

"Older, yes. Not that old. Forty-five or so."

"Yeah, I guess I understand. He's not someone you could... marry?"

"Not at the moment. He's already married. I can't even tell you more about him. He's well known on the island. The house I live in is one he owns under another name, not the place he really lives. Nobody knows about me. Right now he's away in Washington on some war business. He's involved in something with the government because of all the land he owns."

"Do you love him?" Alan asked.

"I don't know," Edie said after a moment. "I guess I do. I'm not sure I'm *in* love with him, if you know what I mean. But he's been good to me."

"So that's what you wanted to tell me? That's not so bad."

"There's more," Edie replied. "I don't know...I suddenly feel like I want you to know everything." Her voice had become a bit shaky.

"Please," Alan said. "I want you to talk."

"OK," she replied. "First of all, my name's not really Edie. It's Ernestine. Ernestine Reick. From a little town in Nebraska called Red Cloud."

"That's the real setting of *My Antonia*!" he said, remembering a high school English teacher he'd had, Miss Richardson, who loved Willa Cather. "That's the real heartland."

"Ah, you're a reader," said Edie. "Yup, that's our claim to fame, one of them. We're also located dead in the center of the United States. I'd never even seen the ocean before coming here."

She paused and then began. "Do you remember when I told you that you reminded me of someone?"

"Yeah, I do."

"That was my husband. Mel."

"Is he...did he die?"

"Yes," she replied. "Here, right here at Pearl. He was in the Navy. He was on duty that Sunday morning."

"I'm sorry," Alan said. "So that's why you were in Hawaii?"

"Yes." She lit another cigarette from the one she was finishing.

"Mel and I were high school sweethearts," she continued. "We were planning to get married back home. Then he decided to enlist in the Navy, so we thought we'd wait and then I'd join him somewhere. This was before the war, in the fall of '41. Anyway, shortly after he left, I found out I was pregnant. So I sailed to Hawaii and we got married here. Then December 7 came."

"Gee, and you really didn't know anyone here, I bet."

"No, not really. And then...then I lost the baby right before Christmas. That's kind of when I went to pieces. I drank a lot. That's when I started to smoke. And other things." She laughed and flicked the ash from her cigarette in the white sand. "I became quite the... party girl.

"I decided not to go home," she continued. "I just couldn't face everyone. But I wasn't a military wife anymore, either. I didn't fit in anywhere."

She traced a little stick figure in the sand. "Anyway, I had... have...one friend, Janie. I'd met her when we worked as temps in an office here in Honolulu. Well, Janie found out she could make a lot of money. Know how?" She looked at Alan. "Going to work in a house. Turning tricks." She rubbed out the stick figure and looked away.

"And...? Alan asked. But he already knew what was coming. He felt a sudden knot in the pit of his stomach.

"And...that's what I decided to do," she replied, looking at him again. "That's where the name Edie comes in. You know, sounds like she'd be kind of a fun-loving gal, right?"

"How long did you, uh, work at this?"

"Well, I hated it, even though the woman who ran the place saved me for her 'best clients,' as she called them. Older locals. Regulars. Nice, mostly. Polite. Couple of wealthy Chinamen, businessmen.

"Anyway, after a few months, this particular man came in and we began to see each other on the sly. And then he asked me to move to my little house. End of story."

They sat in silence. Then Alan said, "Can I ask you how old you are?"

"Sure. I'm almost 22."

"How come you were in the bar that day when I met you?"

"That was a funny coincidence. I'm trying to get Janie to leave what she's doing. I'm worried about her. She was supposed to meet me there, but she never showed up. Then you came in."

Alan took her hand again. "I'm glad you told me. Uh, what should I call you, Edie or Ernestine?"

"Oh God, Edie! I can't stand Ernestine. That was one good result of all this. New name." She laughed and ran her fingers through her black hair, now nearly dry and shining in the sun. "So...I think it's better that we just stay friends, don't you?"

"When did you decide that? You said maybe you'd made your mind up before today?"

"Well, maybe," she said. "But when you mentioned your boys in the car...That made me think. You don't want to get your life all messed up. It could be if we...you know, went on."

"I guess so," Alan replied. But he knew she was right.

They had dinner in a Chinese restaurant, where they ordered drinks in frosted glasses with little paper umbrella toothpicks stuck in the cherries. They kept the conversation light.

"Come on now, try. It's easy once you get the hang of it," Edie said, handing Alan a pair of chopsticks. "Watch me." She deftly balanced her fried rice on the two wooden sticks.

"There's a Chinese restaurant downtown where I live, and they don't even give me chopsticks any more," he replied. "In fact, they take them off the table when they see me coming. I was hopeless."

He told her more about his family, including Belle and Nan. "They all sound nice," Edie said. "Especially your mother. I'm not really that close to mine."

"Yeah, the whole neighborhood thinks the world of her," Alan replied. He wondered what Nan would say if she could see him now. "Anyway, like I was saying, I'm not sure what I'll do after the war. I don't want to go back to my old job. What about you? Is it OK to ask you that?"

"Sure, after what I've told you? I guess you can ask me anything," she replied. "I don't know. I've done a lot of volunteering at the Naval hospital. That kind of appeals to me, nursing or something like that."

"What about your...friend? The man."

"Well, yes, I suppose something could happen there, but he's not free at the moment. I don't know, we'll see."

They drove back in the darkness to the entrance of the landing dock. "I'll leave you here," said Edie. "Let me know when you'll be shipping out, OK? That is, if you can."

"I will," Alan promised. "Except they may not tell us until just before we pull out."

"You know what?" Edie asked. "Somehow I feel a heck of a lot better after talking to you. It's almost like, well, like Mel was here, and now he knows and maybe he understands. I don't mean that it wasn't you I wanted to talk to or be with...It's just...Everything turned out so different after Mel." She turned away. "So different."

"I know," Alan said, reaching for her hand. "I know. You remind me of my wife. Kind of funny, huh?"

"Take care of yourself, Alan," Edie said. "Stay OK for your boys."

"You, too."

"Don't worry about that," she said. "I think I could even take Red Cloud again," she said. "If I had to. But, you know, our home-town gal Willa Cather never came back. She ended up in New York City, of all places. Rich and famous."

They kissed goodbye in the checkered shadow of the high wire gate surrounding the dock. Then Alan watched as the Lincoln slowly turned and moved down the darkened street until its dim rear lights disappeared in the night.

Walking into the barracks a few minutes later, he was surprised to find all the men busy sorting their gear. "Jesus, I thought you'd gone AWOL," Buzz said. "Flew the coop to a little private island or something like that."

"Nope, plans fell through." Alan forced a smile.

"Well, get your shit together, pal. It's 'aloha' time. We're shipping out. Just got the orders. It's bye bye Honolulu, hello who the hell knows where."

Chapter 36: Billy

Billy liked rainy days, when big drops pelted the windows and the wind threatened to blow the yellow blossoms off the forsythias and it seemed like spring really hadn't come after all. When Nan went out shopping late in the afternoon with Gary, he had the house to himself. Other times, he closed the door to his room, a signal that no one, especially his little brother, was to disturb him. Best of all was when he climbed the back stairs, narrow and winding, to the attic.

Book, newspaper, magazine and after-school snack in hand, he'd make his way up, even on sunny days. Covering his lap with one of Nan's discarded quilts— a big throw of gaudy purple and pink squares that Lucille had clawed when she was a puppy—he'd curl up in an overstuffed chair under the dormer window. The late afternoon light filtering through the dusty panes was just enough to read by. There he'd stay until he heard the downstairs sounds of his mother arriving home from work.

Sometimes Angie knocked gently on the door and whispered, "Billy, it's me." That was OK. He and Angie always had stuff to talk about, though lately she'd seemed preoccupied with other things. She'd mentioned a boy in her class named Charlie Flanagan, and Billy wondered if she had a crush on him. He was afraid to ask, though, because he thought she might get mad if it wasn't true. Besides, he really wasn't sure if he wanted to know.

The late afternoon paper today was full of news about the liberation of the eternal city, Rome. A fuzzy picture on the front page showed a huge American tank lumbering past the Coliseum. Astride its big gun sat a scruffy GI, rifle in hand, an unlikely, weary hero riding his oversized chariot.

Sal was somewhere in Italy, working as an aide at a field hospital. Billy wondered if he might be among the crowds of soldiers now moving into the capital. He knew the Allied objective was to push the Germans further and further north. Berlin, where Hitler lived, was the ultimate destination of the forces slowly making their way up the Italian peninsula. Everyone had become familiar with the newspaper maps and diagrams of that big geographical boot, so different from the pretty flowered print of "Bella Italia" that hung in the Mazzarellas' front hallway.

A muffled bark drew Billy's attention to the yard three stories below. Angie was greeting Gary and Lucille, who were playing fetch-the-stick. In one of his letters, Alan had asked the boys to make sure that Lucille got her exercise so that she wouldn't develop arthritis in her legs. She was OK for a few energetic retrievals, but she tired more easily these days. "Like me," Nan said. "We're neither one of us spring chickens anymore."

"Yeah, but Lucille knows when to slow down," Belle told her one night at dinner. "Not like some people I could mention." Mary Mazzarella had reported that Nan fell again on the porch.

Billy wondered if Angie's coming home late from school today had anything to do with Charlie Flanagan. Maybe she'd stop by later. She was supposed to bring over last month's movie magazines, and Laura had a few issues of *Life* and *Time* for Mr. Mazzarella.

Leafing through the latest *Life*, Billy paused at a photo of a wounded solider with bandaged eyes being led down a jungle path by a muscular native in a loincloth. He wondered if the soldier had escaped the malaria that the article said was rampant in the islands. Or the snakes. Billy shuddered.

The next picture spread was of the destroyed monastery atop Monte Cassino, between Naples and Rome. It didn't seem possible anyone could have been left alive after so much bombing, but here was a picture of two scared-looking German soldiers emerging from the rubble, one of them all bandaged up, the other missing a leg. They made Billy think of Roger Bowles.

A few days ago at school, Roger, one of the principal's enlisted sons—the one in the Navy—came to speak to the students. He'd been badly wounded many months ago when his ship was torpedoed off Guadalcanal.

Mrs. Bowles announced at the noon assembly, "And now, boys and girls, one of our war heroes, and, I'm proud to say, my son: Petty Officer Roger Bowles!"

Though most of the kids knew Roger had lost an arm and a leg, it was still a shock when he wheeled himself out onto the stage of the auditorium. Billy had never seen anyone in real life who was missing one limb, let alone two.

Roger spoke about his time in the Pacific and the courage of his fellow sailors and how kind the doctors and nurses had been. He told the kids that it was very important to continue to support the war, and he encouraged them to keep buying bonds and doing all the other things that would lead to victory, like collecting tin and paper and rubber. He even told a funny story about the jokes played on new sailors when their ship crossed the equator.

At the end of Roger's talk, Mrs. Bowles asked, "Any questions, boys and girls?"

"Yes, Candace, what would you like to know?" Mrs. Bowles asked one of Billy's classmates. Billy wasn't surprised that Candace, a big show-off, would be the first to raise her hand.

"Were any of your friends, you know, killed, when your ship got bombed?" asked Candace.

Roger paused for a moment and then said, "A bunch of my friends were killed. My best buddy was blown up when the torpedo hit." Mrs. Bowles put her hand on Roger's knee. "We never even found any parts of him." His voice had gotten loud and shaky, and then all of a sudden he began to sob.

Mrs. Bowles quickly got up and shielded Roger from the audience. You could tell she was upset, too. "Boys and girls, this is a difficult time for all of us. Why don't we all rise and sing 'God Bless America'?" She turned and shifted to the side so that her son could join in. Everyone remained standing after the song, and then they all applauded and cheered as Roger wheeled himself off the stage. He managed a wan smile and a salute as he disappeared into the wings..

Seeing Roger Bowles that day made Billy feel the impact of the war more than anything else so far, except being at Richie's funeral. Of course, everyone was worried all the time about his father and Sal, but that was different. They were still OK.

A slight movement over by the half-opened attic door startled him. He looked up just as Max nudged himself into the room. He padded soundlessly across the bare wooden floor and leaped onto the recessed sill of the dormer window. Satisfied that there were no birds or squirrels in the neighboring fir tree, he turned and focused on Billy's half-full glass of milk.

"Here, Max," Billy said as he carefully poured some out on the plate that had held his Lorna Doone cookies. He placed it on the floor, all the while studying Max up close. He never tired of watching the rapid yet delicate lapping of the cat's pink tongue along the shallow surface of the saucer.

Billy slowly stretched, just like Max, before settling back down in the chair. He picked up his book, a worn copy of *Gone with the Wind* his mother had loaned to many people over the years.

"I don't know," she'd initially said when she saw him reading it. "Maybe it's too...well...too long for you?" Billy had learned that when it came to regulating his reading material, she wasn't quite sure what to do. He'd been reading grown-up novels for a couple of years, though he still liked the kinds of books he got as special gifts, too. Just last week, for his 11th birthday, Mrs. Brown had given him a beautifully illustrated copy of *Robinson Crusoe*.

"Ma," he replied, "I'm telling you, *Gone with the Wind* is easy. Anyway, I already know what happens from the movie." He didn't mention that he'd also been secretly reading *Forever Amber*, a current bestseller he'd found under Laura's bedside table. That, he knew, would get him in trouble for sure. *Forever Amber* had some really juicy parts, but he liked Scarlett O'Hara's story better.

Yesterday, he'd been talking to Mrs. Brown, and she asked him who his favorite character was in the book. "Hmm...Gee, that's hard," he replied. He thought a moment and then said, "Mammy. I like Mammy the best."

"That's an interesting choice, Billy," Mrs. Brown replied. "She *is* a wonderful character all right. What do you like about her especially?"

"Well, she's funny and nice, and she takes care of everyone. She kind of reminds me of Nan."

"That's very perceptive of you," said Mrs. Brown. "But what's the big difference between Nan and Mammy?"

"Oh, that's easy. Mammy's colored and Nan's white."

Mrs. Brown laughed. "You're right about that. But what else does that mean in this book?"

Billy paused and then asked, "That she's a slave?"

"Yes, exactly," replied Mrs. Brown. "Enjoy the book, my dear, it's a wonderful story, but don't forget that Mammy's life is a very hard one. She didn't choose to be a slave."

Billy was recalling his conversation with Mrs. Brown as he read the chapter where Scarlet returns to Tara after the fall of

Atlanta. Mammy is still there, living in poverty with the family. She could have run away after President Lincoln freed the slaves, but she chose to stay.

It was all very complicated, and Billy got lost in thought about what makes people do the things they do. For instance, how was Nan able to leave her parents and brothers and sisters in Scotland and come to America? No one loved her family more than Nan. After she left, she never saw her mother and father again, ever.

"Billy, dinner's ready!. Come on, Nan and Belle are waiting for us. It's one of your favorites, meatloaf." His mother's voice on the landing made Billy realize that he hadn't even heard her arrive home. He put down his book, gathered his things together and, watchful of Max scooting under his feet, made his way downstairs.

⇛⇝

Later that night, after the dishes were done and Billy had taken the trash out and Gary had gotten ready for bed, they all gathered in the living room to listen to the President's special edition of "Fireside Chat." Billy was glad it was being broadcast at 8:30 so he wouldn't miss *Lux Radio Theater*, his favorite show, at 9.

"How come they call this a *fireside* chat?" Gary asked. He was being allowed to stay up and hear the President, though he usually got bored and went to his room. "Is it like when you're at a camp?"

"Well, no, it's from the White House," Laura explained. "Though maybe he's really sitting by a fireplace there. But it's so you feel that President Roosevelt is right here in our living room talking to us, like we were having a conversation by the fireplace."

"But we don't have a fireplace."

"No, but a lot of people do," Billy said. "I heard it was a name that the radio station made up so that people would tune in."

"And it's just like he *is* here with us," said Nan. "He's for the people, FDR. So is Mrs. Roosevelt. What would we do if he weren't our president in these awful days?" As the broadcast started, she moved to a footstool near the radio so she could hear better.

"*Yesterday, on June fourth, 1944, Rome fell to American and Allied troops,*" the President began. "*The first of the Axis capitals is now in our hands. One up and two to go!*"

Billy noticed that during his speech President Roosevelt talked about Italy and the Italians just like they were our friends now. *"Italy should go on as a great mother nation, contributing to the culture and the progress and the goodwill of all mankind."*

"That should make Mary and Salvatore and Nonno feel good," said Belle. "Angie, too," she added, smiling at Billy. "And some of my Italian friends at work. They've had a hard time of it."

After talking about the difficult months that still lay head and hinting at some events that were going to be happening soon, the President ended the broadcast with the words: *May God watch over all of our gallant, fighting men."*

"Amen," said Belle. "And the women. Let's not forget they're over there, too, Franklin." She handed Nan a handkerchief to dry her eyes and said, "What do you say, toots? Let's head back downstairs."

After listening to *Lux Radio Theater* later on in his bedroom, Billy had trouble getting to sleep. He didn't want to get up and go to the bathroom, because he was afraid that Laura wouldn't let him stay up anymore on a school night if she knew he was wide awake from the show. She called it being "all nerved up." He'd had trouble enough persuading her to let him listen late in his room every Monday night.

Tonight's program was an adaptation of the recent movie *Jane Eyre,* with Orson Welles playing the mysterious Mr. Rochester. As he lay in the dark, unable to get the program out of his mind, Billy tried to imagine being blind, like the bandaged solider in the jungle picture in *Life*, and Orson Welles at the end of *Jane Eyre.*

Since there wasn't any moonlight tonight, at first he kept his eyes open and pretended that he was half-blind. That was bad enough, but it was worse when he closed them tight and couldn't see anything at all. None of this made him feel sleepy, though, so he reached over and turned the radio back on, very softly.

Harry James was playing in a late-night remote broadcast from the Hotel Astor in New York. He introduced the next number, "I'm Beginning to See the Light," to be performed by the band's girl singer, Kitty Kallen.

Suddenly the music was cut off by the familiar voice of the announcer Robert Trout: *"We interrupt this program to bring you a special bulletin from London. The Allied invasion of British and American troops on the mainland of Europe has begun."*

Billy's heart began to pound. Maybe the war was ending. He jumped out of bed and raced down to his mother's room. Laura was sitting up in bed reading *Forever Amber*.

"Ma, Ma, turn on the radio! The Allies invaded the mainland of Europe!"

They listened for a while, but there was no further news, except that it was believed that the landings had taken place on the coast of France, in Normandy. "What does this mean, Ma? Is the war nearly over?"

"Well, it certainly seems like the beginning of it," Laura answered. "That'll be good news for Sal, won't it? I wonder if he knows, over there in Italy."

"What about Dad?"

"Well, he'll hear, too, I'm sure," she replied. "But you know, Billy, the Pacific war probably won't be over so soon. That'll take longer. It's a whole different kind of affair over there."

"Yes, I read about that," said Billy. An article in *Life* talked about the thousands of miles between each island and atoll as the Allied forces jumped from one Japanese-held stronghold to the next. Island-hopping, they called it, as though each destination was just a hop and a skip away from the last, but Billy knew better.

∾∿

Though he slept fitfully, Billy nevertheless awoke early the next morning. As he finished dressing for school, he thought he heard a clatter in the yard. He looked out to see a Western Union delivery boy picking up his bicycle from the driveway. Billy waited to see which porch he climbed onto—theirs or the Mazzarells'-and then he ran to the kitchen.

"Ma!" he yelled.

"What now, honey? You're still all nerved up this morning, aren't you?"

"Ma, the telegram boy just went next door to Angie's."

"He did?" Laura ran to the window. "Oh God, what now?" As she said this, the delivery boy walked out the Mazzarellas' kitchen door and down the porch steps, and pedaled slowly away. In a moment, the door flew open and Angie and her mother came running across the yard. Max, grooming himself on the grass, skittered away when he saw them bearing down on him.

"Oh no, something must have happened," Laura said in a low voice. "And Mr. Mazzarella would have already left for work. Belle, too." She raced down the back stairs, Billy at her heels, Lucille picking up the rear. Gary was still in bed.

"Mary, Angie, what is it?" Laura cried. Angie and her mother were already gathered around Nan, who must have seen the telegram boy, too. All of them were crying.

"La santa madre de Dio!" Mary wailed.

"It's Sal," Nan explained. "Sal. He's been hurt. Wounded." She drew Mary to her and began comforting her.

"Angie, may I see?" Laura asked, pointing to the telegram Angie was holding. Angie nodded wordlessly as she handed it to her.

"Ma, what does it say? Please?" Billy asked. He cleared his throat so that he wouldn't choke up.

"Yes, all right," Laura replied. Her hands were shaking as she began to read: *"Regret to inform you that your son Salvatore Mazzarella was wounded in action in Italy. You will be advised as reports of condition are received. Adjutant General."*

Morto? Non morto? cried Mrs. Mazzarella.

"Ma, I told you, no. He's wounded," said Angie. "That's all. *Ferito"*

"Ferito, ferito!" Her cries became louder.

Laura walked over to Billy, whose face had turned white.

"Ma, what does the telegram really mean?"

"I don't know, Billy" Laura whispered. "But at least it's not... you know. At least we know he's in the hospital."

She hugged him and said, "Now you go and take Angie for a ways down in the yard. Talk to her and see if she feels like going to school today. I'm going to stay here with Mrs. Mazzarella and Nan for a minute. Go on, now."

Billy went over to Angie and took her hand. Lucille followed, and the three of them walked slowly toward the swing, where Max the cat was frolicking on his back in the morning sunlight.

Chapter 37: Laura

"I'm so darn sick of the war," Laura said to Helen and Mae as they were finishing lunch on a hot Friday in July. "I'm on my last pair of stockings, and they're about to give up the ghost."

"Same with mine," replied Helen. "And this leg make-up is for the birds." Women were buying colored liquid to paint their legs to look like they were wearing hose. They saved their nylons for special occasions.

"Yeah, especially on a muggy day," said Mae. "Why do we put ourselves through this? You should see the gyrations I go through trying to draw the blasted seam on straight."

"Maybe you can get Captain Lawrence to dig up some nylons," Helen said to Laura. "I hear a lot of officers out at Westover can get just about anything." She was referring to the black market that flourished for hard-to-find items—choice pieces of meat from your friendly butcher, automobile tires if you were lucky enough to have a contact at a garage in town, extra pairs of leather shoes. They were around if you had the right price and the right contact—your own "Mr. Black", as they said.

"Well, you ask him. I wouldn't," Laura replied, giving Helen a look. She was sensitive about John's name coming up in front of Mae, though there was no reason she should be, really. But Laura knew that her older friend disapproved of John, and she hoped Mae understood he was nothing more than an acquaintance who came to hear her sing with the band.

"I just meant that you'd have a better chance than me if you... promised to sing his favorite song or something," Helen said lamely. "That's all." She'd clearly caught Laura's admonishing glance.

"Well, he did say he wants to show the boys and me some of the base," Laura said. "I suppose I could then. I don't know, maybe they sell them at the store there, or whatever they call it. They have their own shops, you know."

"Yes, they say it's like a little town." As the war dragged on, Westover had continued to expand both as a training base and a take-off point for planes heading to the European theater.

"Listen, I'm going to scoot down the hall to the library," Laura said, finishing up her apple pie and milk. "I'll see you girls back in the department."

Billy had asked her to check on the latest young adult mysteries. He'd discovered a new series about a girl detective named Kay Tracy, and the copies at the local public library were always charged out.

"This is a brand new one," the library clerk said to Laura as she selected a cellophane-covered book from the display wall. The jacket depicted a young woman hiding behind a tree, observing a masked man running out the door of a mansion. "Your daughter will be the first one to read this copy."

"Well, actually, it's for my son," Laura explained. "He's already gone through all the Hardy Boys." That was true, but it wasn't why she had offered this extra bit of information. She'd been surprised, and a bit disconcerted, herself the first time Billy had asked her to get a Nancy Drew mystery. He did read everything in sight, but she was aware that most boys probably wouldn't be seeking out stories about girl detectives.

"What's a good new novel?" Laura asked. "For me, I mean. I just finished *Forever Amber*. Maybe something a little less...you know..."

"I understand," replied the clerk, laughing. "But it *was* pretty good, wasn't it?"

"I'll say," Laura replied. She didn't dare tell her that she suspected Billy had read that one, too.

"Here's a new one I really liked. It's about a soldier in a small town in Italy."

"*A Bell for Adano*," Laura read. She'd never heard of the author, John Hersey, but the setting appealed to her. Maybe it would be OK for Billy as well.

She also picked out a title for Nan, a new novel, *Tell Me, My Heart,* by one of her favorites, Faith Baldwin. A "nice little book," as Nan would say.

Laura raced back to the tabulating department and settled in front of her keypunch machine just as the lunch break ended. Four more hours to go. She was looking forward to her upcoming one-week vacation, the first she'd had since she began working last year.

She'd made no special plans, other than a visit to see Ceil. They were planning on taking the kids to the circus in Hartford.

There were a lot of things Laura liked about her job: the nice working conditions, her new friends, getting dressed up every day, and, of course, her weekly pay, meager as it was after taxes. Still, twenty dollars was twenty dollars.

She was bored a good deal of the time, however, and sometimes had trouble staying awake. Helen's sudden "Pssst!" from the adjoining desk had become a familiar warning that snapped her head up more than once, especially on warm, seemingly endless afternoons.

Walking home at five that evening, she thought about what to serve for dinner with the fish she planned to pick up at Perry's Market. Nan was having problems with her leg again, so Laura had insisted on cooking. The band was off on a weekend engagement at a ballroom on Long Island, and, though it would have been fun, she'd persuaded Ray Jardine to let her take a break. Billy and Gary, she knew, were looking forward to having her around more often during the summer.

Fish for the Friday night meal meant that she wouldn't be stopping at Mr. Simka's or the A&P to see what cut of meat she could finagle from the butcher's extra stash. My own little complicity in the black market, she thought with a laugh, but what the heck. Everyone knew someone who could work a deal—or be extra accommodating.

The fact was that she'd become comfortable with Simka's suggestive glances and had grown adept at a bit of teasing with him. Why not? She knew how she affected men, and, besides, it added a bit of excitement to her dull life. *It's come to this*, she thought ruefully as she waited at a corner to cross the street, *flirting with the corner butcher for a choice sirloin.*

Laura walked into Perry's, noisy and hot, the air pungent with the fishy smells she remembered from her childhood summers at the shore. She decided on cod, which everyone liked except Belle, who wouldn't be home for dinner. "Perry, could you wrap that up with some extra paper? Can't afford to get this dress messed up." Laura was wearing a new green chambray that cost ten dollars, way too much, but she hadn't been able to resist.

"Sure thing, my love," Perry replied. "Wouldn't want to spoil that pretty outfit." Perry, who had to be pushing 65, was another of her admirers. She smiled as he jotted the price down with the pencil stub that seemed to be tucked behind the ear of every butcher and fish person and grocery clerk in the world.

"Say hello to Mrs. Stewart, will you?" he asked. Nan had been trading at the market for years. "And next time you write Alan, tell him I've got a big lobster waiting just for him."

As she walked the rest of the way home, Laura wondered what Belle and Abe were doing tonight. She was happy for Belle, who'd had her share of bad apples. She always seemed to pick the good-time Charlies. Abe was just the opposite.

Laura wondered how she herself would have fared if she hadn't met Alan right after high school. She didn't have anyone else to compare him to, really. Besides, once she discovered Billy was on the way there had been no choice, though they'd already made plans to marry.

She hoped he'd be able to get his job back at Westinghouse after the war, though she knew he wasn't all that happy there. Maybe he'd be able to start college part-time. She'd eagerly written him about the GI Bill of Rights that had become law a few weeks ago, providing a lot of money for veterans who wanted to go back to school. If he could hold out at Westinghouse, they'd be all set.

At the dinner table, Laura was glad to see that Billy was more talkative. She'd been worried about him ever since they'd received news of Sal's injury. For a week he'd hardly spoken to anyone except Angie. The two of them had been a mournful pair, sitting for hours on end in the garden swing. Even Lucille and Max had seemed more subdued as they followed the children around the house and in the backyard. Everyone said it was a good sign they'd not had another telegram, though, so the kids' mood had gradually improved.

And then one day the Mazzarellas heard directly from Sal. A German plane had strafed his medical jeep when he was delivering supplies. He wrote that he was going to be all right, but Laura wondered about the extent of his injuries. You heard stories all the time about men coming back with terrible wounds and missing limbs, like the son of the principal at Billy's school. They'd just have to wait and see.

Billy had also received his own short letter from Sal, which he proudly read to everyone. They all laughed when Sal described a little dog he'd adopted. He'd named him Ernesto, in honor of the war correspondent Ernie Pyle, who'd passed through the hospital in Italy.

"Ma, do you think I'd like the book you brought home, since it's about Italy?" Billy asked at dinner. "Maybe the town in the book is where Sal is."

"Well, we'll see. Let me read it first. Not all the books I get are for kids, you know," she said pointedly, but she was glad he was interested enough to ask.

They heard the kitchen door open, accompanied by Belle's voice yelling, "Help!"

"Oh my, what's wrong?" Nan said.

Belle appeared at the dining room entrance in her magenta silk robe, a big white towel wrapped around her head.

"Laura, do you have some Mum I could use? I meant to get a jar at Walgreen's and forgot."

"Belle, how come girls use Mum?" Gary asked.

"Well, it makes us smell better, that's why," his aunt replied.

"How come men don't use it?"

"They have their own, or they use a strong soap, like Lifebuoy. You know, the orange soap?" She added, "And some men don't use anything at all." She made a face and pinched her nose.

Gary laughed. "Oh yeah, Daddy uses Lifebuoy. Mum: I guess that's why they call it that—it's for mums and ladies."

"There you go," said Belle. "Never thought of that." She rolled her eyes. "You're a sketch."

"Hey, Gary," Billy said. "Bet you don't know a commercial about Mum."

"Bet I do." He thought a minute. "OK, wait, wait, I remember! *Stay popular through the evening ahead. Use Mum.*"

"See, that's just why I came dashing up," said Belle. "This is an emergency, for the evening ahead. Can't have Abe running off on me in the middle of the show."

"What movie are you going to, Belle?" asked Billy.

"That new one with Claudette Colbert and Joseph Cotten, *Since You Went Away*, but it's awful long, I hear. See ya later, everyone. Thanks, Laura."

That night in bed, Laura re-read Alan's latest letter. In this one he'd underlined "somewhere at sea," a clue that they'd left Hawaii. She wondered where in the Pacific his ship was headed. She'd read all about LSTs after he'd been assigned, and she was all too aware of the ship's nickname: "Large Slow Target."

The family was following the island-hopping war in the Pacific on a map Billy tacked up in his room. The latest battles had been in the Philippine Sea, and, more recently, on an island called Saipan. These places seemed so far from Hawaii on the map that it was hard to imagine Alan already there. Still, the weeks passed quickly.

It was hard to tell how he was doing from his last few letters. Laura sensed a certain distance, something reserved in his tone, but that could be because he wasn't allowed to say much about what was going on. Also, after all these months, the novelty of writing had worn off, though Laura tried to send a few lines every other day. It was hard to make one letter different from the last.

Sometimes she wondered about the Navy WAVES or other women in Hawaii. One night she had a crazy dream in which Alan was doing a hula around a fire with a bare-breasted native girl. That image had stayed with her the entire next day.

Laura knew he was still unhappy about her singing with the band. He was always a bit jealous, even when they were together. The thought of her practicing new arrangements with Ray Jardine and dancing with various officers during sets probably bothered him a lot. She hoped he knew there was nothing at all to it. Ray was a smoothie but harmless. It was part of her job to rehearse. And dancing with the customers was good for business.

John Lawrence, on the other hand, was another matter. Her relationship with the captain consisted of nothing more than sharing a table and lots of dances on the nights he came in from the base, but Laura knew it could easily change—if she let it happen. So far that hadn't turned into an issue between them, but she wondered how things would go if he became more insistent.

As her vacation week progressed, Laura enjoyed spending more time than she had in months with the boys. Mornings they were busy in the yard tending the victory garden, which was flourishing. They'd all become old hands at staking the tomatoes and weeding the beans and peas and watering on dry mid-summer days.

One afternoon they took the bus to go swimming at Joyland, which provided some relief from the intensity of an early July heat wave.

Nan was getting a good rest, too, at least for her. But it was hard to keep Nan still, even with those leg ulcers that refused to heal. She wondered how much Nan suffered when everyone else in the house was asleep. Belle told her she often found her sitting up in the middle of the night, reading or knitting, her leg propped up on a stool.

"OK, kids, early to bed," Laura said one night toward the end of the week. "We've got a big day tomorrow."

The plan was to take a late morning train to Hartford, and then go to a big bond rally at the Bushnell Auditorium, where Ray's band had been asked to play—to draw some of the Springfield crowd, Laura supposed. She'd sing a couple of tunes they'd already been performing at the hotel. They'd stay with Ceil that night and attend the Ringling Brothers Circus the next day. The kids hadn't seen their cousins Ralph and Sandra in a good while, and it would be fun to spend the afternoon in the big top.

❧

By the time they boarded the Hartford train at Union Station, Laura was already sweaty and cranky from the 90-degree temperature. It was going to be another scorcher, and, according to the radio that morning, there was no end in sight. Though every one of the streaked and dirty train windows was open, the morning sun had already baked the inside of their coach.

"Mommy, this is itchy," Gary said. As he stood up, particles of dust rose from his worn green velvet seat and floated in the humid air.

"It'll be cooler once we start up," Laura said as the conductor shouted *"Alll aboooard!"* Despite her own discomfort and the fact that she was feeling a bit under the weather from a headache, she still experienced that familiar sense of excitement as they pulled out of the station, across the Main Street overpass, and south along the river. There was just something about a train.

In a few minutes, they were in Connecticut, moving at a fast clip past acres of the rippling white gauze that shielded the Valley tobacco crop. Soon busloads of kids from the cities would be harvesting the prized green leaves, to be dried later on in the big old red barns that dotted the landscape.

Arriving at the station in Hartford, they walked slowly across the wide green expanse of the city park to the Bushnell concert hall, its stately Georgian brick and cream-colored facade cool and elegant in the noon heat. The tip of the building's tower gleamed in the sunlight, a much smaller version of the enormous gold dome atop the state capitol on a rise just across Trinity Street.

Laura was pleased by how well she'd organized their trip. The light crepe dress she'd decided to wear at the bond rally wouldn't show wrinkles and had fit nicely into the small overnight suitcase she'd packed for the three of them. Gary was in charge of his storybook and a couple of magazines, and Billy carried a shoulder bag that he was handling with ease. Watching him take up the lead, Laura was struck by how tall he'd become the last few months.

"I see Aunt Ceil!" yelled Gary as they approached the entrance to the theater. Sure enough, there she was, looking fashionable as always in a pink silk Laura remembered from before the war, and a big white brimmed hat that framed her dark pageboy. Next to her stood Sandra, a mirror image of the Ceil Laura had idolized when they were growing up. She was talking to another girl who looked vaguely familiar.

"Peter couldn't get off and Ralph's on a Scouts camping trip with his friends in the wilds of Vermont," Ceil explained. "But here's Sandra's friend, Dorothy, who's staying with us for a few days. She'll be going to the circus tomorrow, too."

"I recognize that pretty charm bracelet from when we met you at Sandra's party last summer," Laura said. Now she remembered Dorothy as a shy girl who'd enjoyed talking to Billy about movies they'd both seen. Dorothy smiled at her.

"What, Sandra, I look that bad, huh?" Laura said to her niece, who was giving her the once-over. Usually Sandra complimented her on her appearance.

"No, I was just noticing those pretty earrings you're wearing, Aunt Laura."

"Thanks, dear. Someone special gave them to me. She winked at Sandra. They'd been a present from her niece on her last birthday.

They walked to where Ceil's black Buick was parked and put their luggage in the trunk. "You should've let us pick you up at the station," Ceil said. "The three of you look like you just got off one of those refugee transports from England."

"Well, that's how I feel," Laura sighed. "Like I've been through the wringer." The back of her peasant-style white blouse was more than damp, and the front was smudged with soot from the train. "Anyway, I've got to rush backstage and get ready. I think we're on first for a number or two, then some speeches, then a movie."

She walked to the stage door, leaving them at the theater entrance. Gary was busy explaining something to Ceil, and Billy and the girls were talking, too. Billy got along better with Sandra than he did with her brother, Ralph, who was a couple of years older and an athletic, outdoorsy type, like Peter, his father. A nice boy, but he and Billy never had much to say to each other.

Laura had just enough time to change, fix her hair and makeup, and check the set-up and microphone with Ray before the house opened to the public. It was fun to explore a bit behind the curtain; though she'd seen many shows at the Bushnell over the years, she'd never been backstage.

She peered out at the crowd from stage left, where Ceil had said they'd try to find seats. The art deco interior of the theater was as beautiful as ever, soft lights highlighting the gold and brass decor, the plush maroon seats, and the lofty ceiling with its painted classical figures. In a way, it seemed a rather incongruous setting for the hard-sell bond rally that was about to happen.

Laura's number went well. They performed "Don't Sit under the Apple Tree," which she could sing in her sleep, and another up-tempo tune, "Chattanooga Choo-Choo," with some of the band members joining her on the vocal. She then joined her sister and the kids, who'd saved her an orchestra seat. Gary had made sure she knew where they were by standing up and yelling to her just before the band began to play. Everyone laughed when she gave him a big wave from her chair at the edge of the bandstand.

The mayor of Hartford and the general manager of the Bushnell, Bill Mortensen, spoke, as well as Ellsworth Grant, who was heading up a USO fund-raising drive. She remembered Grant as the man married to Katharine Hepburn's sister. Laura's mother and father still lived not far from the Hepburn place on Bloomfield Avenue. She'd wondered if there were plans to visit her parents later in the day and was relieved when Ceil told her they were down at the shore visiting old friends at Black Point.

"Shall we stay for the movie or not?" asked Ceil. "It's just some old war thing. I don't know. What do you think, Billy?"

Billy looked at Laura and then said to his aunt, "Oh yes, please!" *As if there were any question as far as my son's concerned*, Laura thought, before they all realized Ceil was only teasing. She knew her nephew well.

The Fighting Sullivans was a perfect choice for the rally, unabashedly calculated to inspire patriotic fervor and the buying of bonds in the lobby after the show. Laura wondered how the boys would react to the sinking of the Sullivans' ship and the loss of all five brothers. The movie, based on a true story that had gotten lots of publicity at the time, gave Laura an uneasy feeling. She hoped the boys weren't thinking of their father.

❧❧

The next morning, July 6, dawned hotter than the day before. Laura wasn't feeling up to staying all day for the circus, so she reluctantly suggested they skip it and go home early. "We can see the circus when it comes to Springfield next week," she said, grateful that Ceil hadn't yet bought the tickets. Surprisingly, even Gary didn't seem that upset. The heat was really stifling, and they'd all had a nice visit already, with a picnic and croquet at Ceil's after the bond rally.

"Enjoy the circus, girls," Laura said to Ceil, Sandra and Dorothy. "Hope it's not too hot under the big top."

The ride back to Springfield was uneventful, though the bumping of the bus from the station as it navigated the potholes on the State Street hill made Laura's headache even worse. She could hardly wait to take a shower and lie down.

As they walked into the yard, Nan and Angie came running to meet them.

"Oh, my dears, oh, thank the Lord," Nan cried. Lucille began barking, and even Max stirred from under the hedge where he'd been dozing.

"It's just us back early, Nan. We decided not to stay for the day. What is it?"

"Lord, there's been a terrible fire at the circus. It's all we're hearing on the radio."

"Oh, God, no," Laura said.

Nan put her hand to her mouth. "No, you don't mean Ceil...?"

"Yes, they're there. She and Sandra and Sandra's little girlfriend."

Laura dropped her suitcase and ran into the house. She tried over and over to place a long-distance call to Peter's office, only to be told the lines were unavailable.

Finally, the operator said, "Ma'am, we're trying to keep all circuits clear due to the emergency situation in Hartford. If you're concerned about someone, I'm sure they will call you when they can."

The reports on the radio were terrible. Flames had destroyed the entire main tent and scores of people were dead or injured. Fire companies and ambulances from all over the region had converged on the scene.

"Dear, why don't we not listen for a while?" Nan suggested after a particularly gruesome description of charred bodies lined up in rows on the circus grounds. "You go and soak in a nice tub. We'll hear if anyone calls."

Nan and Belle brought dinner upstairs so Laura could stay near the telephone. When it finally rang, Belle looked at the boys and said, "Come on, kids, let's stack the dishes in the kitchen."

When Laura joined them a few minutes later, she was crying. "It's bad news. Ceil's OK, sort of. She's got a bad concussion and burns. A falling pole knocked her out, and Peter just found her in one of the hospitals. But they don't know where Sandra or Dorothy are." Her voice broke. "There are a lot of people who aren't... dead...but they haven't identified everyone in the hospitals. There are hundreds. There were over 7,000 people in the tent when the fire started." She began to sob. "Oh, poor Ceil." She ran over and hugged Billy and Gary.

Later that night, Peter reached them again to tell them that Sandra had been located. She was alive but very badly burned. He'd actually been in the same hospital much earlier that evening but hadn't recognized her because all her hair was gone and her face was covered with some kind of medication.

The worst of the news was that Dorothy was dead. They'd identified her from a charm bracelet that had melted into the skin on her wrist. "I can't believe it. I can just see that bracelet on her arm. I think I even mentioned it to her," said Laura.

"You did, Mommy. I remember," said Gary. Billy nodded his head but didn't say anything.

A few days later, Laura took the train alone to see Ceil at Hartford Hospital. Though she'd visited friends there many times over the years, the lobby and corridors seemed different this time, full of somber people milling around and nurses rushing everywhere. A lot of the doors to the rooms on Ceil's floor were closed, "*Do Not Enter*" signs hanging on the knobs.

"I'll be getting out soon," Ceil told her after they'd exchanged teary hugs. Ceil was wearing a green turban to hide the bandages on her head. What remained of her singed hair, she told Laura, had been shaved. She'd apparently been lifted from under a pole and canvas and dragged unconscious through a hole someone cut in the side of the tent. That good Samaritan had saved her life.

"They're not sure if the pole hit me or if it was someone from the grandstand who panicked and jumped. Anyway, the burning canvas fell from the roof on top of us, and that's the last I remember until I woke up in the hospital."

Sandra would recover, but she would need a lot of surgery on her burned face and arms. They were keeping her isolated from everyone since she was prone to infections. Later, Laura was able to peek through a tiny window on the door of her room, though she couldn't manage to get Sandra to notice her.

"I feel so awful about Dorothy, even though I know it wasn't my fault," Ceil said. "Still, she *was* with me, you know? I couldn't even go to the funeral. I tried to hold on to both girls when the canvas fell, but it was no use. The crowds...it was a stampede..."

She looked at Laura. "God, I'm so glad you and the boys went home. "Can you imagine?"

"No, I can't. I can't even think about it." Over 160 people had already died, several of whom had still not been identified. Miraculously, none of the circus animals had perished, though Ceil told her the roaring and screeching were terrifying as they tried to get out of their cages before being wheeled outdoors

"I'm just glad you're all right," Laura said, gently patting her sister's turban. Somehow, Ceil managed to look stylish even with her eyebrows singed.

"Do you remember what you said to us before you left that morning?" Ceil asked. "You said, 'Hope it's not too hot under the big top'."

"Oh, God, I did?" Laura was horrified.

"Don't feel bad. Believe me, that's given me more than a few laughs since I've been lying here." She started to cry, then wiped her eyes and reached up and embraced Laura. "Come down again soon. I bet you'll get to see Sandra next time."

On the train ride home, Laura couldn't stop thinking about the hundreds of people affected by the fire, especially the children. She tried to imagine the lives that had been changed forever in the awful ten minutes it had taken for the huge tent to turn to ashes. Ten minutes.

It's not just in Europe and Asia that people get burned and maimed and killed, she thought. Laura feared more than ever for Alan, a sitting duck in that clunky LST. For the first time since the war began, she had some understanding of what much of the rest of the world had been experiencing for years.

Laura pictured her niece, immobile and unresponsive in that white bed. She hoped shy little Dorothy hadn't suffered too much, though she'd read enough reports detailing the cries and screams of those trapped inside the tent to know that most of the deaths hadn't been instantaneous.

It was all too horrible, as though somehow the destruction and awfulness of the war had spread across the Atlantic and invaded their quiet New England summer. And how ironic, at a circus of all places. She shuddered and tried to concentrate on the view out the dirty train window. One thing she knew: She'd never again look at a newspaper photo of a child wandering in a bombed-out city or a family huddled in a refugee camp in quite the same way.

Chapter 38: Alan

Alan lay in his shorts on the aft deck of the LST, watching the foamy wake slowly disappear as the ship made its way through the tranquil Pacific. A distance off, dwarfed by sea and sky, several other vessels in the convoy followed in line. The layover at Pearl Harbor had made him forget the isolation he'd felt when they'd first sailed the thousands of miles from San Francisco to Honolulu. Now, loaded with supplies, they were headed for scattered island outposts in the vastness of the world's biggest ocean.

There was no real danger from air attacks at the moment, though that would change as they got closer to Japanese-held territory. As usual, they'd not been officially told their destination. Alan had figured out from scuttlebutt in the radar and radio shacks that they were most likely headed for the Gilbert Islands and Tarawa and then maybe further south to the Solomons and Guadalcanal, now under Allied occupation.

But then where? North to Guam and Saipan? That was his guess, closer and closer to the Emperor's homeland. The small landing vessels that crowded the huge lower deck of the LST were an ominous presence, an indication they'd end up in the middle of some invasion. You didn't carry a boatload of LVTs for nothing.

"Hey, this sun is something, isn't it?" The speaker was a young fellow Alan recognized from the engine room, though the sailor's filthy pants and wet torso would have been enough to identify his assignment. "And the ocean's nice and calm today. Not like last night."

"You just get off?" Alan asked. Although water was strictly rationed on board, there was a fresh water hose for the men working below, where the temperatures could exceed 120 degrees. The rest of the crew had to make do with showers every few days. Ocean water was always available, but you ended up feeling sticky and salty and worse off than before.

"Yeah, came up here for awhile to dry off before I sack out," the sailor replied. "Mike Kaplan." They'd all been together for months, but with ninety crew on board there were men Alan still hadn't really talked to, especially those working below deck.

"It's swell up here," Mike said. "Just the peace and quiet and the fresh air." Along with the extreme heat and humidity, the din in the engine room was intense, and the men had to shout to make themselves heard above the continuous roar of the motors. And the smell of diesel oil, pervasive throughout the ship, was particularly noxious below.

"You from New York?" Alan asked.

"Brooklyn. How'd you know?" He laughed. "I can't tell about you. You sound like all the radio announcers—no accent I can make out."

"Springfield, Massachusetts," Alan replied. "So, guess you're a Dodgers fan, huh?"

"You bet. And we're bringing the series back East next year." The 1944 World Series had been all St. Louis, with the Cardinals winning over the Browns.

"Mind if I stretch out here?" Mike stripped to his regulation-issue shorts and lay back on top of a heavily secured, canvas-covered skid of canned food supplies. Before long he was sound asleep, his snoring in rhythm with the mild bumping of the large pontoon fastened against the side of the ship.

Alan returned to the book he was reading, Steinbeck's *Cannery Row*, which he'd picked up from a small library one of the petty officers had fixed up in a recessed shelf in the mess. Soon he, too, succumbed to the sun and the gentle bobbing of the ship as it plowed through the placid sea.

❧

It turned out he was right about their first destination, the battered island of Tarawa. The craft, along with several other LSTs in the convoy, had an easy beaching, despite the wreckage scattered in the reef and on the shore. Palm trees at the jungle's edge bore the ravages of the recent invasion. Their fronds sparse and frayed, the naked trees stood like battered sentinels guarding the dense jungle behind them.

Alan and Buzz watched as supply trucks slowly emerged from the starboard door of a neighboring LST. In a long line, the convoy lumbered through the unusually wide expanse of shallow water and then maneuvered onto the littered beach.

"No wonder the Marines dropped like fuckin' flies," Buzz remarked. "The poor sons of bitches never had a chance if they had to run that far. That's a hell of a beachhead." The very name "Tarawa" had already come to signify a victory won only after fierce enemy resistance and terrible loss of life.

After an overnight layover, the ships proceeded south to the Solomons, where they entered a channel called "the slot," a salt-water graveyard for many Japanese and Allied vessels and their crews. Soon the convoy reached Lunga Point on Guadalcanal, near Henderson Field.

Even though the invasion had ended many months ago, there was a great deal of ongoing activity at the pier, constructed by the Seabees soon after the landing. The base continued to be key to the Pacific campaign, with thousands of troops passing through Guadalcanal as the island-hopping continued.

"Hey, look, bet it's a mail call," Buzz said to Alan as a battered Higgins Boat, perhaps left over from the invasion, pulled up to their ship the morning after they arrived. They hadn't gotten any mail for weeks, and the small craft was loaded with large canvass sacks.

Alan devoured the letters from home, more than 40 in all, including a scrawled drawing from Gary of Lucille and Max. He wondered how those two were getting along. It still seemed funny to think of Max as part of the family, now that Mrs. Herrmann was gone. Everyone in the neighborhood knew that old cat from his perch in her second-floor window.

The big news from back home, which everyone mentioned in their letters, was the circus fire in Hartford. Billy was the only one who told him that they'd actually been planning to attend. Alan wondered what other worrisome items Laura, Belle, and his mother were leaving out of their letters these days.

Though there hadn't been time to call Edie before they left Pearl, Alan had given her his address in a letter he'd scrawled as they were waiting at the dock to ship out. He hoped the sailor he handed it to bothered to post it. He'd have to wait until the next mail call, wherever that was, to find out.

Alan was confused and troubled when he thought about Edie, and he wished he had someone to talk to. Buzz would be happy to listen, but he needed an older ear, someone with more life experience. When he thought about Laura and the boys, Alan knew things had ended for the best, but it still bothered him that Edie represented one more thing he hadn't managed to follow through on. And so she stayed in his mind, a tantalizing memory of something—he didn't quite know what—only half-realized.

That night, he and Buzz carried their dinner trays outside to the upper deck to escape the stifling heat. Alan tried to spend as little time below as possible. Even after the sun set, being in port on the island of Guadalcanal was like sitting in a steam room, minus the steam. Underwear and socks never felt dry. Prickly heat and more troublesome fungal conditions were common.

As he picked at his Spam, lumpy mashed potatoes and corn, Alan became aware of a conversation going on near the pallet where they were sitting.

"Ah tell ya, ah got maself right back in line and by the time ah got back in the door again, ah was good an' ready. Ah did that three times on ma last leave. One was a white gal, the second Chinese or somethin', and the last looked just like one a them hula dancers." The speaker was a pudgy sailor with bad teeth from somewhere down South. Alan recognized him as a gunner whose post was on the aft deck.

"That horsefly's talking about one of the whorehouses in Honolulu," Buzz said in a low voice. "Jeez, I feel sorry for the girls that got him. Who'd wanna end up under that smelly cracker? Bet he got the worst-looking dames."

"Yeah," Alan replied. But he was suddenly thinking of Edie. He tried not to imagine her with someone like that. She'd told him her customers had all been older guys.

"But, you know, most of them were really pretty good looking canaries," Buzz continued. "Come to think of it, I never saw a real crow. Shit, that guy won't be so lucky when he gets home to Georgia. He'll be poking the pigs again."

Alan laughed. "Buzz, I'm telling you, better watch your tongue when you're back in Nebraska."

"Yeah, I know," said Buzz. "Ain't I terrible? It's the fuckin' company I keep."

Later, they carried their bedding to the deck, a nightly routine they'd begun when the extreme heat set in. There was a slight breeze, but not enough, thankfully, to affect the delicate equilibrium of the flat-bottomed LST, gently butting the side of the pier. Evening was always a welcome relief from the sultry stillness of the afternoon.

Once again, it was spectacularly clear and starry, not unusual in the nighttime canopy of the southern hemisphere. Though the effect was not quite as dazzling as when they were far from land, the after-dark blackout on Guadalcanal did create that same seamless blending of earth and sky.

"Look, Buzz, do you make out the Southern Cross?" Alan asked.

"Nah, I can never see that stuff, the Big Dipper and all that. Everything up there looks the same to me. I probably seen it at home and never noticed it."

"No, you wouldn't have seen the Southern Cross in the Midwest. You have to be further south," replied Alan. "Look, follow my finger. See those four bright stars?"

"Nope, nothin'. I told ya." He stared a few more moments. "Wait, wait, yeah, I do see it! Jeez, yeah, I can make it out!"

Buzz was excited, just like a kid, reminding Alan of the time he'd shown Billy an eclipse of the moon. "Daddy, I see it! I see it!" Billy had cried in his high-pitched voice. He must have been four or five, maybe even younger. It was when he was a tyke, when they were more at ease with each other.

The two men were silent, watching the night sky. Although the deck was crowded with sleeping sailors, the only sounds were the gentle lapping of the waves, the faint strains of music from a radio somewhere below deck, and the mild bumping of the hull against the makeshift wooden pier.

After a while, Alan asked, "Buzz, remember what you were saying about the whorehouses in Honolulu?"

"Yeah," he answered. "Why, sorry now you didn't come along?"

"No, not that, but I guess I'm curious. What were they like?" he asked quietly.

"Somethin', they were somethin', no shit. Well, first they sold you a ticket at a booth inside the door. Three dollars for three minutes, five bucks for five."

"Is that all?" Alan was astounded.

"Hey, I don't know 'bout you, but three smackers is a lot to me."

"No," Alan replied, "I meant, just three *minutes?*"

"Yep, that's it. You could make some kind of arrangement for more time. But, for most guys that was enough." He lowered his voice. "My first time, she didn't even get the rubber on before I squirted all over the place. But that was, you know, my first time...I mean, ever. Don't tell that to the other guys, OK?

"So, anyway, every time I went, they were pretty busy, so you really didn't get to pick, unless you asked for a girl by name. Like, if you already knew her from before. Then you could wait for her if you wanted to.

"The rooms are little and real plain—a cot, basin and soap, wastebasket, towels. That's it. There's a smell of sweat and stuff and smoke and some kind of disinfectant they use. While you were taking your pants off in one room, she was finishing up in another. Bang, bang."

"Did the girls tell you their names?" Alan asked.

"Sure they told you, but they have names like Lotus and Lana and Rita. Once I had one who said her name was Scarlett, but she was Chinese, I think. Funny. They make 'em up."

"Were there places where, you know, the girls were special or real expensive?"

"Not where I went, but, yeah, they say there was one where you had to be an officer, and even then I think most of the customers were, like, rich guys on the island. A ritzy place. It was called the Ambassador, I think. Something like that."

"Jesus, will you guys can the talk or keep it down?" came a voice from the next pallet.

"OK, OK," Buzz replied. "Hey, Maloney," he added. "Wank wank!"

❧

When they left Guadalcanal the next afternoon, they took on dozens of the departing 3rd Battalion, 5th Marines, as passengers. These were among the thousands of troops who'd spent months on the island during the bloody campaign. Many were still in the local hospital and some had been sent back to Pearl or the mainland, but others had already been shipped out on various makeshift troop vessels to resume battle.

Because of their extended time in the jungle, most of the Marines on board had skin ulcers or a fungus called jungle rot. They spent as much time on deck as possible, frequently naked and smeared with bright purple medication.

"Gonna be crowded up here at night, ain't it?" observed Buzz. They'd all massed on deck when the ship slowly left the landing at Guadalcanal and headed up the slot toward the open sea.

"Yeah, but imagine what they've been through," Alan replied, observing the men and wondering what their thoughts were as the Solomons receded from sight on the horizon. "That island was 2,000 square miles of torture. Every one of them probably lost a buddy. I bet they hope to hell they never see it again."

From his daily watch in the radar shack up on the bridge, he knew they were proceeding in a northerly direction. They bypassed the Caroline archipelago and Truk and headed north to the Marianas, where fierce fighting had occurred on Guam and Saipan. Now they'd begun to hear of more kamikaze attacks, and Lieutenant Commander Salisbury had increased the frequency of general quarters alarms.

"All those Japs would have to do is see them Marines all painted up purple," said Buzz one day as they wandered back to the deck after yet another drill. "That'd be enough to throw 'em off course, right into the drink. Hey, professor, what does kamikaze mean, anyway?"

"It means 'divine wind'," Alan replied. "It was the name of a typhoon that destroyed a Mongol force against Japan a long time ago."

"So how do they get these friggin' Japs to blow themselves to bits?" Buzz asked. "Beats me."

"They're dying for the emperor," Alan replied, wondering himself what motivated the pilots to give their lives for someone they'd never seen or even heard on the radio. Hirohito lived in isolated splendor in a palace, aloof from his millions of worshiping subjects. "It's part of their religion."

"How come you know all this stuff?" Buzz asked.

"I just read a lot, I guess," Alan said. "I get sick of cards. I never much liked betting." Playing rummy back home was a frequent family pastime, but that was different. Gambling was officially banned on board ship, but most officers chose to ignore this rule. Games were in progress at virtually all hours. Buzz joked about a buffalo nickel with a distinctive green mark that he'd won and lost about a dozen times.

On a sunny morning as they chugged along somewhere north of the Marianas, Alan was heading to breakfast after a night in the radar room. Suddenly, bells rang and horns blew. The captain's voice came over the loudspeaker: "NOW GENERAL QUARTERS! GENERAL QUARTERS! ALL HANDS MAN YOUR STATIONS! THIS IS NOT A DRILL. THIS IS NOT A DRILL. ALL HANDS MAN YOUR STATIONS!" Alan knew lights would also be flashing in the noisy engine room below, to alert the men who couldn't hear the speaker warnings.

Within minutes the ship was battle-ready, with all posts manned. Alan returned to the radar room as back up for Ryan, who had just relieved him. "What's up, Donny?" he asked. Donny Ryan was a smart, freckle-faced kid from Indiana.

"A bunch of planes heading this way," Ryan said, pointing to the radar screen. "Looks like the destroyer anti-aircraft didn't stop 'em." That meant they'd head for the LSTs, whose guns were fewer and far less powerful. "I think we're going to see some kamikaze babies up close."

As Donny spoke, Alan looked out on the bridge. Far aft, he saw two specks high above the horizon, bearing down on an LST three or four ships away. As he watched, one of the planes hit the water, sending a modest geyser spurting into the sky. That happened in silence. What was faintly audible was the ack-ack of anti-aircraft artillery coming from other ships in the convoy.

"Those ain't backabombs, they're the real thing," Ryan said. Backabombs were tiny, glider-like planes the Japanese had begun to transport under the bellies of bombers. When a ship was sighted, the flying torpedo was released, guided by a lone, doomed pilot to its target below.

There was an explosion as the second plane hit one of the ships and then bounced off it into the water. "Shit, I hope they're not carrying an ammo supply on that one," said Donny. "At least he didn't get below deck."

Suddenly their own forward guns began firing, followed almost immediately by the roar of the rear 20 millimeter a few feet away from the radar room. "Jesus, there's one headed right for us," Alan shouted. He'd been so engrossed in watching the activity ahead that he hadn't seen the tiny craft appear, literally out of the blue, bearing down at a steep angle.

The plane, slightly off to the starboard side, managed to right itself a few hundred feet above the water and headed toward the ship. "Jesus H. Christ," shouted a sailor in the radio shack. "Look out, he's coming straight at us."

The pilot couldn't quite regain his control of the steering apparatus, however, and the plane swerved clumsily at the last minute. As it skirted the side of the ship, the red sun insignia painted on the side flashed like a red ball of flame. The plane passed so close to the radar room that Alan was able to see the pilot's goggles and his white scarf waving in the wind.

A few moments later, he'd turned and was bearing down on the ship again, roaring toward the bridge and into a barrage of anti-artillery fire. When the plane was about fifty feet above the deck, one of the guns scored a direct hit. The explosion was terrific, ear shattering and blinding in its intensity. Chunks of burning metal fell everywhere, and pieces of shrapnel flew through the air like so many knives and daggers.

"Jesus, Donny, that was close," Alan said, rising from the floor where he'd been thrown. He turned to Ryan, who was still in a bent-over position at the radar screen. Then he saw blood streaming down the side of the chair. Alan ran over to him, but the thin, oblong piece of metal protruding from his skull was too hot to touch.

He lifted Donny and carefully laid him on the floor. The radar equipment seemed to be intact—pulses pulsing, green lights glowing—so the bridge and manning tower must have escaped damage as well. Alan shouted, "Need help in here! Ryan's hit bad. I think the radar's OK." Taking off his shirt and wiping up the blood as best he could, he took Donny's place in the chair and awaited further orders.

There was chaos on the bridge and deck for some time as small fires were put out and the debris removed, but apparently the ship was relatively undamaged. Several gunners had been burned or wounded by shrapnel, but not like Donny. No further planes appeared, and activity returned to normal.

Later that day, they found out more about the LST that had suffered a direct hit. Two men died, many were wounded, and the deck was pretty much smashed up. But the engine room was intact, and the ship remained afloat.

Donny, under the care of the Hospital Corpsmen in the tiny sick bay compartment, still hadn't regained consciousness. Arrangements were being made for his transfer, along with the other wounded sailors in the convoy, to a fully staffed hospital ship that had recently sailed from Guadalcanal. Donny's absence would mean extra time at the screen for Alan and Stan, the other radar man.

The next morning, as he reported for duty, Alan watched as a sailor and the grim-faced ship medic accompanied the cot carrying Donny up to the deck. Donny was strapped tightly, everything but his arms and face covered. Even from a distance, the blood on the bandage around his head was visible, a bright crimson against the white of the sheet.

Before the cot was hoisted over the rail to the waiting transport ship, the medic leaned over and whispered something to Donny. Alan couldn't tell if his friend responded or not. He and Donny hadn't been close, really, but he was a swell kid. Alan felt himself choking up as the cot and its occupant were slowly drawn along the temporary cable connecting the two ships. He wondered if he'd ever see Donny again.

"What's happening?" Alan asked a moment later as he stopped by the radio shack. Buzz, was just hanging up his earphones after an all-night stint.

"Well, 'member I said something about that island Iwo Jima?" Buzz usually told Alan in strict confidence about messages that went straight to the captain or the bridge. "That's where it looked like we were heading'."

"Yeah, I figured that's where we were taking these guys," replied Alan, referring to the Marines on board.

"Well, it's all changed. We're bypassing Iwo. Guess things are under control there already. Now we're heading toward a bigger island. Here, take a look at the map."

Buzz pointed to a large mass much closer to the mainland of Asia, directly south of Japan. "See, here. Looks like it's the biggest island in the Ryukus, a place called Okinawa."

"What's the name again?" Alan asked.

"Okinawa," Buzz repeated. "Spelled O-K-I-N-A-W-A. From what I'm hearing, every friggin' ship in the Navy is headed there."

Chapter 39: Belle

Belle awoke to the slow, measured cadence of Abe's breath on her forehead. Carefully easing herself from under his extended arm, she studied his face, clearly outlined in the moonlight that streamed through the bedroom window. His wavy hair shone silver, as did the curly tufts peeking above the blanket covering his chest. Gray stubble was visible on his chin. Skipping his daily shave was enough to transform Abe into a Paul Bunyon lumberjack, so unlike the immaculate daytime gentleman most people knew.

It had turned bitterly cold that afternoon, and snow was predicted before the end of the weekend. Raising the sheet and blankets over her shoulders, Belle felt the heat from their bodies escape into the chilled air. She was sorely tempted to stay where she was, but she'd promised to fix dinner. They'd decided against going out, forgoing their usual Saturday night at the movies for an evening of *Inner Sanctum* and *Your Hit Parade*.

Belle felt for Abe's leather slip-ons under the bed and stepped into them. His heavy blue corduroy bathrobe was in its usual place on the hook behind the door. It had seen better days, but it was warm and roomy and she liked wearing it. Scuffing into the hallway, she made her way down the carpeted stairs, glancing into the large, darkened living room on her way to the kitchen.

It seemed funny to her, still, the absence of any Christmas decorations in Abe's house. No manger scene, no window lights, no tree—especially now, with the recent lifting of blackout restrictions.

Finally, after nearly three years, the war was going well. Since the Normandy landings in the summer, the Allied forces were moving steadily eastward, and there were predictions of the capture of Berlin within weeks. On the opposite side of the globe, though there was some progress, the ocean road to Tokyo was turning into a much longer haul.

Belle turned on the pin-up lamp next to the kitchen table, illuminating the copper pans hanging on the wall and the cheery café curtains on the window over the sink. She felt the presence of Abe's wife in this room more than any other.

After one brittle wooden match snapped in two and another nearly burned her hand, Belle finally lit the deeply recessed burner of the old gas stove. Browning the nice rump they'd managed to get at Abe's neighborhood butcher shop, she lowered the flame and added onions, potatoes, carrots and a little water. Though she didn't cook much at home, she wasn't bad at preparing meals she liked. A pot roast dinner was one of Abe's favorites, too.

"Just having something home-cooked is a treat," he'd told her the first time she'd prepared dinner at his house. "Hannah's not much for the kitchen and, besides, she's hardly ever here. And I can just about make coffee." He confessed he often stopped off after work at one of the downtown Italian restaurants on Main Street before boarding the bus for home.

When Belle returned upstairs, Abe was awake. As she walked toward the bed, removing the corduroy bathrobe, he said, "Wait. Just wait there a minute. I want to look at you."

Early on, in the summer months, they used to stand in front of the big bureau mirror together, naked. This began one hot afternoon after they'd made love and Abe remarked, "Wish I still had the build I did twenty years ago."

"What, you were even handsomer then than you are now?" Belle asked. "Here, come here," she said, pulling him off the bed and over to the mirror. "What's wrong with that?" she asked, running her hand over his broad shoulders. She patted his flat stomach, and then tickled his groin. Before Abe, she hadn't been with a man who was circumcised, and she enjoyed studying him, head to toe.

"Hey, watch it, or you know what'll happen," he replied, laughing. "You're the one who should be standing here, all by yourself," he said. "You're beautiful." He caressed the back of her neck and then cupped her breasts in his large, gentle hands.

Though she knew men found her attractive, Belle had always thought she was too tall and a bit heavy. But Abe's obvious pleasure in her body had made her more comfortable with herself. In fact, together they made a pretty good-looking couple.

Now, in the December chill, she stood for a moment by the side of the bed. "OK," she finally said. "Lady Godiva here is going to freeze her little tootsies off." She jumped in next to him, and rested her head on his chest.

After a while, she said, "Abe, what do you think is going to happen at work? I mean, with me?"

"Depends on who comes back after the war. I wish I could say your job is secure. I mean, the one you're doing right now. But there'll be something else if it comes to that, I can see to it."

"Well, I wouldn't want to put you in that position," Belle replied. "It's awkward enough as it is, you being my boss and all. But, anyway, I'm not sure I'd want to have that happen—being demoted."

"I know," he replied. "It's tough."

In a way, she was sorry she'd brought up the subject, since she knew there was really nothing Abe could do. The writing was on the wall. Rumor had it that Elaine Foley, who'd been the first woman in the plant to become a floor lady, was about to lose her job. The man she'd replaced was back from the Army, discharged because of a leg injury. One of the girls had seen him in the personnel office a few days earlier.

"Didn't you tell me that Hannah and Charlotte spoke to you about the bookstore?" Abe asked. "You know they've signed a lease in that space next to the art gallery, where the men's hat shop used to be? They're already working on fixing it up."

"Yeah, I know you've been helping them out a lot. They did speak to me, but that wouldn't be full-time."

"But didn't you want to go back to school?"

"I've thought about it. I did have some experience a few years ago keeping books. And at the Paramount, I supervised a handful of people. If I had a business school diploma or something, I think I could land a really good job."

"I know you could." Abe paused. "And then there's us."

"Yes..." Belle answered.

"You know how I feel about you," he said.

"I know. I just don't know about...It's a big step, Abe."

"Well, we don't have to decide right away," he said. "Say, how's that dinner coming? Smells good."

"Oh, shit!" said Belle. "I hope nothing's stuck to the bottom of the pot. I'm not all that used to your stove." She jumped out of bed. "It'll be ready soon if it's not already overdone. You can use the bathroom first. I need to check downstairs!"

Later, as they were relaxing over coffee and dessert—ginger-bread that Nan had sent over with Belle—they heard the front door open.

"Hello...it's me. Are you in the kitchen? OK to come in?"

Hannah appeared at the doorway, her cheeks and nose rosy from the cold. "Wow, it is *really* bitter out there! And it's starting to snow." She brushed her tweed coat and took off her mittens and red woolen beret, fluffing her unruly black curls. Her hands bore traces of pale purple paint.

"Well, I can see what you've been up to," Belle said. "How's it coming?"

"Fabulous! We're going to have the most stylish bookstore in town. But I guess that won't be hard, considering the number of them." Except for Johnson's on Main Street and the small book departments in the big stores, the only other real bookstore down-town was H.R. Hunting's. But Hunting's catered to a different cli-entele, stocking first editions and maps and thousands of out-of-print titles on their dusty, crowded shelves.

"I like the color," Belle said.

"Yeah, we decided on a scheme of lavender," Hannah replied, waving her fingers. "And lime. With white bookshelves."

"Can I help?" Belle asked. "I'm not handy like Abe here, but I can wield a paintbrush or help put up the books."

"We won't have any stock in for a while, but, sure, we could use a hand. I know it's awfully close to Christmas, but how about some night next week?"

☙❧

After work on the following Monday, Belle braved the cold wind coming up the side streets from the frozen Connecticut and walked over to the new shop. The windowed storefront and glass door were covered from the inside by large sheets of white paper. A faded haberdashery sign still hung above the entrance. Charlotte and Hannah's next-door neighbors were a jewelry and watch repair business and, on the other side, the art gallery owned by Mrs. Brown's friend.

"We've got some old clothes you can change into, Belle," said Charlotte. "I think you and I are about the same size."

"Then people will really take us for sisters," Belle replied. Though they'd gotten used to their similar looks, every once in a while it pleased Belle to realize how much they resembled each other. Somehow it made her feel close to Charlotte and Hannah, and it had helped ease a slight awkwardness she'd initially felt when she realized the nature of their relationship.

"Well, maybe we're like younger and older sisters," said Charlotte, laughing. She didn't appear middle-aged, but Abe had told her Charlotte was in her early forties.

Dressed in ragged jeans, a flowered smock, and a makeshift bandanna she'd fashioned out of an old dishcloth from Abe's house, Belle began to paint a large pine shelf.

"So tell me more about the kind of books you're going to sell," she said.

"Well, we'll have to have the standard bestsellers, but otherwise not a large line of mainstream literature," Hannah replied. "We're going for more of the off-center stuff—women's issues, social concerns, small presses."

"It's a risk, but there's really no outlet in this whole region for that, except further up the valley in college towns like Amherst or Northampton," said Charlotte. "Publishing is already picking up these last few months. And with all the older college students we expect after the war is over, I hope we'll attract a new crowd. You know, the GI bill and all."

"Will you sell other stuff, too?" Belle asked. She wondered how many customers it took to make a little bookstore turn a profit.

"Oh yes, we'll have a few things like notebooks, cards, posters, but with a theme," Hannah explained. She pointed to a large print affixed to the wall that depicted a young woman dressed in a blue jumpsuit and flexing the muscle on her sturdy upper arm. The caption read, *We Can Do It!*

"Ah, Rosie," said Belle.

"Actually, the real "Rosie" poster is a different one by Norman Rockwell," replied Hannah. "This is by a man named Howard Miller. It was done for Westinghouse and then used by the War Production Coordinating Committee. You watch, this one is going to last. It's a classic."

"Upstairs, we're going to have used books and a small area to serve tea and coffee. Maybe if that does OK, we can expand and have sandwiches and small meals," Charlotte explained. "Readings, too. You know, receptions, discussions."

"Oh, and don't forget the children's books," Hannah added. "But we're trying to find material that isn't the usual Dick and Jane stuff. It's not easy, believe me."

"What do you mean?" asked Belle.

"You know, Dick and Jane and Mommy and Daddy and Spot and...was there a cat?" Hannah replied. "That isn't the only kind of family in Springfield."

"Well, it wasn't mine, that's for sure," said Belle, remembering the difficult times they'd had as kids with Nan trying to make ends meet. Had she felt back then that they were different? Poorer than the other kids, for sure. Otherwise, she couldn't remember.

"Gee, maybe Billy could help out if you want a guinea pig for the kids' books," she suggested. "You know, to preview stuff the same way we test games on kids at the factory. He's always buried in a book. Course, he reads a lot of grown-up stuff now, I think."

"Sure, that's a good idea, and he could even help out here in the store. We want to have our customers feel that their kids are welcome, too," Charlotte replied.

"Boy, he'd love that. He already thinks he's twenty years old, you know. He was always that way, just like a little old man."

"Speaking of helping out in the store, what about you, Belle?" asked Hannah. "The war's not going to last much longer, you know. I wonder about all you gals and your factory jobs."

"That's what I'm worried about, too," Belle replied. "I know we did talk about it before, but..."

"We wouldn't be able to offer you anything full-time, and it wouldn't be nearly what you're getting at the factory, but your hours could be flexible. Neither Charlotte or I will be able to quit our jobs right away, so we'll need a third person in the store. Someone reliable."

"I don't think I know enough about...you know, books," Belle replied. "High school was a few years back, and reading wasn't my best subject."

"Listen, you're bright, you'll get to know the stock, and anyway there are other ways you can help," Charlotte said. "Like with the office-type stuff, for example."

Before she left to catch her bus, Belle had promised to think seriously about their offer. She agreed to let them know by the first of the year if they could count on her.

Belle wondered how much Abe had told Hannah about their situation. She suspected father and daughter talked to each other a lot, and with complete frankness. They were close, and neither was one to mince words. But since she didn't know for sure, she'd hesitated to mention Abe at the bookstore. He was part of the decision she needed to make, though. She had a lot to think about.

෨ৎ

The very next afternoon at work, Belle found out that the rumor they'd been hearing all week was true.

During morning break, Gert, the union steward, approached her. "Got some news you ain't gonna like. Just heard officially through the front office that Elaine's being let go. Wilbur Cranston's getting his old job back. I guess his leg injury ain't so bad that he can't work full time. Me and Elaine just met with Personnel."

"You mean, she's been fired completely?" asked Belle incredulously.

"Naw, but the only thing they're offering her is something on the night shift until another daytime job opens up. At her old pay, too."

"Shit. Can't the union do anything?" Belle asked. "I heard that Wilbur wasn't exactly a ball of fire when he was boss."

"You're right. He's lazy and he don't know how to work with the girls," replied Gert. "Sure, we could fight it, but think about it. Family man comes home from war and don't get his job back. On top of it, he's some kind of war hero. And on top of *that*, he's a *wounded* war hero with a bum leg. How's that gonna go over?"

"I suppose you're right. So what's in the cards for me, Gert?"

"Well, nothing's set in stone, but I wouldn't count on being in this here job more than a few months. If Eddie's coming back, well...it'll be his. But, believe me, we're gonna do our damnedest to make sure most of you newer girls stay on."

Belle didn't get a chance to talk to Abe before she left the factory that afternoon. Besides, she didn't know if she wanted to discuss the news with him just yet, since it tied in with other decisions she needed to make. She wondered if he'd known before today that Wilbur was back on board.

"Dear, anything wrong? You seem on the quiet side," said Nan after she greeted Belle in the front hallway that evening.

"No, hon, just a busy day at work," Belle replied. She sat down, took off her fur-lined boots and massaged her feet. They were killing her. "What's for dinner? Smells good."

"I made a nice beef and kidney stew. Mr. Simka had some lovely chunks he saved for me." Nan picked up a letter from the telephone table. "This is for you from California. From someone named Loretta Larue. Do you suppose it's about Flo?" Surprisingly, Flo had written regularly since she'd boarded the Greyhound bus for California last year.

"Beats me, let's see," said Belle. "Wait, this *is* Flo's address! I thought they had a little house of their own, no roommates. Hope nothing's wrong."

She opened the letter and began to read. "No, she's fine," she said, laughing. "I'll wait and read it at the table." Everyone always got a kick out of her friend's chatty notes from, in Flo's words, "sunny Los Angeles."

"OK, everyone, want to hear what our Flo has to say?" Belle asked after she'd helped Nan clear the table for dessert. She began to read:

Dear Belle:

Hello from sunny Los Angeles.

Bet you were surprised to see the name on the envelope. Yep, that's me. It's my new moniker, Loretta Larue. Classy, don't you think? Know why I have it? I AM IN THE MOVIES!

Belle paused and glanced at Billy, who was holding his forkful of apple pie in mid-air. "Wow!" he said. "Go on, Belle!"

Remember that man I told you about who lives next door? Well, sometimes we have a drink or two together—me and him and my friend, Glenda, the girl I told you about who works at Fox—that's 20ᵗʰ Century Fox. Anyway, this guy's an agent and both Glenda and him said I should try to get a job at the studio.

So, to make a long story short, I got all dressed up , went with him for an appointment that Glenda fixed up and the next thing you know I'm getting made up and taking a screen test in color.

A few days later they called me and now I'm in a new Betty Grable movie, The Dolly Sisters! I don't talk or anything like that, but I'm in a big number called "Lipstick, Powder and Rouge." I just kind of stand there with a big lipstick on my head and they say, "And this is Lady Lipstick" and I smile at the camera! The only hard part is making sure I don't move my head much, 'cause the lipstick tends to wobble, at least it did in rehearsal.

Betty's real nice and John Payne is so handsome! I'm going to ask them to autograph a picture to send to Billy.

Gotta go! Sammy—he's my agent now—is picking me up for dinner.
Love ya, Loretta.

p.s. Little Lana is just fine. They told me she walked yesterday but I haven't seen that yet. Gee, they sure grow up fast!

p.p.s. Tommy is somewhere over in the Philippines. Wait 'til he hears my news!

"Gosh, she's in the movies!" Billy said.

"Does that mean Flo is going to be famous?" asked Gary.

"It's Loretta now, Gary. Loretta Larue," said Billy.

"Well, you never know," replied Laura. "Leave it to Flo, I mean Loretta. We'll have to watch for her."

"I just hope Miss Loretta Larue remembers that she is also Mrs. Tommy Flanagan," said Nan.

"How could she forget that, Nan?" asked Gary. "She's got a baby and everything."

"Umm," said Nan.

"Hey, it's hard to say 'Loretta Larue' fast," Gary exclaimed. He rattled it off a few times. "Betcha can't do that!"

They went around the table, and Gary was right. He was the only one who could say 'Loretta Larue' three times in a row without stumbling over the syllables. Nan was the worst. "Oh well, it doesn't matter, to me she's still Flo," she said, laughing and adjusting her upper dentures.

Hearing from Flo and her escapades made Belle feel better, a little more hopeful about the future. If Flo could do what she wanted, then why couldn't she? By the time she was ready for bed she'd decided to talk to Abe tomorrow.

Turning off the light, Belle thought again about Flo's letter. Leave it to that girl. But Nan was probably right. It did sound like Flo was getting in kind of deep.

Lying in the dark, Belle imagined that, instead of a job in a bookstore, she'd gotten a contract to go to Hollywood. Now she had to change her name, too. What would it be? 'Marlene Martine'? 'Rhonda Rogers'? 'Patrice Pascal'? That wasn't bad. Exotic. But then she decided she liked 'Veronica Vanderbilt' best of all.

Veronica Vanderbilt. Now that one had real class. *Yep, just like me*, she thought as she drifted off.

Chapter 40: Billy

"Time for a snack, dear, if you'd like something, " Nan called into Billy's bedroom . "Mrs. Brown's here, too."

When Billy walked into the kitchen, Mrs. Brown motioned him over and gave him a hug. "It's wonderful hearing from Sal, isn't it?"

"I know," said Billy, grinning. They'd all had letters that morning. Sal had even sent Mrs. Brown a short note, so he must really be OK.

"Do you think he'll be able to bring his dog Ernesto back with him, Mrs. Brown?" Billy asked. In his note to Billy, Sal had talked about the little dog he'd adopted who followed him everywhere.

"I don't know about that," Mrs. Brown replied. "Still, you never can tell, that I've learned."

"Mrs. Mazzarella says that Sal's OK because she prayed to St. George. He's the patron saint of soldiers."

"You see, that's just what I mean. You never can tell. Perhaps that's so." Mrs. Brown smiled.

"Ah, Mrs. Stewart, the other war news isn't so heartening," she said as Billy joined them at the table.

"And just when we thought things were going so well, Mrs. Brown," Nan replied, pouring her a cup of tea. Now that Belle had gotten to know Mrs. Brown better and was referring to her as Ada, it seemed all the funnier to Billy that the two older ladies were so formal with each other.

"Those poor soldiers over there in that forest," Nan continued. "Gabriel Heatter said on the radio last night that it's one of the coldest winters Europe has had in years."

"And you've heard the news about our rationing?" asked Mrs. Brown. "They're raising points on everything." She added, with a sly sideways look at Billy, "Sugar included." Everyone joked about Nan's sweet tooth.

"No, you don't mean it!" Nan exclaimed. "This is so much worse than the First War." Billy wanted to remind Nan that her brother Harry had been killed in that war, but he decided that wasn't a good idea. It would just get her more worked up.

The conversation continued on about food shortages rather than the neighborhood or family gossip that Billy liked to hear. He listened for a while, but when he finished his tea he excused himself and went into his bedroom to read the paper.

The news was all about the new German offensive, and Billy was concerned, too. Unexpectedly, Germany had made a significant inroad—what the papers were calling a "bulge"-- in the Allied lines surrounding the Ardennes Forest in Belgium.

Though the new push wasn't anywhere near Italy, Billy was worried about Sal. Maybe they'd shift him from the hospital where he was stationed to the front lines further north. He'd probably recovered from his wounds by now; the letters they'd received were all dated a month ago.

Everyone had been hoping for a more normal holiday, as normal as Christmas could be without Billy's father and Sal. They'd placed a big, bushy evergreen in the usual spot in the living room bay window. With the blackout lifted, the lights of the tree glowed for the whole street to enjoy, and electric candles shone at night from all the front windows. Billy and Gary had helped decorate Nan and Belle's living room as well, though their tree was a small one that sat on a table in the corner.

"Hitler's spoiled everything again," Billy said to his mother. "It's not fair."

A photo in the morning paper showed a group of soldiers shivering around a little Coleman stove in a snowy clearing 'somewhere in the forest'. Atop the stove was a can of steaming coffee. One of the soldiers, cigarette dangling from his lips, was holding a puppy in his grimy hands. Billy glanced at Lucille, asleep on the braided rug next to his bed. He wondered what would happen to Ernie if Sal got sent to the front.

Neatly folding the newspaper, Billy dragged his desk chair over to the closet and retrieved the suitcase Sal had given him for safekeeping before he enlisted. Hoisting it up on the bed, he sat crossed-legged in front of it, running his fingers over the decals, some of them torn and faded, pasted onto its surface: Riverside Park, the Statue of Liberty, two red socks on a baseball, and a World's Fair banner. He could still remember Sal's descriptions of the fantastic sights he'd seen at the fair in New York City. That had been back in 1939, when Billy was six and Sal in junior high school.

After the bad news about Sal came a few months ago, Billy had been tempted to unlock the suitcase. He kept the little key hidden in the wooden box that held his collection of special marbles — aggies too beautiful to play with that he liked to roll between his fingers and hold up to the sun. He'd even gone so far as to try the key in the lock. It worked, and he was about to open the suitcase when he heard Gary tromping down the hallway. He quickly stashed it under the bed.

One afternoon back in mid July, when they'd still received nothing but the War Department telegram, Billy and Angie were lying out in the backyard, next to Nan's roses. Though the blooms were past their peak, a faint fragrance wafted across the lawn, and a bee or two buzzed hopefully from bush to bush.

"Angie, how come we haven't had any more news?" Billy asked.

"'Cause it takes time," she replied. "The telegram said they would let us know more, but I think that means only if things are, you know, worse. I think it's OK that we haven't had any news." But she didn't sound too convinced.

Mrs. Mazzarella was acting like Sal had already died. Angie said she cried all the time. One night when he took the garbage out, Billy could hear Angie's father yelling, even though the kitchen door and windows were closed. The next day Angie told him it was because her mother had told them she'd had a dream about Sal in his coffin.

"I'm going to tell you a secret," Angie said. "Before he left, Sal gave me a letter and told me that if anything happened I should open it."

"What did it say?" asked Billy.

"Whadda mean, what did it say? I didn't open it!"

"Yeah, but something happened, just like he said," replied Billy.

"He meant if *something happened*, like if he died. Billy, you're really dumb!" He'd never seen Angie so angry with him. "If I open that letter, it means he's dead!" She jumped up and ran into the house. Billy could tell she'd begun to cry.

Soon, Angie came back outside and offered him a peanut butter cookie her mother had just made. "Ma just used the last of our sugar for the week."

"Thanks," Billy said. "Angie, I know what you mean about Sal. I'm sorry I said that."

"I'm sorry I called you dumb," she replied.

"Well, it *was* a dumb thing to say."

"Yeah, it was, but that's OK." They both laughed. "Wanna play cards or something?"

Billy was tempted to tell Angie about the suitcase, but he didn't want her to feel bad that Sal had left it with him and not her. From that day on, Billy knew he wouldn't open the suitcase, maybe not even if Sal never came back. But every once in a while he dragged it down from the closet shelf to look at it and feel its surface and wonder what its contents might tell him. Everyone had secrets, and he wondered what Sal's were.

❧

This Christmas would be the second one without Alan and Sal. Small gifts and goodies had been mailed to them weeks earlier, but there was no guarantee the packages would reach their destinations by December 25, especially Alan's ship—wherever it was. Billy knew his mother and aunt and Nan were doing their best to make the holidays cheery for Gary and him, but it was no use. The setback in Europe, the endless battles in the Pacific, and the newly increased rationing had affected everyone.

Except for the easing of blackout restrictions and a big storm that blanketed the yard with a foot of snow, Christmas once again wasn't the holiday of years past. No matter how many times Belle played "Santa Claus is Coming to Town" on the old Philco phonograph in the downstairs living room, Bing Crosby and the Andrews Sisters couldn't lift the gloom that had settled in. Alan's Christmas cards, their envelopes ragged and dirty from postal misadventures along the way, didn't reach Springfield until the week after New Year's, and by then the cold and damp of January had set in.

By mid-February, however, the news was more encouraging. The 1st and 3rd armies came together after their temporary rupture at the bulge, and the march toward Berlin was once again underway. In the Pacific, the Marines, suffering tremendous casualties, stormed Iwo Jima, a volcanic island riddled with inter-connecting tunnels and caves only 600 miles from Tokyo.

"Ma, how come the Japs kill themselves instead of surrendering?" Billy asked. The evening paper had shown a photo of a cliff from which a bunch of Japanese, both soldiers and civilians, had jumped into the ocean. "I know it's supposed to be for the Emperor, but how can they do that? How can anyone kill themselves?"

"Well, sometimes people just reach the end of their rope, and they see no hope. But I think these soldiers believe it would dishonor them and their family to be captured," Laura said. "I don't think they all do that, but some do. Same thing with the kamikaze attacks. It's an honor to die for the Emperor." Billy knew she was worried about the kamikazes, because it had been reported that several LSTs had been sunk after being hit by the suicide planes.

Next to the map in his bedroom Billy tacked a newspaper photo of several Marines hoisting an American flag on Mount Suribachi after the Iwo Jima victory. Later he read that three of those Marines were killed shortly afterwards. Billy often studied the picture and tried to imagine which of them, struggling that day on top of the rocky volcano, had not made it off the island.

He wondered if his father's LST had been one of the many that transported the Marines to the beaches during that furious assault. Whenever Alan mentioned a particular place in one of his letters, the censor's black mark covered it up. They wouldn't know for sure just where he'd been until the war was over and he could tell them himself.

Billy heard Mrs. Brown talking to Nan one day about Joey Raccagni, who lived down the street and had been sent home early from North Africa because he'd lost some toes from shrapnel. Mrs. Brown said that he wouldn't talk to anyone about his time in the Army. Billy hoped that wouldn't be true of his father and Sal, though he'd also read in one of Nan's ladies' magazines that you needed to be careful not to press returning soldiers to go over their war experiences. The article was called "When Your Man Comes Home," and he'd made sure to show it to his mother so she'd know what to do.

෨ books

One Saturday afternoon in March, Billy and Angie were walking home from a matinee at the Strand, where they'd seen *Going My Way* with Bing Crosby.

"Boy, he wasn't like any priest I've ever come across," said Angie.

"I know. Did you ever hear a priest sing like that?" Billy asked.

"Are you kidding? Well, you know they do kinda sing during mass, but it's different. Nothing like "Too Ra Loo Ra Loo Ral"."

"Angie, do you think people go to hell?" asked Billy.

"Well, that's what they say," Angie answered. "I guess some people do, but not for stupid things like missing confession or eating a hotdog on Friday or something like that. I think you have to be real bad, like Hitler maybe."

"What about people who aren't Catholic?"

"Well, that's what I mean about dumb reasons. That's sure one of them. Sister John says they'll all end up in hell, but that's an awful lot of people, if you ask me."

"We'll be going to church on Easter Sunday," Billy said.

"That's good," said Angie. "I mean, you never know."

"Mrs. Brown said your mother asked her to bring back some palm leaves from St. Patrick's Cathedral when she goes to New York next weekend," said Billy.

"Yeah, she did," replied Angie, rolling her eyes. "I guess the archbishop blesses 'em or something."

That night at dinner, Billy asked his mother, "Are we still going to church on Easter?"

"Sure, we always do. And you'll have some new clothes to show off, too. What made you think we wouldn't?"

"Oh, nothing, I was just checking," Billy replied. "But, you know what? Angie said that all people who aren't Catholic might end up in hell."

"Oh, now, I declare!" said Nan. "Why is she putting that nonsense in your head?"

"Well, *she* didn't say it, but she told me one of the nuns at her school did."

"Irish, I'll wager," said Nan. "Really, the nerve!"

"Well, kids, listen, I just thought of something," said Belle to Billy and Gary, who was suddenly paying attention to the conversation. "If that's the case, then I guess we're all going, so it will be just like a big family reunion, see? Won't that be fun? We can roast hot dogs!"

The following week Billy was visiting with Mrs. Brown, showing her two books he'd borrowed from the library, *Drums Along the Mohawk* and *Northwest Passage*.

"Oh, those are grand novels," said Mrs. Brown. "I'm impressed, but I'm not surprised, Billy. You like big historical books, don't you?"

"Yes, I like to read about what happened before. I pretend I'm there, and everything."

"Well, that shows you have a lot of imagination."

"Mrs. Brown, do you think people go to hell?"

"Oh my, that's a big question for a Thursday afternoon," she replied. "But I must tell you, I don't. No, I don't believe that people go to hell."

"So everyone goes to heaven?"

"Now, I didn't say that. I don't think they go anywhere, but you needn't repeat that I said that. I think our time is here on Earth. I think once our time here is finished, all of us"—she pointed to Billy, herself, and to Ashkii, grooming himself on the sofa—"we all of us live on in others' thoughts."

"So you don't go to hell if you're bad or heaven if you're good?"

"That's what I think, but of course that's my opinion. Others would disagree." She peered at him. "Of course, that doesn't mean you should forget about doing good. Remember, I said we live on by the way people remember us."

"Mrs. Brown, how was St. Patrick's Cathedral?" He'd seen the palm leaves carefully arranged behind the painting of Jesus in the Mazzarellas' living room.

"St. Patrick's? Oh, you mean the palm leaves..." She paused. "Well, can I let you in on a secret?"

"Sure, I won't tell."

"Well, on Sunday afternoon when Hattie was seeing me off at Pennsylvania Station—Hattie's my friend in New York—I suddenly realized I'd forgotten Mary Mazzarella's palm leaves. What to do? We weren't near St. Patrick's at all. Then Hattie remembered there was another church around the corner, so we dashed in there and got some lovely palm leaves."

"So, that was OK then," Billy said.

"Well, no, not really, because it wasn't a Catholic church. It was an Episcopalian church. That's Protestant, you know."

"So those palm leaves weren't blessed by the archbishop like Angie said?"

"No, I'm afraid they were not. No, indeed, not at all. But you must promise not to tell Mary Mazzarella—or Angie."

"Oh, I won't, Mrs. Brown," he replied, though he knew Angie would think it was funny. "It's kind of like it was an April Fool's joke, isn't it?" As it happened, the coming Sunday—Easter Sunday—was falling on April 1.

"Well, I wouldn't go so far as to say that," replied Mrs. Brown. "But, yes, I suppose it is, in a way. But I had the best intentions, really I did."

She laughed and leaned over and patted Billy's knee. "Really, Billy, you are a most unusual boy. How fortunate I was to find this house—and you and your family. My dear neighbors and friends. Here, have another piece of cake. And remember, not a word about those counterfeit palm leaves!"

Chapter 41: Laura

"Hello, Mr. Pringle. What's happened?" Laura called out to her neighbor on her way home from work. Mr. Pringle was sitting on his front steps, looking glum, the American flag over his porch flying at half-mast.

"You didn't hear, missy?" the old man asked. "President Roosevelt passed away."

"No!" Laura was shocked. "How? When did it happen?"

"It came over the radio just a while ago. A cerebral hemorrhage, they say. Sudden like."

Mr. Pringle, for once, didn't comment on Laura's appearance. As she resumed walking, she heard his screen door close. Usually, she felt his eyes following her until she turned into her own driveway a few houses down the street.

FDR dead. What would this mean for the war? Roosevelt was the only president Laura had ever voted for. Her parents hated him, so she and Ceil had kept their votes a secret in the '32 election. It just wasn't worth hearing their father go on and on about "that socialist and his communist wife."

"Ma, guess what? President Roosevelt died!" Billy greeted her excitedly at the back porch. "It's on all the stations! Nan's real upset."

"I just heard from Mr. Pringle," Laura replied. "It's awful." Nan would be taking this news hard, she knew.

Sure enough, she found her mother-in-law sitting on the ottoman next to the radio, tears streaming down her face. "Oh, Laura, isn't this terrible? Dear, oh dear."

Laura gave her a kiss and handed her a handkerchief. "How about a cup of tea? I'll bet you forgot your tea."

"You know, I did. And Mrs. Brown's been downtown shopping since this forenoon, so I haven't seen her. She may not even know." Nan twisted Laura's handkerchief. "Oh my, what are we going to do now?"

Laura put together a dinner of leftovers, including what remained of a new "Victory Meal" recipe Nan had tried the night before. It involved peppers, onions, canned potatoes, applesauce, and large cubes of Spam, all cooked in a large skillet. The adults hadn't much liked it, but Billy and Gary had cleaned their plates.

"Ma, aren't they going to have any regular shows on tonight?" Gary asked. "They started talking about the President right in the middle of *Daniel Boone*. And now no *Lone Ranger.*"

"No, I don't think so," replied Laura. "That goes for the programs later on, too, I expect. No *Mr. Kean* or Bing Crosby's show— or maybe Bing'll just have special music or something like that."

"This is a big thing, kids," Belle said. "When I took the bus home tonight, you could tell something bad happened. Everybody was so quiet and sad."

"Poor Mrs. Roosevelt," Nan said. "And all her boys in the service, too."

"I wonder if there's an extra edition of the paper," said Belle. "Think I'll walk down to Joe's and see. Wanna come, kids?"

Later that night, Laura lay awake thinking about how fast things were happening these days. The invasion of the Japanese island of Okinawa, the discovery of horrible conditions in a camp in Germany called Buchen-something-or-other, and now Roosevelt's death. With the Allies closing in on Berlin, the war in Europe was almost over. The Japs couldn't last much longer, either, though everybody said they would hang on until there wasn't one soldier left to defend the homeland.

She didn't know for sure, but Laura assumed Alan was in the thick of it. The newspapers and newsreels had talked a lot about the flotilla of ships at Okinawa, even singling out the boxy, workhorse LSTs for their support during beachhead invasions. Though Laura hadn't heard from Alan much in recent months, neither had she received any other news. The death last week of the fiancé of a girl in her department was a chilling reminder of that possibility.

In the time that had passed since she'd last seen him—coming up to two years in the summer—it bothered Laura that her feelings were so muddled in other ways. The sweatshirt she still kept under his pillow had become like the little kewpie doll she dutifully arranged at the head of the bed after making it each morning—a familiar reminder of the past, but not much more.

What she worried about was the future. She knew how he was going to react to the way things had changed for her—the job at the Mutual, her singing, even the fact that she enjoyed balancing her check book, meager as the figures were. Except for the grocery money Alan used to give her every week, managing the household finances was something she hadn't been involved in at all before the war.

And what about Alan himself? He didn't like his job at Westinghouse—that she knew. And other things, like his drinking. He never mentioned how he was feeling in his letters anymore.

For the first time, she agreed to meet John Lawrence, the captain from Westover, at an hour other than when she was singing. He knew she usually rehearsed with the band mid-day on Saturday and had suggested lunch.

"OK, I can meet you right after we finish, but I need to be home to do things around the house and be with the kids for the rest of the afternoon," she told him.

Thinking about things late at night wasn't a good idea, Laura decided as she sat up and plumped up the pillow one more time . She turned the light on and opened a new library book, *The Egg and I*. It had quickly become a best seller and everybody was talking about how hilarious it was. Maybe it would take her mind off weightier matters.

કોન્ડ

Late Saturday morning, Laura arrived at the hotel. She was early, but she'd missed the first rehearsal during the week and needed to work on the music to a new tune they'd be performing that night. She was a quick study, so Ray pretty much let her get by with minimum practice time.

"You're looking especially nice today, Laura," he said as she walked into the empty lounge and over to the piano. Ray was busy making some notations on the musicians' sheets. He was always changing the arrangement, right up to the last minute.

"Thanks, Ray. I guess getting dressed up makes me feel better."

"I think it'll be all over soon, Laura," Ray said. "Even in the Pacific." He took her arm as he handed over her music. "Hope you'll stay on after your hubby comes home. You've got a pretty loyal following here, you know. That's good for the hotel, too, of course."

"I sure want to, Ray, believe me," she replied. "It just depends." They'd already discussed the possibility that she might quit after the war. "So what's the new song?"

"Sentimental Journey." It's getting a lot of play. Heard it? "

"Sure, in fact, just this morning. Les Brown. And Doris Day does the vocal. She's good. You watch. She'll be leaving to go out on her own soon." She laughed. "Whoops, didn't mean anything by that."

"Yeah, right, they all say that. Anyway, it's going to be a smash hit, I think. Especially if the war ends in the next couple of months." Ray played and sang a few bars. "It's a perfect coming-home song, you know?"

The other tune they rehearsed after the guys arrived was a novelty number called "Mairzy Doats," full of nonsensical words. Laura was joined on the vocals in this one by various members of the band.

"Hey, this isn't fair," she said. "I have to remember these goofy lyrics. You boys can hide behind the sheet music on your stands. "

"Yeah, that's 'cause we're not as pretty as you, kiddo," said Mickey, who'd been playing the clarinet around town for years.

As they finished running through the last of her songs, Laura spotted John out in the lobby. She hoped he wouldn't come in. Already she wondered if his presence the past few months had been noticed, though on Saturday nights he usually showed up with at least one other officer.

Laura said her goodbyes, motioning to John that she'd join him outside. Though he wanted to go to a fancier place, they walked down the street to the Rink restaurant for a hamburger. She'd have actually preferred to stay at the hotel and eat in the luncheon grill there. The band would be rehearsing a least a couple of hours longer back in the lounge, so she knew they wouldn't be stopping in there. Laura hoped she wouldn't bump into anyone from the office or neighborhood at the Rink.

"Ready for tonight?" John asked after they'd ordered. "You sounded good in there, what I heard. Do you get nervous?"

"Always, even though I know I'll be OK once I get into the song," Laura replied. "I guess the two things I worry most about are not coming in at just the right time and then forgetting the words.

I've done that a few times — had my mind go blank — so I just make up something."

It seemed strange to be sitting with John somewhere other than in the crowded lounge, always smoky and noisy on a Saturday night. She sensed he felt that, too. He was unusually quiet.

"Laura, I have some news," he suddenly said.

For a wild moment, she thought it had something to do with Alan, but how would he have gotten information about that? Before she could ask, he said, "I'll be leaving Westover. Just got word."

"Leaving? When?"

"Monday. For the West Coast. We're getting ready for a big transfer of pilots to the Pacific. Lots coming back from Europe now."

"Will you be going over, too? I mean, to the Pacific?"

"I don't think so, but it's a possibility." He laughed ruefully. "Anyway, no more Westover. Sorry I never showed the boys the base."

"That's all right," Laura replied. "I bet it'll be open afterwards. You know, for special celebrations and things."

"I'm sure it will be. Westover's become a very big installation. And it's going to get bigger. The world is going to be a whole lot different after this war. It's all about air power now."

There was silence. Laura wasn't quite sure what to say. Just last night she'd been thinking about all the things that seemed to be happening at once. Here was another. John was right. More was ending than just the fighting.

"Laura, you know how I feel about you, I know you do," John said, taking her hand. "Look, I'll be staying in town tonight, at the hotel. Could you manage to be with me?"

She smiled and gently moved her hand. He'd never been so direct before. She took a sip of her coffee and waited as the waitress arrived with their burgers. "I couldn't, John," she finally said. "It's my birthday tomorrow." She realized that was a rather lame answer. "I mean, I promised my mother-in-law I'd be there for dinner and, I imagine, a little party."

"Well," he replied. He smiled wryly. "Happy Birthday. I didn't know."

"I haven't talked about it much. One more year. Sometimes I feel, you know, that time is passing so fast." She shrugged. "Getting old, I guess."

"I wouldn't say that. You're the type of woman who gets better looking with the years."

"Well, I'm not *that* old," she said, laughing. "John, about what you said, it's not just that it's my birthday. It's not even easy for me to be here in this restaurant...I'm not...I'm not sure just what I *am* doing..."

"I know," he replied. "And I understand. Look, I won't say anything more. But if you change your mind after you get off, I'm in room 33."

That night Laura took special care getting herself ready for the lounge. She wore her hair in an elaborate upsweep with lots of curls in front. A simple black silk gown she'd had for years showed off her white shoulders and the bright red of her new lipstick.

As she was coming out of the small backstage office that served as her dressing room, Evelyn, the cigarette and candy girl, came up her. "Here, Laura, for you," she said, handing her a small lightweight box. "From your captain admirer, you know, the handsome one with the mustache. He's back at table 20 with a bunch of officers and their dates."

"Gee, thanks, Evelyn," Laura replied. So Evelyn had been noticing all along. She wondered who else had. "Wait and sec, I think it must be flowers."

Laura opened the box and held up a white gardenia. "Here, help me with this, would you? I've got to get out there." She showed Evelyn where to fasten it in her hair.

"That looks swell, Laura," Evelyn said. "Wow, you look real New York tonight."

The band was in the middle of an upbeat rendition of "I've Got A Gal In Kalamazoo" as Laura took her seat on the side, next to Red, the tenor saxophonist. It was hard to see beyond the couples jitterbugging on the small dance floor, but she briefly caught John's eye as he raised his glass and smiled. She pointedly patted her hair near the gardenia and smiled back.

Waiting for the number to end, Laura opened the small envelope that had been inside the flower box. *To remember me by*, the note read. She looked up and realized John was watching her. She felt a rush of emotion as he held his gaze, this time a long, serious look that seemed to pierce the noise and smoke of the crowded room. As the band finished and the dancers dispersed, she looked away and tried to concentrate on the words to the new song Ray was introducing.

There was something special about this tune, that was for sure. By the time she sang the last notes of "Sentimental Journey," most of the couples on the floor had left off dancing and were gathered in front of Laura in rapt attention. When the song finished, they burst into loud applause.

"You hooked 'em on that one, honey," Ray whispered to her as she sat down. "Only time I've seen that before is the year after Pearl Harbor when we played "White Christmas" and everybody started to bawl."

"Oh, it's the song, Ray," Laura said. "It just gets to you."

"Yeah, but you put something extra into it. Like you meant it."

During the rest of the evening, when Laura wasn't singing, she was busy talking to people who came up to the bandstand to compliment her. She noticed that women seemed to like her singing as much as the men. Ray had told her once that was the sign of a good singer, when it was more than your looks that made them listen.

She had a few dances, but none with John. His party was whooping it up in the corner of the room, and now he seemed to be purposely avoiding her. She wondered how many of the other men in the small group were leaving for the coast as well.

At the end of the night, for their last number, Ray launched into "Sentimental Journey" again. As she began singing, she noticed John and his friends stand up to leave. Just before exiting into the lobby, he turned and raised the cap he was holding. He tipped it in her direction and then disappeared.

"Gonna take that sentimental journey...sentimental journey home." As she finished the song, Laura began tearing up. Alan, the boys, the tune itself, John...She wasn't one to lose control easily, but she was filled with something she couldn't explain: sadness, happiness, a terrific awareness of feeling, of just being alive.

She blinked a few times to clear her eyes. As she took a last bow, Laura wondered if John had sensed when she sang the song earlier that she wouldn't be meeting him. She herself had known it then. She couldn't, when all she was able to think about was

Alan somewhere out there in the Pacific, waiting to return, going through God knows what. She didn't know what the future held, but he was part of hers.

"Ride, Laura?" asked Mickey, who lived up the hill a couple of blocks from Nan's house. He carefully placed his clarinet in its battered case.

"Sure thing, Mickey," Laura replied. "Just give me a minute to get my coat."

Though it was after one before Laura got to bed, she knew she wouldn't be able to sleep. Her mind was whirling with thoughts of the crowd's response to her songs tonight, and of the handsome pilot with the mustache who'd flown in and, it appeared, out of her life. She really hadn't known much about John. Was he single, as he'd claimed, or did he have a wife back in—where was it—Ohio? Now she'd never know.

She tuned in to a broadcast of Count Basie from the Savoy Ballroom in Harlem and opened her half-read copy of *The Egg and I*. She surprised herself when she was able to concentrate on the story. It really was a very funny book, all about a transplanted urban housewife trying to manage a chicken farm in Oregon with her difficult husband and assorted relatives.

At one particularly outlandish bit involving a chaotic supper with two eccentric neighbors, Ma and Pa Kettle, and their 15 kids, Laura let out a loud guffaw, and then tried to stifle her laughter so she wouldn't disturb the boys. But in a few minutes, Billy appeared at the door.

"Oh, Billy, did I wake you?" She turned off the radio and put the book aside.

"That's OK, I wasn't too tired anyway. What were you laughing at, Ma?"

"This book. There are some grown-up things in it, but I guess you could read it if you want. It's a riot!"

"Even with President Roosevelt dying and everything?"

"I know, maybe I shouldn't be laughing," she said. "You're right. But you know, sometimes you can't be a Mr. Sobersides all the time. Life can be funny and full of surprises, you know."

"Ma, what's this?" Billy pointed to the dresser, where Laura had placed the gardenia in a cereal bowl full of water.

"Oh, that's a flower I wore tonight."

"Where did you get it?"

"Somebody gave it to me. It's so pretty, isn't it?" She paused. "Remember that captain from Westover, Captain Lawrence? Him. He's leaving on Monday."

"Leaving for good?" Billy asked.

"Yes. He says he's sorry that you won't be able to go over to Westover."

"That's OK, I don't mind. So you—we—won't see him any-more? Ever?"

"That's right. I don't know how we would."

"Ma, you know how you were saying it was too bad you didn't get a birthday card from Dad?"

"Yes, but I understand, with the mail and all."

"Well, pretend you don't know I told you, but there really is a card that we're going to give you tomorrow at your birthday party."

"There is?! Well, I promise I won't let on." Laura was aware of Billy's serious gaze. Turning her head, she wiped her eyes. "Oh, that book is so funny it nearly made me cry!"

"OK, I'm going back to bed now," Billy said. Laura drew him to her for a quick hug, though she knew that wasn't his favorite thing. Unlike Gary, Billy wasn't one for easy displays of affection, even when he was a very little boy. "'Night, Ma," he said.

As she lay in the dark, Laura imagined what it would be like if she and Alan and the kids moved out to the country. Just like in *The Egg and I*. Well, maybe not quite as cuckoo as that particular chicken farm. Nan and Belle and Abe and everyone could visit, but it would be a place for just the four of them after the war was over. Lucille and Max, too, she reminded herself, right before she dozed off.

Chapter 42: Alan

"Think this is what a London fog's like?" asked Buzz in a raspy voice. "Christ, I can't fuckin' breathe and I got a wicked sore throat."

While the crew of LST 1717 waited offshore at Okinawa, the fog generator on the fantail was working overtime. Thick white smoke hung over the ship, making visibility next to zero. Several five-gallon smoke pots strategically arranged along the main deck added to the eerie sense of isolation created by the heavy camouflage.

They were in fact surrounded by Allied ships, all part of what Captain Salisbury said was probably the largest naval flotilla gathered in the Pacific since the war began. The day before, as they'd approached the island, battleships, destroyers, transports and other LSTs and smaller landing craft had been visible everywhere. Some bobbed as close as a few hundred feet away, others dotted the seascape as far as the eye could see.

Now they needed to be wary of aircraft or small boats the enemy might launch from the beach, or even swimmers with explosives strapped to their backs. Several times guards patrolling the decks of front-line ships opened fire on pieces of debris floating just below the fog line, fearing they might be hiding suicide bombers.

Even though the LST was still too far offshore to be concerned about human bombs, every irregular lapping of a wave or unusual clang on deck made the hairs on the back of Alan's neck stand up. It was the waiting and the not knowing and the creepy fog, fake or not, that got to you.

"Some way to spend Easter Sunday," Buzz said. "Waiting to unload some Marines on an island full of Japs holed up in all them caves."

"Yeah, sure is," replied Alan. "Hey, guess what else it is today? April Fool's Day. April first."

"Shit, you're right," said Buzz. "Never thought of that. That's even worse. Now you got me scared."

As it turned out, the first landing they made, to discharge the Marines who had sailed with them from Guadalcanal, had gone without incident. They'd begun preliminary beaching procedures hours earlier—warming up the auxiliary diesels for extra electric power, testing the ramps and doors. Then came the call to General Quarters. Alan's GQ station was always in the radar shack, where he often had nothing to do but wait. With all the fog above deck, only the constant artillery fire from the larger vessels reminded him that an invasion was going on. There had been surprisingly little resistance from the beach.

At one point, Chief Petty Officer Sloan stuck his head in the radar shack. "How are things going in here, men?"

"OK, sir, nothing much happening," said Stan, Alan's partner on watch. "How's it going out there, sir?"

"We're lucky so far," replied Sloan. "Hardly any resistance, though a craft a few hundred yards away on the port side just got hit by a suicide plane. Problem is, there's a big reef here and we can't go too far in or we'll hit the coral heads. We can only discharge at high tide for a few hours at a time."

About an hour later the beaching alarm sounded. "Guess we're going in," said Stan.

"They'll probably just launch the LVTs," Alan said, referring to the small landing vessels carried on the lower deck. "They'll want to get those Marines on the beach first."

"Glad I ain't them," said Stan. "Jesus, their gear would be enough to sink you, never mind a mine or bullet."

"Hope the LVTs hold up on the coral. I think they're made more for sandy landings," said Alan.

"Yeah, but at least we don't have those old Higgins boats. They can't make it across reefs for shit. Lot of guys get killed in the water that way—dumped off too far out."

At the order to disembark, the bow doors were opened and the ramp lowered to about six feet above the waterline. The compact LVTs eased out onto the reef one by one, each loaded with approximately 20 marines. The smoke from the generators had been temporarily stopped, so Alan was able to see the men crowded into the small boats as they maneuvered their way toward the beach. When they got closer to the shore, the amphibians' rear ramps would be lowered for the troops to wade a few feet onto dry land

After delivering the Marines in the LVTs, the ship moved to a stretch of volcanic ash dubbed Green Beach. Over the next several days, the crew unloaded the rest of the contents of the ship along pontoon causeways that had been hastily constructed directly after the invasion.

The lower tank deck was cleared first, then elevators lowered more equipment from the main deck to the open bow door. Off went four trucks, ten jeeps, and a dozen water trailers. These were followed by the unloading of barbed wire, telephone equipment, ammunition, gasoline and water drums, tent furnishings, kitchen utensils, and canned food—all materiel that had become part of the standard first wave of supplies delivered to an invasion site.

At this point, the island was still far from taken, so most of the supplies were stacked on the beaches. Only later would the Seabees move in to construct more permanent installations.

Alan had never been so tired. When not on duty in the radar shack, he did extra time helping unload and standing watch as raids from Japanese planes along the shore became increasingly frequent. Everyone got used to eating cold food, and there was no time to shave or wash. Sleep was limited to a couple of hours at a stretch.

Although the General Quarters alarm sounded regularly, it was only when an LST that was anchored next to theirs sustained a direct hit that Alan fully understood the danger they were in. He was topside when the kamikaze plane smashed into the stern of the other ship. Men were blown across the deck, and he could hear the cries of the dying and wounded. His mind flashed back to the incident on his own ship months earlier. He wondered how Donny, with that chunk of shrapnel in his neck, had fared after being evacuated. They still hadn't heard.

❧❧

Despite the chaos, the initial unloading at Okinawa was completed with relatively few casualties. The crew of LST 1717 rested for a couple of days offshore and set out in the second week of April for Saipan in the Marianas to pick up more troops and supplies.

Soon after they lost sight of the island, a crew member from the radio shack ran into the radar room waving a piece of paper.

"Hey guys, take a look at this. I just delivered the original to the bridge."

"Oh, boy," said Stan as he read the radiogram aloud. "Roosevelt's dead. My mom'll be upset about this."

"Mine, too," Alan replied. He could picture his mother leaning in front of the radio, intent on hearing every bit of commentary about her beloved FDR. Alan found himself thinking about Fala, the Roosevelt dog, and he wondered how old Lucille was doing these days. Then he wondered if the President's death would have any effect on the progress of the war. Things had been going pretty well.

During the several runs the LST made between Saipan and Okinawa over the next several weeks, there was little apparent danger from Japanese ships and large airborne convoys. Those days of the war seemed to be over.

The kamikazes continued to wreak sporadic havoc, however, both in human casualties and damage to ships. The psychological impact was significant as well, an ever-present fear that became instilled in the crews of the vessels poised like sitting ducks on the open sea or at anchor. It was even worse during hours spent below deck.

Nevertheless, life on board proceeded as normally as possible during the early summer of 1945. LST 1717, like most vessels in the Pacific war zone, had a movie projector and screen. While in transit, blackouts prevented the showing of movies on deck, but in port they were standard fare after dark. Ships anchored near each other in Saipan's Tanapag Harbor or in Buckner Bay on the eastern side of Okinawa exchanged films regularly.

You'd love this part of the war, Billy, Alan wrote in a letter home. *We see a different movie just about every night and not always old ones. Sometimes we have to stop the film mid-way if there's a blackout alert. We race to our General Quarters stations and then back topside when it's all clear. Last night we saw Dorothy Lamour in "Aloma of the South Seas."*

What he didn't mention was that something went wrong that night with the sound as the projector was running. At first there were boos and catcalls on deck, but when the movie proceeded silently, some of the guys began to shout out their own dialogue.

"Let me give it to you, I'm so horny!" pleaded one of the sailors on the rear deck as the bare-chested hero on the screen gazed longingly at Dorothy/Aloma.

"I'm sorry, my daddy warned me if he caught me screwing I'd be sacrificed!" Dorothy/Aloma replied in a disembodied falsetto, modestly lowering her gaze.

"But I'll go crazy!" came a deep voice from somewhere in the crowd.

"Well, I guess it's OK then, but first let's see what you're hiding under that skirt, Big Boy!" Dorothy/Aloma replied sweetly as the couple embraced under the moonlit shadow of a swaying palm. Everyone cheered.

"Jeez, we should make a record of this and send it back to the states," Buzz said to Alan. "Beats the real show any day!"

∽∾

A few weeks later, on a still, overcast August afternoon, they were proceeding at sea in a southeasterly direction toward the Marianas. The ship had left Okinawa at noon for the usual return run to Saipan. Its main and tank decks were now empty of the materiel delivered the day before, much of which was still sitting exposed or in makeshift tents and temporary warehouses near the pier back at Buckner Bay.

Jimmy, a radioman in the shack next door, stuck his head in the radar room, waving a pale yellow message in the air. "Hey, guys, this looks bad," he said to Alan and Harold, the other radar man on duty.

"TYPHOON WARNING," the radiogram began, followed by details pinpointing the storm's exact location and probable course. It had been bearing down from the northeast, away from them, but was suddenly shifting in a southerly direction, on a straight path for Okinawa.

By the time LST 1717 and several other transports in the small convoy adjusted their course, the weather had begun to change. The wind velocity was picking up by the minute, accompanied by a torrential rain. The sky to the north had turned an ominous dark gray.

All they could do at this point was ride out the storm and hope to remain on the periphery of its unpredictable fury. By good luck they'd at least escaped the more dangerous anchorage at their crowded berth back in the harbor, never a good place to be when a big storm swept in.

Alan peered out the porthole, but the pelting of the rain and the piercing whistling of the wind threatened to smash the little window. Sticking his head out the door, he had to hold on to the sides so as not to be swept out on the deck and possibly overboard.

Off the port side, another LST in the convoy was thrashing dangerously close to them as both vessels were buffeted by the monstrous waves. The ship rose so high before it slammed down on the crest of a descending wave that Alan could see its propeller, called the screw, whirling crazily against the dim horizon all too visible underneath its stern. It was an awesome, unnerving sight. He quickly retreated into the relative safety of the radar room.

"Holy shit," he said. "I just saw daylight under the ship next to us."

"This is really awful," said Harold, a normally placid young man who had left his studies in engineering school to enlist right after Pearl Harbor. He knew more about radar than anyone on board. "I've never been seasick before, but this may be it."

"Yeah, but can you imagine what it's like below?" Alan replied. "Guys must be tied to the bunks. And remember, we don't have supplies and equipment on board anymore for extra weight down there."

"You're right, I guess," said Harold in a shaky voice. But he was pasty-faced and sweaty, and he didn't look convinced.

"Be careful if you have to go outside," Alan shouted. "Try to stand facing downwind if you're really going to be sick. I'm not kidding, you'll get it right back in your face. And stay away from the rail." At this point the din was terrific: rain battering the deck in steady horizontal sheets, a howling wind, and angry waves crashing over the signal bridge.

"What's that whining noise?" Harold asked.

"I think that's the mast," Alan replied. The sound was eerie, like a monstrous, off-pitch tuning fork that wouldn't stop vibrating.

"You mean, it's really moving that much? Oh, Jesus," Harold groaned, "We're going to sink for sure."

Amazingly, all the electric equipment was holding, despite flooding in the engine room. Several sailors were already in sickbay as the result of bad falls taken on the narrow stairs and collisions with moving objects. Others were too sick to leave their bunks because of the pounding the ship was taking. The tank deck was off-limits, its vast space a shooting gallery of flying skids, platforms, jacks, and big empty containers.

In the shack, Alan hung on for dear life to the radar table. Harold was a couple of feet away, but the din was too ferocious for conversation.

Alan was reminded of the '38 hurricane back home. The storm had raced up the Atlantic seaboard, hitting landfall with hardly any warning on Long Island and the Connecticut and Rhode Island shore towns. Then it roared northward into Massachusetts.

By the time Alan was sent home from Westinghouse late that afternoon, the hurricane was reaching its peak. As he made his way up the front path, struggling against the force of the wind and rain, a rocking chair suddenly took flight from the second floor porch. It careened crazily in the air for several seconds, and then landed upright with a thud directly in front of him, as though beckoning him to take a front-row seat to witness the fury of the storm.

Although everyone was glad to see him home safely that day, the big concern was the absence of Lucille. In her prime back then, she'd been roaming somewhere in the neighborhood and hadn't returned when the storm began.

Suddenly, Billy, anxiously watching for her at the kitchen window, shouted, "There she is! I see her under the bushes!" Sure enough, there was Lucille, cowering under the huge lilac at the far edge of the yard. She'd apparently made it home but was afraid to negotiate the big expanse of open lawn, where an evergreen had already fallen and debris was flying through the air.

They'd all crowded in the back porch doorway, encouraging Lucille to make a race for the house. "Come on, Lucille! You can do it! Come on, Lucille!" Billy shouted in his little boy's voice. He must have been about five then. Gary hadn't even been born yet.

Just as Alan was about to make an attempt to brave the elements and rescue the terrified dog, Lucille made a dash for the house. At every few leaps forward, she was buffeted back by the howling wind. Once she actually appeared to be airborne, landing on her rear in the branches of the fallen pine tree. With a mighty effort, she righted herself, took off again, and made a flying leap onto the porch, bounding into Alan's arms, whining and smothering him with kisses.

A sudden blip of the radar jolted Alan back to the present. He could tell from the screen that vessels were not far away, too close in fact, and he wondered how the other ships in the small convoy were doing. The LST that had nearly landed on top of them had disappeared from sight. There had to be a good chance that at least one of the ships wouldn't make it, or that anyone caught above quarters would be swept overboard.

After the storm ended, however, and all the damage was assessed, the crew of LST 1717 counted themselves lucky. They'd come out of the typhoon relatively unscathed. The most serious injuries were a broken leg suffered by a sailor who fell through an open hatchway, and the loss of a finger by another man whose hand had gotten jammed between a steel container and the wall it had crashed into.

Flooding, a few bent railings, and a battered signal mast constituted the major structural damage sustained by the ship, along with general chaos involving anything that wasn't bolted down — utensils, food supplies, and the like. Below deck it looked like, well, it looked like a typhoon had passed through.

Buckner Bay, where they'd been just a few hours earlier, was a disaster. Ships had smashed into each other, and many were blown ashore and wrecked. The storm had actually doubled back and hit Okinawa again the following day. The devastation was tremendous: virtually all the Army installations near the beaches destroyed, many planes at the five airbases on the island wrecked, food and water supplies gone. All told, nearly 300 ships in the region were sunk or damaged beyond repair. Loss of life was in the hundreds, including many American troops.

As a result, the radiogram that came into the shack a few days later seemed almost anticlimactic — at least to the troops who had lived through typhoon Louise. *For your information*, it began, *the State Department has received official Japanese acceptance of surrender documents*. The sudden capitulation had come quickly after the destruction of two Japanese cities, Hiroshima and Nagasaki, with a weapon unlike any that had been used before: an "atomic" bomb. The war was over.

All available transport ships immediately became part of the massive operation to occupy Japan. Finally, after many more weeks of ferrying troops to offshore islands, as well as directly into

Yokohama Bay, LST 1717 received orders to proceed homewards. Alan assumed that meant directly stateside to the West coast, but Buzz told him that he'd delivered a message from the shack to the captain that indicated otherwise.

"We're heading back to Honolulu," he said. "Switching us over there to one of the big carriers, it looks like. So guess we'll get to see some of the sights again."

He grinned at Alan. "That's just fine with me, the idea of sailing into Pearl again. How about you?"

"Yeah," Alan replied. "I guess so." But he wasn't sure.

Chapter 43: Billy

"Ma, can I go downtown with you and Belle?" Billy asked. "Everybody's going to be there for the celebration."

"Oh, I don't know, Billy, it'll be kind of wild, I think," Laura replied. "And those two kids over in West Springfield who came down with polio...I don't like you in such a big crowd." She thought for a moment. "What about Nan and Gary?"

"Nan said she didn't mind being alone. And maybe Mrs. Brown'll come over. Please, Ma, please? Angie's going with her parents."

"Well, OK," Laura replied. "But you have to promise to stay with us every minute."

The war with Japan was over. Billy knew this was a special day in history, even more so than the day the fighting in Europe ended three months ago, on May 15. On that afternoon, the school principal had come to his class and told the kids that they would always remember where they were when victory was declared.

"Now, think of the same thing, boys and girls, on the day the Japanese are defeated as well," said Mrs. Bowles. "Soon, we hope and pray." Now it had finally happened.

Everyone was so excited they forgot all about having a regular dinner. "I'll make some sandwiches and we'll invite the Mazzarellas and eat out back," Nan said. It was a pleasant, still evening, but the August twilights were growing shorter. The air, too, had a hint of cooler nights to come.

"Now your papa will be home, too," Mary Mazzarella said to Billy as they all sat at the picnic table. "Just like Salvatore." Though Sal hadn't yet arrived back in the USA, they were expecting him sometime in the coming weeks. He'd sent them a postcard from London, saying he was waiting for a transport ship.

As the sun faded and the crickets began to chirp, Billy went in the house to put on his long trousers for the bus ride downtown. The newspaper said that big crowds were expected, but he wasn't sure what everybody would actually be doing. Maybe there would be a parade, but even if they all just stood around he wanted to be there.

"You take good care of Nan, Gary," Laura said.

"Aw, she's just going to listen to the news," Gary said. "Can I play in the yard?" Nan was already sitting by the radio waiting for her favorite broadcaster to begin his report.

"Bet you know what Gabriel Heatter's going to say on his show, Gary," Billy said.

"Yup, *'There's good news tonight, folks!'*" Gary replied in a deep, clipped voice. Over the course of the war they'd gotten used to that familiar greeting, though often there had been bad news to report first. Not tonight.

The downtown bus was mobbed, every seat taken and riders crowded in the aisle. Billy clung to the worn leather overhead strap, which he could reach easily now. He'd grown a couple of inches in the past year and was the second-tallest kid in his sixth grade class.

The mood was jubilant, with much joking and chatting among the passengers. Even the creaky old bus seemed to have picked up new life as it careened bumpily down the hill, spitting out thick exhaust. The driver tooted out a syncopated chorus on the horn each time they passed another bus.

Halfway downtown, they came to a stop in a long line of traffic near the armory, its windows uncharacteristically closed and all lights out. "That's a sign of what's to come," Belle said. "I know some girls who've already gotten their notice."

Cars were backed up even on the side streets. As they inched toward Main, the crowds of walkers became denser and rowdier. Lots of people were waving flags and blowing on horns and other New Year's favors available at hastily assembled vendors' wagons.

"Jesus, this is for the birds, let's get off and walk from here," said Belle. "I bet we'd make better time."

They joined the throngs descending on the downtown area, normally populated on a weekday night only by moviegoers and people out for dinner. Though they were now close to the river, the air was warmer than up on the hill. Billy was half sorry he hadn't kept on his play shorts, but he'd moved on to long pants year-round a while back, and he wouldn't have wanted anyone to see him looking like a little kid, especially at night.

Turning the corner at Main Street, they could hear the sound of band music coming from the big square near city hall. "That'll be Ray and the boys," Laura said. "A bunch of bands are playing, but he knew I'd want to be with you all tonight." She squeezed Billy's hand and put her arm around Belle's waist.

"You know, I told Abe I'd see him down here," said Belle. "He's coming with Hannah and Charlotte. Fat chance in this mob." Billy thought the same about meeting up with Angie, who was also somewhere in the crowd.

They managed to inch their way close to the barricades in front of the outdoor stage. Billy ended up standing next to a chunky lady wearing a sleeveless pinafore dress that exposed a splotchy, star-shaped vaccination mark on her left upper arm. A tied-up bandanna hid her hair, but you could see the tightly fastened pin curlers underneath.

Nan wouldn't approve of that, Billy knew. "Try to look your best whenever you step off your porch," she always said. "You never know what's going to happen." He knew she was referring to getting hit by a truck or something, but he could never figure out why you had to be dressed up, even with clean underwear, if you ended up all covered with blood and dirt and stuff.

The lady with the vaccination mark smiled at him and blew some air his way with a newspaper she was using as a fan. Billy recognized it as the extra edition of the *Daily News* that had been delivered late in the day. Its headline read in big black letters: **WAR ENDS; WORLD WILD WITH JOY.**

Mayor Anderson, amid cheers and whistles, stepped to the microphone and began to speak. "We have lived through days and years that have tested the security of our civilization," the mayor said, his voice reverberating off the buildings surrounding the large square. "To most of us the war has meant hard work, rationing of the essentials of living, worry for our kinfolk in the armed services. Others have suffered deep grief at the loss of a loved one. But the ones to whom the war has meant everything are those men who had a rendezvous with death."

As the crowd quieted for a moment of silence, a steady honking of horns continued in the background. Somewhere in the distance a factory siren began to wail. Billy became aware of another noise, the sniffling and the blowing of noses among the people in the crowd. He looked up at his mother and aunt, both of whom had tears running down their cheeks.

"Look, there's Ray on the stage," said Laura, pointing over the head of an elderly man waving little American flags in each of his upraised arms.

As the mayor finished, Ray took the mike. "Ladies and gentlemen, following our distinguished mayor's inspiring words, we'd like to do a song that is particularly appropriate for this wonderful night. But we'll need the help of someone I see out there among you. She's the lovely gal with our band, Laura Stewart. Laura's with her own family tonight, but I'm sure she'll join us for this one number."

"Oh boy, I wasn't expecting this," Laura said. "Look at me, I'm not dressed or anything."

"Go on, Laura, you look just fine," Belle said.

"Yeah, go ahead, " Billy whispered to his mother, giving her a slight nudge. He always loved the chance to hear her sing, and tonight was a really special occasion. Everybody would get to see her.

Laura made her way to the makeshift wooden stage that had been erected in front of the campanile, a tall Italian bell tower, that rose between the columns of the twin municipal buildings. A bright spotlight illuminated the band as dusk approached.

Billy saw Ray whisper to her, and she nodded. Then he said into the mike, "Laura, thanks for being up here. Anything you'd like to say to these folks?"

"Gee, Ray, just that I'm awful glad to be here, and I'd like to dedicate our song to all the men—and the women—who've been serving and who'll be home soon. Especially my husband, Alan, Alan Stewart, who's a radar man first class on an LST in the Pacific."

The crowd cheered as the band began a song everyone knew, "When the Lights Go On Again All Over the World." Though his mother was wearing a simple yellow summer dress with a wide matching ribbon in her hair, Billy thought she looked really pretty as she sang into the big microphone. Her voice seemed magnified a thousand times by the huge cone-shaped amplifiers pointed into the square.

Laura finished her number amidst loud applause and whistles. As she made her way down the wooden steps of the stage, the lady next to Billy asked him, "That your older sister, sonny?"

"No, my mother," Billy replied. He looked up at Belle and smiled. No one had ever made that mistake before.

"Well, land's sake, ain't she pretty," the lady said. "Sweet voice, too. She belongs on the radio."

From further down Main Street, toward the railroad station, the sound of a marching band could be heard. The parade was coming. "Now I'm sorry that Gary and Nan aren't with us," Laura said. "This isn't as crazy as I thought it'd be."

The police were having trouble clearing the street, but eventually one of the high school bands came into view, followed by a lot of men and a few women in uniform. Most were young and clearly still in the service, some of them from the base at Westover.

With them were several soldiers and sailors from the Great War, marching as they did in the Memorial and Armistice Day parades every May and November. An old fellow carrying a sign that read **REMEMBER THE MAINE** walked all by himself. "Wow," said Billy, "he must have been in the Spanish-American War!"

Later, heading for the bus to go back up the hill, they realized it would take forever even to get one to stop for them, so they ended up walking the two miles home. Police were evident everywhere, trying to keep more cars from entering the center of the city, directing others that were trying to leave the downtown area, and keeping pedestrians out of the clogged lanes.

As the traffic thinned out at the top of the hill, more than one car sped by overloaded with teenagers stuffed inside, sprawled on the hood, and standing on the running boards. One boy was even wrapped around the trunk wheel of an old roadster. A lot of kids were clinging to the backs of city buses, faces pressed sideways against the dirty windows, arms and legs splayed against the hot, metal-covered motors.

"You wouldn't ever try that, would you, Billy?" Laura asked.

"No," he answered. "That's mostly the tough kids who do that stuff." He had, in fact, recognized one of his friends from school, but he didn't mention that after Laura's remark.

"Ma," he said, "a lady standing next to me asked me if you were my older sister."

"Get out!" Laura said.

"Nope, she did," said Belle. "I told her, no, *I* was his older sister!"

"Well, she just said that 'cause *you're* getting so old looking," Laura said to Billy, though he could tell she was pleased.

"Laura, that was swell that you mentioned the women overseas, not just the men," Belle said. "Unlike our mayor."

"Well, I wonder if I would have thought of that before you got involved in those meetings," Laura replied. "Now I seem to notice these things, too. It makes me mad."

As they neared the Strand Theater, Billy was reminded of the night they'd walked home after seeing the Donald Duck cartoon about Hitler. "Hey, 'member when we all marched up the street doing that funny Nazi step?" he asked his mother and aunt.

"Gosh, yes, that seems like such a long time ago," said Belle.

They walked the rest of the way mostly in silence, passing several groups of people congregated on street corners. Others sat on the steps of the tenements along stretches of the wide thoroughfare. Making their way down their own quiet street, they greeted neighbors sitting in the darkness of their front porches.

Nan was alone, reclining in the big Adirondack chair Mr. Mazzarella had made many years ago. After telling her all about the events on Main Street, Belle and Laura went indoors. "Hope I hear there's no work tomorrow," Belle said. "Wouldn't that be nice?"

Billy sat down on the steps near his grandmother. Lucille circled, sniffing the floor, then sprawled out at his feet. Max's eyes gleamed in the dark from under a bush a few yards away.

"Nan, there were a lot of men from the First World War in the parade downtown," Billy said.

"Aye, I expect there would be. They're not so old, you know," she said. "A lot of them younger than me."

Billy remembered that Nan was older than her brother, Harry, who'd been killed in that war. "Were you thinking of your brother, today, Nan?"

"I was. Harry. Fancy that you would remember, Billy. You're a good, kind laddie."

"Can you think of where you were when you heard he got killed?" Billy asked.

"I can indeed," Nan replied. "Of course we didn't know right away over here, Harry being in the British army and all. But one day I got a letter from my dear mother, and the border was all in black, so I knew someone had died. That's what we did in those days," she explained. "I thought, *No, not our Harry*...Handsome Harry we called him...but sure enough, that's who it was, dear Harry." Nan sighed, and though he wasn't sure, Billy sensed she was crying in the dark.

"But at least Dad is coming home," Billy said.

"Aye, we have that to be thankful for. And Sal, too. But so many will not be thankful, sad to say. That's the shame of it." Nan sighed again. "And think of all the poor homeless children everywhere."

"Maybe this will be the last war," Billy said. He was trying to think of something else that would cheer Nan up.

"Ah, dearie, that's what they said the last time," Nan replied. "I just hope you and little Gary will be spared. But perhaps you're right. Maybe this is the end of it, after all."

Then Nan leaned over and slapped his knee and said in a cheery voice, "Now tell me, did you see Mrs. Brown down there in all that hullabaloo?"

"Didn't she come over to see you?"

"She did, dressed to kill." Nan laughed and wiped her eyes. "She declared she wouldn't miss going downtown if she had to walk the whole way, high heels and all. Now, you're sure you didn't see a lady with red hair sitting on the curb rubbing her old corns?"

PART IV

Summer 1945-Summer 1946

*Fifty square miles of Tokyo are leveled in incendiary raids by B-29 bombers

*The #1 song on the *Billboard* charts is "Sentimental Journey" (Les Brown Band, vocal by Doris Day)

*The #1 best-selling books are *Forever Amber* by Kathleen Winsor (fiction) and Ernie Pyle's *Brave Men* (non-fiction)

*By war's end, five million copies of the iconic, over-the-shoulder pin-up of Betty Grable are in print

*The bikini bathing suit, named after the atomic bomb test on Bikini Atoll, is introduced

*Jackie Robinson debuts as 2nd baseman for the Montreal Royals, a farm team of the Brooklyn Dodgers

Chapter 44: Belle

It was a Saturday afternoon in early September, nearly a month after V-J day. Belle and Nan were sitting on the front porch, enjoying the last of the summer weather. There had already been a few cool nights, and in the front yard the leaves on the red maple, always the first to turn, were showing the faint hues of pink that would soon deepen to blazing scarlet.

Suddenly, with an exasperated cry, Belle flung her magazine across the floor. It stirred the air above the sleeping Lucille, who yawned, scratched her ear, and then resumed her nap.

"Oh my, Belle! What is it, a wasp?" asked Nan, stopping her knitting in mid-stroke.

"No, Mother, it's not a wasp," replied Belle. "It's a goddam stupid ad I just read in that goddam stupid magazine." Belle got up and retrieved the copy of *Women's Home Companion*, now flattened against a potted geranium at the bottom of the steps. "I'm sorry. Didn't mean to startle you."

"My goodness, dear, what was in it?" asked Nan. She'd already resumed her knitting, shaking out a few more feet of the tightly balled red yarn resting on the floor. The tube-like piece she was working on would somehow turn into the arm of a sweater she was making for Gary. Belle could never figure out how this happened.

She quickly leafed through the wrinkled magazine. "OK, listen to this ad for vacuum cleaners," she said, slapping the page. *"Like you, Mrs. America, we will put aside our uniform and return to peace.'* And, see," Belle continued, her voice rising, "it shows a picture of this nice, neat housewife—who used to be the scruffy factory worker in the little picture in the corner here—vacuuming her living room. See, now she's happy as a clam, and she's just *vacuuming*, for Christ's sake."

"Well, I guess she's glad the war's over," said Nan. "And that her husband's home safe."

"Sure, we'll all be glad of that, but what about all the Mrs. Americas whose Mr. America got killed?" Belle asked. "Or the ones who aren't Mrs. at all? Like me, for instance."

"I know, dear, you're right. It doesn't seem fair when you put it that way. But don't get yourself all worked up."

Nan would be sympathetic to anyone who was upset, but it was no use trying to explain things like this to her. Belle wondered if her mother really approved of Laura's working, when it came right down to it.

In any event, Belle didn't want anything to upset Nan these days. She was so happy at Alan's impending return. Belle just hoped he'd arrive safely, whenever that was. No time soon, she feared. There were too many others waiting who'd been in longer and earned more service points, guaranteeing them a faster discharge.

"Mother, I've been meaning to ask you," Belle said, smoothing out the magazine. "What do you think about the idea of me going back to school?"

"Oh my, I think that would be grand," said Nan. "But do you really expect you're going to lose your job at the plant?"

"No, not fired anyway. But for sure I'll end up on the line with the other girls, or something not so terrific, believe me. And I don't want to do that."

"Where would you go to school?"

"I'm not sure, business school downtown, or maybe some courses at AIC. They're already offering a lot of night stuff this fall." She'd noticed an ad in the paper the other night for American International College, right down the street.

"What does Abe think about all this?" Nan asked. "I mean, if..."

"If what?" asked Belle, laughing.

"Well, I was hoping that maybe, you know, you'd be making plans. He's a lovely man."

"That he is. But he still would want me to do whatever I want as far as a job. Anyway, I wouldn't stop working, you know, whatever happens."

"No, I guess not," replied Nan. "Things have changed since my time."

"Meanwhile, I'm planning to work with Abe's daughter, Hannah, in her new bookstore," Belle said. "The thing is...will that be OK as far as the household finances? I'd probably have to cut back a bit." Belle gave her mother a good chunk of her paycheck each week, but Nan still paid the bills.

"Oh, don't worry about that, " Nan replied. "Your dear dad saw to us in that respect." Nan had not only received life insurance money, she still got a monthly check, part of the settlement after the accident back in 1922. Negligence by the construction company, or something. It wasn't a heck of a lot, but Nan was thrifty.

"Thanks, Mother," Belle said. "You stay out here, I'm going to fix lunch." She had no idea what Nan had in the refrigerator, but she'd find something.

After talking things over once more with Abe later that night, Belle gave her two-week notice the following day. She was pleased that Mr. Webster, the head of personnel, seemed truly sorry to see her leave. Still, she wasn't surprised when he acknowledged that he couldn't have guaranteed that her present job would continue much longer.

"You understand, Belle. So many of the men are coming back, it's not possible for us to keep things as they've been. And we won't be having most of these government contracts renewed."

"It's a hell of a note to see you leave, Belle," said Gert, the union steward, that afternoon. "It's gals like you we need."

"I know, part of me wants to stay and fight it out," replied Belle. "But there's a lot of stuff going on. I have plans to go back to school. And I don't want to make waves for Abe, you know?"

"I wish all the bosses were like Abe," Gert said. "We're in for some tough times, I can see it coming. Tell me again exactly what Webster said to you."

ॐॐ

That weekend Belle worked for the first time at the bookstore. Hannah and Charlotte had decided to open it for business without any fanfare. Sometime later in the fall they'd have a big celebration—after the local colleges were in full swing and everyone had a chance to settle down from the excitement of the war's end.

As she approached the shop, Belle noticed a new sign hanging above the storefront window:

WOOLF'S DEN
BOOKS

Charlotte had explained to her that Virginia Woolf was a British author who was very influential not only for her novels but her ideas about women. "Here, read this," she said, handing Belle a slim volume. "This is a good book to give you a sense of what we're trying to do in our store here. For women. It's called *A Room of One's Own*."

"Is Virginia Woolf still alive?" asked Belle.

"No, she died at the beginning of the war, in England."

"In the blitz?" Belle asked.

"No, actually, she walked into a pond," Charlotte replied. "Drowned herself."

"Jeez," said Belle. "That upset, huh?"

"It's complicated," added Hannah, smiling from behind the counter. "It wasn't just the war. Read her book and we'll talk more about her. Charlotte's right, you'll like it, believe me. But take your time, she's got a lot to say."

Later in the day, as Belle was checking some inventory lists, Charlotte asked, "Do you think you could manage while we go over and sign a few more papers at the insurance agency?"

"Sure," Belle replied. "Go ahead. If people ask about some writers, I can always tell them to wait or come back." She was pleased that they felt comfortable leaving her in charge.

After a few minutes, a middle-aged woman who'd been browsing some of the shelves in the back came up to the front counter. "Excuse me, but I take it you don't know much about the books being sold here? I couldn't help but overhear."

"Well, that's true," Belle replied. "I'm not familiar enough yet to recommend anything, but I could find out if we carry a title."

"What I mean, miss, is that you may not be aware of what you're being asked to sell." She held up a book. "For example, one such as this."

"Radclyffe Hall, *The Well of Loneliness*," Belle read. "Nope, that's one I don't know. Sounds sad. What about it?"

"What about it?" the woman exclaimed. "It's a disgusting book, from what I was just reading. It's about women who love..."

"Women who love? Sounds nice to me," replied Belle, although she'd already figured out where the conversation was heading.

"Women who love *other women*," the woman said, carefully placing the book down on the counter. She stepped away, as though it might fly back at her. "You know. They call them lesbians! Did you know that?"

"I didn't know about this book. But, sure, I know about lesbians. Don't you, ma'am?"

"Unfortunately, yes, I do, I know all about them, and it's a disgrace. Your sister should be ashamed of herself."

"My sister? Who's that? Oh, you mean one of the women who just stepped out who looks like me?" Belle laughed. "Look, lady, I don't know who the hell you are, and I don't care. But I think there's something you *don't* know all about, and that's good manners."

"Well, I never!" the woman cried. "This store should be closed!" She turned and walked toward the door.

"Well, we don't need your business anyway," Belle said. She was getting mad. "And you know what? That woman may not be my sister, but I hope I'm a hell of a lot more like her than I am like you, you narrow-minded old fart!"

Belle was still mumbling to herself when Charlotte and Hannah returned. "Here's a Pepsi from Walgreen's," Hannah said. "Boy, it's kind of warm out there. In here, too, I guess. Your face is all red."

"That's not from the heat," Belle replied. She told them about her encounter with the customer. "I swear, I was ready to kick her in the ass."

"Well, maybe that would have been going too far," said Charlotte, laughing.

"But was I wrong to say what I did?"

"No, you weren't, really. She was worse than an old fart," replied Hannah. "But I guess this is what we're going to have to expect. Charlotte would have tried to get her involved in a conversation. I think I'd have done just what you did, Belle."

"It's probably good there was no one else in the store, Belle," said Charlotte. "But thank you for standing up to her." She gave Belle a brief hug. "Abe is going to love this story!"

❧

Charlotte was right. "Boy, I wish I could have been a fly on the wall," Abe said that night over dinner at the Student Prince. "But you probably should be a little more careful when it's a customer. Then again, I guess I haven't been in that position when stuff has happened with Hannah. I mean, having to be polite. And she usually deals with it just fine all by herself."

"You mean, things like that have gone on in front of you?"

"Sure, occasionally, though mostly it's stuff she's told me about. You can't have a daughter as outspoken as Hannah and not feel the backlash. Remember, everyone's not as open-minded as I hope we are. And a lot of prejudice is from people who just haven't experienced folks who are different."

"But that woman was plain nasty," Belle said.

"Sure, she's an extreme case, but sometimes I've heard jokes and things from people who aren't really bad, and then I think, *should I say something?*"

"I bet you do," Belle said.

"Now I usually do, yes, but sometimes I still let it pass. Then I usually regret it afterwards. But imagine hearing stuff about *yourself*, the way Hannah and Charlotte do." He paused, and then said, "Well, I guess I have experienced that, too, now that I think about it. You know, being Jewish. Right in the factory, in fact. But not to my face, at least not any more."

"It's funny," said Belle. "You know, there couldn't be a kinder, more caring person on this earth than my mother. Yet she has this thing about the Irish."

"Everyone's fallible, Belle, but your mother's about the best person I've ever met."

"She is," replied Belle. "Really, not a mean bone in her body. That's why it's hard to decide...I hate to think of her alone."

"Have you discussed it with her?"

"Yeah, I have, and the funny thing is, she was surprised we haven't already moved ahead. That's Nan for you. It's just that I got kind of used to feeling responsible for her, in a way. It's been the two of us since Alan got married. That's a long time."

"You know she could always live with us."

"Thanks, I know, but I'm not sure I'd want that. I don't think she would, either. And she seems to be fine when she's alone. I mean, like tonight. She knows I'm staying over."

"What about Alan and Laura? If Laura keeps working, wouldn't your mother be taking care of the kids?"

"Yes, but that's not so simple, either. She would, and I know Laura really cares about her. But I have a feeling Alan's not going to be too happy with Laura working and all. That's the problem. It'll be interesting to see how everything turns out." She didn't mention that she was also worried about Alan if he got upset about everything, though she'd discussed his drinking with Abe before.

Later that night, while Abe was reading the evening paper, Belle picked up the copy of the book Charlotte had loaned her. She got through the preface, which was helpful in giving her a sense of what Woolf was going to talk about: Women and the writing of books. Then she began to read.

"Oh, boy," she said a few minutes later. "I don't know about this."

"What?"

"This book Hannah gave me to read. It's hard for me to make heads or tails of it. If it wasn't for that introduction, I wouldn't know what the hell it's about."

"Well, just remember," Abe replied, "I'd be in the same boat, even worse. You haven't been in school in what—15 years? Maybe it's good you're waiting until January to start taking classes."

"But how will I do then? It's kind of scary, Abe."

"It won't be the same thing. You're already familiar with some of that business stuff they'll be telling you about."

"Yeah, I guess. But, boy, do I feel stupid right now."

A few minutes later, she glanced up to find Abe looking at her. "What?" she asked, smiling.

"You must have just read something interesting," he replied. "Your whole face lit up."

She was flattered that he'd been watching her. "Well, yeah, I decided to jump around the pages," she replied. "Want to hear the sentence I liked?" She searched for a moment and then read: "'*There is no gate, no lock, no bolt that you can set upon the freedom of the mind.*' I had to think about that for a while, but now it makes sense. No one can stop you from thinking the way you want to, really, can they, Abe? No one."

"That's right, they can't," he replied. "But the trick is to live that way, too. That's the hard part." He got up from his chair and walked over to the couch.

"No, stay there," he said, as she started to make room. He carefully eased himself down on his knees and took her hand. "I think I'm a little old for this," he said, "but now that I'm in this ridiculous position...How about marrying me?"

Belle leaned forward and put her head on his shoulder. "Oh, Abe," she said, "I love you." She kissed him for a long time and then said, "Yes, I'll marry you. I will."

"Well," he said, holding her tight, "I'm not sure what I would have done if you'd said no. Asked you to help me get up, I guess."

"Get out!" she replied, laughing and pulling him down on top of her. After a few moments she whispered, "Now if you really want to show how much you love me, you'll sweep me up in your arms and carry me up the stairs and ravish me. Just like Clark Gable and Vivien Leigh in *Gone with the Wind*."

"Tell you what, Scarlett," Abe said with a drawl. "How about if we pretend all that happens and just do it right here?"

Chapter 45: Alan

As Alan's convoy sailed into Pearl Harbor, the differences between this arrival and last year's were striking. No escort planes accompanied the fleet's approach this time, and no tugs were waiting to sweep the security nets aside. As they neared the entrance to the harbor, small civilian craft cruised offshore, their passengers cheering and waving as each ship passed.

At Pearl itself, there was less evidence of the December 7 attack than before, though an empty berth in Battleship Row was black with oil where the remains of the Arizona and its crew still lay just beneath the surface of the murky water. Alan wondered if there were any plans to raise the ill-fated ship and its doomed crew.

LST 1717 was scheduled to return to Japan, loaded with supplies for the occupation, but Alan and most of the present crew would be heading in the opposite direction. The length of his stay in Hawaii depended on when he could get placed on a transport home. The logistics of organizing the hundreds of thousands of troops scattered over the entire Pacific were staggering, but with luck he and Buzz would be leaving within a week. There was talk that they might even get on the big carrier Hornet.

"You seeing your lady friend?" Buzz asked after they'd docked. It was late morning, and they'd been given a pass for the rest of the day.

"Yeah, I think I will, but just to say goodbye. I didn't get a chance when we left." This was the first time he'd admitted to Buzz that there had been someone special

"Yeah, sure," Buzz replied without comment. "I'm gonna say some goodbyes of my own, too."

"No, I mean it," Alan replied. "That's all over, just like the war, you know? Got a nickel for the phone?"

He dialed the number Edie had given him, but an operator interrupted to say that it had been disconnected some weeks back. He tried again, with the same results, and then stepped out of the booth to make way for the next sailor waiting in the long line.

"Hey, guess what I just heard?" Buzz asked Alan when he returned to the dock. "All the whorehouses been closed. They had some kind of crackdown."

Though he couldn't imagine that Edie had gone back to that life, Alan wondered if there was a connection between her disconnected telephone and the shutdown of the clubs. "Still planning to go into Honolulu?" he asked Buzz and a couple of other guys standing in the cab line.

"Oh, yeah, for sure," Buzz replied. "They say what you do now is just ask a cab driver or a bartender and he'll fix you up. Some of the girls work outta their houses now. Costs more, though," he replied. "Did ya get in touch with...you know?"

"Uh, yeah, I did. I'll ride in with you," Alan said distractedly. He decided to go directly to Edie's place. He was glad he'd kept the address along with the telephone number, though he'd probably have been able to find the house by retracing his steps from the main square. He'd been pretty much sober by the end of that drunken afternoon.

Once the cab let them off in downtown Honolulu, Alan headed on foot toward the Punchbowl. Excavation for the new cemetery on its slope was visible in the hazy distance. It would have to be pretty big if it was meant to commemorate even a fraction of the thousands of troops killed in the Pacific.

Alan wondered if there would be a marker for Donny Ryan. They'd recently heard that Donny had died on the hospital ship from his shrapnel wound on the day of the kamikaze attack. Alan wasn't surprised, though he'd held out some hope that Donny might be OK once they'd moved him to a decent treatment center.

Skirting the muddy puddles left over from a morning downpour, he recognized Edie's bungalow by a blue metal chair on the front porch. He remembered the vivid contrast between it and the bright orange of the bird of paradise flowers in the little front yard.

Though the windows were open, the blinds were down and the door shut tight. The house had an unkempt, unoccupied look. Browned palm fronds lay under the blue chair, and a pungent odor of some kind of fruit well past its prime wafted out into the unpaved street.

Alan knocked on the door and waited. He thought he saw the blinds move, so he knocked again. Soon a woman's voice called out, "Yeah, what? You're supposed to call first."

"I tried, but the number I had was disconnected. I'm looking for Edie."

The door opened slowly. In the shadows stood a pretty blonde, barefoot, wearing a silk bathrobe. "Who are you?" she asked in a little-girl voice.

"I'm a friend of Edie's. I'm sorry, does she still live here?" Alan asked.

As the young woman's eyes became accustomed to the outside light, she said, "Oh my God, I know who you are. You're the guy who looks just like Mel. Jesus, she was right." She stared at him and then stepped back, waving her hand in an unfocused gesture.

He walked tentatively past her into the living room, its furnishings vaguely familiar in the semi-darkness. The air was surprisingly cool inside, though there was a strong smell of old food and smoke and perfume. A radio played somewhere in another room.

"Uh, so, is Edie around?" Alan asked again, holding his white cap in his hands. He felt awkward, like he wasn't meant to be there.

"No, Edie isn't around," the young woman said. "She's gone."

"Gone?" Alan asked. "You mean she's gone home?"

"Yeah, home," she replied, laughing harshly. She took a deep breath and whispered, "Edie's dead."

"Dead?" He couldn't believe it. "She's dead?"

"Yeah, a few months ago. Gone." She snapped her fingers and stumbled back against a table. Alan suddenly felt sick to his stomach and slowly eased himself onto the sofa.

"I'm sorry," the young woman said after a moment. She sat down next to him. "I know you and her got kinda close. I didn't mean to do that so sudden-like." She put her hand on his arm.

"You know what, I still can't believe it either," she whispered after a moment. "You're Alan, right?"

"Yes," he replied. He raised his head. Edie must have talked about him more than once.

"Janie. I'm Janie," she said.

He remembered the name. "You two worked together," he said. Without thinking, he added, "What was the place again?"

She laughed and said, "Hah, so she mentioned me to you, too. Edie." She sighed. "Yeah, we worked together. It was the Ambassador."

He nodded. The Ambassador. So it *was* the house that Buzz had said was the fancy one. Somehow that made him feel better.

"Can you tell me what happened?" he asked, though he wasn't sure he really wanted to know. How could she be dead?

She took a drag on her cigarette and looked past him. "Sure, OK. Hey, you want a drink?"

"Yes."

"What?"

"I don't care. Whatever you've got."

She rose, tightened the sash on her robe, and left the room. When she returned, she had a fresh cigarette in her mouth and was carrying two large ruby-colored tumblers frosty with moisture.

"Singapore Slings," she said. "Just made a new batch." She looked at him. "Boy, I can't get over it. I'd swear you were Mel. He was a real nice guy, her hubby. He died, too," she added, handing Alan his drink. "But I guess you know that."

She sat back down. "I don't how much Edie told you," she began. "More than a little, I guess, if you know about the Ambassador."

"I know about her husband, and she told me what happened later on with the baby," Alan said. "Then she worked at the club for a while. And then she had a friend, a man. I thought maybe she was planning to leave Hawaii."

"Yeah, that's right," Janie said. "She was. With the guy who owned this house. Still does, he's letting me stay here.

"Anyway, one night about six months ago, she said to me—I was living here with her by then, she'd gotten me to quit the Ambassador—anyway, she said she was taking a ride up to the Pali. You know the Pali road?" she asked.

"Yes, we drove up there one time," he replied.

"Yeah, that don't surprise me. She had some kind of thing about that place. Kind of a creepy thing, you know?"

He remembered Edie had talked about how she loved the desolate lookout high above the valley. 'I kind of thought that, too," he said, recalling the screaming wind that made it almost impossible to talk.

"Well, she took off in that fancy car," Janie continued. "She told me not to wait up, and I went to bed a couple of hours later. The next thing I know the cops are at the door. It was early the next morning. They drove me down to the morgue."

"What happened?" Alan asked.

"Car went off the cliff." Janie took a gulp of her drink and hiccuped.

"Jesus," Alan replied. "I remember how fast she drove up there that day."

"Yeah, well...," Janie began.

"What?"

"Well, it wasn't like that. Just before the car went over, someone else happened to be coming along the road and saw the whole thing. Otherwise they probably wouldn't have even known about it for a few days."

"And?"

"Well, it wasn't like the car skidded or nothing like that. They said it was stopped and then it started up and drove straight over. No skid marks or nothing."

"You mean, she...?"

"Yeah, they think it was on purpose. They didn't say that in the papers or nothing but that's what they think. I got a friend in the police department and he told me. Case closed." She began to cry. "If only I'd known. I thought she was OK, leaving the island and all. I mean, she wasn't crazy in love with that guy, but he was decent to her. Boy, he was real broke up."

Alan emptied the last of his drink and buried his head in his hands. He wasn't used to drinking gin, and he was feeling dizzy.

"I know," Janie said, patting his hand. "It's terrible, isn't it? Edie was real good to me." She moved closer to Alan and laid her head against his chest.

Without thinking, he began to stroke her thigh. She was naked under the silk robe, and it was easy to slide it off her shoulders.

"Here, lemme help," she murmured, unbuckling his belt. She lay back, still sobbing softly. Alan buried his head in her hair and then kissed her roughly, stretching himself out awkwardly on the edge of the sofa. She moved against him and guided him into her. Their sharp cries and the noisy vibrating of the tumblers on the glass table broke the muted sound of the radio in the next room. It was over in a couple of minutes.

"Jesus," Alan whispered, sitting up.

"It's OK," Janie said. "It's OK. Know what? Edie would be laughing if she knew. Maybe she does. That was the kind of thing Edie liked, figuring out why people do the crazy stuff they do."

Alan suddenly thought of what Edie had mentioned about the Hawaiian warriors who threw themselves off the ridge at the Pali. *They did what they had to do*, she'd said. He shivered, sure now that Edie's death hadn't been an accident.

"You don't have to worry," Janie said. "I mean, 'cause we weren't careful. I'm clean." She stood up. "I'll be back in a sec."

He was adjusting his white jumper and black silk neckerchief when she returned. "Are you staying on here?" he asked.

"Yeah, for a while," she replied. "I got a good wad stashed away and I still do OK, 'cept I have to be, you know, quiet here. Meantime, I can stay as long as I want. I gotta get myself straightened out first. Lay off the booze. I will, you know," she said to him. "I never touched the stuff before I came to Honolulu."

"I hope so," Alan said. "Same thing with me. I have to kind of watch it, too, or it gets me into a whole lot of trouble." Even though he felt a bit loose from the gin, he was surprised he'd told her that. Then he thought, *Why the hell not, after what just happened*. "Anyway, I guess I'd better go." He moved toward the door.

"Can I help, or anything?" he asked, reaching into his pocket for his wallet.

"Naw, but that's sweet of you," she replied. "Like I said, I'm OK in that department. And this was nice," she said. "You kiss good. Sounds funny, don't it, me saying that? But I don't ever kiss anyone when...you know, when I'm working."

Before she opened the door, she gave him a hug, holding him close for several seconds. "Now, don't you go feeling bad about what we did," she said. "Like I said, Edie would understand perfect. That's how she was."

He kissed her on the top of her head. "Take care of yourself, Janie," Alan said as he moved quickly through the open door.

Before she closed it, he turned back. "Wait. I don't know how long I'll be in Honolulu, but I'd like to visit Edie's grave. Is the cemetery around here?"

"Nope, her parents paid to have her ashes shipped back," Janie replied. "A place in Nebraska. Red Cloud. Funny name for a town, huh? Different. Real pretty, though. Red Cloud."

Chapter 46: Billy

Billy was visiting Mrs. Brown on a Saturday morning in October. The sun was shining, though silvery dew was still visible on the leaves of the hardy purple asters in her flowerbed. Autumn had arrived and with it, as Nan would say, "the frost on the pumpkin." This was Indian summer, that short interlude between the first real frost and the chilly days of late fall. It would warm up even more by the afternoon.

"Indian summer" was a term Billy liked. It always got him to thinking about the tribes that used to rule the Pioneer Valley, when Springfield was a little river town with a fort and a stockade fence. Settlers in those early days faced the fearsome chief Metacom, also called King Philip, in the first Indian war in America.

"Now, you must tell me about Sal, " Mrs. Brown said as she handed Billy a cup of tea. "I haven't seen him yet." She gave Ashkii a cat treat and then dropped a cube of sugar into her own cup. Billy noticed her hand was shaking slightly.

"Come and sit with me here in the heat of the sun," she said, pointing to a sofa in a large bay window facing east.

"Sal's good...I guess," Billy replied.

"Oh? Hasn't he recovered fully from his wounds?"

"Well, you can tell something happened to his shoulder 'cause it's kinda stiff. But it's more that he's quiet or something."

Mrs. Brown nodded. "You know, we have to remember that our men and boys—and servicewomen, too—have been through things we can't even imagine. We have to be patient and give them time to re-adjust."

"Yeah, I guess so," Billy replied, though he wondered how long that would take. Sal had already been home four days.

Since surprising everyone the afternoon he appeared in the driveway, duffel bag on his shoulder, Sal had hardly left the house. Angie said he stayed in his room a lot. Once, when his door was open, she'd noticed that he was just lying on his bed, staring up at the ceiling.

"And how is school going, Billy?" Mrs. Brown asked. "Do you like junior high?"

"It's fun," Billy said. It was different this year, not being in one classroom all day with the same teacher. He'd already decided he liked Miss Lester, his English teacher, best. "I'm reading *Oliver Twist* by Charles Dickens for my first book report," he told Mrs. Brown.

"Ah, Dickens! What a world of wonderful characters he created," she replied. "And how he brings London to life! And what else? What are your other subjects?"

"Arithmetic, science, geography, music, and art." He added, "Oh yeah, and gym."

Mrs. Brown smiled. "Well, it's important to exercise your body, too. But I wasn't partial to physical education either, when I was a girl," she said. "Especially the silly outfits we had to wear. You could hardly move your arms and legs, much less throw a ball. Thank goodness that's all changed nowadays. Are your other classes difficult?"

"Nah, they're all pretty easy," Billy replied. Even though he didn't like arithmetic that much, he was still just about the fastest in the class reciting the multiplication tables. Science was OK. They were learning about how things grow.

"Do you know what photosynthesis is, Mrs. Brown?"

"I believe it's got something to do with how plants take in light and stay healthy," she replied. "I've always remembered that particular word." She repeated it slowly: "Pho-to-syn-the-sis. Some words just stay in your head, don't they?"

"Like Constantinople," Billy said. He'd been reading about capital cities of the world in geography. "It's Istanbul now. Before that it was Byzantium."

"Oh my, yes, those are all good examples," Mrs. Brown replied. "As our poet Emily Dickinson said about certain words, 'Now there's one to tip your hat to!'"

"I like Damascus, too," said Billy.

"Oh, yes, and Madagascar and Baghdad and Zanzibar and Timbuktu!" She exclaimed. "Don't those grand names just make you want to pick up and go? My, they do me!"

"Were you ever in those places?"

"No, never in those particular exotic locales we've named, I'm sorry to say," she replied. "But, as you know, I did my share of traveling in Europe." She often talked about her visits to England and Italy. "And, of course, my time out West."

"Maybe Sal will tell us about being overseas," Billy said.

"Oh, I do hope so, but we should wait until he wants to talk about it. You know, some things he saw he may not want to remember."

"Like what?" Billy asked.

"Oh, things like seeing some of his comrades killed, or the damage that war can do to the people and animals whose land has been destroyed. Things like that."

As he left Mrs. Brown a few minutes later, Billy turned and said, "Marrakech!"

"Kathmandu!" she replied, laughing. "Borneo! And Bora Bora!"

Ashkii the cat followed Billy to the white fence that separated the two yards. Though he held the gate open, Billy couldn't persuade the cat to go any further. He and Max didn't get along, though both were so old Billy had never seen anything come of their occasional encounters. Intense staring and occasional hisses seemed to be the extent of it.

Later, lying on his bed, he worked on his homework, a few arithmetic exercises and a chapter on ancient Egypt for his history class. He'd already finished the book they were reading for English, *The Red Pony*, so Miss Lester suggested another novel by John Steinbeck, *The Grapes of Wrath*.

"You can check with your parents to see if it's all right for you to read that," Miss Lester said. "It may be too adult."

"Oh, I know it's OK," Billy replied. "I can read anything. I even read stuff my mother brings home from the library for herself." He was going to mention *Forever Amber* but decided it might give Miss Lester the wrong impression, since he really hadn't gotten permission for that one. "My father's not home from the Navy yet, but I'll ask my mother," he promised.

After lunch, Billy went outdoors and joined Angie, who was reclining in the swing chair at the far end of the yard. The arbor grapes, resplendent in their purple luster only a couple of weeks earlier, were gone. Nonno and his Sons of Italy friends had completed the harvesting, followed by a day of wine making in the Mazzarella basement. Now the gnarled posts of the arbor, depleted of fruit and leaves, were already beginning to take on their sinewy, wintry look.

"Hi, Angie, want to come with us to the movies tonight?" Billy asked.

"I'm going, too," Gary said. He'd followed Billy from the porch, Lucille trotting beside him.

"Nah, I can't," Angie replied, standing up and straightening her pleated skirt. "Look how wide this is." She twirled around a couple of times. "It's a new peasant look. Fiesta dirndl," she explained. "I'm going to my friend Peggy's later on. She's having a pajama party."

"What happens at a pajama party, Angie?" Gary asked.

"Oh, we sit around and talk. Sometimes we dance, and then we eat. Peggy's mom always has good stuff, like pigs in a blanket and chow mein candy clusters"

"Arggh!" yelled Gary, rolling on the grass pretending to gag. Lucille, still game to play, leaped on top of him.

"I thought boys didn't go to those parties," Billy said.

"They don't," Angie replied. "Why?"

"'Cause you said you danced sometimes."

"Yeah, we dance with each other. We practice so we'll be good when we *are* dancing with boys."

"That sounds funny, dancing in your pajamas," said Gary, giggling.

"We don't dance in our pajamas," Angie replied. "We get ready for bed later."

"Then how come they call it a pajama party?" he asked.

"Because we stay over. Later we put on our pajamas or night-gowns, OK? Anyway, mostly we talk."

"What do you talk about?"

"Boy, this kid asks a lot of questions!" Angie said. But she laughed and continued, "Well, we talk about some of the boys at school. Like who's a drip and who's dreamy."

"What about Billy?" asked Gary, pointing to his brother. "Which one is he?"

"Oh Gary, shut up," said Billy.

"Well, Billy doesn't count, 'cause he's too young," Angie replied. "Anyway, he's my friend." Gary seemed satisfied by this explanation and wandered away with Lucille.

Billy, however, wasn't sure what Angie really meant. He was glad she described him as her friend, but he wondered if she just didn't want to say what her girlfriends thought of him. He would probably be included in the "drip" category, because at school some of the kids used to call him a teacher's pet. Sometimes someone said "sissy" behind his back, but that hadn't happened yet in junior high, as far as he knew.

Angie reached into the pocket of her skirt and pulled out a small leather purse. She rummaged around and held up a lipstick in a black tube. Removing the top, she gave the bottom knob half a twist and, holding a small mirror in her other hand, carefully applied orange coloring to her lips.

"Tangee," she announced, deftly tossing the tube and the mirror back into her purse.

"'Member when we used hide in the bushes and shine a mirror up at Mrs. Herrmann when she was looking out her window?" Billy asked. "And then she'd come out on her porch and yell at us?"

"Yeah. Gee, that seems like ages ago, huh?" Angie replied. "Well, gotta go," she said. She leaned closer to Billy and said in a lower voice, "Hey, here comes my brother. See if you can get him to talk or laugh or something. My ma's all worried about him."

Billy looked up to see Sal walking down the steps of his back porch. He waved to them but headed over to the garage, which he entered from the side door.

"Guess he must want to look at his car," Angie said. "That's good. See ya later." She headed down the driveway, a bit wobbly in her new red wedgies. Nan said she was going to break an ankle for sure.

Billy sat on the chair swing watching Gary and Lucille playing in the leaves. When the wind swirled a few of the small ones in the air, Lucille chased them and then rolled around like crazy on the ground. Billy knew in a few minutes she'd lumber off and take a long nap, but for now she'd forgotten she wasn't the puppy she used to be.

Soon they'd be busy raking, but not before the big sycamore down by Mrs. Brown's fence was bare. It was always the last to lose its yellow leaves. Billy wondered if this year he'd be allowed to burn the big piles without supervision. Maybe his father would be home by then, or Sal would want to help.

He glanced over at the garage, closed up and silent. He thought Sal would have opened the doors by now. When they'd gotten word that he'd docked in New York, Mr. Mazzarella had re-mounted the old tires, newly inflated, and tried starting the motor. Maybe Sal would suggest going out for a ride.

Billy walked over and peered in the window of the side entrance to the garage. It was hard to make out anything in the gloomy interior, but in the front seat of the car he could see the orange glow from Sal's cigarette. He hesitated, then pressed his face against the garage window and tapped on the glass.

He was pretty sure he could see Sal's hand beckoning him, so he opened the door. The garage smelled of smoke and oil and rotting leaves. "Hi Sal," Billy said in a loud voice. "Is it OK?"

Sal reached over and opened the passenger door slightly so that Billy could inch his way in. The inside of the car was surprisingly free of dust and smelled like Windex. "Gee, it's nice and clean in here," Billy said.

"Yeah, I guess my ma was busy. They've been telling me to take a spin."

"Don't you want to?" Billy asked. "Won't the car start?"

"It'll start OK. Just need to get some new plugs and be sure the oil and gas and water are OK."

"It's not so hard to get gas anymore," Billy said. "Most of the rationing is all over."

"Yeah, I heard," Sal said.

They sat in silence for nearly a minute. Then Billy said, "The first time Angie and I came and sat in your car it seemed real funny that you weren't here. That was the day Richie came over..." He stopped, realizing that maybe he shouldn't have mentioned Sal's friend.

"Yeah, I remember you said that in one of your letters, " Sal replied. "Maybe sometime you can tell me more about Richie's funeral and all."

Billy watched a spider who'd spun a web above the dirt-encrusted garage window. "Hey, do you want me to help you roll the car outside so it'll be easier to work on it?" he asked.

After a moment, Sal said, "Sure." He got out of the car and stuck his head back in the window. "OK, you'll need to scoot over here and steer. I'll give it a push." He swung open the wide front doors, letting in a flood of light and fresh air from the outside.

"But what about your shoulder, Sal?" asked Billy. He also wasn't sure if he could manage his part. He'd never been in the driver's seat for real.

"Yeah, I know, I'll be careful," Sal said. "It'll be OK." He stooped and leaned carefully into the window again, his hair, still short and bristly, brushing against Billy's forehead. He adjusted the steering wheel and made sure the clutch was in neutral. "Now, when I tell you, put your foot down hard on this pedal and just hold on to the wheel like this so the tires don't change direction. I'll tell you when to ease your foot back up."

Sal squeezed in front of the car, took off his flannel shirt, and leaned his good shoulder against the hood. "Now!" he shouted.

Billy concentrated on the steering with all his might, practically willing the car to move slowly backwards in a straight line. In a few seconds they were out in the driveway, sunlight reflecting off the chrome and shiny red paint of the Ford.

Sal yelled, "OK, raise your foot!" The car lurched and stopped. "Now, just put on the hand brake. We're all set," said Sal, leaning on the hood.

"Boy, I'm out of shape," he said as they walked further into the yard and sat down in the leaf-covered grass. "I haven't done any real stuff like that since the accident," he said, gingerly rubbing his shoulder.

"Do you have any scars?" Billy asked.

"Yeah," Sal replied. He wiped his forehead with the bottom of his t-shirt, now sweaty and stained, then pulled it over his head and rolled it up into a ball. "Here," he said, pointing to a thick, mottled pink cleft that extended from the middle of his collar bone to his vaccination scar. You could see where some of the hair on that side of his chest still hadn't completely grown back

"Gee, does it hurt?"

"Yeah, some. I don't talk about it much, though, so don't let on, OK?" He ran his finger along the scar. "I got burn marks on my legs and backside, too, but the doc says they'll fade."

"Did you really almost die?" Billy asked.

"Nah, not really," Sal replied. Then he looked away and said, "Well, yeah, guess I did." Billy remembered what Mrs. Brown had said about not asking too much, so he said nothing.

They lay back on their elbows in the grass, enjoying the warmth of the late morning sun. Suddenly, without looking at Billy, Sal began to speak.

"I usually drove a motorbike, but I had a jeep that day. That probably saved my life, except that this one didn't have the red cross painted on the hood, so it looked like a plain old military jeep.

"All of a sudden," Sal continued, "I heard a plane somewhere to my left. I figured it was one of ours, but then I saw the yellow nose. A Stuka. When it got closer I could make out the cross and swastika.

"I ended up going off the road into a marsh. I must've hit one of the tires on a rock 'cause I couldn't steer. I think I got hit then, too, 'cause the whole engine started steaming up." Billy slowly looked over at Sal, but he was still staring straight ahead.

"I kept driving through the marsh. I was trying to keep low in the seat, so I couldn't see much. Then he hit me for sure and I lost control. The jeep exploded—that's how come I got the burns—and I ended up flying out into the water. I think I banged my head on something and part of the jeep smashed against my shoulder." Sal rubbed his arm and turned his head toward Billy.

"The pain in my shoulder was something awful. The last thing I remember before I passed out was that I was going to drown in that friggin' marsh." He gave a funny laugh. "But I didn't." He looked away again, and they both remained silent.

"Hey, Sal, what about your Italian dog?" Billy hoped it was OK to ask, since Sal hadn't mentioned anything about Ernie yet.

"Yeah, Ernesto," Sal said. "Well, he was OK when I left. I'm hoping he'll get shipped over. They kind of promised me, a guy I knew at the airfield. If they can just get him on a plane to Westover, he'll be right here in no time."

"Does he understand English?" Billy asked.

"Oh, yeah, I spoke to him in both Italian and English. But maybe he's not even Italian. We think he came ashore with the troops at Anzio, 'cause he was found wandering on the beach 'way up there. So...if Ernie got to Italy that way, it could've been from who knows where—North Africa, who knows? Maybe he's from Casablanca."

"Wow," Billy replied. Now he was even more intrigued by Ernie. He wondered how Lucille would get along with a dog from Casablanca who could understand English and Italian and even the language they spoke over there in North Africa. Arabian, like in *The Arabian Nights*? He wasn't sure. Mrs. Brown would be real interested in hearing about all this.

"Sal, are you going to get a job someplace?" Billy asked after another few moments of silence. "Like with Doc Jenkins at the drugstore?" Sal had worked there part-time when he was in high school.

"Yeah, sure, guess I got to," Sal replied. "Angie told Doc I was on my way back and he said to come over and see him. Maybe I can get full-time work there, I don't know." He hesitated, then said, "You know what? I was thinking of going back to school, too, like to work in a hospital."

"You mean, to study to be a doctor?" Billy asked.

"Doctor? Jeez, no, like an assistant or aide, something like what I did at the field hospital in Italy" he replied. "Anyway, I got to think it over. What about you? How's school?"

"School's OK. Junior high's not so hard."

"Not for you, maybe," Sal replied. "I had a heck of a time. You're a brain."

Though he was used to having people tell him that, Billy liked hearing Sal compliment him. And he was glad Sal was beginning to talk more.

"Did you make new friends over in Italy?" he asked.

"Sure, I got to know some of the local people. I spoke Italian a lot."

"What about other soldiers?"

"Yeah, sure. There was a guy, Gus Poulos, from right here in Springfield. His sister was in my class. He was my buddy, and then we got separated. But he's back now, too. And..." He hesitated, and then said, "And there's a guy I got to know. He's a college professor. I'll be seeing him."

"Oh, an older guy?" Billy asked.

"Not real old, but, yeah, almost 30. But he's like you, kind of. He reads books and stuff all the time."

"Where does he live?" Billy asked.

"In New York City. He teaches at a college. But he's still in Italy."

"Oh," replied Billy. "Do you think he'll come to Springfield sometime?"

"Maybe," Sal said. "Or maybe I'll go down to New York."

"What's his name?" Billy asked.

"Will, it's Will. It's really Willem, like your name but in Dutch. His family came from Holland back when."

Max wandered up and sniffed Sal's pants. "Isn't this Mrs. Herrmann's old cat? The one you took?"

"Yeah, Max," Billy replied. Max rubbed the side of her chin against Sal's loafer. "That means he likes you," Billy said. "He's putting his scent on you."

"Thanks, Max," Sal said. He scratched one of Max's ears and for the first time smiled in the way that Billy remembered from before the war.

"My mother said to ask you if you wanted to come for supper tonight or tomorrow," Billy said.

"Um, maybe. Not tonight, but maybe tomorrow, OK?"

"Sure," Billy said. "Well, I promised her I'd get some stuff at the store, so I'd better go." He got up and felt in his pocket to make sure the money was still there. He wondered if Sal had noticed that he was wearing dungarees now.

"Sal," he said, "You know your box? I still have it in my bedroom."

"Oh, yeah, I forgot," Sal said. "Thanks, I knew you'd take care of it."

"It's locked and everything, just like you gave it to me."

"You can bring it over tomorrow."

"OK." Billy started to walk away. "Sal?" he said.

"Yeah?" Sal looked up, shielding his eyes from the mid-afternoon October sun.

"Nothing...just that I'm glad you're back home safe."

Sal got up and walked over to Billy. "Thanks," he said. "Me, too. Say, you want to go for a ride after? If I get the car started?"

"OK, Sal," Billy replied. "See you later!"

Walking down the street, he kicked at the red and gold leaves that were piling up on the tree belt and the sidewalk. He decided he'd stop in at the drugstore on the way to the A&P and look at the new movie magazines. If Doc happened to ask about Sal, he'd tell him that Sal was home and ready to go back to work.

Chapter 47: Laura

"What a walk!" Laura said as she collapsed into her chair at work. "Mae, can you give me a hand? I'll never manage, I had such a heck of a time getting these things on." She held on to the arms of her chair and raised her feet, snow still clinging to the bottoms of her fur-trimmed ankle boots.

"I love the feel of that rabbit fur," said Mae, getting a grip on one of the platform heels and tugging at the boot. "I can't believe we're already having snow." It was only early November.

"I know, but it was so pretty when I looked out in the yard this morning," Laura replied. "The kids were all excited when they woke up."

"Any word from Alan?" Mae asked.

"Well, if things went according to his last letter, he should be sailing from Honolulu on a ship right now," Laura replied. "But who knows?" V-J day had been months ago, and it seemed to have taken him forever to get from wherever he was to Hawaii. The government was asking everyone on the home front to be patient.

"Then I suppose it'll be at least a couple of weeks getting cleared in California and onto a train," Laura added. "How about Tim?"

"He's stuck in the Philippines, Subic Bay," Mae replied. "He and about a million others, he said. They've been using aircraft carriers as transports, but there are so many men waiting." She checked the seams on her stockings. "But then you never know with the Seabees. They could send him off on some other construction thing. He still belongs to the good old Navy."

"It'll be swell when they're both back and we can all get together and meet each other," Laura said. She was hoping that the two men would hit if off. Tim's being older might be a good thing, too—a positive influence on Alan. She'd never asked Mae if Tim was the partying type, but she suspected not, if Mae had anything to say about it. She'd never told Mae about her flirtation with John Lawrence.

Since the captain's transfer to the West Coast, Laura had been less inclined to mingle with the customers at the hotel. The end of the war and the subsequent departure of a lot of the Westover officers had brought a different clientele back, older couples who preferred to dance to slower numbers, staid old tunes like "Beyond the Blue Horizon."

"Can't get 'em up for 'Boogie Woogie Bugle Boy' so much anymore," remarked Ray early one Saturday night as they ran through a new arrangement of "My Dreams Are Getting Better All the Time," a Les Brown/Doris Day number that had just made last week's Hit Parade.

"Well, they'll like this one," Laura replied. "It's almost as good as "Sentimental Journey"."

"I've seen people here the past month who haven't been around since the war started," Ray said. "They even *look* different." He motioned to an empty table near the back. "You know those two that asked for 'Stardust' last night? I remember them from the early days, right after Prohibition."

"Well, they looked pretty good on the dance floor," Laura replied. In fact, during the bridge in the song, she'd watched that couple and the way they still seemed all wrapped up in each other. It was nice.

Later, they'd approached the bandstand and complimented her. "Thank you, 'Stardust' is one of my favorite songs," Laura replied. "And my husband's, too," she added quickly, though she really couldn't recall that he'd ever mentioned it in particular. "He'll be home from the Pacific any time now."

❧

"Any time now" didn't come for a few weeks. In mid-December a telegram arrived: SAILED UNDER GOLDEN GATE STOP HOME SOON STOP WILL CALL STOP LOVE ALAN.

"Will Daddy be here by Christmas?" Gary asked.

"Maybe. Even if he isn't, we know he's coming soon now, don't we?" Laura replied. But she was sure he wouldn't make it by the 25th.

"Tell you what," she said. "Instead of waiting 'til Christmas eve, let's put up the tree this weekend. Then we'll be all ready whenever he gets here."

She knew Gary would be disappointed if Alan were delayed. Though he'd been only five when Alan enlisted, he talked about his father all the time. With Billy she wasn't so sure. He rarely mentioned Alan, and since he'd started seventh grade he seemed more distant and to himself than ever.

"He's just at that age, Laura," Belle said to her when she mentioned it one night at dinner after the kids had left the table. "He's in junior high school, remember. With older kids. He's probably going through puberty himself right now."

Puberty. It didn't seem possible, but Belle was right. She'd just been too preoccupied to see it herself. Once she'd surprised him reading something in bed that he quickly hid under the covers. She hadn't questioned him, nor had she objected when he kept his door closed and asked everyone to knock before entering. Had she been too busy with her own concerns to notice what was happening in her kids' lives?

Resolving to spend more time with both boys, Laura also began to focus on Alan's return. "Won't it be swell to have him back?" she asked. "Gary, you'll have someone to play catch with again."

She tried to think of something to say to Billy, but there wasn't much she could remember that he and his father had done together. "And, Billy," she finally added, "Dad will be able to help you with school more than me." That much was true. Laura knew she was smart as far as the practical things in life were concerned, but she'd never been an outstanding student. Doing her homework without being prodded hadn't been her pattern in high school. She much preferred trying out a new hit tune on the piano or learning the words to the latest popular song or practicing a new dance step with her girlfriends.

Remembering those days got Laura to thinking about the early years of her marriage, when Billy was a baby and she could hardly wait for Alan to come home at night from his new job at Westinghouse, rushing in the door like he'd been gone for a week. Over the past months, her letters to him, though steady, had settled into predictable accounts of life at home. His were even more routine, since he couldn't talk much about the war. But had things begun to change even before Alan enlisted? She wasn't sure.

"I can't imagine going back to my old routine," she told Helen one day over lunch. "It would seem kind of funny now, with my mother-in-law downstairs and the two of us home all the time. I like what I'm doing. Plus, the kids love her taking care of them."

"You don't have to explain all this to me. The question is, when are you going to let Alan know?" Helen asked. "You need to think about what to say. Who knows, maybe he's changed, too. He's been through a lot himself. More than you realize, probably."

"I just hope the strike'll be over by the time he gets home," Laura said. Workers at Westinghouse had been out for several weeks, and the walkout was turning into a long and bitter struggle. The huge plant was nearly shut down, and there had even been a few ugly confrontations on the street. But even if they took him back, she wondered if Alan would cross the picket line if the strike wasn't settled. He had a lot of old friends in the union.

As she'd expected, the holiday came and went without his arrival. They spent Christmas Eve with the Mazzarellas, Mary bustling about, insisting that everyone have second and third helpings of her antipasto and meatballs and Italian cookies. She fussed over Sal, who seemed to Laura as quiet and withdrawn as he'd been since his return from Italy in the fall. Perhaps older and a bit more confident, but still not one to talk much. He was a nice guy, but hard to figure out.

They went to bed early that night, with no snack set out for Santa Claus for the first time since Billy was a little boy. Gary had announced a few weeks earlier that he knew for sure that Santa wasn't real.

"No one could go all around the world in one day," he informed everyone at dinner. "And, besides, reindeers can't fly."

"Reindeer," Billy said. "There's no 's'.

"But there's more than one reindeer," Gary replied.

"Yeah, but that's the grammar rule," Billy said. "Anyway, how do you know that the elves don't help him?"

"They're too little and there aren't enough of 'em," Gary replied. "Ma, tell him there's no Santa."

"Well, I'm sure Billy already knows that," Laura said. "It's just that it's fun for all of us to pretend, isn't it? And isn't it a nice thing for all the children to believe in?"

"Yeah," Gary replied. "It's OK for the little kids."

They opened a few presents on Christmas day, leaving most unwrapped under the tree. For dinner Nan baked a ham. Laura bought a small turkey and crammed it into the small freezer compartment of the fridge. They'd have a real Christmas dinner after Alan got home.

A few days later, he telephoned from Chicago. The connection was poor, with a funny time delay that resulted in awkward pauses in their conversation. They weren't able to exchange more than basic information about his arrival time in Springfield, and she didn't even bother having one of the kids run downstairs to get Nan and Belle.

"That didn't sound like Daddy," Gary said. "It sounded like somebody different."

"I know," Laura replied. "It'll be better once he's here. Imagine, in two days!" But the phone call and Alan's disembodied voice only increased a certain anxiety she was already feeling. They'd been separated a long time, and she hoped they could pick up like before. Like before, but with some changes.

⤙⤚

The Saturday of Alan's expected arrival dawned dark and wet. A morning rain had turned to sleet by the time they were ready to leave for downtown.

"Are you sure it's safe for the three of you to drive, dear?" Nan asked. Though Laura had assumed they'd all be part of the welcome party, Nan and Belle had decided to wait at home.

"It's better that just you and the boys be there," Belle said. "We'll be here with a big lunch ready. Nan wants to make everything Alan likes, all in one meal. She's driving me nuts!"

Despite the weather, Laura was determined to take the car. She wanted to show Alan she could do it. Besides, it didn't seem right to have to hop on the public bus to get home after you'd been thousands of miles away for two years.

The sleet pelted the windshield and slid down into the crevices of the clunky wipers as she backed the big Packard out of the garage. Laura's skunk coat was getting in the way of her driving, but it was much too cold in the car to take it off.

"I want to sit up front!" Gary yelled after he helped Billy close the garage door.

"We'll all fit up here," Laura said. "Just keep your legs away from the shift, Gary." This was probably the last time the kids would be sitting in the front seat for a while. And she wouldn't be driving much anymore, either, at least not when Alan was in the car.

As they proceeded slowly downtown to the train station, Laura wondered what other changes they'd have to get used to. Alan tended to be the disciplinarian, and she'd probably been a bit lax in that regard, especially with Billy. A potential problem, she feared, especially with their already strained relationship. Another thing to worry about.

Though most of the Saturday excursion riders to New York had taken trains much earlier in the morning, Union Station was still crowded with other weekend travelers. There was a noticeable difference in the number of servicemen. Hardly any seemed to be waiting to depart, though significant numbers of men in uniform, as well a few women, kept arriving on incoming coaches.

The train was late, and they waited on the uncomfortable benches for over an hour. When the announcer boomed out the arrival of Alan's train—"*Chicago*" was the only word that came through clearly in the muffled, rapid-fire delivery—Gary ran ahead to the doorway leading upstairs to the outdoor track. "Come on!" he yelled.

"We'll wait here, boys, don't go any further," Laura said, grabbing his hand and reaching out for Billy's as they joined the throngs of people at the front of the enclosed staircase.

As soon as the conductor opened the door at the top, a gust of cold, damp wind whooshed down the stairs and into the station lobby. Soon Laura heard the sound of a train whistle and then the hiss of released air from the brakes as the engine pulled into the station.

Suddenly, finally, she felt a crazy rush of excitement. He was really here. The words of a Peggy Lee tune she'd recently practiced with the band came into her head: *"Waitin' for the train to come in..."* She laughed to herself, remembering how she used to feel sitting at her second-floor bedroom window, watching for Alan to arrive in his old roadster for a Saturday night date. He was never on time then either, but she didn't care as soon as his car pulled into the driveway.

"There he is!" Billy shouted, pointing to the top of the stairway, now filled with men in uniform, both khaki and navy blue. Most had big duffel bags over their shoulders.

Alan, fit and tanned and, as usual, towering over the rest, was easy to spot. He was halfway down the stairs before he saw them, but when he did, he smiled broadly and waved.

Laura struggled to hoist Gary up so he could see his father. She hadn't lifted him in some time, but she managed so that he could wave as the mob of mostly servicemen inched its way down the stairs and into the station. Water from Gary's yellow raincoat splashed her face, and his surprising weight, as well as the crush of the crowd, was making her sweat. She probably looked a mess.

And then Alan was there. He set down his duffel and threw his arms around her. Gary, still in her arms, was caught in their embrace. Laura's fur tam fell off, and she was vaguely aware of Billy, standing behind them, struggling to pick it up.

"And here's Billy!" she said, moving back.

"It can't be, he's so tall!" Alan said, at first extending his hand. Then he leaned down and hugged his older son.

"Let's get out of here so we'll get a seat on the bus," Alan said. "It'll probably be crowded."

"We came in the car," Laura said, handing him the keys. "Here."

"In this weather?" he asked. "You never liked to drive even if it was just raining."

"Well, that was before," Laura said, laughing. "I can do a lot of things I didn't used to do before. Like taking care of the furnace, for example. Right, kids?"

"Yeah, she even goes downstairs at night alone," Billy said.

"And sometimes we see a mouse down there, Daddy," Gary added.

"One time we changed a flat tire," Billy said.

"Well," Alan replied. "Looks like things have changed, all right!"

Backing out of the parking space, he stalled the car twice. "Boy, It's been a while," he said.

"Maybe you should let it run a minute," Laura said. "I think it needs a tune-up. That I didn't do."

"Everyone at home OK?"

"Yes, Nan's having a good winter," Laura replied. "No flu or anything like that, and her leg's pretty good. Belle's real happy.

Lucille's OK, kind of stiff, but still the same old Lucille. She's missed you, I know."

"We have Max now," Billy added.

"That's what you said in one of your letters. That was lucky for him. It'll seem funny not to have old lady Herrmann looking out her window. How about Mrs. Brown, and Angie?"

"Well, you may notice a change in Mrs. Brown, but she's making out." Laura looked at Billy, wondering if he'd noticed how their neighbor had aged in the past few months.

"Angie has a boyfriend now," Gary said.

"A real boyfriend? Little Angie?!" Alan replied.

After a while, he asked, "What's the story on gas? No more rationing, right?"

"Yes, not for a while," Laura replied. "And the price didn't go up, either, the way everyone was afraid it would. The last time I got some at the Atlantic station it was 20 cents a gallon. Those speed limits are gone, too. No more 35 miles an hour on the highway."

"I'm sorry I missed Christmas," Alan said.

"That's OK, Daddy," said Gary. "Know why? The tree's still up! And we have a lot of presents to open!"

"Gary, that was supposed to be a surprise!" Billy said.

"Well, it was, you just told me!" Alan said. "I thought I'd missed everything."

"I think the Mazzarellas are having us over for another New Year's party," Laura said. "Just like always. We had a little celebration last week, but they wanted to do it again when they heard you were coming."

"That'll be good. So, Sal is settled back at home?"

"Yes, he's been back since the fall. But I'm not sure just what he's doing these days. Billy, what's Sal up to?"

"He's working at the drugstore, but he's looking for something else," Billy replied. "Maybe he's going to go to school somewhere."

"Anyway, he's awful quiet, I think," Laura said. "Of course, he had that bad injury in Italy. He doesn't say much about the war or anything."

"I can understand that," Alan replied. "What about Westinghouse?" he asked as they passed the Armory. "Looks like there's still working here on the weekends."

"On Saturdays, I think, but they don't have three shifts anymore." She paused and then said, "Westinghouse is still out on strike."

"I was afraid of that. Have you talked to anyone? Fred? Joe?"

"I saw Fred's wife, Betty, at the A&P. He got home a few weeks ago but he won't cross the picket line. Joe's working, I think. He's a boss now. But he might be out, too. They've closed most departments, I think. It's kind of an ugly situation." She didn't mention that Betty had told her there was no settlement in sight. He'd find that out soon enough.

"Daddy, how come your hair's so blond?" Gary asked.

"You forget, it gets that way out in the sun," he replied. "Like yours. Remember, where I was it was sunny and hot just about all the time. Even in the winter."

Alan's hair was still shorter than usual, but not as clipped as Laura remembered from his leave two years ago. Maybe that was because he was still in boot camp then, or perhaps they hadn't been as strict with regulations after V-J day.

She watched him as he concentrated on his driving, both hands on the wheel, not his normal way of steering. He did look good, his light hair and tanned skin contrasting with the navy blue of his pea coat. Maybe a few more wrinkles around his eyes, and he had a stubble from not shaving. But he was as handsome as ever.

"Almost home!" Laura said as they turned and headed down the street toward the house. "Lucille's going to turn herself inside out when she sees you. I hope her old heart can stand it!"

She reached over and patted Alan's leg, quickly, not wanting to distract him from his driving. Mixed in with the slightly rank odor of all their damp clothes, she could smell his tobacco smoke, though he'd put out his cigarette before getting in the car. When he'd kissed her, she thought she'd also gotten a whiff of beer or liquor, but maybe not.

In any case, she wouldn't worry about that now. Tomorrow maybe, but not now.

Chapter 48: Billy

"Hey, guess what?" Billy asked Angie as they rode home on the bus after a matinee at the Loew's. "Roy Roger's coming to the Paramount in a few days."

"I know. You still like him?" Angie asked. "His singing voice is OK but he's not like Van Johnson or Alan Ladd." They had just seen *Thrill of a Romance*, in which Van played a dashing war hero Esther Williams fell for on her honeymoon after her busy tycoon groom got called away on urgent business. They were staying at a fancy resort, so Esther got to swim a lot in the pool while she was trying to figure out what to do.

"Well, I still like to listen to Roy sing on his radio show," Billy replied. He felt funny admitting that he still eagerly awaited every new Roy Rogers movie. The comic books and the gun and holster set and all the Roy Rogers shirts and pajamas of earlier years had disappeared or been handed down to Gary. But Billy still had a big collection of old movie magazines in his bedroom closet that featured Roy and Trigger and Dale Evans, his cowgirl co-star and real-life wife.

On the Saturday of Roy's personal appearance, Billy left the house early. "I'll be gone most of the day, Ma," he said as he walked through the kitchen. If he really liked Roy's new movie, *My Pal Trigger*, he might sit through it twice. Last summer he'd watched *Bells of Rosarita* three times and missed dinner altogether.

Billy got to the theater in plenty of time to see Roy arrive in a big black car, followed by a silver-colored horse trailer. Shorter than Billy had expected, Roy was resplendent in white pants, stitched black boots, and a bright red shirt with white fringe.

Roy shook hands with a few kids at the edge of the crowd. Up close, he looked just the way he did on the big screen. He was only a few feet away from where Billy was standing before he turned back toward the truck.

Trigger was led down a ramp, where he waited patiently for Roy to mount him. They pranced around the blocked-off street in front of the theater for a while, the big palomino's thick hooves clicking on the pavement. Finally, as Trigger reared and neighed, Roy took off his white cowboy hat and waved.

Billy managed to get a seat in the first row of the orchestra. He was too close to watch the movie comfortably, but he wanted to get another good look at Roy. Carl DeSuze, the famous Boston announcer from station WBZA, came out on stage and, in his familiar radio voice, said a few words about Roy. Then he announced, "And now, ladies and gentlemen, boys and girls, here's the King of the Cowboys!"

Acknowledging the whistles and riotous applause, Roy quieted the crowd and, guitar in hand, sang his current hit, "Don't Fence Me In." Then he put down his guitar and said, "OK, amigos, I need one of you to help me out."

Billy didn't raise his hand, though he had been staring at Roy during the entire song. "Hey, how about you, young fella?" Roy asked, pointing directly at him. Though he really didn't want to, Billy awkwardly made his way up the wooden steps and into the bright circle of light shining down from the back of the balcony.

"What's your name, pardner?" Roy asked.

"Billy, Roy. I mean, just Billy." Roy smiled and everyone laughed.

"OK, Just Billy, now you stand there and be as still as a jackrabbit on the prairie," Roy said. He moved back, took a lariat from an assistant in the wings, and carefully spun the braided rope.

The lariat whirled through the air, scattering particles of dust in the glare of the spotlight. When the lasso dropped over his head, Billy knew what to do next. He dropped to his knees and hung his head.

The audience suddenly became quiet as Roy ran up to him. "Are you OK, pal?" he asked in a low voice.

"Yes," Billy whispered. "I'm just being your prisoner."

Roy laughed and said in a louder voice, "Say, this young fella should join my tour! Let's hear it for our Springfield outlaw here!" He took off his black neckerchief and handed it to Billy. Then he sang another song, "Tumbling Tumbleweeds," and left the stage to cheers and stomps and a lot of clapping.

After sitting through a second showing of *My Pal Trigger*, Billy waited until everyone exited the theater. At the door just inside the lobby, he paused in front of a life-sized cardboard image of Roy, eyes narrowed, body tensed, six-shooter in hand. Billy looked over his shoulder, and then checked to make sure no one was in the box office cubicle. Heart pounding, he grabbed the cutout and walked as fast as he could out of the theater and up Main Street.

He wasn't sure if he could manage boarding the bus dragging Roy behind him, and, besides, he was afraid all the other passengers would stare at him on the ride up the hill. Walking, he avoided acknowledging the momentary looks of surprise and amusement from passersby as he struggled along, trying to keep the cardboard figure from touching the ground.

By the time he arrived home, everyone was at the dinner table. "What in blazes is that?" Alan asked, as Billy carried Roy down the front hallway, knocking over the telephone and bumping into the wall.

"It's a souvenir they gave out from the movie," Billy yelled. "A life-size cutout of Roy Rogers."

When he returned to the table, Gary said, "Wow! Can I keep him some of the time in my room?"

"Never mind now," Alan replied. Then he added, "No, you can't. And you, Billy, wash your hands and sit down. No more about your hi-jinks. We're nearly done." Billy was surprised and relieved that he said no more, but his father had been quiet with everyone lately. At least he didn't yell, and he *was* home more these days.

☜☞

After dinner, Billy decided to visit Mrs. Brown. She hadn't been out at all since Christmas, and he'd heard Nan tell Belle that she was "failing." As far as he knew, she didn't have any special disease except for her recent pneumonia, but she did seem pale and thin and kind of weak.

"How nice to see you, Billy," Mrs. Brown said when she came to the door. Though it was still early evening, she was dressed in a long purple silk robe. "I'm afraid I've been a bit lazy. I've been resting in bed most of the day."

Walking slowly, she led him into the living room, dimly lit by two floor lamps with fringed amber-colored shades. The soft glow cast shadows on the picture above the fireplace, a bold oil of a rugged mountain range in New Mexico by her artist friend, Marsden Hartley. Except for the painting of the young man who looked like Sal, it was Billy's favorite of all the pictures in her house. He liked to stand in front of it and imagine himself somewhere on one of those mountains, riding through a deserted ravine or camped out with a cowboy friend under the western sky.

Ashkii was sprawled out on a chair near the radiator. He opened his eyes and acknowledged Billy with a cursory meow before stretching lazily and resuming his nap. The room was very warm, accentuating the familiar smell of the potpourri that Mrs. Brown kept in jars throughout the house.

"You seem a bit quiet tonight, Billy," Mrs. Brown remarked as she settled back on the sofa. Before she covered herself with a blanket—a maroon and blue lap robe that she'd once told him was made by the Taos Indians—he noticed that she was wearing light brown moccasins with yellow stitching. These he'd never seen before.

"Um, I'm OK," he replied, but Mrs. Brown was right. She could always tell when he was thinking of something else.

"And your dad, how is he doing? It must be difficult with the strike still going on."

"Yeah, he doesn't say too much about it," Billy replied. "He doesn't talk much at all." He hesitated, and then asked, "Mrs. Brown, remember the book of pictures by that artist? I think his name was Hopper. You said you knew him."

"Edward Hopper. I don't *know* him, really, but, yes, I did meet him several times in the city." Mrs. Brown always referred to New York as 'the city.' "That book is in my room, beside the bed. Why don't you run and get it?"

In all his times at Mrs. Brown's, Billy didn't remember ever being in her bedroom. Though the room was in semi-darkness, he noticed that the walls were covered with pictures, mostly paintings of cliffs and big rock formations in the desert, though there were some black and white photographs, too. Nan had told him that Mrs. Brown knew a famous photographer and his lady friend, the artist whose first name was Georgia.

Turning on a small lamp at the bedside table, Billy nearly knocked over a large silver-framed photograph. The picture was of a little boy kneeling outdoors next to a cactus, squinting as he smiled shyly at the camera. Though he was light-skinned, he had long black hair and Indian features.

Lugging the big book back to the living room, Billy squatted down next to Mrs. Brown and leafed through the pages. "What do you think about this picture, Mrs. Brown?" he asked.

The painting depicted a couple in a living room, seen through an open window. The man sat in a chair reading a newspaper. The woman was perched on a stool in front of a piano, and, though her body was toward the man, her face was turned away, one hand idly toying with the keyboard.

"Ah, yes. That picture is called 'Room in New York.' Well, let me look." Mrs. Brown examined the picture and then said, "I think I'd like to know first what you see, Billy. I'm curious."

"Well, the colors are nice."

"Yes, the lady's red dress and the yellow wall. But tell me more about the people."

"Umm...they're in the same room, but they don't seem really settled down. They seem to be waiting for something."

"What do you suppose they're waiting for?"

"I don't know. Maybe they're waiting to talk to each other, or for things to change."

"You know, I think you've caught just what Edward Hopper was trying to depict. It looks to me like they're waiting for the right moment to begin a real conversation. What do you think?"

"Maybe," Billy replied. "But, still, it's kind of a sad picture."

"Yes, perhaps sad because of how they're feeling now. But maybe they haven't been used to talking, or maybe what they have to say is difficult. But to me, it looks like they're going to talk. They're together, in the same room, after all."

"Yeah, they are," Billy replied. "Maybe it will be better. Do you think he painted anything that shows them later on?"

"Perhaps he did, that's a good thought to keep in mind. He did many paintings, you know." She reached down and patted Billy's head. "You have a good eye, Billy. You see things. Just remember that we're all complicated creatures. Life isn't any easier for us adults than it is for you younger folks."

Billy put down the book. He always felt better after talking to Mrs. Brown. "Did you get those moccasins in the West?" he asked. "Are they real, I mean, are they really made by the Indians?"

"Yes, indeed, they're quite old, as you can imagine. This robe is from my time in Taos, as well." She ran her hand slowly across the blanket on her lap.

"Mrs. Brown, who is that boy in your bedroom, the one kneeling by the cactus tree?" His mother would probably say that he shouldn't be asking personal questions, but he wanted to know.

She looked away for a moment and then said quietly, "That boy is someone from a long time ago, from my years in New Mexico." She stroked the blanket again and added, "A long time ago."

They talked a bit more, and Billy told her about his afternoon at the movies, being on stage with Roy Rogers and then carrying the cardboard cutout all the way up State Street. "Goodness, that must have been something to see," she said, laughing. "Good for you, though I won't tell anyone you snitched it. I generally don't go to western movies, but I do think Roy is a pleasant chap, at least from his radio program. And he sings nicely, too."

"Why don't you go to western movies, Mrs. Brown?" Billy asked.

"I can't bear to see how the Indians are portrayed," she replied. "They were never the marauding savages we see on the screen. I know that."

"I'd better go now," Billy said a while later. When he took the Edward Hopper book back to the bedroom, he looked again at the photograph of the little boy. This time he noticed how old the picture was—faded and turning shades of pale brown—just like some of Nan's photos from the old country.

"Billy, your visit has done me a world of good," Mrs. Brown remarked as they said goodbye. She took his hand, something she'd rarely done in the past. "You won't regret having spent time with an old lady."

"But that's not why I come over...," he began to say.

"I know, my dear, I know that." She patted his hand, the band of her huge turquoise ring tapping his knuckles. "You have a fine sense of wonder, Billy. When we talk it rekindles that spark even in me. Next to kindness and understanding, it's the most important quality you can have in life. A sense of wonder. Don't ever lose it, my dear, your sense of wonder."

"OK, I won't."

She smiled. "What I meant just now, Billy, when I said you won't regret visiting me, is that soon you'll be wanting to go to college, and I mean to help you do that."

"Gee, thanks," he replied. He didn't know what else to say and, besides, the idea of going to college seemed so far away. No one had ever mentioned that to him before.

"Tell your grandmother I'm determined to have tea with her next week," she said. And in *her* kitchen!"

As Billy walked down the shoveled path between the two houses, he turned and waved. He couldn't see Mrs. Brown's face, but her frail figure was outlined against the light from the kitchen, just as he knew it would be, and her hand was raised.

Though the vapor of his breath was visible in the cold February air, the night was clear and there was no wind. The pale yellow of the full moon cast long shadows on the frozen ground. A little creature scurried through the snow beneath the spruce, maybe a squirrel looking for breadcrumbs overlooked by the birds.

Billy spotted Nan through the curtained window as he climbed the back porch steps to go upstairs. He stamped his feet on the horsehair mat, opened her door, and walked in.

"Hello, dearie," she said. "I'm making myself another cup of tea. Have one with me. Belle may join us when she gets home from her class." It still seemed funny to Billy to think of his aunt being graded just like him on papers and tests, but he knew she was having a good time being a student again.

After he gave Nan a report on how Mrs. Brown was feeling, Billy asked, "Nan, I had to go into her bedroom and I saw a picture of an Indian boy on the table next to her bed."

"Did you, now?" Nan replied. She busied herself with pouring their tea, careful to place the strainer over each cup. Even so, tea leaves always escaped and ended up stuck to the sides and bottom of the china.

"Do you know who that boy is?" Billy asked.

"What did Mrs. Brown tell you? Did you ask her about that little boy?"

"Yes. She didn't say much, just that it was someone from a long time ago."

"Aye, that's a fact," Nan replied. She put the teapot back on the stove and returned to the table with the two steaming cups.

"Yes, well, I suspect that maybe she didn't want to get herself to thinking too much about it all. Not on a cold winter's night."

"But do you know anything about that boy?"

"I do," Nan replied. She spooned out three teaspoonfuls of sugar, slowly stirring as it melted in the steaming cup. "I guess there's no harm in telling you. You're such good friends, you and Mrs. Brown, and you're not a wee lad anymore."

Nan poured milk into her cup and continued stirring. Billy could tell she was settling in to tell a story.

"Now then," she began. "You know that Mrs. Brown was born here in Springfield. When she was a young girl, she pestered her parents to send her to art school in Boston. I guess she was quite the painter, though I don't believe anything hanging in the house now is hers.

"After she finished her schooling, she wanted to go to New York. Her father said 'No, my girl, that's not for you.' Of course, that just made her want to get away all the more.

"One of her friends was from New Mexico, or maybe it was one of her professors." Nan paused and thought. "Never mind, it doesn't matter, Mrs. Brown just up and took a train out to the desert. I can't remember the little town she settled in."

"Taos?" asked Billy.

"Taos! That's the one." Nan said. "She lived among the painters out in Taos for a number of years, some of them famous artists, I think. She had a high old time of it. And then she met a young man, and they became sweethearts."

"One of the other artists?" Billy asked.

"Oh no, far from it. A kind of cowboy, I think, but it so happened he was a full-blooded Navajo. Fancy that, Billy, a real Indian. I don't know his Indian name, but Mrs. Brown calls him Joseph."

"Wow!" Billy said. "What happened?"

"Well, dearie, here's where the story takes a sad turn. One day Joseph was found dead of a broken neck in a lonely stretch of country. They said his horse had thrown him, but Mrs. Brown wasn't so sure. There had been a lot of talk about them being together, you know, him being an Indian and all."

"You mean, maybe he was murdered?"

"Aye, I do. But, mind you, that's just speculation."

"So then she was left all alone?" Billy asked.

"No, not exactly. You see, she was in the family way. Do you know what that means?" Nan asked.

"That she was going to get a baby?"

"There you are. And that's the little boy in the picture. And do you know what his name was? It was Billy! Can you beat that?"

"Billy, wow! So then what happened?"

"Well, more sadness, I'm afraid. Mrs. Brown and Billy lived for some years in Santa Fe, New Mexico. I think she owned a little shop, selling jewelry and vases and knick-knacks, things like that. And then when he was ten years old, Billy died, too. He had typhoid fever, poor wee thing."

"That's what Sal said a lot of people in Naples got when he was over in Italy."

"Yes, but then it was even worse. They had nothing to treat it with back in those days."

"So then Mrs. Brown was really alone?"

"She was. Of course she had friends. But sometime after that Mr. Brown came to town, to Santa Fe. He was some kind of wealthy businessman, and he took a shine to Mrs. Brown. And she married him. And sometime later he died, too, and she came back here to Springfield. And there you are." Nan sighed and finished the last of her tea.

The noise of the front door opening stirred them both. "There's our Belle now, home from her school. Best not to say any more, Billy dear. And I wouldn't let on to Mrs. Brown," Nan cautioned. "I expect she'll tell you herself some day."

Belle appeared at the doorway, her face flushed from the cold night air. "Jesus, I'm not only getting smart, I feel like I'm in training for the Olympics," she said. "The damn school is just near enough that I feel guilty taking the bus, but I think I'm too old for this!"

Belle plopped down wearily at the table. "Billy, you gotta give me some homework tips. You're not the only one in this family who can get good grades!" She kicked off her shoes and groaned and rubbed her feet, but Billy could tell she was pleased with herself. He was glad to see her so happy.

❧◈❧

Later that night, lying in bed, Billy thought over what Nan had told him about Mrs. Brown. Her romance with an Indian out

West made her more interesting than ever in his eyes, but he felt bad about what happened to the two people she loved—three, if you counted her husband, Mr. Brown, too. Nan had never talked to him like this, either. It made him feel like he was really grown-up.

Billy opened his eyes and looked at the cutout of Roy Rogers, positioned directly in front of him across the room. He'd tied the black neckerchief Roy had given him around Roy's neck, making the image eerily life-like. Roy's crouching stance was alert and rigid, eyes hooded and uncharacteristically cold, mouth tight and determined. His silver colored six-shooter, held low against his body, gleamed in the moonlight streaming through the window.

Billy looked at Roy for a long time. He wasn't sure what he was feeling, but it was making his heart beat faster. He lay staring across the room, gradually relaxing as his body eased into that hazy limbo between drowsiness and sleep.

Hours later, he dreamed he was lying in a tepee. When he tried to move, he realized his wrists were bound together. Suddenly, the flap of the tent opened and Roy Rogers appeared. He untied Billy's ropes, swooped him up in one arm, and jumped onto his horse.

Off they galloped, Billy in front clasping Trigger's powerful neck, his face buried in the thick mane of the palomino. The wind blew his hair, and he tried without success to keep his light brown moccasins from flying off his feet.

Billy tried to say something, but the words wouldn't come. He tensed and tightened his grip on Trigger. He didn't know where they were headed, but it didn't seem to matter as he and Roy sped faster and faster and faster into the darkness.

Chapter 49: Alan

"Christ, Fred, I can't take much more of this sitting around," Alan said. He refilled their coffee cups and returned to the kitchen table. Though sunlight streamed into the room, sudden gusts of a bitter January wind rattled the windows and stirred the sheer curtains. Alan stretched his legs so that his slipper-clad feet pressed against the grated vent. The furnace heat felt good.

"Drive over with me today," Fred urged. "It's not that cold when you're moving. And they got doughnuts and all the coffee you can drink."

"Hell, I'm not even employed at Westinghouse anymore. Why would I join the picket line?"

"Come on, Alan, I'm not back either, yet. But you know your job's still there, that was the deal. We'll be re-hired the day this is over."

"Even if I'm spotted on the line? How that hell would that look? Remember, I'm not in the union anymore," Alan replied.

"Yeah, I know, but this is different. Practically the whole plant's shut down now. We're all affected. You don't have to actually join the picket. I've seen some foremen standing across the street. Everybody's involved."

They talked for a few more minutes. Fred had been with the Merchant Marines and had spent some time in Hawaii.

"Shit, it's like another world, isn't it?" Fred asked rhetorically. He shook his head and drained his coffee cup.

"You can say that again," Alan replied, though he wasn't sure if Fred was referring to Hawaii or the Springfield they'd come home to. As exotic as the palm trees and purple mountains had seemed when he'd sailed into Pearl that first time, life at home wasn't the same anymore either. That was for sure.

"Look, maybe I'll stop over this afternoon," he said as Fred rose to leave. "I just don't want to screw things up."

Alan put the dirty cups in the sink and walked slowly back into the bedroom. He wasn't feeling so good. As he eased himself onto the unmade bed, Lucille made a valiant effort to jump up next to him. He leaned down and gave her hindquarters a boost, pain shooting through his head like the sudden tightening of a vise. He didn't think he'd drunk that much the night before, but maybe he'd lost count. Or maybe he couldn't handle it like he used to. Lately, he seemed to have a hangover nearly every morning.

"That's a good girl," he said as Lucille burrowed her head on his stomach. Since his return, she seemed to have reverted to their old relationship, before the kids came along and became her best friends. Maybe it was the boys' increased attention to Max. Maybe she just felt sorry for him. He'd once read that dogs could sense when things weren't going right with their human companions.

Last night had been a disaster. He'd been edgy all day and didn't want to hear Laura's questions when she got home from work. Though she'd initially supported his waiting out the strike, the past few days she'd been prodding him about looking for work.

He'd been happy enough the first couple of weeks at home, sleeping late and being waited on by Nan during the day and Laura at night. Now he was becoming tense and irritable, and he had too much time on his hands. He'd started drinking again, not much at first, but there had been a couple of recent long visits to the bar. Though he knew Laura wasn't happy about that, nothing had been discussed. At least not until last night.

It had started as soon as Laura got home from work. "Did you find out anything more from Mr. Green?" she asked as she took off her gloves and coat. Walter Green was his old boss at the plant.

"No, he wasn't home," he replied. In fact, he'd only tried once, and the line was busy. When he also admitted that he hadn't looked at the classifieds in Sunday's paper, she turned away and went into the bedroom.

Nan had invited them down for the evening meal. "I made something I think you'll like, dear," she'd told him earlier in the day.

The aroma was unpleasantly familiar when they walked down the stairs at dinnertime. When Nan brought in the big platter, he almost gagged.

"There!" she said, placing it next to Alan and wiping her hands on her apron. "They call it Spam Aloha!"

And there it was, two identical blocks of pineapple-covered, processed pork, the browned yellow fruit sizzling in the fatty juice of the meat. Underlying the sickeningly sweet aroma of the hot pineapple was the unmistakable smell of baked Spam. Surrounding this concoction were wedges of avocado shaped like palm leaves.

"Look, it's all yellow and pink and green!" Gary exclaimed.

"The recipe calls for maraschino cherries for the top, but I just couldn't find them anywhere," Nan said.

Alan looked at Laura, who avoided his glance as she adjusted her napkin, then at Belle, who was rolling her eyes. He moved the platter toward the center of the table.

"Uh, Mother, I don't think I can eat that," he said.

"Why ever not?" Nan asked. "I even made some rice to go along with it, instead of potatoes. Do they even grow potatoes in Hawaii, I wonder?"

"Nan, remember how Alan used to joke about having to eat Spam all the time?" Laura asked after a moment of silence.

"Well, yes, I do, but I thought he might like something that would remind him of his pals, you know, the other boys on the ship."

"Mother, it looks real pretty and I'm sure it's delicious, but let me cook up a hamburger for Alan," Belle said.

"Dear, I'm sure you'll like it if you just try it," Nan said, ignoring Belle and moving the platter back toward Alan.

"Jesus Christ, Mother, no!" he yelled. "If I never see another goddam slab of Spam in my life it won't be long enough!" Alan pushed his chair back, bumping into Lucille, who yelped and ran out of the room. As he moved to get up, his knee hit the edge of the table, knocking a glass of water to the floor.

"Alan, sit down!" Belle got up and practically forced her brother back into his chair. He looked over at his mother, who said nothing but had tears in her eyes.

"Let me clean this up and I'll see what's in the fridge," Belle said. "I'll be right back." As she left the room, she turned and said, "Now don't everyone eat all the Spam before I get back. I happen to like the stuff!"

Belle heated up some leftover tuna casserole, Lucille meandered back into the dining room, and they finished the meal without further incident. Afterwards Belle suggested they play a game of rummy.

"That's a grand idea," Nan said. "My, I don't remember you folks having a real family evening of cards since before the war.

Come on Gary, you can read me one of your stories in the kitchen while I do the dishes."

For a while the game went smoothly, although there was little small talk. That was fine with Alan, who tended to get annoyed when Laura and Belle began a conversation in the middle of a hand. What irritated him even more was Billy's lack of concentration, but tonight he seemed to be paying more attention. At least he didn't have a book open on his lap.

Laura was humming a song under her breath, probably a new one that she was learning. Normally, he enjoyed hearing her. Tonight it only reminded him that she was still singing with the band. But he kept quiet, and he didn't say anything later when he noticed that Billy was occasionally turning the pages of a copy of *Life* that he'd placed at the edge of the table.

Alan liked to surprise everyone and show his winning cards all at once. Now, after a few bad hands, he was ready. Belle picked a card, shrugged and discarded, as did Laura. Then it was Billy's turn. He picked up the three of hearts Laura had put down and carefully arranged his cards. "Rummy! I won!" he exclaimed. He fanned his cards on the table—three jacks and a run of hearts—and smiled triumphantly at Alan. Then he went back to perusing his magazine.

"OK, that's it!" Alan yelled, scattering his cards on the table. "I don't like smirky winners, and, besides, I can't concentrate with that goddam incessant humming!" He got up from the table, not before noticing Billy's stunned expression and the look of anger on Laura's face.

Storming out of the room, he nearly ran through the kitchen, almost colliding with his mother. Alan ignored her questioning look and slammed the back door behind him. Fumbling for his keys, he got into his car, hardly aware that he was still in his shirtsleeves. He gunned the frigid, groaning engine into unwilling life, nearly hitting a passing car as he backed into the street.

☙☙

Returning home a few hours later, Alan navigated the Packard slowly up the dark driveway. Nevertheless, he managed to clip the side of one of Nan's lilac bushes as he headed toward the garage. He knew better than to attempt to park inside, so he turned off the motor, stumbled out of the car, and weaved his way to the porch and up the back stairs.

He got to the bathroom and snapped on the light just before falling to his knees and throwing up. Still heaving, chin resting on the rim of the toilet, he heard a slight noise behind him. He turned and recognized the pale blue of Laura's nightgown and the red of her painted toenails just visible under the folds of silk. She wedged her way in and quietly closed the door.

"Guess I don't have to ask where you've been," she said, seating herself on the edge of the tub. "And I suppose there's no point in saying too much to you tonight."

Alan flushed the toilet and, with some difficulty, stood up. He rinsed his mouth and splashed water on his face. Then he pushed past Laura and started to open the door.

"No, wait, don't walk away just yet," she said, holding his arm. He sat down next to her, eyes closed.

"Look, I know you've been through a lot, and that it isn't so easy right now. But, you forget—it hasn't been easy for any of us."

"I know, but..." He started to rise.

"Wait," Laura replied, getting up and leaning back against the door. "It's one thing to act this way to me, though I don't think I deserve it. But you're forgetting that Billy is still just a boy. And Gary shouldn't be seeing you behave this way. And certainly your mother and sister are trying to help."

"I know, I know," Alan said. "I just don't know what..."

"I don't know, either. But I do know that before anything else, you've got to stop drinking. Period."

"I know, I'll try," Alan said. He reached out his hand.

"No, I'm not in the mood to be friendly," she said, her voice still calm. "And it's got to be more than trying. Things change, Alan, and I don't want them to change even more between us. Do you know what I'm saying?" She got up. "Sleep on the couch. There are sheets and a blanket on the chair."

She left the bathroom and then stuck her head back in the door. "By the way," she said quietly, "don't look for the bottle you hid down in the basement. Billy found it tonight when he went down to take care of the furnace."

All that had happened last night. Now, as he lay on the bed with Lucille snoring by his side, Alan thought about what Laura had meant by "things changing." Was she really threatening to leave him? He tried to think of anyone he knew who was divorced. There had been a scandal at the plant involving one of the bosses and his secretary, but there were no children involved when that marriage broke up.

Talking earlier with Fred about Hawaii was making him think of Edie. He went over and over the details of their time together, realizing that they really hadn't had more than a few hours, even when you added it all up. There wasn't much to think about.

It was crazy, he knew it, but he couldn't help wondering about what might have been. One more thing in his life that didn't turn out, though what he'd been hoping for he wasn't sure. What exactly was it that "might have been"? He'd hardly known her. An image of her car plunging over that dark and windy precipice played over and over in his head.

He carefully placed his hand on Lucille's rough fur, feeling the rhythmic rising and falling of her noisy breathing. The warmth and steady motion comforted him and he tried to go back to sleep, but it was no use. He felt too nervous to sleep and too blue to stay awake.

Suddenly he remembered what Laura had said about the bottle, and his stomach churned. He wondered what Billy thought when he found it. One thing for sure, he would have known exactly what it was and why it was hidden away. Sometimes he looked at Alan as though he understood him better than anyone. Now, with last night's outburst, things would be more awkward than ever between the two of them. He had hoped that it would be different with Billy after he'd gotten home from the service. Things hadn't changed after all, but whose fault was that?

Lucille stirred and whined to be helped off the bed. Alan decided to get dressed and take her out for a walk in the backyard. The vet had said that her eyes were slowly failing, and she seemed to want someone to be with her when she ventured outdoors.

It had turned cloudy, the sky a bleak backdrop to the stark outline of the bare oak and elm trees. The spruces usually provided some color, but even they looked cold and lonely as the wind whipped their branches, normally silvery green but today a dull gray.

Alan glanced ruefully at the Packard, still positioned at a zigzag angle a few feet in front of the garage. Visible along the side of the driveway, for all the world to see, was the swerving tire track that had flattened the hard crust of remaining snow. A couple of branches of the lilac had snapped off, but not enough to destroy the big bush. He'd make amends to Nan by taking her to the cemetery as soon as the snow melted. Those visits meant nothing to him, but they were important to her.

Lucille lumbered slowly ahead of Alan, clumping down the porch stairs and stepping carefully along a trodden path they'd made from their walks down to Ada Brown's fence. Alan had been shocked at how their neighbor had aged, but Billy told him she'd been sick since Christmas. He'd always admired Mrs. Brown's spirit and style, and it had bothered him to see her so changed. Just like everything else.

Though it was bitterly cold, Lucille seemed to be in an inquis- itive mood, avidly sniffing several patches of yellow snow along the way. Alan had forgotten his gloves, and his ears hurt, but he lin- gered at the edge of Mrs. Brown's yard, watching a few birds eating crumbs near her back door. That was a good sign—it meant she was still putting out scraps.

Alan watched the frantically darting sparrows, who seemed oblivious to Lucille's nearby presence, or too hungry to care. He admired the little birds for their tenacity, their determination to survive, and he felt a deep sadness at the harshness of their mean lives. Something caught in his throat and he suddenly started to cry, the warm tears stinging as they trickled down his face.

Pausing by the garage on the way back to the house, Alan hesi- tated. He really should get the car inside before everything froze up. And he hadn't forgotten that there was a pint of whiskey stashed in the trunk. But after a moment, he decided he was too cold. The car could wait, and a drink was the last thing he needed.

Walking up the porch steps, he stopped again and turned around. Maybe he'd move the car inside and just sit in the garage for a while. In the darkness. If he had just one nip and left the bottle in the glove compartment, he was pretty sure he'd be OK for the rest of the day.

He half-ran back toward the garage and struggled to open the wide doors, aware of Lucille, now on the porch, whining and wag- ging her tail inquisitively. With a determined pull, he yanked open the doors and swung them apart.

He turned around and walked back the few steps to the car. Shivering, he felt for the ignition key in his pocket with his stiff fingers, opened the driver's seat door, and stepped in. The motor eventually turned over, and Alan drove slowly into the dark garage.

Chapter 50: Belle

Belle had a late breakfast of toast and coffee and took her time getting dressed. It was nice to be alone in the house for a change. She wasn't scheduled to work at the bookstore, and she planned to spend the afternoon reading a few chapters in her business marketing class textbook. Maybe she could pick up some good ideas for the bookstore.

Though The Woolf's Den was developing a steady and enthusiastic clientele, Belle knew there was no guarantee Hannah and Charlotte would be able to succeed in their venture. She loved being in the store, and she wanted to help them in any way she could. It also made her feel good to have established a bond with Abe's daughter.

She could tell by the steady heat from the kitchen floor grate that the furnace was all set for the day. Alan's being home meant that she and Laura didn't have to worry about that anymore. Nan was off until late afternoon, shopping and then meeting an old friend for lunch downtown.

Belle was finishing her second cup of coffee when she heard the sound of Lucille scampering down the inside back stairs from the second floor, followed by the heavier tread of human footsteps. She wiped the moisture from the window in time to see Alan walk out into the backyard, his breath visible in the frigid air.

Lucille, energized by the cold weather, had trotted ahead and was down by the garage, heading in the direction of Ada Brown's. Alan's Packard was already parked outside. He must have been out and about already. Funny that she hadn't heard him earlier.

She returned to her room and made a halfhearted attempt to tidy up. Nan had long given up on trying to turn Belle into a good housekeeper, and she mostly looked the other way when she passed Belle's bedroom. "And don't get any bright ideas about swooping in and cleaning when I'm at work, hear?" she warned her mother. "The shock'd kill me."

As she hung up some of the clothes she'd been wearing the past few days, she found herself thinking about Alan. Maybe she'd ask him up for coffee. It was always hard to get him to talk, but he'd been especially withdrawn since coming home. She knew things weren't going well, and she was concerned that he'd started to drink again.

Nan had mentioned his problem the other night, and Belle had promised she'd say something to her brother. "But don't get your hopes, up Mother. He has to decide for himself," she warned Nan.

Suddenly she remembered being awakened by his car late last night. That's why it was still in the yard. He'd at least been sober enough not to attempt to drive it into the garage.

Belle opened the porch door to give him a call to come upstairs. Lucille greeted her, barking frantically and hopping down the stairs and then back up again. She noticed with surprise that the car was gone now. Odd that he would have left Lucille outside in the cold, and why was she acting so crazy? She rarely moved around so fast anymore.

"What is it, Lucille, what's wrong?" Sensing Belle's attention, the dog nudged her and ran toward the backyard.

Belle looked up and noticed puffs of vapor coming from under the closed garage doors. At first she thought it was smoke from Alan's cigarette—he must be inside--but she immediately realized there was too much of it. With a sudden sense of dread, she raced down the porch steps and across the yard and opened the side door to the garage.

Exhaust was swirling around the car. Through the window of the passenger seat, she could see Alan sitting behind the wheel, his head slumped to the side.

She covered her face with her sleeve, ran outside to the front of the garage and opened the two doors. Clouds of vapor surrounded her as the exhaust met the full force of the frigid air. Belle grabbed a rag from a hook on the wall, covered her face, took a deep breath, and ran to the driver's side of the car.

"Alan! Alan!" She shook him and slapped his face. She was relieved when he seemed to stir. She managed to reach over him and turn the ignition off.

"Come on! Get up! Get out! Alan, the fumes!" He opened his eyes and looked at her with a dazed expression. Nevertheless, he was able to lean over on his own as she pulled him out of the car.

He stumbled as she dragged him by the arm out of the garage and onto the frozen grass next to the drive. The wind was blowing the exhaust in the opposite direction, away from them.

"Here, sit here! Can you breathe?"

"Yeah, it's OK. What happened?" He still had a glassy expression on his face, and his hair was damp and disheveled. He put his hand over his forehead. "Christ, my head. What happened?" he asked again.

"You were passed out, and the motor was running. Lucille was barking, that's how I knew to look back here."

"I was putting the car away. I must have dozed off." He took several deep breaths and tried to sit up.

"Keep doing that, I'm going to get help."

"Wait, wait, don't call the ambulance. I'm OK."

"No, you need to go to the hospital or something. Let me see if Sal's home. Stay right here."

He didn't object, so she stood and started to run back toward Sal's. She turned around and yelled, "Don't lie down! Keep taking deep breaths!" She didn't know if that was the best thing to do, but it seemed right.

She raced up the Mazzarellas' back porch and banged on the door. She could see Sal sitting at the kitchen table.

"Belle, what's the matter?" She realized she didn't even have a coat on, and her hair was still in bobby pins.

"Alan was in the garage and the car was running and he got overcome. I've got him out on the lawn."

"Jesus!" Sal threw Belle a coat from the rack by the door, and raced out past her.

Alan was still sitting on the grass, holding his head with both hands. Lucille stood next to him, whimpering.

"Sal," he said. "Jesus, that was stupid."

"How do you feel?" Sal asked. "Dizzy?" He scooted down and felt Alan's forehead. "Can you breathe OK?"

"Yeah, but my head. And I feel like puking."

"Let's stand up and walk around. Come on." Sal hoisted Alan under his arm and raised him up. Belle watched as they walked slowly down to the grape arbor and back again. Sal seemed so grown-up, not the kid she remembered from before the war.. She hugged her arms together, trying to bury her hands in the sleeves of the lightweight jacket Sal had tossed to her, one she recognized as Angie's.

"Come on, got to get you down to the hospital," Sal said, looking first at Alan and then at Belle. "We don't have to call an ambulance. We can drive down in my car."

"Do I really have to go? I'm feeling pretty good now." Alan raised his head, then winced. "Jesus, my head. But otherwise..."

"Yeah, I think you're OK. Your color is good and you're breathing OK and you're making sense. And no chest pains, right?" Alan nodded. "But you need to get some oxygen and have your blood checked just to be sure. Can't fool around with carbon monoxide. I seen some bad cases working in the field hospital with guys in jeeps and trucks."

"We need to do what Sal says, he knows from his experience overseas," Belle said. "Sal, thank God you were home."

"Let me get my wallet and keys. Alan, you go up and sit outside on the porch. Better yet, keep walking. Don't lie down. Belle, you get yourself ready and meet us here."

"Lucille, come on, that's a girl. We'll be right back." Belle grabbed Lucille by her collar and gave her a nudge toward the house.

There was little conversation on the way to the hospital. Belle sat in the back of Sal's Ford as they made their way down the hill to Wesson Memorial. She watched her brother for signs of grogginess, but he appeared to be alert. He'd wanted to have a drink of water before they left, but Sal suggested they wait until he'd been checked. "Suppose I shouldn't smoke, either," Alan said as he began to pull his pack out of his pocket. Sal nodded.

He'd tried to tidy his hair, but it still stuck out a bit at the top, just the way it had when his butch cut started to grow out at the end of the summer when they were kids. He could never get the cowlick completely tamed, even when he spent hours in front of the bathroom mirror before going out on a date.

Belle wanted to ask him more about what had happened but decided to wait until later. She hadn't smelled any liquor on his breath, but he must have been drinking the night before. She'd noticed the tire tracks and the lilac bush as they'd backed out the driveway. She hoped they'd have some time to talk in private later on.

Sal slowed down as they passed the high school and the big Masonic temple, and then they turned into the entrance to the hospital emergency room. He kept the motor running and ran inside. Soon an attendant came out with a wheelchair, and Alan was whisked away.

After filling out some forms and answering a few questions from a nurse, Belle and Sal sat in a waiting room occupied by an elderly man who was coughing incessantly. *Sounds like he should be in the hospital*, Belle thought, before realizing that he'd come to just the right place. She wasn't thinking straight.

"Not much business today," Sal said.

"No. Guess everyone's pretty healthy." She didn't quite know what to say to Sal. After a while, she asked, "What do you think they'll do? I mean, to check out Alan?"

"Well, there's not much they can do to treat carbon monoxide. The good thing is, it doesn't look like he was in there long. He probably hadn't really lost consciousness, from what you said. They'll want to get some oxygen in him and they'll test his blood. Boy, it was good that the doors were open and you saw the exhaust."

"Yeah," Belle replied. She hesitated. "Well, the thing is, I did see the exhaust, but the doors were closed."

"How could the doors have been closed? Didn't you say he had just put the car in? The doors would have been open. Or was he taking the car out?"

"The car *was* outside. Before. I saw it earlier. He said he was putting it away. But he must have closed the doors after he drove in."

"Oh." Sal looked at Belle. "So you think..."

"I don't know what to think, Sal. Look, you know Alan's had to watch his drinking. But I'm sure he hadn't had anything this morning. It doesn't make sense that he'd..."

"Gee, I didn't even think of..." Sal shook his head. "Well, a lot of guys come back and they have trouble, you know? It ain't easy. I was pretty low, too, but now I've made some plans. He's still out on strike, right?"

"Yes, but it looks like they might be settling. I heard that last night from a friend. Look, I'm not sure what's going on. I'm going to talk to Alan, but maybe if you didn't say anything to anyone, Sal..."

"Oh, jeez, don't worry about that, Belle. My ma's out and Nonno wouldn't have seen or heard a thing. Don't worry."

Belle wondered if there was any chance they might want to admit Alan. She'd have to call Laura at work and deal with Nan. And what about Billy? Her thoughts started to race, so she picked up an old *Look Magazine* and tried to concentrate on a tribute to war correspondent Ernie Pyle, who'd been shot by a sniper on a Japanese island last year.

Eventually, a doctor came into the waiting room and told them that Alan was OK. His blood was normal, and as soon as he'd taken a bit more oxygen, he'd be released.

"You'll be with him, Mrs. Stewart?"

"Actually, it's Miss Stewart. I'm Alan's sister. But someone will be with him the whole time."

"Good, I'll be seeing him again in a few days. I have an office up your way. Take good care of your brother, now, hear?"

It was still early afternoon when they got back to the house. Alan had talked little on the way home. "I really feel stupid," was all he said about what had happened. "I guess I'm lucky that Lucille was there and that you happened to look out," he told Belle.

When they got out of the car, he thanked Sal. "I really appreciate it, Sal. That was a really dumb thing."

"Well, stuff like that happens. I won't mention it," Sal said. "Hey, Alan, anytime you want to talk, I'm around." He patted Alan on the shoulder and gave Belle a hug. Once again, she was aware of how he'd changed since he'd been away. She'd have to thank him again in private and maybe ask him a few things about the war... how it affected people who were right there in the middle of it, things she didn't really understand.

Nan wasn't home yet, so Belle suggested they have a snack downstairs. "I'll boil some water for tea. Are you at all hungry?"

"Actually, I am, a little. I wasn't before, but I'm feeling better."

As they sat at the kitchen table with their tea and some cheese and crackers, Belle said. "OK, let's talk."

"About what happened?"

"Yeah, about what happened. I don't think you were drinking this morning, were you?"

"No, not this morning. I was last night."

"That I figured. So, tell me, how did you end up in the car with the garage doors closed?"

He sighed. "OK, I was feeling pretty bad this morning. Not just a hangover, bad about everything. I...well, I knew there was a bottle in the car, but at first I wasn't going to get it. Then I decided if I had just one snort..." He shook his head.

"I drove the car inside the garage," he continued.

"But the doors were closed when I got there."

"Yeah, well I got out of the car and closed them," Alan replied.

"Why?"

"I don't know, it was so cold. The car was still running. I got back in and kept it on for heat."

He paused. "I remember I could hear Lucille barking. I guess I got to thinking. I know I decided not to take a drink, I'm sure about that, but then I must have leaned back. It was warm and I guess I just wanted to rest."

His voice began to break. "The next thing I remember is you yelling my name."

Belle put her hand on Alan's arm. "You weren't thinking of something else?"

"Belle, I swear, I wasn't. But I can see how you'd think that. Believe me, I wouldn't have done that with Laura and the kids and..."

"OK, I believe you. What about your drinking? What about that?"

"I know I have to stop."

"I'm going to tell you something. Mother would kill me. You know what I remember about our father as much as anything else?"

"What?"

"Well, what I remember is that he drank. He drank a lot. He was nice and kind to us. And to her. Not abusive or anything. But he was quite the drinker."

Alan looked at her. "He was? I never knew that."

"No, you were too young to remember, and no one ever talked about it later." She lit a cigarette. "That's the thing with this family, we don't talk about the uncomfortable stuff. We skirt around it and pretend we're happy. Nan has never mentioned it to me, ever." Belle flicked the ashes into the ashtray and smoothed the tablecloth with a nervous gesture.

"You're sure about our father? You know, I've heard that can run in families."

"Sure I'm sure. I can remember lots of scenes. Like I said, it's kind of what I do remember. Anyway, I wanted to say that." Belle wasn't sure why she had brought up her father. Something to do with making Alan see that he wasn't the only one who ever had a problem, but also to remind him that he wasn't the only one in the family affected by it, either. And she didn't want Billy and Gary to have some of the memories she had.

"You were lucky this time. I'm not saying your drinking had anything to do with what happened directly, but you were probably not in great shape when you drove into the garage. Maybe somewhere in your mind you even wanted to...I don't know...escape?"

"Maybe. I do remember thinking that it felt awful good just to lie back and stay warm in that dark place."

"So. Did you tell the doctor any of this?"

"Well, sort of. Yeah, I guess I did. He wants to see me in a few days, and I got the feeling maybe we'll talk. I liked him, and I kind of felt I wanted to. Talk, I mean. He seemed like someone you could confide in."

"That sounds good. Are you going to tell Laura?"

He looked at Belle. "I thought I wouldn't, at least right now. Why, are you going to say something?"

"I won't. That is, if I can really believe you're going to pull yourself together. Only with that condition." She took his hand. "Look, Alan, I'm not telling you anything you don't know. You've got a wonderful wife, the best. You've got two great kids. OK, Billy and you don't exactly see eye to eye, but he's an exceptional boy, you know that, and he's your son. Be proud of him."

"I wish I wasn't hanging on this goddam strike. It's driving me nuts."

"Abe knows someone who was saying it's probably going to be settled soon. Go back there for a while. You make good money at Westinghouse. With the GI bill you could go on to college. Especially if Laura keeps working."

"Well, that's another thing..."

"Look, she got used to it. It's been over two years, Alan, two years. She learned a lot. Let her at least do that. Times have changed. And it makes sense for the two of you, for the whole family."

"I suppose. Boy, you're really big on the advice today," he said, laughing uneasily.

"Yeah, guess I am. But I *am* your big sister, remember that. And I guess I've learned to say what's on my mind. Not that I ever was the quiet type exactly," she added when he raised his eyebrow. "But I just want my brother to be happy."

"Thanks, Belle, thanks for everything. I'm going to have a talk with Sal, too. He was always a good kid. I wonder what he went through in Italy."

"A lot, I'll bet, but he's like you. Have to pry it out of him. OK, Nan'll be home any minute. Guess I should tidy up the kitchen." She rose. "Just do this for me, too. Let me know how you're doing. You know what I said about no one in the family really talking. Let's just talk more, OK?"

"I promise," he replied. "I think I'll call Fred. You know, Fred from the plant. He wants me to help out on the picket line. And maybe he heard something today. I'd sure like to be back there by spring."

He gave Belle a hug. "Thanks, Belle. I think you saved my life, maybe in more ways than one." He hugged her again and turned to go.

"Hey, don't forget Lucille, too. That old girl is pretty sharp. I'd even say she's the one who saved your life." She wiped her eyes. "Go. Jesus, I forgot all about what I'm supposed to be studying for that class tonight. And at my age I need to read everything over at least twice. No, make that three times. Hell, even then I'm not sure!"

Chapter 51: Laura

"Hey, Ma, can we live in one of these when we move?" Gary asked. Laura and the boys were browsing the furniture floor of the Forbes & Wallace department store, where a Quonset hut had been put on display, complete with decorated rooms and a tiny front garden planted with tulips and daffodils. Now that the war was over, thousands of these government-owned, prefabricated structures were being sold to small businesses, churches, colleges—and as homes to families feeling the effects of the acute housing shortage.

"No, I'm afraid not," Laura said. "It's cute, all right, but I don't think there's really enough room or privacy for all of us." The hut, designed in the shape of an Iroquois council lodge—Billy told them he'd read that somewhere—was partitioned off into separate rooms, one leading into the next. It was selling for $1,000.

"Besides," she asked Gary, "who said anything about moving?"

"I heard you talking to Belle," he replied.

"Well, that was just a conversation." She glanced at Billy, who was giving her an alarmed look. "There aren't any plans to move, honest." Gary had apparently been in the next room when she and Belle were talking. Laura wondered what else he'd heard.

She'd had a discussion with Belle a few weeks ago, when things weren't going so well with Alan, about their living arrangements. She still wondered if being in Nan's house, even with their big upstairs floor, was the best thing for them. But now wasn't the time to move. Both she and Alan had decided that he needed to get situated work-wise before they considered buying anything. The GI bill would still be available later on.

"I was worried about you and Alan, you know," Belle had said to her. "Even before he enlisted."

"You were right," Laura replied. "I'd just about had it, Belle, with his drinking. And it's hard to know what's on his mind."

"He never was a talker, even as a kid."

"But it was worse after he got back, Belle. I suppose I could manage that, but not the other."

"Things seem better lately."

"They are," Laura replied. "We kind of had it out one night. Things seemed to change right after that. I don't know...Maybe what I said made an impression, or perhaps something else happened."

"Well, maybe he'll talk about it," Belle said. "Tell him you'd like to know how things are really going with him. Maybe he'll surprise you."

"I don't think he's crazy about the idea of being back at Westinghouse after the strike," Laura continued. "He's been going on interviews. But I think he's coming around. He can always get something else later. Places will be hiring again."

"I'm glad to hear you say all this," Belle said. "Remember one time you told me that you always felt a little jolt, a little shiver, when Alan came into the room, even after you'd been married a long time? I never forgot that."

Laura smiled. "Know what? I still do. And I know he feels the same, too, even though it's hard for him to say it. We'll be OK. What about you and Abe?"

Belle thought a moment. "Well, it's a different feeling. I guess. More like a warm glow than a jolt." She laughed. "Not the same as with Dan Flanagan. Jesus, I was crazy about him, fool that I was. Did I tell you I saw him at Riverside? What an eye-opener. And remember Artie Simms a long time ago?"

"Sure I do," Laura replied. Artie Simms sold cars at the local Studebaker dealership and was the spitting image of Cary Grant. "Boy, was he good-looking."

"Yeah, but that was about all that was good about him," Belle said. "Well, he had a snazzy car, too. But Abe is one in a million. I couldn't ask for a nicer man. Maybe I'm not ready to jump out a window over him, but I love him in a, well, a more secure way, you know?"

"He's a great guy," Laura said. She poured Belle another cup of coffee. "Life's funny, isn't it? Remember the day I first met you and Nan? Boy, was I scared. Seems like a long, long time ago."

Now, walking away from the Quonset house toward the appliance department at Forbes, Laura and the boys joined a crowd watching a demonstration of a new RCA television. It looked just like a big table radio, with a glass screen about ten inches wide in the middle.

"This will be the first television brand to go on sale in the United States, folks," said the salesman standing next to the set. "It'll be available in this store sometime in the fall for only $486! Reserve yours today!"

"Who'd pay almost $500 for that little thing?" Billy said. "I'd rather go to the movies."

"But, just think," Laura replied, "You don't have to get dressed up and you could even have a snack while you were watching the program or run quick to the bathroom. And no tickets to buy for everyone. After you own it, everything's free!"

"Can we get one?" Gary asked. "Please?"

"Well, no," Laura said. "Billy's right about the price. Maybe they won't be so expensive next year."

They exited the store through the big revolving doors, Gary the first to jump between the slowly moving glass panels. Emerging onto Main Street, they were blasted by the usual wind blowing up from the Connecticut River a long block away. Still, they had no trouble hearing the newsboy at the corner stand.

"Extra! Extra!" he shouted. "Westinghouse strike over! Extra! Read all about it!"

"Oh, gosh!" Laura said, pausing at the kiosk to read as much as she could of the front-page news. "Come on, kids, let's hurry and catch the bus. Your dad said he thought they were close to settling. I wonder if he knows about this yet." Alan had gone out for another interview, his fifth in as many days, but so far there had been no offers that approached what he'd been making at the plant.

Just as they got off the bus at the corner near the house, Alan drove up beside them in the familiar green Packard. "You heard?" he yelled. "Come on, get in! We're going out to celebrate!"

The boys wanted spaghetti, so they drove to Rovelli's out at the edge of town on Boston Road. As she walked behind the boys and Alan into the big, noisy restaurant, Laura noticed the worn shine of his brown gabardine suit. But his shirt was starched and white, his hair neatly combed, and his cordovan shoes unscuffed and polished.

That morning, helping him with his tie, she'd asked, "Nervous about today's interview?" There was still a piece of tissue stuck to his chin where he'd nicked himself shaving.

"I was for the first couple," he replied. "Then I thought, Christ, I've been through a typhoon, kamikaze attacks, and Navy food, and I'm worried about this?"

Now, as they ordered from the huge Italian menu, he seemed relaxed and happy, a big change from a few weeks ago. After he'd come home drunk that night, Laura had stuck to her guns. She was sure he hadn't had a drop since then, and she was determined it would stay that way. But she knew it all depended on him.

A few days earlier, she and the girls—Helen and Mae—had gone out to dinner and a show. Helen liked Ray Milland, so they ended up taking in his new movie, *The Lost Weekend*. Seeing the harrowing film about a few days in the life of a real alcoholic was an eye-opener for Laura.

"You know, I feel funny saying this, but that movie really hit home," she said to Mae the next day at work. "I mean, the way that things got out of control for that man."

"You think Alan has a problem like that?" Mae asked. "Sure, he drinks, so does Tim. But he's fine the next day. I never saw him drink in the morning like that man."

"It's different with Alan," Laura said. "I don't think he really enjoys it. It's like, once he starts he can't stop. Remember the line in the movie, 'One drink is too much and a hundred aren't enough'? That's Alan when he starts."

Though she hadn't mentioned this to him yet, Laura wanted to suggest that he try to get in touch with someone from Alcoholics Anonymous. There must be at least one meeting place in Springfield. If there were any more episodes, she'd make the call herself.

In the meantime, she did sense that perhaps he'd turned a corner. He'd made an appointment to see a doctor and had even gone back for some follow-up visits, "to talk about some things," he said. She suspected the things were his drinking and his bad moods. Whatever they talked about, it seemed to be working. He'd tell her when he was ready.

That was all several weeks ago. Now, arriving home after eating too much pasta, veal and cannoli at Rovelli's, they stopped in to see Nan and Belle. Abe, a frequent guest these days, was there for dinner. He and Nan had become great friends.

"It's not like you have to stay at Westinghouse forever," Belle said after they all congratulated Alan about the end of the strike.

"This way you can keep looking around. Meantime, you've got your supervisor job back again. Not like me," she added. "But don't get me wrong. I wouldn't go back."

"You're right about Westinghouse, I know that," Alan said. "Abe, do you know my big sister usually has pretty good advice? About a lot of things? Just don't let her get her way *all* the time."

"Don't worry, I think Abe can take care of himself," Belle replied. "I can't even get him to change his taste in ties," she added. "Did you see that hideous red and yellow number he had on the other night? Good God! But I'm working on it."

"Dears," Nan said, putting her arms around Belle and Abe. "Tell them *your* news!"

"Well, I've asked this beautiful, though bossy, woman to marry me," Abe said. "And she said yes."

"Oh, Belle!" Laura cried. She felt a rush of happiness. With Ceil living her own busy life in Connecticut, Belle had become another sister. And she was the best aunt any two boys could have.

Before they went upstairs, Belle said, "Hey, I've got an idea. Why don't the two of you go away for the weekend and celebrate? You could take a two-day excursion to New York. We'll watch the kids." She looked over at Abe. "I mean, Abe, do you think it would be OK if we watched the kids?"

ॐঔ

The next morning Laura and Alan were on the 10 o'clock New York, New Haven and Hartford train to Grand Central. She'd never have even thought of going away this weekend if Belle hadn't suggested it, but she was glad for the break. Billy was emerging slowly from a mood he'd been in for some weeks. She suspected that, like her, he was relieved to see the change in Alan, but she also sensed it was still hard for him to get used to having his father home. Suddenly another male was in charge, and Billy was never one to take orders.

Gary was being particularly irksome these days, constantly testing to see which of his parents was in control. Last night at the restaurant he'd behaved badly, changing his mind several times about what he wanted to eat, then picking at his food when it arrived and kicking Billy under the table when he'd been asked to move over a bit. When he noisily began sucking up long strands of spaghetti from his plate, Laura told him sternly to behave himself. But it wasn't until Alan loudly said "Gary, enough!" that he stopped. She gave him a meaningful look, and he was fine for the rest of the meal.

The train ride through Connecticut and down into the city went by quickly. As the towering Manhattan skyline came into view, Laura felt a familiar thrill of anticipation. There was nothing like New York. The sun glinted off the Empire State and Chrysler buildings, their spires soaring above the other midtown towers. When the train glided into the darkness of the tunnel at Park Avenue and 96th, she resolved to stop thinking about home.

They took a yellow cab from Grand Central to the Dixie, a Times Square hotel where they'd stayed on their honeymoon in 1934. Carrying their big alligator pattern Samsonite, a uniformed bellboy escorted them to a room on the 20th floor with a view across 43rd Street to the Times building. Alan tipped him a quarter and closed the door. He took off his sports coat, loosened his tie, and lay back on the bed.

"So, want to rest or go exploring?" he asked as Laura returned from the bathroom. She closed the blinds, feeling the welcome heat from the radiator under the windowsill, and joined him.

"It feels so good to have some peace and quiet," she replied, snuggling up close. "Let's just stay here for a little while." She couldn't remember the last time she and Alan had been alone, really alone.

The room was quiet except for the occasional closing of a door in the corridor outside. Feeling the slow, measured movement of Alan's chest under her arm, Laura wondered if he'd fallen asleep. She was happy to see him relax. The strain of the war, the strike he'd come home to, getting used to the differences in the kids...Laura knew it must be difficult, especially now with his new resolution to face it all without his usual escape. She closed her eyes and soon dozed off to the distant sound of a siren somewhere in the streets far below.

"Hey, sleepyhead, wake up." Alan was leaning over her, wet hair slicked back. A big white towel circled his waist, and he smelled of an unfamiliar soap. "It's already the middle of the afternoon."

They had a quick lunch of franks and beans at a nearby Automat, then walked over to Fifth and strolled north along the crowded sidewalk, past Saks and Tiffany's, then across Central Park South. Though the late winter day was sunny, the harbor wind was fierce as it blew up the wide avenues from the lower part of the island. Laura drew her heavy skunk coat close to her face. Her nylon-clad legs were freezing.

After buying tickets at the Imperial Theatre box office for the hit show *Annie Get Your Gun* with Ethel Merman, they walked the few blocks to Mama Leone's on 48th Street. "This is just about as good as Mary Mazzarella's," Alan said as he twirled his pasta and sauce on an oversized fork. "But we won't tell her that."

"Hey, we'd better hurry," Laura said. "Curtain is at 8, and we don't want to miss the overture. It's Irving Berlin." Laura loved any Berlin tune, from "How Deep Is The Ocean" to "Alexander's Ragtime Band." Everything he wrote was a pleasure to sing.

It was 11 by the time they left the theater, but Times Square was blazing with neon, passersby jamming the intersections as cabs scrambled to beat red lights. The atmosphere was intoxicating, charged with energy, pulsing with the stimulation of the big city.

They passed under the marquee of a movie palace showing a new film that hadn't yet come to Springfield, *Tomorrow Is Forever*, with Orson Welles and Claudette Colbert. Laura glanced at their reflection in a mirror in the brightly lit outer lobby, Alan towering over her, handsome in his camel hair coat and white silk scarf. She didn't look so bad herself. Though her feet were killing her, she was glad she'd worn her new black suede spikes.

Later, as they got ready for bed, Alan said, "Funny to be listening to a broadcast on the radio when we could be seeing one over at the Roosevelt or Edison."

"I know, but you don't mind that we didn't go? I guess it would feel like a busman's holiday," Laura replied. Besides being tired, she was conscious of how much money they'd already spent. The tickets for *Annie Get Your Gun* cost nearly five dollars each, more than she'd ever spent for a show. And she wasn't particularly comfortable with Alan's urging her to have a drink when he'd be having ginger ale. Better to avoid that for a while.

"That Ethel Merman is something, isn't she?" Alan asked, arranging his slacks on a big wooden hotel hanger. "What did you think of her voice?"

"I never heard anyone who could project like that. And without a mike. She wouldn't be so good with a band—she'd drown 'em out."

Laura decided this was as good a time as any to talk about her own future in show business. "Honey, I've made up my mind about something," she began. "I'm not going back to the band. I mean, I may sing a few more weekends, but that's it."

"Are you sure that's what you want to do?" Alan asked. She was surprised that he seemed genuinely concerned.

"I am. I've sort of got a plan." She took a deep breath and continued. "What I really want to do is keep working during the day, at least for the time being. With Nan all alone after Belle leaves, I know she'll be happy to keep watching the kids. And they love her as much as they do me."

"You really like it at the Mutual?" Alan asked.

"All in all, I do. And things are going to be changing there. They're getting some big computer machines in and I think there might be good opportunities for me." She waited for him to say more.

"Well, OK, that's OK by me, I guess." He added, "I suppose I'm not really sorry you'll be away from the band. Guess you know that."

"Well, there *is* something else," she began, "but it's different, really different. Someone from WBZA was at the hotel one night and he asked me if I'd be interested in being on a Saturday morning radio show they're starting downtown in the fall. Kind of a talk thing, except sometimes I'd sing a few of the hit songs, too, with a piano or a small combo. He even said they might be moving into television in a few years, if it catches on."

"That would just be on Saturdays?" Alan asked.

"Yup, I don't even think I'd have to rehearse, except before the show. I'm sure there'd be a script for the other stuff. And no live audience."

"Hmm, sounds like you do have it all planned out," he said, turning and hanging his pants in the closet. She couldn't gauge the tone of his voice. He came back and sat on the edge of the bed. "Just don't take off for Hollywood on me," he said as he stroked her cheek. She realized that things were going to be OK.

"Anything else to tell me?" he asked, taking her hands in his.

"Nope, that's it," she replied. "Well, I do have two boys and a couple of pets. Oh, and a husband. He just came back from the war, and I'm very proud of him."

Alan lay down and ran his fingers through Laura's long black hair. "You're prettier now than when we were going out," he whispered. "I almost said 'younger,' but I like you better all grown-up."

"You're still that tall, handsome guy on the beach in Rhode Island," she replied. "I was noticing you on the street tonight and thinking that. Not as skinny as back then, but I like the extra muscles." She ran her hand over his shoulder and pulled him over to her, realizing as his body moved on hers that he was ready. Sometimes, since his return from the Pacific, that had been an issue, but clearly not tonight.

Far from the kids and high above the city, the radio playing softly next to the oversize bed, they melted into each other. Their lovemaking was both tender and intense. For the first time in as long as she could remember, Laura felt a bit like the girl she used to be, head over heels in love, her whole life before her.

"Boy, I hope no one heard us," Laura said as they lay in the semi-darkness.

"Aw, if they did, they'd just be jealous," Alan replied. "Anyway, they're probably occupied, too."

After a while, he asked, "When I was away, did you ever, you know, see anyone you kind of liked? Or did anyone try to make a pass?"

"Sure, guys, especially from the base, they made passes all the time. I just flashed my ring," Laura said. Then she added, "There was an officer, a pilot, who used to come in all the time. I think he liked me. Actually, the boys met him, even Belle and Abe one night."

"So you saw him a lot?"

Laura wondered if she'd made a mistake in mentioning John. "Only when I was singing," she replied. "He had his own circle of friends. He's long gone to California. I think he was heading off to the Pacific. Who knows what happened to him?" She actually hadn't thought much about John in recent weeks.

"And what about you?" she asked. "You weren't always on the high seas with your buddies." She laughed, a bit nervously.

"Well, I really was, most of the time after boot camp anyway. Except for Hawaii."

"Hawaii?"

After a pause, he said, "One time on leave in Honolulu I met this girl..."

"Yes?" she murmured, holding her breath.

"And, well, something could have happened maybe, 'cause I'd had a hell of a lot to drink, but it didn't. Anyway, her husband had died at Pearl Harbor and she was kind of, you know, confused about everything."

"What happened to her?"

"I think she went back to her folks in Kansas or somewhere."

"Did other men on the ship, you know, play around?"

"Some, but you'd be surprised at how much time we spent talking about our wives and sweethearts and kids. Everyone knew what you looked like from pictures."

"The one of me in the evening gown at the club?" Laura secretly liked that particular shot, a glamorous pose with her head turned sideways and her hair and skin glowing. Her Hollywood photo, Billy called it.

"That one, plus a few others I had. Of the kids, too."

Laura reached down and pulled the sheet and blanket up over them. Then she moved closer to Alan, her cheek tickled by the hair under his arm. He smelled of sweat and smoke and Old Spice.

"Comfortable?" he asked.

"Yes," she whispered. "Yes."

Chapter 52: Billy

Billy was letting Max in the back door when he saw Sal walking up the driveway in the dusk. He hadn't talked to him for over a week.

"Hi Sal. Did you have a good time?" Besides working at the drugstore, Sal had been spending almost every weekend in New York.

"Yeah, the city was good. Hey, how about if we go down to Doc's for some pie and ice cream after supper? My treat."

An hour later they met in the backyard and began to walk the short distance to the drugstore. Ernesto, Sal's newly arrived dog, tagged along behind them. He'd arrived safe and sound on an army transport from Italy, just as Sal had hoped. Billy had ridden out to Westover Air Base with him to claim the open crate containing the little dog, who had practically turned himself inside out when he saw his American friend. And Billy had never seen Sal so happy.

"So, what's up with you?" Sal asked as they walked along the street. It still seemed funny to see so many cars on the road, especially at night. Everyone was eagerly awaiting the unveiling of new models, the first since early in the war.

"Well, school's OK," Billy replied. "It's still pretty easy for me. And I have a new friend, Sammy, a kid who moved here from New York. He knows all about Broadway shows and movies and stuff like that."

"Hey, that's great," Sal replied. "Angie's kind of busy these days, I hear. She don't say much to me, but my ma talks about her boyfriend all the time. She's not so happy about it, but at least he's Italian."

"Yeah, Angie is with Rocco a lot, but we still do things together sometimes."

They walked into the drugstore, Ernie following behind. It was OK, because Sal knew the kid behind the fountain, and Ernie had been trained to stay close by when he and Sal were in Italy. They sat down at one of the small marble-topped tables near the soda fountain, Ernie settling himself underneath the table at Sal's feet.

Above them, the ceiling fan rotated slowly, surrounded by a ceiling of blue sky with clusters of fluffy clouds that Doc's artist daughter had painted one summer.

"How's your dad doing? Don't get to see him much. Is he glad to be back at work after the strike?"

"Yeah, he is. And he's...home more now. At night."

"He's a good guy, your dad. And how 'bout Mrs. Brown?" Sal asked "I never see her anymore either. She must be up there in years, like Nonno, even though she acts younger."

"Well, she's not so good, she stays in bed a lot." Billy wanted to tell Sal how frail Mrs. Brown had become, but he didn't like to think about that. "Know what? She told me that she's going to help me out if I go to college."

"Jeez, wish I had a fairy godmother," Sal replied. "That's real nice of her. I always liked that lady. I bet you she had some life when she was younger. I bet she always did what she felt like doing."

Billy wanted to tell Sal what he knew, but he'd promised Nan. "Yeah, I'll bet she did, too," he replied. "One time she said to me, 'Billy, when you're not sure whether to jump or not, don't look down. Look up instead and just take the plunge'."

"See, I was right. That's real good advice."

"Yeah, well I gotta do something like that soon, like what Mrs. Brown told you," Sal finally said. "I been thinking of going to New York."

"For another weekend?" Billy asked. Then he looked up from his apple pie and vanilla ice cream. "Oh, you mean like..."

"Yeah, like moving there. You know my friend Will? He said there are a lot of ways I could get into doing work in a hospital, or even going to school."

"Oh." Billy fiddled with his dessert. After a moment, he added, "I guess there are a lot of hospitals in a big city, not like here in Springfield."

"Listen, if I do go, I want you to promise something," Sal said.

"What?" asked Billy in a quiet voice, not looking up.

"That you'll come up and see me and Ernesto and Will. You can take the train or the bus and I'll meet you at the station. Promise?"

"OK," Billy replied. "Would Will be living there, too, with you and Ernesto?"

"Yeah, sure," Sal said. "You'll like talking to Will, he knows a bunch of stuff. You're like him in a lot of ways."

"Hey," Sal continued, "you're the first one I've told any of this to, so mum's the word, OK? Even to Angie."

"OK, I promise." He looked up at Sal. "Do you think I can come down sometimes over school vacation, too?"

"Sure. You won't be having a job for a couple of summers yet, right? You can take Ernesto for walks when we're at work. He'll probably have to stay in the apartment a lot."

On their way home, Billy mentioned his new friend, Sammy, again. "Right now, we're having a contest to see who can read the most books in a month," Billy said.

"Oh boy, so he's a brain, too? Too bad I won't be able to ask you to help me with my homework when school starts. I'm kinda scared about that."

"My Aunt Belle already asked me to help her, too."

"That's 'cause we know how smart you are."

It seemed colder on the way home, the kind of February night that made you think spring would never come. Billy wondered just when Sal would be moving away.

"Stop over at the drugstore anytime after school and I'll fix you up at the fountain with a soda or sundae," Sal said as they parted in the driveway. "And remember what I said about New York."

"OK, Sal, I will. 'Night."

Sal smiled and tilted his head in that way of his and walked toward his back porch. Billy waited until he turned and waved again just before opening the storm door. As it slammed shut, he caught a glimpse of Mrs. Mazzarella washing dishes at the sink. She'd miss Sal when she found out he was leaving for good. They'd all miss him.

☙❧

Billy kept waking up during the night. He'd lean down, adjust the tangled sheets and blankets, and check to see if Max was in his usual spot at the foot of the bed. Lucille was sleeping in his parents' room these days, or with Gary. He heard the mantle clock in the living room chime two and then three before finally falling into a fitful sleep.

What awoke him in the morning was a dream in which he and a crowd of people were running away from a fire. He'd had this dream before, ever since the Hartford circus fire last summer. The sounds of the sirens were everywhere, and when he opened his eyes, the wailing continued.

With a start, he sat up in bed. It was morning, and a real siren was sounding somewhere near the house. He ran to the window but couldn't spot anything down below. Racing into the kitchen, he looked out the back pantry window and saw an ambulance at the far end of the backyard, over in Mrs. Brown's driveway. Its siren was turned off now, but the headlights were reflected off the windows of Mr. Mazzarella's shed.

Heart pounding, he dressed as quickly as he could, grabbing his clothes from yesterday, crumpled on the floor. His mother wasn't in the house, though she wouldn't have left for work yet. Gary, he noticed, had slept through the noise. He wondered if Nan was at Mrs. Brown's already.

As he raised the latch of the gate that separated the two yards, Mrs. Brown's back door opened, and a man came out, holding up the end of a stretcher. Before the front of it came into view, Billy had a glimpse of a foot sticking out from the blanket, its ankle circled by a shiny gold bracelet. Mrs. Brown's ankle bracelet. He caught a glimpse of her face—he couldn't tell if she was awake—before they whisked her into the ambulance.

Nan came down the porch steps and got in the ambulance with the attendants. With a screech, it backed out the driveway and sped away down the street, siren at full blast.

"Billy!" His mother was coming out of the house, locking the door behind her. She quickly walked up to him. "It's Mrs. Brown, she's had some kind of shock. Nan found her when she went over to fix her breakfast. She's gone with her in the ambulance."

"I know, I saw them. What about Ashkii?"

"Ashkii's inside. It's too cold for him to be out. I made sure he has enough food and water, but you can check on him later." She put her arm around Billy. "Come on, it's cold. Let's go back and get ready for school."

"Is Mrs. Brown going to be all right?"

"Well, we'll have to see. She's asleep right now, but they'll help her all they can at the hospital. Come on, honey, we'll catch cold."

Billy wanted to ask his mother if he could stay home, but he really didn't want to be alone. Maybe Nan would be at the hospital all day.

They had a hectic breakfast, and he was almost late getting to school. Because he'd rushed, he had some trouble breathing all the way through the end of the first period—geography—but he managed to get through the day. Instead of packing lunch, his mother had given him some change, so he bought a scoop of mashed potatoes with gravy, chicken noodle soup, and a piece of chocolate cake in the cafeteria.

Billy walked home slowly in the afternoon, his scarf protecting him from breathing in the cold air. He'd thought about Mrs. Brown all day. She'd looked very white and still, and he couldn't get the image of her exposed foot and ankle bracelet out of his mind.

As he climbed the back porch steps, he could see Nan through the window in the back doorway. He didn't know whether that was a good sign or not.

"Come in, dear. I've been waiting for you, and I've got a nice cup of tea ready for us." Nan helped him off with his coat and took his glove, hat, and scarf. "Gary's off playing with his friend. Go wash your hands and we'll sit down."

"But what about Mrs. Brown, Nan? How is she?"

"Well, now," Nan replied, taking his hands in hers. "Our Mrs. Brown has left us." Nan gave that funny sigh under her breath that meant she was really sad. "She had a peaceful end. I do think she was with us until we arrived at the hospital. I sat next to her, holding her hand, but she just faded away from us. She looked at me once, and I know she was glad I was there, the dear."

Billy felt like crying, but Nan was so calm he didn't want to get her all upset. He wasn't sure what to do or say. His stomach felt funny, like he was going to have to run to the bathroom. He wondered why Nan had cried so much when President Roosevelt died and was so composed now.

"Nan, how come you're not crying?"

"Oh, I shed my tears, dearie, at the hospital and when I came home. One of the people at the emergency room was kind enough to drive me back here, and I'm afraid I wasn't good company all the way up State Street."

She paused and dabbed at her eyes with her handkerchief. "But sometimes, we go just when, well, when we're meant to. Mrs. Brown lived a good long life, and lately she wasn't at all happy. She wasn't one who was meant to sit at home all day in her bathrobe, even that fancy one she had. Not at all, not our Mrs. Brown."

Nan took Billy's hand in hers. He could feel the sharp edge of the narrow wedding band she still wore. "It was just her time, dear. You'll understand when you're older and you've lived a good long life, too."

Later, he walked over to Mrs. Brown's and let himself in with Nan's key. Nan told him that Mrs. Brown had once asked her to take care of things if anything ever happened to her, but he didn't want to ask her about Ashkii and all of Mrs. Brown's paintings and stuff.

The cat greeted him at the door, so he sat on the kitchen floor for a while, petting Askii on his lower back, just the way he liked. Wandering through the house, Billy stopped and looked at the pictures on the wall in the living room. He stood for a long time before the painting of the mountains that her artist friend, Marsden Hartley, had sent to her.

He glanced around for the other painting, the one of the man who looked like Sal. He hadn't seen it since the day Mr. Brown showed it to him, and it wasn't hanging anywhere. He'd search for it another time.

In the bedroom, he saw that Nan had made up Mrs. Brown's bed. Everything was still and silent and neat, the Edward Hopper book on her table just where he'd returned it a few weeks ago, the night they'd talked about the picture of the unhappy man and lady.

Carefully, Billy picked up the brown-tinted photograph of the Indian boy, Mrs. Brown's son. He wondered if they were together now, up in heaven, and if the boy had recognized Mrs. Brown as his young mother from a long time ago. He decided he'd ask Nan if he could have that photo to keep.

"I'll be back later tonight, Ashkii," he said, as he opened the back door. "I'll bring over some treats." He wondered how things would work out for the old cat. Maybe they'd just leave everything at Mrs. Brown's the way it was, and he'd come and stay over sometimes. In the warmer weather Ashkii could be outside in the yard most of the time.

As he looked back at Mrs. Brown's window, Billy thought about the last time he'd visited her. He'd turned around when he left, just like this afternoon, and he'd seen her faintly outlined against the curtains. Billy couldn't remember now if she'd waved back or not. He thought she had, but he wasn't sure.

Returning home, Billy saw someone coming up the drive, a youngish man dressed in a double-breasted topcoat. He was walking briskly but with a pronounced limp. As he got closer to Billy, he smiled and waved.

"You must be one of Alan's boys!"

"Hi. I'm the older one."

"I figured that. You look even bigger than the picture I saw. I knew your dad on board ship." He reached out and offered his hand, just as though Billy were a grown-up. "Bill Jones."

"Hi, Mr. Jones. My name is Billy, too. I'm glad to meet you. My dad's not home yet from work, but he should be here soon." He added, "Do you want to come upstairs and wait?"

"Well, OK. Can't stay too long. I had to come up from Hartford for a funeral, at some parlor down near Winchester Square, so I thought I'd look up your dad."

"A lady we know died today, too. She lived there." Billy pointed to Mrs. Brown's house.

"Gee, I'm sorry. Was she a good friend?"

"Yes, she was. She was one of my best friends." He suddenly thought he might start crying, but he didn't want to do that in front of Bill. "She was elderly, and it was her time."

They sat in the living room and waited for Alan to arrive. He usually got home before Billy's mother these days, often bringing a treat for dessert.

Billy was wondering about Bill's lame leg when he raised his foot in the air and said, "See this?" He was wearing polished cordovans and red and blue argyle socks.

"Oh, I didn't mean to..."

"Naw, I know, but I don't mind talking about it. I got about a pound of hardware in there. My ankle, foot, everything was just about shattered. It happened in New Guinea. Shrapnel. They sent me stateside to San Diego. Then I got discharged after about six months in the hospital."

"My dad came back from the Pacific on the Hornet," Billy said. "The flight deck was 800 feet long, and there were thousands of other sailors. Then he took the train from California."

"Yeah, I took a train, too. I only knew your dad when I was being transported on his LST. I was in the Marines. He was real nice to me, real kind, but we haven't seen each other in a couple of years. I owe him a lot"

Bill leaned close to Billy. "So, anyway, we left San Diego on the train and we're somewhere in the desert in Arizona. All of a sudden, one of the guys says, 'Hey, take a look out the window.' On both sides of us there are all these planes, just lined up and sitting in the desert. Hundreds, thousands. Later they told us it was a storage area. Didn't need nothing to protect 'em due to the dryness. But it looked more like a graveyard to me

"Just like an airplane graveyard," he continued. "One of the guys said that it took us more than 10 minutes to pass by all of 'em. He timed it. And we weren't crawling either. Imagine that—10 minutes. Then I started thinking about all the planes and crews that didn't make it back."

"We had a friend named Richie who was a Marine, but he didn't even finish training," Billy replied. "He got killed in a plane crash near Parris Island."

"Yeah, Parris. Well, it's been tough."

"I think I hear my dad coming up the stairs," Billy said. He was curious to see his father's reaction when he spotted Bill.

"Bill! Holy...Bill Jones!" Alan walked over and they shook hands. "I wouldn't hardly know you—that's a pretty snazzy get-up."

"Yeah, well I got rid of them olive greens as soon as I could. Anyway, I wanted to look you up. I still had your address in my wallet, can you figure that? That piece of paper went through a lot, I can tell you."

"So, Bill, how are things with you? I mean, your wife..." He looked over at Billy.

"I'd better do some homework now," Billy said. "I'm glad to meet you, Mr. Jones." He held out his hand.

"Same with me, Billy. Funny, I remembered you in particular from your picture, 'cause of your name. Your dad was always talking about you."

Alan followed Billy out of the room. "Billy, Nan called me about Mrs. Brown. Are you OK?"

"I guess so. She was real sick, and Nan said it was her time."

"Well, I know she was your good friend. We'll all miss her." He gave Billy an awkward hug. "We'll talk later."

Billy walked to his room and shut the door. But he didn't want to be alone in his room, and he was curious about what his father and Bill were going to say to each other. He carefully opened the door and sat on the floor halfway down the hallway. He hoped Lucille wouldn't waddle in from the living room and cause a fuss.

"One of the reasons I wanted to look you up was to tell you that Carol and me, we're back together," he heard Bill say. "And now there's three of us. I'm a dad as of last month."

"That's swell. I'm glad everything worked out for you."

"Yeah, me too. How about you?"

"I'm back at the plant. I've had some rough spots since I got back, but things are better. The pay's good. I even got a raise."

"I'm glad I met your older boy. He's real adult-acting."

"Yeah, Billy's growing up fast. He's a fine young man. Gary's off playing somewhere. He's a good little kid, too. Both of them mean the world to me."

There was a pause, and then Alan said, "Sometimes it's hard, Bill, and you don't know what to say to them. You'll find out with your own. Especially when they start to get older, like Billy. But I think he knows I love him."

Billy had never heard his father talk like this. He never said how he was feeling or anything. There was more silence, and then Bill said, "Hey, another reason I guess I wanted to stop by is to thank you."

"Me? What for?" Alan asked.

"Jeez, for saving my life, that's what for. I guess I never did tell you this right out, but I think you suspected it. I really was about to jump over that night."

"Yeah, I wondered, but then I didn't think that would happen after we talked," Alan replied. "You seemed OK."

"Well, yeah, that's it. It was because of what you said. I mean it. You weren't old enough to be my dad, really, but I kind of looked at you in that way. I thought a lot about what you said during my whole time over there."

"Thanks, Bill. That means a lot to me. I had a bad time here one day a while back. Sort of like you that night on board. You telling me this is kind of funny, you know? Me giving you advice. But it makes me feel good."

Billy wondered if his father was talking about a particular day several weeks ago. He'd come home from school and found Belle and him having a serious conversation in the kitchen. He'd gone over to Angie's, and Sal had asked him in a concerned way how his father was, like something had happened. But he wouldn't say anything more. Billy had never mentioned this to anyone, not to his mother, not even to Angie.

He moved further down the hallway, straining to hear what the men were saying. They'd lowered their voices and he couldn't make out the words. Just then, he heard the downstairs front door open. His mother. He scooted back into his bedroom but left the door ajar.

"You must be freezing," he heard his father say.

"Just my legs. Honestly, they need to make some kind of wool nylons or something. Oh, sorry, I didn't realize..."

Alan introduced Laura to Bill, explaining who he was and that he lived down in Connecticut. They exchanged some small talk about Hartford, and it turned out they'd both gone to the same high school.

"Mrs. Stewart—Laura—I was just telling Alan here how much I owe him," Bill said.

"Owe him?" Laura asked.

"Yeah, I was in a bad way at the time, though all that's changed now. But Alan, he's kind of an example to me, with his family and all."

"So he talked a lot about us?"

"Well, not too much at first. I think he was more concerned about me getting *my* head turned around. Even so, I could tell that he was someone to listen to, with his family and job and all. Like I said, a good example."

"Thank you, Bill. We're thankful Alan is back with us, and you with your family."

"Thanks, Laura. You know, hope you don't mind my saying this, but well, you're even prettier than your pictures. I didn't think you'd look this..."

"Young?" Laura laughed. "Well, you've just made an old lady happy."

"I didn't mean..."

"Hey, you just gave me a nice compliment, Mr. Jones!"

"I'd better get going, I suppose," Bill said, laughing. "But how about if you walk a ways with me, Alan, and I'll buy you a drink? I promise I'll send him home after that, Laura, 'cause I need to be back at the funeral parlor myself."

Billy crept further down the hallway, straining to listen.

"Sorry, Bill." His father's voice had gotten lower. "Thanks for offering, but I think I'll take a pass." There was silence and then he continued. "See, well...I'm on the wagon now. For good."

"Oh, jeez, I didn't know. I mean, I didn't realize..."

"That's OK, don't worry about it."

"Hey, listen, I know what you're talking about," Bill said. "My dad don't take a drop, either. Well, he did until a few years ago and then we had some trouble, and now he don't at all. But he's a lot older than you. Wish he'd decided that when we were growing up."

He said all this in a rush, and then added, "That don't change what I said before about you...I mean I think it's real smart of you... Shoot, I don't know what I mean."

"Come on" Alan said, laughing. "I'll walk you down to the end of the driveway."

After the men left, Billy walked into the living room. "Billy!" his mother said, rushing over and hugging him. "How are you? I called home during the day."

"I'm OK."

"Mrs. Brown is at rest now. She wasn't enjoying her life any more, was she?"

"No. Nan says her time had come." Billy stifled a sob.

"It's OK to cry, dear. Don't be ashamed." Billy remembered that Sal had once told him the same thing.

"Nan's right about Mrs. Brown," his mother said. "But we'll always remember her." She picked up her coat and started to walk down the hall. "Did you meet your dad's friend, Bill Jones?"

"Yes. He said some nice things about Dad. Ma?"

She stuck her head back in the doorway. "What, dear?" She looked especially pretty tonight, her face still flushed from the February wind.

"Dad is kind of his hero, isn't he?"

"Yes, I'd say he is. And your father never told me a thing about it."

Laura walked back into the room and set her coat down. She put her hands on Billy's shoulders.

"Pretty soon I'll have to reach up to do that, you're getting so tall," she said. They looked at each other for a long moment.

"You're like him. You're like your dad." Laura said. "The silent type. Gary and I are...well, we're the chatterboxes. But you're your dad's son. And you know what? I'm glad."

She smiled at Billy and left the room.

Chapter 53: Finis

As soon as Alan stopped the car in front of the garage, Billy and Gary jumped out, the soles of their dress shoes tapping on the asphalt of the driveway. From the back seat, Belle, Abe, and Laura emerged, smiling and shading their eyes from the midday sun. It was surprisingly warm for April. The women smoothed their silk dresses, checked to see that their corsages were still pinned on straight, and adjusted the small flowered hats they'd bought especially for the occasion.

"Belle and Abe are all married!" Gary shouted to Nan as she appeared on the back porch, wiping her hands on her ruffled apron. They'd just returned from City Hall, where a justice of the peace had made it official. Belle was now Mrs. Abraham Sherman, though she'd jokingly told Billy that she wasn't crazy about the business of changing her name.

"But you're still Belle, too," Billy replied.

"Yeah, but when I see the whole name written down somewhere, I know it'll seem funny. Losing your last name is bad enough, but your first one, too? Come on! I told Abe I'd go so far as Mrs. Belle Sherman, and that was it!"

"We couldn't have asked for a more perfect day," Nan said as everyone stood, spring coats in hand, breathing in the warmth of the new season. "It's almost a shame to go inside."

It had been a cold winter, but now spring was finally here, and without the specter of war for the first time in five years. Daffodils and tulips sprouted near the front porch, and the forsythia bushes down by the garage were in full bloom. Even the lilacs had buds.

"It's so nice, why don't we just set up a couple of tables and have the buffet out here?" Alan suggested. "Come on, boys, give me a hand."

Billy had overheard his mother and Nan making plans the previous week. "Sal's going to be here then," he'd said. "Angie told me. Can he come?"

"Of course. We'll ask the Mazzarellas to join us," Nan replied. "They've been such good neighbors, I'm sure Belle will be happy

with that. But that's all. I promised her it would just be family."
She was about to say something else, but caught herself and sighed
instead.

Billy figured she was probably thinking about Mrs. Brown.
She'd have been invited, too. She came to all the parties.

It was still hard for Nan to talk about her friend, especially
after they found out what she'd done for the family. In letters from
Mrs. Brown's lawyer, they learned that she'd left her house to Nan,
as well as $10,000 in a trust fund for Billy, more than enough to
pay for all his college expenses. She'd also added a special bequest
to him of the Marsden Hartley painting of the man who looked
like Sal.

"Did you know what was in Mrs. Brown's will?" Billy asked his
grandmother one afternoon while they were having tea.

"No, nothing about the house, she never said a word," Nan
replied. "I suppose she knew I had to pinch my pennies back in the
days just after your grandfather died. Of course I never talked to
her about that."

"What about my painting?"

"No, I wasn't even sure what that picture was, from the letter.
I don't think I ever saw that one hanging in her house. I know you
like it, dear, but I'm afraid it's not my cup of tea. I'm a wee bit more
old-fashioned in my taste."

"What about my college money?" he asked.

"Now, I'd be telling a lie if I didn't suspect that maybe she had
something up her sleeve there. She often told me she hoped you'd
go off to college, and I remember she once said 'We'll make sure
he's able to attend, Mrs. Stewart, don't you worry.'"

"She kind of told me, too," Billy said. "Just before..."

"Imagine, Billy, all that money," Nan continued. "My, Mrs.
Brown's full of surprises, even after she's gone, isn't she?" She sighed.
"Poor thing. I miss my afternoons with her."

"I'm still here to have tea with you, Nan," Billy said.

"Aye, that's a fact. You are, and I'm a lucky woman for that."

"What about her house?" he asked. "Are you going to sell it?"

"Your dad advises me no, to hold on to it. You know, I asked if
maybe all of you would like to live there, but your mother and dad
think I should rent it out to get a little extra money."

Billy was reminded of what Nan had said when he saw Abe's daughter, Hannah, and her friend, Charlotte, walking up the drive for the party. He'd heard Belle talking to his father about having them as the tenants in Mrs. Brown's house.

"Hi there, Billy," said Charlotte. She was wearing slacks, but even Nan had stopped talking about ladies in pants. The war had changed all that. "So, did you give the bride away?" Charlotte asked.

"Well, I was there, but I was just watching," Billy replied. The ceremony had been really short, only a few minutes, not like the wedding in St. Michael's, the big Catholic cathedral downtown, that he'd been to last summer when one of Richie Reilly's sisters got married.

"I'm sure my dad and Belle were really happy to have you there. Your aunt talks about you all the time."

"My brother started giggling when the justice of the peace was talking, 'cause everyone was so serious, so I tried to make him stop. Then he got me going. But then Belle and Abe started laughing, too, so it was OK."

"You know, that's what we need, a few laughs down at the store. You going to come and help us out during your spring vacation?" Hannah asked.

"OK, that would be keen." Billy liked Charlotte and Hannah, and he loved browsing through all the books at the shop. He wondered if anyone had asked them about living in the house yet.

"Our neighbor Mrs. Brown died," he said. "That's her house right back there." He added, "It's a real nice house."

Charlotte and Hannah looked at each other. "Guess what?" Hannah asked. "I suppose it's OK to tell you, even though it's not official yet. I think we're going to be living there. Your dad and Belle talked to us about it."

"Gee, that's swell!" Billy replied, not letting on that he knew anything. "That's her cat, Ashkii, sitting on her porch. My grandmother's been taking care of him here, but he still thinks that's his real house. Do you like cats?"

"We love cats," Charlotte replied. She smiled at Hannah. "I wonder if Ashkii would consider moving back into his old house?"

"I know he would!" said Billy. "He's over there all the time."

"Well, that's settled then, as long as Mrs. Stewart says it's OK," Hannah said.

"Oh, my grandmother does, I already asked..." Billy began. "I mean..."

"Hey, Billy, forget the bookstore, would you consider joining our Voter's League?" asked Hannah. "I think you'd be a terrific organizer."

They turned as an old red Ford entered the drive and parked by the Mazzarellas' back door. Lucille, dozing in the sun, perked up her ears and, with some difficulty, rose and made her way slowly toward the car. The sound of another dog's loud barking could be heard from the back seat.

"It's Sal. Hey, look, he brought Ernesto!" Billy said. "Ernesto's a war refugee, you know."

Sal waved as he got out of the car and headed toward his house. "I'll be right down," he yelled, nearly tripping over Ernie, who scooted past him to greet Lucille. During Ernie's first weeks in Springfield back in the fall, he and Lucille had become great friends, the younger dog circling and nudging her along when she was having trouble with her stiff legs and bleary eyes.

"My grandmother says Ernie must be part Scottish border collie, even though he ended up in Italy," Billy said as they all watched the two dogs give each other front-to-rear personal inspections.

"So, how's my friend?" Sal asked Billy after he'd briefly greeted everyone else. He was wearing a dark blue gabardine suit that Billy didn't remember, along with a white shirt and dark green silk tie. Though he hadn't often seen Sal all dressed up, there was something else different as well, maybe his hair or the way he was smiling, Billy couldn't tell. But Sal seemed older, more at ease.

"I'm OK," Billy said.

"How are things, with Mrs. Brown gone and all? Bet it's still hard..."

"Yeah," Billy replied. "Sometimes I still..." He hesitated.

"What? Feel bad? Feel like crying?"

"Well, yeah, but I try not to."

"Why not? Remember what I said once. Just go ahead and do it You've seen us Mazzarellas cry plenty of times," he said, nodding toward his house and laughing.

"Yeah, I know," Billy said. "Well, Nan cries a little sometimes. But mostly we talk now about the nice times we had with Mrs. Brown."

"I heard she left your grandmother the house."

"Yeah, we were real surprised. And she gave me a lot for college. And she donated her paintings and stuff to the museum and some other places, except she left one picture to me." Billy would have liked Sal to see the painting, but it was still at the lawyer's office, or somewhere, until everything was settled

"That's swell about college. What about her cat? He must be pretty old."

"Well, Nan has Ashkii right now, but I fixed it all up. Hannah and Charlotte are going to keep him when they move in."

"Yeah, I just met them. They're moving in? Together?" He looked over at the two women, who were talking to Belle.

"They're real good friends," Billy replied. Sal nodded. "They own the bookstore where Belle works. I help out there sometimes, too."

"How's your mom and dad doing? She still singing?" He motioned toward Laura, who was laughing at something Abe had said, her pale violet dress billowing in the spring breeze. "Your mom looks real pretty today."

"She's not with the band, but she's going to be talking and singing on a radio show," Billy said. "And my dad is good, too. He's taking Gary and me to Boston in a few weeks for the day. Everyone's fine."

"That's real good to hear. I bet your dad don't even think much about the war."

"Maybe not," Billy replied. "He doesn't talk about it."

"He's doing real good, though, huh?"

"Yes."

"Well, I'm real busy now myself," Sal said. "There's a heck of a lot to learn at my job." Sal was at a big hospital in New York, working with veterans recovering from war injuries.

"How's your friend?" Billy asked. "Will."

"He's doing good. He's always correcting tests and stuff."

"Do you have a big house?" Billy asked.

"Naw, it's an apartment. It's up near Columbia University, where Will works." He looked at Billy. "But there's room for you on the couch in the living room. You still coming down? Will said he wants to meet this smart kid he's heard about."

"He did? Yeah, that would be neat. We have spring vacation soon."

"I know," Sal replied. "Angie said she'd like to come down, too, but only for a day 'cause of her boyfriend Rocco. But you could ride with her on the train and stay longer."

"OK!" Billy replied. This time when Sal smiled at him, he seemed more like the same old Sal.

"How's school?" he asked Billy. "Betcha everything's OK in that department."

"Yeah, my English teacher wants me to send in an essay I wrote to a contest. It's a story about a refugee who's coming over from Europe, but then you find out at the end that it's really a dog. It's the story of Ernesto."

"No kidding! Send it to me so I can read it. Will, too." He loosened the knot in his tie. "Jeez, I hate dressing up like this. At the hospital I get to wear a real comfortable shirt, like a smock."

"When do you start school, Sal?"

"In the summer. Not especially looking forward to that. That's not me, studying and all." He pointed his finger jokingly at Billy. "You be sure to go straight on to college, now that you got that money. Wish I'd done better in high school."

"Yeah, but I bet all that stuff you learned in the hospital in Italy will be a big help," Billy replied. "Mrs. Brown says there's no teacher like experience."

"Well, guess I'd better get myself over and talk to the family," Sal said. Angie and her parents and Nonno had just come out the back door. Nonno wasn't able to walk so well anymore, so he'd moved down from his third floor quarters to a room off the Mazzarellas' kitchen. Sal ran over and helped his father carry him to a chair near the picnic table.

Billy walked around taking pictures of everyone with a Brownie camera his father had brought home for him a few weeks earlier. He noticed that Sal was having a big conversation with Hannah and Charlotte. They seemed to be talking about something serious, and he wasn't sure if he should interrupt them. But Sal motioned him over, and the three of them put their heads together and smiled into the camera.

Later, after everyone had eaten Nan's ham and Mary's lasagna and a Jewish noodle pudding recipe called kugel that Laura had found in a cookbook, Alan carried out a big sheet cake with vanilla icing. Written in red frosting were the words *"Abe and Belle, April 6, 1946."*

Mr. Mazzarella poured small glasses of wine from one of his own bottles, even tiny sips for Gary and Billy to sample. They both looked over at their mother, who gave a slight nod.

Raising his glass, Alan said, "If it's OK with Belle and Abe, I want to make this a toast in honor of a couple of other things, too. First, I want to remember our neighbor, Ada Brown, who would have loved to be with us today. No one liked a party better than her." Billy gazed past the forsythia at Mrs. Brown's house, its kitchen windows glinting in the afternoon sunlight, the curtains drawn and still.

He looked back at his father, who was still holding his glass in the air. "And I want to say that we're grateful to have Sal back with us, safe. And it looks like he's on the road to a medical career in the big city. Sal's been a good friend to all of us. So... to Sal, and to his family—our neighbors since Belle and I were kids—and especially to our senior Mr. Mazzarella, Nonno."

He reached out and took Laura's hand. "I'm thankful to be back home, too, with my wife and sons and my mother." Nan smiled, dabbed at her eyes with her handkerchief, and pretended to be busy adjusting the corsage Belle had bought for her to wear.

"Now, to our bride and groom." Alan turned to his sister and brother-in-law. "Today seems like a new beginning, especially for Belle and Abe. Belle, you've always been my big sister, watching out for me way back when Nan was at work. And you still do. I'm so happy that you've started a new life. Going back to school, and helping to run a bookstore." He smiled at Hannah and Charlotte. "Never thought I'd see that!

"But most of all, I'm happy that you met someone like Abe. And, Abe, you know what you've found in Belle. She's one in a million. Our love to you both."

"Just want to add this, everyone," Abe said, stepping forward. "I think Hannah here would agree with me when I say that we both feel lucky. Lucky to have become part of such a fine new circle of family and friends. And whoever made that delicious kugel, I've got a few more dishes I can recommend! *Shalom*, peace."

"So, to Abe and Belle." Alan raised his glass higher in the air, and then put it aside. Billy looked over at his mother, who smiled back at him. He noticed Nan watching his father. She was smiling, too.

Billy took a sip of the wine, but it tasted bitter. He noticed that Gary had tried his, too, and was coughing. But Nonno smacked his lips, and Nan was dabbing at her mouth with her handkerchief. Angie seemed to be enjoying hers, too. Maybe you just needed to get used to it.

"OK, everyone," Belle said. "Before we cut the cake, a certain young lady asked if I was going to throw a bouquet. Well, sorry, Angie honey, I don't have one, but I'm going to borrow something from here." She plucked a red rose from her corsage and raised her arm. "All right, anyone looking for romance, here we go!" She tossed the rose in the air.

Suddenly, Ernesto, who'd been sitting under the picnic table with Lucille, leaped up, caught the flower, and raced away. He circled the yard in a mad dance, the rose dangling from the side of his mouth. As everyone roared with laughter, he returned to the circle and deposited his prize at Sal's feet.

"Now we know where Ernesto really came from," Billy said. "Spain!"

"I taught him to play fetch in Italy, in the fields at Paestum near the old Greek temples" Sal said. "Sometimes if I forgot the ball, I threw a wild rose in the air."

Belle reached down and patted Lucille, who'd wobbled out from under the table to see what was the fuss was all about. "Well, I hope this old girl here at my feet wasn't too put out. I think she figured she and Ernie already had an understanding. Men!"

As the afternoon waned and the sun began to set, the adults moved inside for coffee and tea. Billy and Angie waited outside as Sal got ready for his drive back to New York. When Sal opened the car door, Ernie jumped in and positioned himself in the passenger's seat, his right paw neatly extended on the window armrest.

"Guess the next time I see you two it'll be in Manhattan," Sal said.

"Hey, can you give me a ride over to Rocco's house on your way?" Angie asked. "I promised to help him with his homework later on."

"Sure, hop in," Sal replied. "Be good," he said to Billy. "And remember what I said. About school and about..." He pointed to his eye, and Billy knew he meant about not feeling ashamed to cry if he felt sad.

"OK, I won't. Bye, Sal. See you later, Angie."

Billy watched and waved as the car eased out the driveway and up the street. It was nearly dusk, but Daylight Saving Time would be starting again soon, for the first time in four years. It was funny not to hear the radio announcers saying "Eastern War Time" anymore, but all that had changed back in September, soon after V-J Day.

Billy walked slowly to the end of the yard. There was a sudden coolness in the air, but he didn't want to go back indoors just yet. He sat down on a little marble bench that had come from a quarry in Vermont long before he was born, when his grandfather was still alive.

From here, he could see Mrs. Brown's back porch, just beyond the gate his father had built. Ashkii was still reclining in his usual spot, on the cushion of a weathered metal chair.

"Hi, Ashkii," Billy called. But Ashkii remained absolutely still, his head half turned away, eyes focused intently on the lilacs near Mrs. Herrmann's house. Soon, Billy saw the reason why, as Max appeared from underneath one of the big bushes and sauntered over to the gate. The two cats glared at each other. Finally, Ashkii, with exaggerated nonchalance, stretched and began to fuss with his coat. Max slowly retreated and jumped up on Billy's lap.

Gently petting the cat, he suddenly felt Max's fur bristle. Billy looked down and saw that Max was staring over at his old second-floor kitchen window, where Mrs. Herrmann used to sit for hours on end. Max's ears pointed upwards, and his eyes were wide open. A slight movement of the shade was all that Billy could see, but Max continued his unblinking stare, his body as motionless as a carved sphinx.

Had something triggered a memory of his life with Mrs. Herrmann? Did cats remember? Billy wasn't sure about that. Dogs did, like the day Lucille greeted his dad when he returned from the war. But it was hard to tell with cats. If they did remember, they were more particular when it came to letting you know about it.

He glanced over the fence at Ashkii, now curled up on his chair in a furry ball. Did Ashkii think about Mrs. Brown? Would he be happy with Hannah and Charlotte, or would he just tolerate their presence in his house? They'd all just have to wait and see.

Billy was sure that he would never forget things that happened in his own life, just the way Nan still talked about the olden days when she was a young girl in Scotland. He decided that he'd concentrate hard so that he would always remember everything about today, especially this moment—the dusky pinkish gray of the sky, the coldness of the marble beneath his legs, the feel of Max's coarse, bristly fur, Ashkii asleep on Mrs. Brown's porch.

Belle and Abe's wedding was the best thing that had happened in a long time. Billy thought of all the things that weren't so good, like Richie getting drowned and Mrs. Herrmann slumped over her kitchen table and Sal moving away to New York and Angie having a boyfriend and the trouble between his parents and, most of all, Mrs. Brown. As Nan always said, *When we pick up one end of the stick, we pick up the other end, too.* Today was a good-end-of-the-stick day.

They remained silent, Billy and the two old cats, as darkness fell and lights came on in the surrounding houses. Dew began to settle on the new spring grass and the surface of the bench.

Max stirred again, pawing Billy's trouser leg. "It's OK, Max," he said, as the cat gave a plaintive meow from somewhere deep in his throat. "It's OK. Let's go in now."

From the open living room window, the faint sounds of radio music drifted through the night air. Walking slowly with Max toward the house, Billy glanced back, unable now to see Ashkii in the darkness. Ashkii wouldn't come indoors until much later, and then only when Nan let out that funny, off-pitch yoo-hoo of hers, the same one she'd used for Billy when he was just a little kid.

Epilogue

Laura and **Alan** moved their family to the suburbs not long after the end of the war. Laura's radio show was a hit, and she later enjoyed considerable success as the host of a local afternoon television program. Alan was eventually promoted to an executive position at Westinghouse.

Billy graduated from an Ivy League school on a full scholarship and used the money Ada Brown left him to attend graduate school in New York. He stayed on in Manhattan and became the film critic for a national magazine. He and his partner visited Massachusetts often, especially in the years following his father's death.

Belle received an associate degree in business and became regional director of the International Ladies' Garment Workers' Union. She and Abe managed the political campaign of Abe's daughter, Hannah, who was elected to the Massachusetts House of Representatives on the Democratic ticket.

Nan lived into her mid-90s, traveling back to Scotland with Billy for a visit when she was 83. She eventually sold her two houses and made her home in her later years with both her children's families.

Gary studied the piano and guitar, writing his own songs and performing with a rock band in the early 1960s. He later married, taught high school music, and had five children.

Angie married her high school boyfriend Rocco at 18 and became the mother of four: Rocco, Salvatore, Maria, and William.

Lucille, **Max**, and **Ashkii** lived well into old age, much loved and indulged by their human companions.

Sal remained in New York. His story is continued in the forthcoming novel, *Morningside Drive*.

Acknowledgments

I would like to thank members of my writing groups for their invaluable help and support: Christine Andersen, John Avignone, Lynn Chirico, Marion Cullimore, Janet Dauphin, Debbie Feingold, Marsha Howland, Sarah Karstaedt, Brenda Kaulback, Carolyn Kolwicz, David Tow, and Linda Yates.

Thanks also to friends whose reading and observations provided many helpful suggestions: Linda Duncan, Paul Lorenzo, and, especially, David Kapp.

I appreciate the valuable and detailed recollections of family, friends, and acquaintances who lived through the war years: Lynette Angel, Irving Brown, Robert Gagnon, Larry Gormally, Mae Heath, Koz Lachowski, Sally Lussier, Dave Raines, Joe Riling, Connie Sternberg, and Hal Sternberg. Special thanks to Helen (Heddie) Lachowski for the many memories of Springfield in the 1940s that she so vividly brought to life.

Thanks to the members of Project Team 5 at CreateSpace for their technical advice and to Chris Huestis of Photosynthesis LLC, Manchester CT for his expertise.

I appreciate the help I received from staff at the Springfield (MA) City Library, the University of Connecticut Libraries, and the public libraries of Manchester (CT) and South Windsor (CT).

Although the characters depicted in this novel are fictional, I want to acknowledge, in memory, the following members of my family: Ruth, Jim, Sarah, and Sadie; and my brother, Greg.

38011053R00303

Made in the USA
Middletown, DE
11 December 2016